Carnival of Shadows

R.J. ELLORY

First published in Great Britain in 2014 by Orion Books,
an imprint of The Orion Publishing Group Ltd
Orion House, 5 Upper Saint Martin's Lane
London WC2H 9EA

An Hachette UK Company

1 3 5 7 9 10 8 6 4 2

Copyright © Roger Jon Ellory 2014

A CIP catalogue record for this book is
available from the British Library.

ISBN (Hardback) 978 1 4091 2420 7
ISBN (Export Trade Paperback) 978 1 4091 2421 4
ISBN (Ebook) 978 1 4091 2422 1

Typeset at The Spartan Press Ltd,
Lymington, Hants

Printed and bound in Great Britain by
Clays Ltd, St Ives plc

The Orion Publishing Group's policy is to use papers
that are natural, renewable and recyclable products and
made from wood grown in sustainable forests. The logging
and manufacturing processes are expected to conform to
the environmental regulations of the country of origin.

www.orionbooks.co.uk

Carnival
of Shadows

Also by R.J. Ellory

Novels

Candlemoth
Ghostheart
A Quiet Vendetta
City Of Lies
A Quiet Belief in Angels
A Simple Act of Violence
The Anniversary Man
Saints of New York
Bad Signs
A Dark and Broken Heart
The Devil and the River

Novellas

Three Days in Chicagoland:
1. The Sister
2. The Cop
3. The Killer

Dedicated to all those who asked questions
and never feared the answers . . .

Psychological Fitness Evaluation 19-409
Subject: MT-051027-096N
Date: Monday, August 4, 1958—15:38 p.m.
Transcription by SA Paul Erickson

Q. You understand why you are here, Special Agent Travis?
A. I do, sir, yes.
Q. Take a seat, or would you prefer the couch, perhaps?
A. The chair is fine.
Q. Very good. So let's begin with some personal details. How old are you?
A. Thirty-one.
Q. Married?
A. No.
Q. Engaged?
A. No.
Q. Sexually or emotionally involved with a member of the opposite sex?
A. No.
Q. Very good. Tell me about your personal background, your childhood.
A. The fact that my mother killed my father. Is that what you want me to talk about?
Q. We need to address that area, of course, but we don't need to start with that.
A. Well, if we need to talk about it, then we should talk about it. I don't think there's anything else of great significance.
Q. Very well. We shall begin there, then. You were fifteen at the time, correct?
A. Yes, sir.
Q. Tell me what happened, as best you can recall...

SUMMARY

From initial observation, subject is emotionally restricted. Where there should be significant emotional response and activity, there appears to be little. Such an affected disassociation is not uncommon in cases where severe mental and emotional trauma has been experienced in formative years. Subject's answers appear somewhat practiced and formal, as if he has constructed a means by which he can deal with his emotions. Divergence from that construct is unsafe and would open the subject to alternate interpretations and unpredictable responses. That is unproven and untested territory and therefore—to the subject—needs to be avoided. Conversely, he may simply have adopted a manner he believes best suited to such interviews, in this way presenting as professional a persona as possible. Travis evidences an inability to engage and empathize with others, though he does not see this as a failing, certainly not in his professional capacity. This is not uncommon in orphans, into which category the subject could be loosely placed.

In light of his proposed promotion to lead field operative, I am erring toward the view that this sense of disassociation and emotional distance might not actually hinder his work, but rather simplify it. Emotional engagement with suspects under investigation has proven to be an obstacle in many instances, and I understand that Section Chief Gale is keen to avoid utilization of field operatives who demonstrate an inability to remain wholly objective.

Clearance is granted for active duty per the cover memorandum of Monday, August 4, 1958 (Reference: Psychological Fitness Evaluation 19-409)

STATUS REPORT
Reference: MT-051027-096N
Originator: SA Raymond Carvahlo
Recipient: SSA Tom Bishop
Re: Mandate (Psych Eval 19-409)

—*SA Michael Travis has been granted clearance for active duty*

STATUS REPORT
Reference: MT-051027-096N
Originator: SSA Tom Bishop
Recipient: SA Raymond Carvahlo

—*Acknowledged. Please submit copies of all interview
transcriptions to the office of Assistant Special Agent in Charge
Monroe, copies also to Section Chief Gale and Executive Assistant
Director Bradley Warren.*

COMM EXCHANGE TERMINATED 08.04.58 AT 17:42 p.m. BY
SSA TOM BISHOP

1

"This is an unusual case, Agent Travis, and we don't quite know what we're dealing with, to be honest."

FBI Supervisory Special Agent Tom Bishop stood just inside the doorway of his office. He leaned against the frame, an unlit cigarette in one hand, a plain manila folder in the other.

"You've been in the club a little more than eight years now, Travis, and it's time we threw you to the lions."

Bishop took a seat at his desk. He set the manila file down and then lit his cigarette.

"Twenty-eight U.S.C. 540A0, Violent Crimes Against Interstate Travelers sort of covers it, we think... but we're not so sure. We're dealing with a murder; that much we know. However, all we have right now is a small-town sheriff with a dead body, and he's in need of our help."

Michael Travis shifted in his chair. His neck was a little sore. Occasioned, perhaps, by the invasive nature of the previous day's meeting with the Bureau psychologist, he had not slept well. He tried not to think of his own past, and he certainly did not care much to discuss it, especially with strangers. The conversation with the psychologist had required that he focus his attention toward things that he would have much preferred to remain dormant. However, his humorless, perhaps even *human*-less performance, had evidently satisfied the psychologist, for he knew he'd been given clearance for this assignment. Nevertheless, recollections of his mother's execution, the death of Esther Faulkner, other such events from his past, had left him unsettled, and—in among all of the long-forgotten feelings and thoughts and conclusions—there had been one thing that had stayed with him. The fear that he *was* perhaps his father's son, that the tendency to violence *was* in the blood, a hereditary relay, if you like, and that the baton had been passed.

Also Travis had dreamed again, the same dream that had plagued him for years—the shadow of an unknown man, a cracked and arid field, the sound of a laughing crow. Nothing more nor less.

Notwithstanding his current frame of mind, he also knew how far he had come. He was thirty-one years of age, he had an apartment in Olathe,

5

just outside of Kansas City, eight years of dedicated and exemplary service in the Federal Bureau of Investigation behind him, and was about to be given his first lead assignment. Though he had known such a thing was inevitable, it was still both challenging and significant.

"There is, literally, a carnival in town," Tom Bishop said. "The town is called Seneca Falls, not to be confused with Seneca up on 63 near the state line. This is a small town at the edge of the Flint Hills, sits between El Dorado and Eureka, just to the east of I-35. You've heard of it?"

"No, sir, I haven't."

"Oh, by the way, you can skip the 'sir' business now, seeing as how they've seen fit to give you a senior special agent rank for this one."

Travis's chest swelled. "Really?"

"Oh, come on... You knew it was gonna happen any day now." Bishop smiled, reached out his hand.

Travis reached back and they shook.

"Welcome to the executive washrooms, Senior Special Agent Travis."

Travis smiled. "Heard rumor you have real hand towels in there, sir."

Bishop laughed dryly. "Just a scurrilous rumor, Travis, I assure you. SSA is probationary, of course. You still have to earn your stripes on the frontline, but I don't think anyone has any doubt in your ability to run an investigation of this nature, strange though it is."

"Strange?"

"As I said, we are dealing with a carnival, Michael, and not figuratively speaking. We have a real-life honest-to-God traveling carnival with gypsies, sideshow freaks and the like, and right now it appears that someone within it may be responsible for the death of a man. From what little we have, the victim appears to be a non-national. We don't know for sure. We have very sketchy information from the local police, but due to the simple fact that the travelers came in from Oklahoma, and as soon as they arrived, a dead guy happens to show up, we are treating it as a potential federal case. It might not be. It might be something else entirely. All we know is that the locals are out of their depth and that they've asked us for help."

"You said something about U.S.C. 540A0, Violent Crimes Against Interstate Travelers, but what you're telling me suggests it might be a violent crime *by* an interstate traveler."

"Well, maybe, if this guy had nothing to do with the carnival itself, but the Seneca Falls sheriff says that there are a whole bunch of foreigners down there, and this guy might have been one of them. If he was killed by one of his own people, then it becomes a federal matter."

"I see. So it's a fact-finding operation, first and foremost. If I conclude that neither the victim nor perpetrator had crossed state lines, then surely it would cease to be a federal concern?"

Bishop shrugged his shoulders. "We shall make that adjudication as and when we have sufficient information. I know that Chief Gale works very much with a view that once the Bureau has begun something, it should not leave the matter unresolved. Sort of like the fire department going out to a fire and then deciding not to extinguish it, if you know what I mean. Even if it does turn out to be nonfederal, Chief Gale may just wish it closed up for public relations reasons."

"Yes, makes perfect sense."

"So, you better get your bags packed."

"When was the body found?"

"That's all in the file here," Bishop said, sliding the manila folder across the desk.

"And do I take a second?"

"No. As you said, right now it's nothing more than fact-finding. If it turns out to be a full-blown federal investigation, then we'll send a second, but for the moment, you're on your own."

"And when am I leaving?"

"Oh, around about last Saturday, I should reckon."

"Which, presumably, was when the body was found," Travis replied matter-of-factly.

"That's correct," Bishop said, and made to rise from his desk. He paused then, as if struck by a secondary thought, and resumed his seat. "One other thing."

"Sir?"

"When you get back, we need to talk about something else."

Travis frowned.

"Mr. Hoover, as you know, is a dedicated Freemason." Bishop smiled. "As am I, as is Chief Gale. In fact, it would be fair to say that there is a direct relationship between one's active participation in the humanitarian and philanthropic activities of the Freemasonry fellowship and the speed and certainty with which one ascends the ranks in the Bureau. Did you know that George Washington was a Master Mason?"

"No, sir, I did not."

"Well, Mr. Hoover has been a Master Mason since 1920. He has accumulated a vast collection of medals and awards for his work." Bishop paused for a moment. "Do you know anything of the Freemasons?"

"A little, sir, yes. I knew of Mr. Hoover's devotion to the organization, of course. I understand that he was granted a very senior office just a few years ago."

"Well, this is something we will discuss in greater detail upon your return. Meanwhile, if you have a chance, do secure some literature on this. You might find it useful."

Bishop walked to the door and opened it for Travis.

"Do us proud, Senior Special Agent Travis," Bishop said.

"Absolutely, sir."

Travis gathered together a few things from his office, took the car, and headed back to his apartment outside of Olathe. Here he studied what little information was available in the file that Bishop had given him, a photograph of the main drag of this Seneca Falls, photos of a somewhat disheveled carnival troupe, canvas tents and the like. There were pictures of vehicles, registration numbers, and then the dead man himself. As Bishop had said, the man was evidently a non-national. There was something Germanic, even Slavic about his features, a heaviness that belied mainland European influence. Beyond that, a few notes had been taken—names of people who were part of this traveling circus, but that was all. It was scant information, but then, the lack of information was the reason for Travis's dispatch.

He packed some clean clothes into an overnight bag—a second suit, a pair of shoes, three clean shirts, some heavy boots, a flashlight, other such things he considered needful. It was as he was packing that he glanced over at the bookcase. Somewhere, he had a volume on the Freemasons. Perhaps he should take it with him, study it somewhat. He could not find it, but what he did find was something else of significance. A copy of *The Grapes of Wrath* by John Steinbeck. Travis had bought it for Esther, Christmas of 1943. She had loved the book, though Travis himself had never read it. It was the only thing he had kept from the Grand Island house they'd shared. There was the book, and—more important—there was the letter within. That letter, given to him by Esther with the entreaty that he not read it until after she was dead, had now remained unopened for more than eight years. He believed he would never open it, had in fact come close to just burning it several times, but had always stayed his hand. He knew what it would say, that she was sorry for everything, that perhaps it had all been a mistake, that she was to blame. But that was not true, and Travis knew it. It had *not* been a mistake, and she was *not* to blame. Between the lines of that letter would be his own unwritten confession, his own guilt, his own heartbreak. He was the one who'd betrayed her, he was the one who'd left her, and had he not done so, he knew she might still be alive. Perhaps she might have died anyway, but the ghost of what could have been still haunted him. No, he was not ready to relive those emotions. Not yet. Perhaps not ever.

Travis returned the book to the shelf, Esther's letter safely within it, and hurriedly packed the remainder of his things. He knew he was feeling such a weight of loss because of the interviews with the psychologist. Memories had been stirred up, memories that would have been better left just exactly where they'd been put to rest.

Travis started out just a handful of minutes before midday. It was a dogleg run, southwest along 35 for a hundred miles to Emporia, then south-southwest for another fifty or so into Seneca Falls. He stopped for lunch at a roadside diner outside of Emporia, took a BLT, a cup of coffee, a slice of blueberry pie, and he was back on the road by quarter past two. Traffic was sparse and he made good time, reaching his destination close to half past three.

Travis's first impression of Seneca Falls was of a relatively nondescript and characterless town, much as had been indicated by the one photo in the file. The main drag, at the end of which he found the Sheriff's Department office—itself a low-slung plain-looking building, just one story high, painted a kind of off-white that had not weathered well at all—was populated by a dozen or more of the regular outlets and establishments one would find in such a place. A barbershop, two saloons (the Tavern and the Travelers' Rest), a drugstore, two hotels (the Seneca Falls Hotel and the McCaffrey Hotel), the Seneca Falls Bank, a general mercantile, a grain and seed store, a car showroom, a tractor and farm machinery franchise, a post office, and a small bus depot that appeared not to have seen a bus for some considerable time.

Travis pulled up in front of the Sheriff's Department office and got out of the car. He looked back along the street, feeling at once both anachronistic and strangely unwelcome, and yet he shrugged off the feeling. He did not need to like the place or the people; the people did not need to like him; he was here to do a job, and do the job he would. This was his first lead assignment, and it would be textbook, professional, flawless in its execution. This would be the first of a great many exemplary assignments, of that he was sure. He had no doubt that his reports would go through Bishop, Gale, and Warren, all the way to Mr. Tolson and Mr. Hoover. The director was keeping track of all that happened in the unit, and what happened here meant a great deal to Travis, not only for his career, but also personally.

Before Travis had a chance to lock the car and make his way up the steps to the front door of the building, the sheriff appeared.

Travis introduced himself, felt a certain pride in giving his new title of *senior* special agent.

The sheriff's greeting was at once welcoming and unaffected, almost at variance to the impression Travis had received upon arrival. Travis had suspected that there might be a degree of resistance to federal involvement, but there was certainly no indication of this in the sheriff's manner.

Sheriff Charles Rourke was—at a guess—in his late thirties or early forties. He was slim of build, but broad in the shoulders. He had the kind of open and uncomplicated features found so predominantly in the Midwest, at once trusting without being naive, perhaps believing that other folks should always be afforded the benefit of the doubt until there was reason enough to afford them something else.

"Charles Rourke," the sheriff said, "though everyone here knows me as Chas."

Travis shook hands with Rourke. "Here to assist you with your situation," he said.

"Well, that was fast. You guys are really on the ball, eh? Glad to have you, Agent Travis, and don't let anyone else suggest otherwise," Rourke said. "Folks around here can be a mite suspicious of strangers, and they sure as hell weren't happy when this crowd of gypsies and freaks showed up, but they're a good sort in the main." Rourke nodded back and to the left as if indicating the location of the *gypsies and freaks*.

"The carnival people," Travis said.

"Hell," Rourke replied, "that'll do for want of a better description. Looks like something from the end of last century if you ask me, kind of thing you'd see show up around the edges of the County Fair. Kind of thing we'd encourage to move on, if you know what I mean."

"When did they arrive, exactly?" Travis asked.

"You come on in," Rourke said. "Let's get you a desk and a chair and a cup of coffee and whatever else you need, and then I can give you a full rundown of what's been goin' on."

"Appreciated, Sheriff," Travis said.

"Oh hell, just call me Chas like everyone else does."

"I think it's better if we stay official," Travis replied, smiling. "You're the sheriff, and as such should be afforded the due respect of your position."

"Well, I ain't never heard it put that-a-ways, but whatever you say. And what should I be callin' you?"

"Agent Travis, Mr. Travis, either one will do."

"Well, Mr. Travis, let me welcome you to Seneca Falls, and I can assure you that you *are* welcome, and the facilities and personnel of the Sheriff's Department are at your disposal. We don't make a habit of havin' a murder here, and though some folks around here consider it's exciting and scandalous, still the fact remains that someone got killed, and though that's mighty bad news for him, it ain't such good news for us either."

"Let's go inside," Travis said, "and you can get me up to speed."

Rourke led the way, introduced Travis to the deputy at the front desk with, "This here's Lester McCaffrey. His brother, Danny, and his sister, Laura, run the hotel down the street, which is as good a place as any for you to stay."

Rourke told Deputy McCaffrey to call ahead, to arrange things for Travis at the hotel, and then Travis was shown through to the offices in the rear of the building.

"This here's the throbbing nerve center of the whole operation," Rourke said, a sardonic grin on his face. He showed Travis his own office, nothing more than a plain-deal desk, a chair on either side, against the right-hand wall a half dozen file cabinets, the drawers labeled alphabetically—*AA–CA, CE–FA, FE–KI*, and so on. On the wall was a photograph of Rourke with another man.

"That's George Docking," Rourke explained. "Governor of Kansas. Met him while he was doing his rounds before the election. Nice enough feller for a Democrat."

Rourke sat behind his desk, indicated the second chair for Travis.

"You a political man, Mr. Travis?"

"The Bureau operates in the same way regardless of who's in the Oval Office," Travis said. "The director's answerable to the president, of course, but I think some of those conversations might be a little one-sided."

Rourke smiled knowingly. "Oh, I can imagine that would be the case. I think your Mr. Hoover there is a somewhat forceful and determined individual and not unused to getting his own way. People may know us out here for *The Wizard of Oz*, but we've had our fair share of G-men down here looking for the likes of Alvin Karpis and Ma Barker's boys. You know Karpis?"

"I know of him, of course," Travis replied. "He's been in Alcatraz since thirty-five or thirty-six, as far as I remember. I know that he was very much at the forefront of the director's attentions in the early thirties."

"Well, your Mr. Hoover got him all right, and got him good."

Travis smiled. He didn't understand why they were talking about Prohibition-era gangsters. Maybe such things were of interest to small-town sheriffs. Travis was interested only to hear the details of this most recent case.

"So to our current situation," Rourke said, as if prompted by Travis's thoughts. "We had this crowd show up early on Thursday morning, like some sort of bizarre motorcade. Half a dozen trucks, a handful of pickups, three or four cars, even a couple of caravans."

Travis took his notebook from his jacket pocket and started to write down details.

"I got everything you need to know already written down in a file," Rourke said. "But there ain't much."

"Just for my own recollection," Travis said. "I find it easier if I make my own notes as well."

"Anyway, they show up, this troupe of strange-looking characters. At first I think they're just on a layover for food, a night's rest perhaps, but then they set themselves to erecting tents and Lord knows what else just on the outskirts of town."

"Whose land?"

"Well, it isn't land that belongs to anyone as such. It's town land, I suppose. Just a few acres that run down to the edge of the river. It's no use for farming, not big enough to build much of anything, and it kind of just sits there. It's where we sometimes have a livestock market. One time we even tried to get a Christmas sort of festival thing going, but that flew like a dodo. So, like I said, it ain't anyone's."

"And a cease-and-desist warrant, an order to move on?"

"Well, that was all in progress. Takes a few days to sort out that kind of thing, making sure it's all legal and aboveboard, but before we even had a chance to discuss it, this thing happened, and now we got ourselves a crime scene. Until we figure out what the hell happened, the last thing in the world we want 'em to do is move on, right?"

"Okay, so they showed up on Thursday," Travis said, aware that Rourke would elaborate and head off course if he wasn't corralled somewhat. Travis had taken an immediate liking to the man. There was something altogether unassuming in his manner. Travis, both personally and professionally, considered himself a good judge of character, even from initial impressions, and Rourke came across as an honest and decent man.

"Yes, Thursday, sometime late morning, and then they're working all day, all night, on into the middle of Friday, and then the late afternoon of Friday there's about a dozen of them, some of them just the weirdest-looking folk you ever did see—"

"How so?" Travis asked. "Weird-looking in what way?"

"Too tall, too thin, too many fingers—"

"Sorry?"

"There's a guy down there with too many fingers, Mr. Travis. I've seen some odd things in my time, but that wins a prize somewhere, I'll tell you."

"So we are talking actual physical anomalies here... people who are—"

"You'll see for yourself soon enough," Rourke said. "So, Friday afternoon, here they come, walking through town, handing out flyers, asking

12

if they can post bills in store windows and whatever. The carnival is opening on Friday night and everyone is welcome, don't you know? And you know what they call themselves?"

Travis looked up.

"The Carnival Diablo, of all things. That's like Spanish for the devil or some such, and here you got a God-fearing, churchgoing little community, all about getting on with one another and minding each other's business, and this motley crew of oddballs and misfits descends upon them. Of course, the kids are all electrified, running up and down, laughing and hollering and making a racket, and they all want to go down there and see this freak show. I got phone calls coming in every fifteen minutes. What am I going to do about this? Why haven't I moved these people on already? I'm trying to explain that the law is the law, that you can't just throw people out, that even crazies and weirdoes have rights too, but no one wants to hear that. They just want me to get these people out of here, and that's that."

"No one wants to talk to you until there's trouble, and then trouble arrives and you're the best friend they ever had," Travis said.

"Oh, you can say that again, Mr. Travis."

"You didn't understand it the first time?" Travis said, his expression deadpan.

"No, Mr. Travis... that's just an expression..." Rourke started, and then he saw Travis's smile. "You're jokin' with me."

"Go on with what you were saying, Sheriff Rourke. So the carnival opened."

"Seven o'clock sharp, Friday evening. I went on down there. I'd seen them putting up the tents, erecting that carousel, and it all looked pretty rundown and shabby, to be honest. The tents were old, the stands and sideshows were pretty bashed up and the whole thing needed a scrubbing brush and a lick of paint, but I have to say that when nightfall came, when they had all those lights out around the field, they had that calliope music playing an' all, well it was a very impressive sight."

"And the carnival ran smoothly that first night?"

"No trouble at all. Even the adults seemed to take to it. They had all the usual things. Toss-the-hoop, a little shooting range, some guy doing that card-switch trick, a chicken in a cage that could tic-tac-toe like you never did see. There was the usual popcorn, cotton candy, hot dogs, root beer floats, all that kinda thing. There were a couple fellers doing fire-breathing tricks and an acrobatic troupe made up of five guys that looked exactly the same as one another. It was one busy place, even if I say so myself. I mean, I know about all that sort of thing from the County Fair, where they have the ten-in-one show and you get some

13

guy with elastic skin and some woman with feet the size of suitcases, but this was kind of different. They had the old Bonnie and Clyde death car, you know? Now, if Bonnie Parker and Clyde Barrow had owned as many Fords as I have seen in my time, they'd be wealthier than old man Henry Ford himself, but this one they have here… I don't know what it is, but it looks spooky as hell. You look in back there, through the broken window, and you expect to see Clyde himself taking his last dying breath. They had that over to one side, and then they had people coming on, like this human skeleton guy, and I have never seen anyone as much a skeleton as that. That was just disturbing. They had a giant rat, the Fiji mermaid, the skeleton of a two-headed dog, a midget guy, the guy with too many fingers who turned out to be the best darned magician I ever did see. The whole catalog was there, and they were good. This wasn't no two-bit, flea-ridden ragtag collection of drunks and conmen. These people were good, Mr. Travis, real good. They entertained the townsfolk, I'll give them that much, and when Saturday morning came, I never got one phone call of complaint. Not one."

"Not even from the Federal Surplus Fingers Department?"

Rourke hesitated and then smiled again. "You know, Mr. Travis, you should probably go on down there and get yourself a job as resident comedian."

"So what happened on Saturday?"

"Ah well, Saturday was even busier. We had folks comin' in from Eureka, El Dorado, Augusta, Marion, even as far north as Emporia. Presumably, folks here were making calls, telling their friends and relatives that Seneca Falls had one fine show going on, and they came in like I ain't never seen before. I mean, this town has a population somewheres in the region of four or five thousand, but Saturday night must have seen maybe a quarter as many again comin' on by car and busload. Seems like half the state wanted to see what the Carnival Diablo had to say for itself."

"And when was the body found?"

"That was late, maybe eleven o'clock or so. Most folks had gone. They were only the teenagers hangin' around, some of the younger couples who ain't got kids to get home to bed, and that's when they found him."

"Where was he found?"

"Seen, more than found, so to speak. He was sort of under the platform of the carousel. Neck was broken, but the coroner, Jack Farley, thinks that happened postmortem. Cause of death was a single knife wound to the back of the neck, sort of upward into the base of his brain. Jack said that death would have been instantaneous. Couple of people there said they saw the victim on the carousel itself, as if he were up there having a ride, but when I got to asking further, it looked like they was drunk enough to see Santa Claus and Popeye the Sailor Man up theres as well. So I don't know what to make of it, to tell you the truth."

"Who found him?"

"Well, he was just there, see? It wasn't like he was hiding anyplace. It was a young woman called Frances Brady. Came up here the few miles from El Dorado. This Brady girl was walking back toward the carousel, says she was looking for her boyfriend who'd wandered off someplace, and she saw this guy under the carousel."

"And she saw nothing else . . . no one approaching, no one leaving, nothing at all?"

"Not a thing. She just saw the guy down there, started hollering for them to stop the carousel, and then he was pulled out by a couple of the carnival people."

"And he has not been identified?"

Rourke shook his head. "Not as yet. We've had him on ice, so to speak, since Saturday night, and no one has come forward. I got a picture and sent it to my contemporaries in half a dozen surrounding towns, see if anyone knew who he was, but nothing has come back as yet."

Rourke reached into the drawer of his desk and produced a photograph, no more than five-by-four. It was the same image as that which had been provided by Bishop. He also produced a fingerprint card from the same drawer.

"And there's his prints. Understand you boys have some kind of fingerprint archive or some such. Maybe you got him on record somewhere."

Travis took the card. "Do you have more copies of the picture?"

"Sure do," Rourke replied, and furnished Travis with another photograph of the dead man.

"Anyway," Rourke continued. "I have questioned everyone who works for the carnival to see if any of them recognize him, but there's been nothing. We got ourselves a dead body, no name, no details, nothing in his pockets save a packet of playing cards, a pack of cigarettes, a lighter, and all of nine dollars and forty-two cents. I have all his personal effects and his clothes bagged and labeled down at the morgue."

Travis made a note on his book. "So, best we go take a look at him, then."

"Sure thing, Mr. Travis. You want a cup of coffee or anything before we go? You want us to take your stuff to the hotel?"

"No, that'll be fine, Sheriff. We'll deal with all of that later. I just want to see the body. I want to get going on this thing as soon as possible."

"Good 'nough. Follow me," Rourke said. He led the way out of his office to the front of the building.

They took both cars, Travis following Rourke down the main drag, then left at the end and then a good half mile to a low building on the right-hand side of the highway. *County Morgue* the sign on the front said, and a tan-colored dog with one ear missing raised its head dolefully and watched them exit their respective vehicles and come on up to the front door.

"That's Wolf," Rourke said. "Coroner's dog."

"Hell of a wolf," Travis said, smiling.

"Animal less like a wolf you could never hope to meet, but that's his given name," Rourke replied. "Coroner's name is Jack Farley, like I said. He's a little deaf. Was a medic in the war, but they put his station next to an artillery position, and his ears got a hammering."

Rourke pushed open the screen and went on through the door.

"Jack!" he called out. "Jack! It's Chas Rourke. Got a federal feller here to see our John Doe!"

There was no response from anywhere within the cool and silent building.

"He'll be in back," Rourke said. "This way."

The corridor was painted off-white, the floor was tiled, and the smell of Lysol hung in the air. It reminded Travis of his first day of training at the FBI facility. Everything was sterile, neat, orderly, far more so than it had ever been in the army. There was a comforting element to such surroundings, as if in such a place there was serious work being undertaken.

Rourke opened the door at the far end of the corridor, and there was music. Dramatic, dark even, perhaps Beethoven, but Travis was not sure. He was no classical aficionado.

Jack Farley saw them then. He raised his hand and motioned for them to come on in. He took a moment to step back and lift the needle from a record on a small phonograph turntable in the corner of the room.

Travis placed Farley in his midfifties. He was shorter than both Travis and Rourke by a head, and when he walked, he sort of rocked left to right slightly, as if one leg was rigid at the knee. Farley's hair was ash gray and scalp short, his shoes were inspection clean, and when he stripped off his glove and came forward to greet Travis, Travis noticed that the fingers of his right hand were badly stained with nicotine.

"Apologies for not welcoming you," Farley said. "I'm Jack Farley, Greenwood County Coroner. Pleased to meet you, Mr....?"

"Travis. Special Agent Travis."

"So we got ourselves a federal drama, have we?"

"Perhaps," Travis replied. "For the moment this is just a fact-finder." He glanced at the cadaver upon which Farley had been working.

"That's not your man," Farley said, indicating the body. "That's a-few-drinks-a-day-too-many Stanley Jarrett. Had it coming a long while, and I'm surprised he made it this far. Your man is out back on ice, but I can't keep him for much longer as he's gonna start reekin' something terrible."

Jack Farley put his right glove back on and indicated a door at the back of the room. "Let's go to the icebox."

It was as Michael Travis walked down the corridor to view the dead man that he remembered the death of his own father, the way he had looked as his body cooled and stiffened at the dinner table that evening so many years before.

And the memory came, a memory he had tried ever harder to bury, and yet he knew now, as he'd always known, that they were memories from which he could never be free.

The previous day had dredged these things to the surface, and there was nothing he could now do but face them.

2

Perhaps some people exist simply to remind the world that the devil is real.
This, simply stated, was the thought that gave Michael Travis some small degree of comfort.

Michael was merely fifteen years old when the Terrible Rage came to an end. It came to an end suddenly and unexpectedly and gave him barely sufficient time to catch his breath.

It was a warm August evening, some last vestige of high summer present in the atmosphere. The day had stretched lazily from dawn to dusk and filled each hour between with a sense of strange anticipation. Insects gave up their buzzing and bothering, finding respite from insect business in the deep-shadowed eaves of barns and haylofts. It seemed as if the world and all it offered had come to some unspoken and tacit consent that no manner of work would be undertaken on a day such as this. It was still too darned hot, there was too darned little air, and a cool breeze was something so indistinctly remembered that it might have been a figment of universal imagination. Such was this day: quiet, slow, airless, and as dry as bones.

And so the Terrible Rage came to its conclusion, yet had you asked Michael if such a thing was expected, he would have eyed you with an expression as revealing as a pail of milk. And had you told him that his mother would be the one to bring it to an end, he would have called you a barefaced liar.

So, telling it as it occurred, so very different from the embellished narratives that would late be spun by those who had no business spinning such things, this was how it happened:

Michael Travis was an only child, born on Tuesday, May 10, 1927, born of two people who should never have wed at all, but small-town Midwest farm life being what it was, there was a narrowness of view and an ever-present yearning to see the end of being alone in such a vast and wide-open flatness. There was the earth and the sky, merely two or three kinds of weather in between, and not a great deal else to discuss. People fell in together by default, by external determination, by the divisive collaboration of those possessed of vested interest and ulterior motive.

This was Flatwater, Nebraska. It sat within a stone's throw of the Howard County seat, St. Paul, and—as such—no different from a million other American towns where happiness found sparse and awkward welcome in the lives of its residents.

So Michael's mother-to-be, Janette Alice Cook, her simple cotton housedress decorated with a handful of self-embroidered flowers, married James "Jimmy" Franklin Travis on Wednesday, December 15, 1926, in St. Paul. Though Janette did not yet show her pregnancy to any great extent, the mere fact that her first and only child was born but five months later explained the actual necessity to marry, for neither the Cooks nor the Travises, presently or historically, had ever owned anything worth a hill of beans. Jimmy Travis was predictably drunk for the occasion and proceeded to drink so much afterward that he could not perform his husbandly duties on the marriage night. Janette sat in the bathroom of their apartment and cried for a little while, and then she steeled herself, told herself that all would be well, that Jimmy would change, that fatherhood would do him good, and she prayed that she was right.

She was not.

Fatherhood did not suit Jimmy well, and whatever Janette might have believed her husband to be, he was far worse.

Jimmy Travis was a bullheaded, bigoted, misogynistic asshole of a man. His own father had described the teenage Travis as "a hundred pounds of raw hamburger with the charm and sense of a fence post."

Soon after they were married, Travis angled and maneuvered his way into a foreman's position in a migrant labor camp out near Flatwater. He got the job because he could drink and tell dirty stories. He got the job because he had no problem kicking coloreds and Poles and Germans and Czechs. It was a hard decade, no question, and the camps that sprang up across the Midwest were merely depositories for those who could still heft an ax or swing a hammer despite the lethargy occasioned by broken dreams. Homes were nothing but makeshift sheds built from tar paper and roofing tin; everywhere there was the smell of oil-soaked timber, cheap liquor, sweat, shit, and failure. Travis's camp was an offshoot of the Great Migration, the Germans and the Czechs thus outnumbered by the coloreds, and yet they'd all come in the sure belief that life just got better the farther north you walked. They soon learned that life was no different in the north, that the liquor tasted the same but cost a nickel more a quart, that work was hard and getting harder, that happiness was as rare as hummingbirds and hailstorms, that they were destined to spend their lives building railroad lines between nowhere special and someplace less so.

Jimmy Travis didn't care for much else but sufficient dollars to drink, a few hands of cards, and the feeling that here he was master of his own territory. He was sufficiently confident and expressive of his ill-founded opinions that those of less intelligence believed he knew best, but—in truth—he knew very little at all. Maybe Jimmy Travis was worth little more than his own weight in hamburger, and charmless to boot, but he had himself positioned as a boss, a leader of men, and he got them to work by threats and hollering and the promise of a good beating. When men are already broken, it doesn't take a lot to subdue them completely. So Travis ran the camp, and the men laid the lines, and the Midwestern Standard Railroad Company paid Travis enough to get drunk and stay that way.

It has to be said that meeting Janette Cook was the both high point of Jimmy Travis's life and the low of Janette's. Neither deserved the other. Janette deserved someone decent and kind, whereas Travis deserved a bitter and twisted harridan intent on making his life a misery. But love being what it is—so often misguided, misunderstood, misconceived—those who have no business falling for each other yet fall like stones. Janette had married someone who perhaps represented security, a replacement father, a strict uncle who would keep her in check but yet allow her to blossom. She married an idea viewed through rose-tinted glasses and then discovered that fine ideas and reality were never one and the same thing. In truth, Jimmy Travis was not even a handsome man. His skin was dark and leathery from sun exposure, his hands calloused and rough, his wrecked teeth like a mouthful of broken crockery, and his eyes were just too damned close together to make anyone feel at ease in his company. Plumb the depths of his personality and you discovered almost no personality at all.

Janette, however, was a different arrangement altogether. She was a beautiful child grown into a beautiful woman, perhaps not sufficiently beautiful for every man who saw her to secretly wish his own wife were dead and deep-sixed, but she was something quite special neverthe-less. Jimmy Travis didn't see beauty the way others did; Jimmy Travis simply saw a cute brunette with a fine ass and a great rack, adequate decoration for his arm when he walked down the street. It was not fair to say that Jimmy Travis did not love Janette Cook. It *was* fair to say that he neither understood love, nor knew how to express it. Where she was gentle, patient, and kind, he was domineering, opinionated, and aggressive. Where she was quiet, discreet, and compassionate, he was a bully, a loudmouth, an insensitive boor who believed that anything worth doing in life was best accomplished by force, by manipulation, by deception. Even before Michael was born, Jimmy was screwing around. He had always screwed around. He screwed around on every girl he'd ever known. He'd also beaten pretty much every girl he'd ever known, and though it was no saving grace, he did not start beating Janette until after Michael was born. Perhaps that was some small testament to a dim light of decency that still resided in the dark embers of his heart.

At first Jimmy beat Janette because the dinner was cold. Then he beat her when the baby cried too much. Sometimes he beat her simply because he was drunk and there was no one else to beat. Eventually he beat her because he enjoyed it. It made him feel like the big man, the boss at work and the boss at home, and Janette—petite, almost fragile—took it wordlessly, resiliently, endlessly.

To his credit, Jimmy Travis never actually beat his own son. He threatened to, but he never carried that threat into action. It seemed he had energy enough for the Germans, the Czechs, the coloreds, his wife, but by the time it came to his own son, he was plumb worn-out. For everyone else, Jimmy Travis had a hard word, a clenched fist, but for Michael, he kept his tongue in his mouth and his fists in his pockets. For that, and that alone, Janette had something for which to be grateful.

Had you asked Jimmy, had you *really* asked him, he would have admitted something strange.

"Kid worries me," he would have said. "Kid don't say a damned word, but sometimes when he looks at me, I feel like he sees right through me. There's just somethin' not right there, like I don't feel nothin' for him, like there ain't connection at all."

Jimmy never voiced this thought, nor did he even really think it, but he *knew* it. Somewhere beneath the paper-thin superficiality of his day-to-day thought processes, he believed there was something wrong with that kid. The kid spooked him, plain and simple.

Michael, however, just got on with the routine business of growing up, knowing nothing much of anything beyond the reality of the Travis household. He heard the raised voices, he saw the violence inflicted, and perhaps he believed that this was just the way things were. He was unaware of anything else, and thus any other way of life would be purely imagined.

Sometimes, Michael, all of six or seven years old, would sit with his mother as she nursed a cut lip, a bruised eye, a dislocated finger, and he would ask her why his father hurt her so bad. Was this normal? Were all husbands and fathers this way?

"It's nothing but a Terrible Rage he feels, sweetheart," she would say. "It's not your fault, nor mine, and in a way it's not even your father's fault. Some people are just filled to bursting with this Terrible Rage. They feel that life has done them badly, that there are things that they've been denied, and they try to deal with it the best way they can."

"But why does he blame you for them, Mom?"

"He doesn't blame me, darling."

"So if he doesn't blame you, then why does he hurt you?"

She would hold Michael close then and say, "Because I'm here, baby, because I'm here. That's why."

Michael did not understand his father, and he suspected his mother did not understand the man either, but he never said as much.

There was one thought, however, that did trouble Michael, and it sat beneath his thoughts like a shadow that he did not dare to view. Sometimes he himself would perceive some sense of madness. Sometimes he would feel a bitterness and resentment building inside him, and then the slightest thing would cause him to snap. A sudden flash of anger, brilliant and searing hot, a firework in his mind, and he would want to break something, smash something, do something truly wicked. He did not. He contained and restrained and withheld himself, but the fear was there: that he carried something of his father in his blood and that he would inevitably grow to be the same.

And so, when the Terrible Rage came to an end—finally, indefatigably—it was as much a surprise to Michael as anyone else.

August of 1942, as US forces were preparing to raid the Japanese-held Gilbert Islands, as Winston Churchill concluded his meeting with Stalin at the Kremlin, Jimmy Travis had far more significant things on his mind, one of which was a twenty-two-year-old waitress called Mary Pulowski. Mary was a simple girl from a simple family. Her father, Josef, was on Travis's railroad crew, and Mary came on up one time to bring her father some sandwiches. Travis was in his makeshift office, and Mary caught his eye as she crossed the site perimeter and started down toward the work zone.

Travis called her back, asked about her business, eyed her up and down like a hungry man stares down a T-bone, and with his sharp line in smart quips, his Dixie-Peach-Pomade-slicked coif and his mischievous grin, he got her to fall for him in ten minutes flat. Whatever he might have promised her would only ever be known by Jimmy Travis and Mary Pulowski, but it was enough to get her skirt up around her waist right there and then in the Midwestern Standard Railroad Company Team #31 foreman's office, and Jimmy gave her everything he got. Half an hour later, Jimmy Travis himself delivered the sandwiches to Mary's father, and as the old man thanked him, Jimmy took a moment to marvel at his own magnificence.

That was not the first time he and Mary Pulowski broke a sweat over bullshit promises of better lives and bigger futures, Jimmy having convinced the poor, gullible girl that it was merely a matter of *right timing* before he announced the details of his desertion to his wife. From that moment and for all the years Mary could envision, it would be the high road for them both. The future was as bright as the sun-blessed horizon in the east, and Jimmy Travis and Mary Pulowski would be making their way toward it, smiling high, wide, and handsome, their pockets full of cash, their hearts full of love, their spirits uplifted by the sheer joy and wonder of how good life had become. That was the story, the narrative spun, the tale told, and it was about as worthless and insincere as an eight-buck bill.

Jimmy Travis had no intention of leaving his wife. He just wanted to keep on fucking Mary Pulowski until he tired of her, and then he would find someone else. He even joked about her with his drinking buddies, referring to her as *Merry Pull-Off-Ski*, his *Polish hand job*. This was his way, and there was nothing wrong with it as far as he could tell.

That evening—the evening the Terrible Rage finally ended—Jimmy Travis came home from one such illicit rendezvous smelling of cheap liquor and cheaper perfume. The perfume he had bought himself and given to Mary as some sort of tangible token of the future he'd promised her. It was nothing more than rosewater, but he'd peeled off the label and told her it was *Channel N°55 or somesuch, from Paris near France, you know?* Mary believed him. She wanted to believe him. She'd been saving every hard-earned cent and dime for as long as she could recall, had all of fifty-three dollars and change stowed someplace safe, and she was waiting for the right moment to give it to Jimmy as a pledge for their tomorrows.

That evening she'd walked down to the site and hid out in Jimmy's office until the crew had disbanded and headed home. She'd prepared her father's evening meal, left him a note to say she was with friends, and once the coast was clear, she and Jimmy had driven out toward the railroad station. There was a field behind the station where they could park undisturbed, and here Jimmy had her do things for him that a good Polish Catholic girl should never have done for any man.

Once Jimmy's carnal needs had been satisfied, he drove her back to the main road, no more than half a mile from her home, and sent her on her way. She had wanted to talk to him, to ask him again when he was going to leave his wife and run away with her, but she had seen how much he'd drunk, and she didn't dare make him mad. She knew he had a temper, a short fuse, and she knew better than to light it. She had convinced herself that once they were away from Flatwater, he would be different, that his temper was merely due to the frustration he felt about their not being together all the time. That's what he'd told her, and she believed him. She *needed* to believe him, because if he was lying, then everything

23

of which she'd convinced herself was worthless, and that would have been too much to bear.

So Jimmy let Mary out of the truck, and she started walking home. He drove back to his own house, and there he found Janette waiting for him, his dinner cold, her own temper frayed, and Michael—all of fifteen years old—wondering whether he would be witnessing yet another drama of violence and madness unfold before his eyes.

"Don't even open your freakin' mouth," was Jimmy's greeting as he entered the house. "Long day, dumbass workers, problems you could not even comprehend, and the last thing I need is to hear some bullshit whiny freakin' bitch going on at me about how I'm late."

And then he turned to Michael and added, "And I don't need to see you sharing sideways fucking glances with her like you think you're better than me. Don't think I don't know what you say about me, you pair together like snakes in a freakin' basket. Get my dinner, get me a drink, and leave me the hell alone, all right?"

Michael fetched a bottle and a glass, Janette fetched a plate and some cutlery, and they set those things down before Jimmy and backed away to the kitchen.

"This is freakin' shit!" was the first comment.

"This is some goddamned cold fuckin' shit you're giving me!" was the second.

The third was delivered in person as Jimmy came into the kitchen and roughly pushed his wife against the edge of the sink.

He turned to Michael. "Get the fuck upstairs, boy!" he hollered.

Michael stood there. He hesitated. Perhaps for the first time, he really hesitated.

Jimmy's expression changed, as if the shadow of a cloud had passed over a field and left part of that shadow behind.

The immediate sense was one of disbelief that the kid would have the nerve to disobey him. Then there was something else, as if Jimmy Franklin suddenly became aware of the fact that Michael now stood level with him, that he wasn't looking down at a little boy any more, but a young man.

"Why you—" he started, and then, as if realizing that words were all so much wasted air, he grabbed a knife from beside the sink and brandished it.

"Git!" he snarled. "Git, boy! Now!"

Jimmy lunged once, and though he missed Michael with the blade of that knife, the intent was all too clear.

Janette screamed. "No, Jimmy! Leave him alone! Don't hurt the boy!"

She grabbed Jimmy's arm, but Jimmy pushed her aside.

He advanced on Michael, one step, another, and Michael held his ground.

"You dare to challenge me?" Jimmy seethed.

"No, Jimmy, no!" Janette screamed again, and this time she forced herself between her husband and her son, pushing Jimmy back toward the sink.

"Go, Michael!" she said, her voice an entreaty, a plea. "Please, Michael. Please go... now!"

And it was not the knife in his father's hand that made Michael back up and turn away; it was the look in his mother's eyes.

Michael left the kitchen. He crouched in the shadows at the top of the stairs, and he listened as Jimmy Travis seethed venom and hatred through gritted teeth. He felt as if he had betrayed his mother, and yet he felt that he could not have done otherwise.

It was not long before he heard the rending of fabric, and he knew without a shadow of a doubt what his father was doing to his mother.

She would not cry out; she would not scream. She would close her eyes and clench her fists. That was what he did. That was what he always did.

And when Jimmy was done, he went back to the table, drank another glass of whiskey, lifted his fork, and continued eating.

But that evening it went a little differently.

Once Jimmy had seated himself at the table, Janette composed herself for a few minutes. She breathed deeply, thought of her past, her present, her future, considered what might ultimately happen to Michael far more than what would become of herself, and then she walked calmly through the front room, stood just a foot or so from her husband, and—much to his disbelief and wonder—delivered the following speech:

"I hate you with a passion so fierce I cannot even describe it, James Franklin Travis. You are an ugly man, not only physically, but right through to the very core of your being. You are a shameful blight on the face of the earth, and you are breathing air that does not deserve to be poisoned by your presence—"

To which Jimmy Travis said, "You stupid freakin' bitch. You dumbass, motherfucking stupid freakin' bitch. How dare you talk to—"

Janette smiled then, and there was something so strange about that smile that Jimmy just stopped talking.

That's when Janette picked up the knife from the table, held it firmly in her fist, and—with every ounce of strength she could muster—drove it into his left eye.

Jimmy Travis sat there for a while, his right eye staring at her, that sense of disbelief still present in his expression—doubled now, for there was disbelief that she had talked back to him and a second helping when he realized she'd stabbed him through the eye. But maybe his nervous system had already started to shut down. Maybe the simple fact of finding three inches of cutlery through his frontal lobe was enough to warrant such an expression. He continued to sit there for a good ten seconds more, and then the body surrendered. Whatever electrical impulse might have still churned through his mortal frame gave up the ghost, and Jimmy Travis just sort of rolled forward, his head meeting the table, that knife burying itself a further three inches into his head. If he hadn't been completely dead before, he was then.

For a single second it seemed as though Jimmy Travis had finally come to rest, but—as if in slow motion—his head turned and almost rocked back and forth. It stopped moving, the side of his face on the plate from which he'd been eating only moments before, his left eye nothing more than a raw socket from which protruded an inch of the knife handle, his right eye wide with disbelief and shock, whatever final vestiges of awareness might still exist trying to come to terms with the fact that this was it. He was done for. His life, as he had known it, was a wrap.

Janette Travis then sat down beside her husband and breathed deeply. For an hour, maybe two, she would be a free woman, and she was going to savor it as best she could.

After a couple of minutes, she called Michael down.

"Michael," she said. "Your father is dead. I done killed him with a knife. You have to take your bicycle and go on over to Sheriff Baxter's office now, and you have to tell them to send the coroner's wagon for your father and a police car for me. They gonna hang me for this, I'm pretty sure, but I want you to know that I done it for both of us. I may spend the rest of my life in a jail cell, or they may just wanna save some money and have me done for as soon as possible, but there's every likelihood that this here is gonna be the last time we see each other, certainly as mother and son. So don't fret, don't cry, and don't even think that this was because of you. It was *for* you, sure, but it was for me as well, so don't go beating yourself to death with any kind of guilt thing, you hear me?"

Michael just stood there in shocked silence.

"Michael, you answer your mother when she asks you a question. I don't want you carrying on with any kind of guilt for this, okay?"

Michael nodded. "Yes, ma'am."

"I am counting on you to be the best you can be wherever you wind up," Janette went on, "and never forget that I did this out of love for you and for no other reason. I could have borne this alone, son, but I knew that one day he was gonna kill you, and that I could never have suffered."

She paused then, reached out and stroked her dead husband's

Dixie-Peach-Pomade-slicked hair, and added, "Anyways, whatever else happens, this is done now, and it can't be undone."

She turned and smiled at Michael. "Now come here and hug me good, and then off with you, boy. You go get Sheriff Baxter and tell him I done killed your daddy with a table knife. If John Baxter ain't there, then you get Harold Fenton, okay?"

And Michael stepped forward, and he hugged his mother, and he closed his eyes and seemed to draw every inch of warmth and comfort he could from her, for he knew that this was perhaps the last time he would ever be able to do so. And then he fetched his bicycle and rode the mile and a half to the sheriff's office to deliver the message.

The sheriff came out personal, brought Deputy Harold Fenton with him, put Michael's bike in the trunk of his squad car and drove him back.

When they arrived, they found Janette Travis standing on the porch waiting for them. She had changed her torn dress for her Sunday best, and she had her coat all buttoned up.

"He's in there, John," she told the sheriff. "Deader 'an roadkill. I done killed him for his cheating, his lying, his infidelity, and his cruelty. No excuses, no sympathy needed. I just done what I figured was best for the boy long-term, and that's all I have to say about it."

"Appreciate you didn't try to run, Janette," Sheriff John Baxter said. "Only have had to come after you, and that'd have done nothin' but make it worse for all concerned."

"Nowhere to run to, John," she replied. "Everythin' I ever wanted was here, 'cept I didn't find it. Wasn't for lack of lookin' though."

"You understand this ain't gonna go easy on you, Janette."

"I know, John. I considered all o' that 'fore I done it."

"Shouldn't be sayin' these things to me, Janette. That smacks of premeditation, takes it out of the realm of self-defense. Have to let you know I'm obliged to write up anything you tell me, so's best if you keep your lips tight for now."

"Was premeditated, John. No use hidin' from the truth. Been thinkin' about killin' him for just the longest time."

"What do you want here, Janette? You wanna fry for this?"

She turned then, tearless, almost expressionless, and she smiled like Mona Lisa.

"I was dead three weeks after I married the son of a bitch, John, just no one had the decency to bury me. Left me to rot away here all these years. Now I'm gonna get buried, and maybe I'll get some rest. I can lie to you now when I knows the truth, but whatever punishment I get here on earth will just mean an eternity in hell. Better just face it as it

27

is, take the punishment due, and maybe I got a chance of forgiveness in the afterlife."

Sheriff John Baxter didn't know what to say in response, so he said nothing. He read Janette Travis her rights, he told she was under arrest for the first-degree murder of Jimmy Travis, and then he put her in the back of the squad and locked the door.

Michael had watched the entire exchange unfold in disbelief and silence.

"Maybe better if you just wait here for the county coroner," Baxter said. "He'll be along before you know it. But stay outside the house. Don't go on in there. If you wanna take a ride back to the morgue with your daddy and the coroner, that'd be fine. Maybe you can have a few moments with him when you get there, say your goodbyes an' all."

And with that, Sheriff John Baxter left Deputy Fenton behind to keep an eye on the boy and the body and drove Janette Travis away.

Michael stood for a few minutes, and then—in defiance of the sheriff—he walked on into the house and stood in the hall. Deputy Fenton, a pasty-faced little man with a wife as wide as a water tower, seemed entirely unsure of the protocol in such a situation, and so he simply walked on in after Michael to make sure he didn't touch nothing.

Michael looked through the doorway, could clearly see his father there, his head on the dinner plate, a mess of cold mashed potato and blood squeezed up around his cheek. A wide pool of blood had spread and was now dripping over the edge onto the wooden floor. *Drip-drip-drip*, like a metronome. It precisely matched the beat of his own heart. He wondered if fathers and sons always had the same heartbeat. He wondered if the baton had been passed.

Jimmy Travis's right eye was open and staring. It was a bold blue, bolder and bluer than Michael ever remembered it. The expression—strangely—was one of reconciliation, resignation perhaps, a wordless acceptance of his own fate. And yet there was something else, almost a challenge, a prompt for Michael to say something, to give him one final word of backtalk just to see where it darned well got him.

It was a long time before Michael heard the sound of a car, and when he turned and walked back to the veranda, when he saw the coroner's wagon winding a dusty path down toward the house, he knew that this day had been a special day, an important day, perhaps the most significant day of his life.

He did not know it yet, but this would also be the day when the dreams and the headaches began—dreams he did not understand and headaches that came and went so fast that they might almost have never happened. Ghosts of pain. That's what they were like. Ghosts that haunted his sleeping thoughts, much the same as he himself had haunted the thoughts of his father.

Michael Travis went back inside. He stood once more in silence, listening to his own breathing, feeling the beat of his own heart, watching the ever-widening trail of blood as it *drip-drip-dripped* onto the floor beneath his feet.

3

"Agent Travis?"

Travis looked up.

"You all right, sir?" Rourke asked.

"Yes, of course."

"Got the body here," Rourke said. "Ready for your examination."

"Absolutely," Travis replied, taking the gloves that Farley offered him.

Travis removed his jacket, pulled on the gloves, and stood aside as Farley opened the drawer.

It took the three of them to lift the dead man onto a trolley, and then Farley wheeled him to the mortician's slab. Again, it took three of them to transfer him from the trolley.

"Two hundred and forty-five pounds," Farley said. "Give or take. He's six foot one inches in height, he takes a size twelve shoe, and from the look of him, he's either a gangster or a soldier."

Farley stripped back the sheet, and the dead man was revealed in all his damaged splendor. The right side of his body—mainly focused on his shoulder, his hip, and his upper thigh—were badly discolored.

"Laking here," Travis said.

"Precisely, and a considerable amount of it. As far as I can gather, the weapon of choice entered at the base of the skull." Farley lifted the dead man's head and turned it toward Travis. The hair was cut short in back, and the entry wound—now black and rigid—was little more than an inch wide.

"Whatever kind of blade was used, it went right up through the cerebellum into the temporal lobe. Two or three more inches and the tip of the blade would have touched the internal roof of the skull. It wouldn't have taken a great deal of force. Could have been done by anyone with a modicum of strength."

"And the lapse of time between death and discovery?"

"I'd say twelve to twenty-four hours. I'd like to be more specific, but that's tough. As I said, there is a considerable amount of laking, so he was dead and laid on his back for a good number of hours before he was moved."

"And the scars and the bullet holes are the reason for your assumption that he was a gangster or a soldier?" Travis asked.

30

"From what I can see, he has been through the mill, physically speaking. He appears to have been shot three times, once in the right shoulder, once in the right thigh, another time a through-and-through on the left side of his stomach. The oldest is the right thigh; the newest is the shoulder. Those wounds go back ten, maybe fifteen years. There are indications of defensive knife wounds to the hands, a stab wound in the lower back that narrowly missed his spine, a scar on the upper-right side of his head above the ear that would correspond to a blunt trauma injury, perhaps a tire level, a hammer even, and a host of other minor injury indications that really put him in a class of his own."

Travis seemed to disconnect then, seemed to enter a world of his own. Farley and Rourke just stepped back and watched him as he pored over the body, literally inch by inch. He lifted the dead man's right hand and turned it over. He inspected the wrist, the forearms, the shoulders, beneath the arms, the back of the neck. He felt along the hairline, behind the ears, along the collarbone, and across the chest. Then he inspected the lower half of the man's body, getting Farley to help him turn the body over, looking every place possible for anything that would assist in identifying the man. He inspected every scar, every mark, every blemish.

"This means something," Travis finally said, indicating the back of the man's right knee.

Both Farley and Rourke came forward, and there they saw what Travis was speaking of.

It was a tattoo, no doubt about, but so small, so insignificant, that it could have been very easily overlooked. The simple fact that the tattoo was nothing but a series of small dots also meant that it could have been taken as a scattering of minor skin blemishes, perhaps lentigines or freckles.

"What the hell is that?" Rourke asked.

"Uncertain," Travis said, "but it looks like a reversed question mark."

Travis took his notebook from his pocket and carefully drew a precisely scaled diagram of the mark.

Travis set the diagram aside and continued to inspect the body. It was between the toes that he found further tattooed dots—seven in all, one dot at a time, three on one foot, four on the other.

He made a note of this in his book and then asked Farley to assist him in turning the body faceup again.

"So this bruising," Travis said. "This appears more post- than pre-mortem..."

"Hard to tell, yes," Farley said, "but I'd go with post as well. If it is post, then at this stage we can assume that he was killed by the insertion of the blade into the brain, and then he was put under the carousel. The fact that he was under the carousel platform and on his left side indicates that the bruising on the right side came from being hit by the platform as he lay there. Truth is, we don't know. All I can say is that from the extent of the laking, he was dead for a good while before he was found."

Travis turned to Rourke. "The Brady woman reported seeing him beneath the carousel and got them to stop it, right?"

"Exactly," Rourke said.

"And a couple of people from the carnival dragged him out."

"Just like I said."

"Okay," Travis replied, closing his notebook. "That confirms that he could not have been on the carousel before he died, as was reported by some. That's all for the body right now, Mr. Farley. Let's get him back in the drawer."

Once the body was returned, Travis asked for the man's clothes and personal possessions. Again, with the same fastidiousness with which he had inspected the body, he pored over every inch of the man's effects. He asked Farley for several sheets of paper and drew exact outlines of both the left and right shoes.

"You have fingerprinting ink and a roller?" he asked Farley.

"I do, yes," Farley said, and handed them over.

Using the roller, Travis applied a thin layer of ink to the sole of each shoe and made an impression of them on two more sheets of paper. He then cleaned off the soles and returned the shoes to the bag from which they'd come.

Travis washed his hands thoroughly, smelled them, and washed them again without soap. Once satisfied that his hands carried no discernible odor, he went back to the dead man's clothes, holding them merely an inch from his face, his eyes closed, attempting to determine anything telling. He inhaled, but as he exhaled, he turned his face away so as not to taint any existing aroma with that of his own breath.

"Cheap fragrance," Travis said, his eyes still closed. "Coffee, oil, tobacco, sweat."

Travis spent more time looking at the blood patterns on the back of the man's shirt collar and the collar of the jacket. He asked for a magnifying glass, went through every pocket, turning it inside out and brushing whatever lint and fragments he found within onto a sheet of white paper and then viewing them closely. Every once in a while, he paused to make further notes in his book.

Though he seemed unaware of Rourke or Farley, he nevertheless glanced up at them and smiled knowingly.

"You've done this before, then?" Rourke said.

"No, Sheriff… First time for everything though, eh?"

Rourke looked at Farley. Farley just stood there, seemingly fascinated by the entire process.

Once Travis was done with the man's clothes, he folded them again neatly and returned them to their respective bags.

"We're done for the moment," he told Rourke. "There are no manufacturers' labels on his clothes or shoes; he walks heavier on the right than the left; he had low blood pressure; he was a heavy smoker, obsessively chewed his fingernails; low-protein diet, signs of diabetes, drank far too much alcohol for his own good—probably for anyone else's as well—and when it came to crooners, he erred more toward Bing Crosby than Dean Martin."

Rourke shook his head, unsure of whether Travis's final comment was actually a joke or not. "I don't know what to make of you."

Travis smiled wryly. "You don't have to make anything of me, Sheriff Rourke."

Farley gathered up the paper bags and walked them back to the lockup.

"I'd like to go to my hotel now," Travis said. "I want to take a shower, and then I want to head out to the carnival and begin questioning the personnel."

"Very good," Rourke said.

"How long do I gotta keep your friend here?" Farley said.

"A while yet," Travis said. "We have to identify him before anything further can happen with the body. And I'll need a copy of your autopsy report."

"No problem. I got one ready for you."

Farley gave Travis the report. Travis thanked him for his assistance, and then he and Rourke made their farewells and returned to the cars outside the building.

"Got you the best room the McCaffrey has," Rourke said. "It ain't the Plaza, but it should suffice."

"I am sure it'll be just fine," Travis said.

*

The McCaffrey Hotel certainly wasn't the Plaza. The young man who greeted Travis and Rourke at the desk was Danny McCaffrey, the brother of Rourke's deputy, Lester.

"Honored to have you here, sir," Danny told Travis. "And I hope you'll be comfortable." He insisted on taking both Travis's overnight bag and his portable typewriter.

Rourke asked how long Travis would need.

"Forty-five minutes," Travis said.

"I'll be back in forty-five minutes precisely, then."

Michael Travis and Danny McCaffrey made their way upstairs, taking a left along the landing toward the front of the building, and here—with seeming pride—McCaffrey showed Travis a room no more than eleven by fifteen, a single bed against the right-hand wall, a small desk and chair beneath the window, a tired armchair, a floor lamp standing sentry beside it, and a threadbare rug on the floor.

In that moment, Travis was reminded of the first time he had seen his given room in Esther Faulkner's house.

He felt a twinge of something, something deep, something unidentifiable, and he pushed it aside. Once again, further memories floated up from the shadows of his past.

"This will do just fine," Travis said, appreciating that he had no choice in where he stayed. To ask of the other hotel would be dismissive of the McCaffreys' hospitality.

"Sorry to say that none of the rooms have their own bathrooms, so you'll have to use the one down the hall. Third door on the right."

"No problem at all," Travis said.

"Breakfast you can have here in the morning," Danny McCaffrey explained. "Dinner in the evening too, and we own a small diner in town, so you can take your lunch there if you wish. You'll find my sister down there. Her name is Laura. She knows you're expected."

"That's very good of you," Travis said.

"More than welcome," McCaffrey said. "Anything else you need, just holler."

"Much appreciated, Mr. McCaffrey."

"Please call me Danny," he said.

"Danny it is," Travis replied.

Danny left the room, closing the door gently behind him.

Travis laid out a clean shirt and underwear. He went down the hall, found the bathroom, and got undressed.

The first minute beneath the shower was bracingly cold, and then he increased the flow of hot water to a comfortable level and washed quickly.

34

He dried himself, redressed in his suit trousers and shirt, bundling his underwear into the towel and checking that the hallway was empty before he hurried back to his room. Once behind the door, he changed into his clean clothes, dried and combed his hair, and unpacked the remainder of his things. He set his typewriter on the small desk with a towel folded beneath it to reduce the noise. He put Farley's autopsy report next to the typewriter. He glanced over his extensive notes, made another copy of the diagram from the back of the dead man's knee. It was very definitely akin to a reversed question mark. He did not pause to consider it further. He would find the significance of it, but everything in its own time. Now he had to begin the process of questioning all those who worked at the carnival.

Travis checked that he had everything he needed—his notebook, his pens, his camera, the shoe outlines and prints, a photo of the victim—and then he locked the door and went on down to the lobby.

"Danny, how many keys are there to each room?" Travis asked.

"Well, we have three or four as a general rule. Guests are pretty forgetful when it comes to keys."

"Okay, if you could take any copy you have of my room key and put it in the safe, that would be appreciated."

Danny frowned. "The safe?"

"You don't have a safe?"

"No, sir. No safe."

"Okay, well, put them in a lockable desk drawer or something, somewhere secure, and don't give them to anyone but me, understand? And there will be no need to clean the room on a daily basis. I will attend to that. You can change the bedclothes on the usual schedule, but forewarn me so I can be there when it's being done."

"Yes, sir, of course."

Travis glanced at his watch. Rourke had another handful of minutes before he'd be late.

"Can I get you anything, Mr. Travis?" Danny McCaffrey said, interrupting Travis's thoughts. "A cup of coffee while you wait for Chas, perhaps?"

"No, thank you," he replied. "I'm good."

Travis turned back to the window. The street was empty of people, strangely so, and it reminded him of another day, another town, another empty street. That had been an important day, and though he tried not to think of it with pride, he could not help but think of it with a sense of accomplishment. Things had changed that day, and—as such—its importance could not be underestimated.

February 11, 1953, a Wednesday, a day when Michael Travis, special agent, had been mentioned in dispatches to the director himself.

But the significance of what had happened that day in February of 1953 bore a far greater weight due to the events that immediately followed the death of his father, the blunt reality of the Nebraska State Welfare Institution, and his first meeting with Anthony Scarapetto.

4

For Michael Travis, it was a change, and a hard one at that. Looking back, it was as if he had two distinct ranges of memory set against the horizon of his mind: the *before* and the *after*. The first was dark, the second darker. *Before* meant the ever-present threat of liquor-fueled violence, the ferocity of his father's outbursts, all of this tempered by the two sides of his mother, the beaten, bloodied, swollen-faced wife, possessing barely strength enough to breathe, and on the other side his *real* mother, loving, somehow ever-forgiving, convincing herself that all it would take was to believe *enough* to make it all change for the better. It never did and now never could. The *after* was something else entirely, though equally strange, immeasurably new, and frighteningly real.

For a long time after his father's death, Michael did not speak. Already a quiet one, he became silent. People with letters trailing their names said he was *emotionally traumatized*, understandably so, and would eventually come back to reality. They asked him about his thoughts, his feelings, what was really going on *inside*. He did not care to answer their questions, and so he did not. He did not speak of the dreams, for there was little he could recall of them once he woke, and he would not have known what to say anyway.

Michael became a ward of the state of Nebraska: the court his father, due process his mother, and he the bastard child that fell through the gap in between.

Janette Alice Travis, a mere thirty-one years of age, was charged, arraigned, and remanded for trial. As the county prosecutor and public defender prepared their cases, she was held west of York in the State Reformatory for Women. There had already been intimations that the state would press for the death penalty. Sheriff John Baxter, if nothing else, was a man who understood law as needful for the survival of a society and thus was duty bound to relay precisely what Janette Travis had said to him upon his approaching the scene of the crime. It was to be those few words that damned her.

Was premeditated, John. No use hidin' from the truth. Been thinkin' about killin' him for just the longest time...

37

Had she not said such a thing, there might have been a prayer, but it seemed the state prosecutor had blood on his teeth, and he wasn't going to fall victim to pleas for clemency, mitigating circumstances, et al. The previous two governorships had seen no executions. Before them, Governor Arthur J. Weaver, back in May of '29, had seen only one murderer pine-boxed out of death row. If Janette Travis went such a way, then it would be the first execution under the current governorship of Dwight Griswold, the first woman ever to take her place in the Big Chair up at Nebraska State Penitentiary in Lincoln.

Maybe the state prosecutor, a bullfrog of a man called Frederick Wyatt, and the state's DA, Lyle Samuelson, figured such a thing was worth brownie points on the old career scoring card.

Whatever went on in the minds and hearts of the bureaucratic and judicial collective responsible for the expedition of Janette Travis's case, none of it gave a thought for Michael, even then sojourned in the inappropriately named Nebraska State Welfare Institution, for institution it may very well have been, but *welfare* could not have figured any less in its concerns.

State Welfare was an ex-military facility a couple of dozen miles north of St. Paul. There were no armed guards or watchtowers; there were no dogs or alarms or gun galleries. The doors were locked, and the custodians, as they were known, were uniformed and carried whistles and nightsticks. The big boss of the hot sauce during Michael Travis's period of tenure was Warden Seymour Cordell, ex-cop, ex-penitentiary governor, head as hard as a pool ball, face like a worn-out leather mailbag, absent of pretty much any kind of feeling save a gritty and downbeat pragmatism that was doled out by the handful to anyone within arm's reach.

Michael Travis was inducted at State Welfare on Monday, August 24, 1942, just five days after the death of his father. He had not seen or heard from his mother during those five days and had not been given any information regarding her circumstances or whereabouts. Those five days had been spent in the holding cells of the Flatwater Sheriff's Department, simply because there was nowhere else to put him. A perfunctory inquiry into existing relatives had turned up nothing. It appeared that both maternal and paternal grandparents were deceased, as was Janette's one maternal aunt, Clara Pardoe, herself a liquor-widow. Clara had had a son, Bernard, who was Janette's cousin, though he was dead. Bernard had been briefly married to a woman called Esther, though she could not be easily located.

So, five days of jail food and serge blankets later, Michael Travis was driven twenty or thirty miles upstate to Welfare, and once he had been stripped, deloused, clippered and uniformed, he found himself standing before Warden Cordell, a custodian behind him, another at the door.

Warden Cordell sat behind a beat-to-shit desk as wide as a football field. The chair within which he sat was a wooden roller, and each time he shifted, it creaked like a ship. He read through the single sheet of paper that sat in the manila file in front of him, and then he leaned back and looked at Michael for what seemed like half an eternity.

"When I was a boy," he said, "and not a great deal younger than yourself, I did something wicked. I killed a cat. It was a mean cat, a vicious little son of a bitch, and it sat on the veranda of my folks' house like it owned the place. I would shoo it away, kick it every once in a while, but it was a tough creature, and it just kept on coming back for more. My ma used to throw it tidbits, you know? Encourage it. I hated the thing. Hated it with a passion. But I'll tell you this now, son, that cat was not a quitter. No matter the times I kicked it or pelted it with rocks, it would just keep on coming back for more. Seemed the urge to survive was a great deal stronger than the fear of pain."

Cordell paused for a moment, as if caught in reverie, and then he looked back at Michael and went on talking.

"Anyways, one day, I got tired of this cat, and I coaxed it up on the veranda with a piece of chicken and then I bashed its head in with a stone. That was that. The cat was dead. And you know something? I damned well missed that son of a bitch. I missed him something bad. Real sorry that I killed him, but—"

Cordell waved his hand dismissively.

"What you gonna do, eh? The past is the past, and there ain't no reason for cryin' on it, right?"

Michael stood impassive, implacable. He didn't want to say anything in case it was the wrong thing.

"Well, believe it or not, son, there's a coupla reasons for tellin' you that story. Firstly, like I said before, there ain't no use cryin' on what's been an' gone. Life kicks us this way and that, and kicks us good. You may think that you're the only one who ever got kicked this hard, but I can assure you that there's a good deal of kids here that has had it as tough, some even tougher. Okay, so your ma is up at the reformatory for killing your pa, but at least you got a ma, son. At least for a while."

Cordell smiled like he was delivering some good news in among all this other business.

"Anyways, second reason I told you about the cat is perhaps more relevant to your present situation. I learned from that experience that cats is tough. Well, I learned from working here that kids is tough too, often tougher than cats. There is rules and reggerlations. They is ironbound and immovable. You break those rules, we gonna fix you up so you see the error of your ways. You break the rules a third time, well, that's when we put you in the Choke Hole, and that ain't a place you wanna go, believe me now, son. That is *not* a place you wanna go visit."

Cordell paused and squinted at Michael.

"You hearin' me, son?"

Michael nodded. "Yes, sir, I am."

"You got nothin' to say for yourself?"

"No, sir, I have nothing to say."

Cordell smiled. "Polite, I'll give you that. Respectful. I'm just sayin' that I don't want to have to bash your head in with a stone, you see? Figuratively speakin', o' course. But from what I can see, it appears we're gonna have very little trouble gettin' you settled in here, son."

"No trouble at all, sir."

"Well, okay. So I done read your paperwork, I understand you had some difficulties, but seein' as how there ain't no one to look after you, you get us. You ain't no thief as far as I can see. You ain't never been in trouble with the law, right?"

"No, sir."

"Well, let me warn you about some of these here boys. Some of them are all teeth and claws, and those you gotta watch out for. They feel threatened by change, threatened by newcomers, threatened by things only they can see, as far as I can tell. And then some of them are just noise and nothin' else, and you don't gotta be afraid of them. They bark, but they don't got no teeth to bite with. Then there's the quiet ones, and they's the most dangerous of all. We have ourselves a couple of really crazy ones, but we keep them out of the main circulation of events, and that makes life a lot easier for everyone."

Cordell rose from his creaking chair and walked around the desk.

"I hope you ain't gonna be a troublesome one, son, because I just got enough on my hands without all of that. It don't never get you nowhere 'cept the Choke Hole, or Chokey, as they see fit to call it now, and—like I said afore—that's a place you don't wanna go once, let alone twice. I understand you ain't here because of some bad thing you did, but still, if you figure that our own lives are our responsibility, then you ended up here 'cause of yourself and no one else, right?"

"Yes, sir."

Cordell smiled, and for a moment his awkward leather face took on an almost avuncular warmth. He extended his hand, and Michael took it—warily at first—and then when he realized that Cordell was doing nothing but shaking his hand, Michael returned that gesture with a firm response.

"Good handshake says a lot about a man," Cordell said. "And you done looked me in the eye while I was talkin' to you. You ain't no regular delinquent, son. I can see that plain as day. Don't let them see your weaknesses. If you let them get a foothold, they climb all over you and kick you to pieces before sundown."

Michael Travis felt his hand being released, and then Cordell gripped his shoulder, wished him a final "Good luck, son," and then he was escorted out of Cordell's office and down the hallway.

The custodian who walked with him stopped at a locked door. "My name is Officer Hibbert," he said. "Through here we have something called the cubes. They are little rooms, cells if you like, and they ain't got nothin' in them but four white walls, a bed, a chair, a locker for your clothes, and a towel. You gonna be in here for two weeks. This is just the way it is. You get your food through a mailbox in the door, and you come out for an hour's walk around the yard between ten and eleven in the morning. If you have some difficulty or problem while in your cube, then you knock on the door three times. You then wait fifteen minutes. If there is no response, then you can knock on the door again. You wait until you are attended to. Any violation of that routine or any violation of any other regulation means a full day in Chokey. A full day is twenty-four hours. You will receive a copy of the facility regulations tomorrow, and you'd be advised to read it."

Hibbert paused and looked at Michael closely. "You do read, right?"

"Yes, sir, I can read."

"Good, 'cause I am dog-tired of having to read that whole thing out loud and explainin' all them words. Anyways, that's the deal, kid. This is for your own good. This is so's you get used to the idea of your own company. This is so's you learn how to mind your own business and no one else's. Now, I am gonna take you on through there and put you in your cube. You'd be advised to not start thinking about minutes or hours or days. Just makes it worse. Just get your head down and sleep as much as you can, and these two weeks will go like nothin'."

Hibbert took his key chain from his belt, found a key, opened the door, and walked Michael through. The corridor was painted white and stretched for a good eighty or ninety feet. On each side, spaced perhaps eight feet apart, were doors facing each other. The doors had a single lever handle, and low to the ground was a bolted shutter perhaps a foot wide and three inches deep.

Hibbert walked half the length of the corridor, Michael right behind him, and then he stopped to open the door.

"I will not be on duty tomorrow morning, and so another officer will come to supervise your exercise time. Dinner is at six." Hibbert looked at his watch. "Three and a half hours from now."

Hibbert opened the door and ushered Michael in, and before Michael even had a moment to turn and look at the man, the door had closed tight behind him and he was locked inside.

"Like I said, son," Hibbert said through the locked door, "you try and sleep as much as you can. Don't do no good to be thinkin'."

He heard Hibbert's footsteps retreating all the way to the hallway door, heard it open, slam shut, heard the key turn with a sharp finality, and then there was silence.

Hibbert's advice might have been wise, but Michael was a thinker. He had always been a thinker. His mother figured he thought too much. *Some people just are that way*, she'd say. *Some people want an answer for everything. They want to know why and how and when and where. That's a double-edged sword, mind. Sometimes you wind up with a whole basket of answers you'd have done better without.*

Michael did not believe that there was such a thing. Any answer, even a bad one, was better than no answer at all.

But, as was often the case, there were questions that would forever be nothing but questions, because no one had the answer.

Michael thought about his mother. He knew she was in the State Reformatory for Women just west of York. He did not know what kind of room she was in, whether she was alone or with other women. He did not know if she was well or sick or if someone had already beaten her half to death. Such things happened in prison. He knew this.

That first night, the few hours of fitful rest he managed were disturbed by dreams. As was always the case, those images that assaulted his sleeping mind were gone as soon as he woke, and trying to recall them was like snatching smoke rings from a breeze. The only thing that recurred, the only thing he ever remembered, was a single shadow against the dry, cracked earth of an arid field. And the sound of a bird. A crow, perhaps a grackle, its cawing more like the laughter of some old woman than any real creature. But even that image, the strange feeling that accompanied it, was gone within minutes.

That first morning in the cubes, as with all subsequent mornings, breakfast came through the mail slot. A pressed-metal tray, four sockets, within them a piece of corn bread, a spoonful of blackstrap molasses, a handful of beans, and a thumb-sized strip of dried pork that was tough and salty. There was a cup of water as well, and it possessed a brackish and metallic taste. Michael did not think as he ate. He simply ate. Ten minutes passed and there was a knock on the door.

"Yes?" Michael said.

"Tray and cup, fucknuts," a voice from the other side said, and Michael saw the mail slot open at the base of the door.

He passed the utensils back through the aperture and heard it slam shut.

"Got a schedule," the voice said. "Be ready next time."

Footsteps moved on, the sound of the adjacent door being knocked, the tray and cup being returned, and on it went until the footsteps were silent and the opening and the closing of the aperture in each door was nothing but a whisper of sound that he had to strain to hear.

Michael returned to the thin mattress and lay down.

He knew that someone would come and collect him for exercise time at ten o'clock. He did not know what time it was and thus had no clue as to how long he would have to wait. He closed his eyes and fought his way back into an agitated and restless sleep.

At first he could not see anything but that single blue eye, the way his father looked back at him from the surface of the table. He had not seen it then, but was there a flash of fear in that eye? Was his father actually afraid in his moment of death? Was he able to see what was waiting for him on the other side, his reward for a life of lies, infidelity, and violence?

Michael could then see himself standing on the veranda of the house. Somewhere beyond the horizon he could see heat lightning. He could see the curvature of the earth. A sudden flare of distant color erupted in silence, and he knew it was a tree bursting into flames.

He was aware of a metronomic sound, something almost subliminal, and though he at first believed it to be his pulse or his heart, he soon realized that it was the echo of his father's blood—*drip-drip-drip*—as it fell to the floor beneath the dinner table. He wondered whether that sound was now part of him, as if there were a chamber within his mind where such sounds would be forever stored.

And then Michael woke, and he lay there for some small eternity, listening to the sounds of the corridor, the distant footsteps, the closing and opening of doors. The world went on without him, and he was no longer part of it. At least for now.

Unbeknownst to Michael, he would reside at State Welfare for merely ten months, but those ten months would mark his passage from boy to man. His sensibilities and preconceptions about himself and life would be challenged by many people and in many ways, but by none more so than Anthony Scarapetto, he of the *Tray and cup, fucknuts. Got a schedule. Be ready next time.*

Scarapetto was all of seventeen years old, the seventh of nine children.

The Scarapettos were among the original birds of passage who had immigrated to America at the beginning of the 1900s. How and why they had settled in New York with their plan to open a small restaurant, perhaps a delicatessen within arm's reach of Mulberry Street, and how such a dream had collided with reality in such a way as to leave almost none of that dream intact, was a different story and did not need recounting, but Anthony Scarapetto warranted a mention considering his influence and effect on Michael Travis, both at State Welfare in 1942 and then again in February of 1953.

Anthony Scarapetto killed a man before he was fourteen. No one knew this, and Anthony would never speak of it. Though he felt no shame in having committed the murder, a murder that he felt was both provoked and justified, he was somewhat ashamed regarding the circumstances that forced his hand. The man (his name was Forrest Young), was a rent collector in Little Italy, back before the Black Hand and other such outfits took everything over, and he walked the streets and collected dollars, taking a particular interest in the youngsters. Boys or girls, it didn't matter to Young. He possessed a seemingly insatiable appetite for the attentions of children, and Anthony Scarapetto, all of nine years old, inspired in Young a fervent obsession that was beyond anything Young had experienced before.

The details of Young's entrapment of the boy in the confines of his car one Thursday afternoon in the summer of 1934 are vague and uncertain. Police reports later stated that Young's car was found parked in an alleyway at the north end of Mulberry, and within it lay the deceased. He was discovered on the backseat, his stiffening corpse drenched in blood, not only from the wide incision in his throat, but also from the terrible and vicious assault that had been perpetrated on his genitals.

"Like a tiger had mauled him," the first-at-the-scene officer had reported. "Like a wild animal had gotten in there and just torn everything apart."

There was no tiger. There was merely a nine-year-old Anthony Scarapetto with a switchblade and a vengeful temper. He had agreed to Young's invitation to sit in the backseat of the car because he figured he might be able to rob the man. When the doors had been locked and Young had started his billing and cooing, Anthony had been well aware of the man's indecent intent. Nine years old he might have been, but he was no spring chicken. Nine years of life in Little Italy was worth twenty or more anyplace else. Anthony carried a switchblade, had done so since he was five, and though he'd only ever used it as a threat to escape beatings and suchlike, now was a time when the blade might see some blood.

When Forrest Young tried to stroke Anthony's hair, Anthony told him that he wanted a dollar. Young produced the dollar from a wallet so thick it could have been a telephone book. Anthony took the dollar, tucked it into his pocket, and let the man stroke his hair. When Young tried to kiss him, he said he wanted another dollar. Young handed over the second dollar, smiling to himself, perhaps thinking that this was turning out to be a great deal easier than he'd imagined. They knew—these kids, with their flirtatious ways, their sly and coy glances—exactly what they were doing and why. But still so many of them gave the pretense of resisting. But this one? This Anthony Scarapetto was not hiding anything. He was going to do everything Forrest Young wanted him to do, but he was going to get paid for it. In a way, that made it less of a challenge, but the boy was so beautiful it didn't matter.

When Forrest Young put his hand on Anthony's thigh, Anthony asked for a third dollar. This was now slightly insulting. Two dollars was a lot of money.

"You better give me another dollar, mister," Anthony told him. "You plan on doin' that thing to me, then there better be another dollar."

"And what is it that you think I'm going to do, Anthony?" Young asked. He wanted to hear the boy say it. He wanted to hear those dirty little words from the boy's own lips.

"You want to stick your thing in my mouth, right? Or maybe you wanna stick it someplace else?"

Young's heart started beating so hard he could barely breathe.

"Well," Anthony went on, "if you wanna do that stuff, then you better give me another dollar."

Young fumbled with his wallet. He gave the boy a third dollar. He set his wallet on the dashboard and started unhooking his belt.

"Come on, mister," Anthony said. "Get it out and show me."

Young couldn't manage the buttons; his hands were shaking so much.

Anthony reached over and rested his left hand on Young's thigh. He moved his hand slowly toward Young's crotch. Young leaned back, his eyes closed. He moaned softly, little more than an exhalation, and with his right hand, Anthony Scarapetto drove the switchblade into the center of Young's throat.

Young couldn't speak. He couldn't utter a sound. His eyes screamed, however. They screamed with an agony so unbearable that there would have been no words to describe it anyway.

Young was dead within a minute, but that did not prevent Anthony from withdrawing the blade and actually cutting the man's throat from ear to ear. Then he went to work on the man's crotch and upper thighs, stabbing and slashing until Forrest Young did in fact appear to have been savaged by some wild and ravenous beast.

Anthony Scarapetto took the contents of the wallet, all of eighty-six dollars, and stuffed it inside his shirt. He exited the vehicle, ran to the end of the alley, snatched a pair of pants from one washing line, a guinea tee from another, and when he was safely from view of the street, he stripped and changed. The pants were three or four sizes too big, but he buttoned and then rolled the waist, also turned up the legs, and thus looked no different from a hundred other kids who were dressed in their father's worn-out pants for want of anything better. The knife itself was kicked into the first storm drain he encountered, the shirt into the second, the pants into the third. By the time he reached home, there was little evidence of his recent experience but for the blood beneath his fingernails and in the welts of his shoes.

Anthony Scarapetto, thus having drawn first blood, began a swift downhill run into all things criminal and violent. Safe to say that by the time he was arrested for grievous assault and mayhem in Lincoln, Nebraska, in the late winter of 1939, the Scarapetto boy that had stabbed Forrest Young had become a hardened, inveterate thief and liar.

To Michael, the seventeen-year-old Scarapetto seemed more intense and threatening than any of the custodians, perhaps representing two sides of the same deal, nothing so simplistic as good guy and bad guy, but something close enough. Michael Travis understood that he had found himself an inmate of State Welfare due to fate, bad luck, even human error, whereas Scarapetto knew he was there became of the calumny and weakness and vindictive persecution of others. Michael knew he was in trouble because of himself, in essence, and thus knew it was up to him to get out of it. Scarapetto knew he was in trouble because of everyone else.

On the day that Michael was released into general populace, Scarapetto watched him as he arrived for breakfast. He waited until Michael had taken a tray, joined the queue, been served his single piece of corn bread, his ladle of watery oatmeal, his spoonful of reconstituted egg. Michael—as all the greenhorns did—stood for a second away from the end of the queue and surveyed the mess hall before him. The noise was strange to his ears. There had to be a thousand people there, and each of them was talking in hushed voices. It gave the impression of far-off thunder, some distant sound beyond the horizon, a sound created by something that remained unseen.

Eventually, Michael chose a table to the left near the corner. The table was occupied by one person and one person only—a teenager, perhaps sixteen or seventeen, who looked sufficiently unthreatening. Michael sat down. It was no more than thirty seconds before the teenager got up and walked away. He did so suddenly and swiftly, almost as if he had been directed by some unknown command.

Michael frowned, looked over his shoulder, and was confronted by Anthony Scarapetto.

"Oh," Michael said.

Scarapetto grinned and then walked around the table and sat facing Michael.

There was an immediate change in the air. Tension perhaps, a coolness, a feeling of imminent danger, and it emanated from Scarapetto like a bad smell.

"Hey, fucknuts," Scarapetto said.

Scarapetto was a little shorter than Michael, a little narrower in the shoulder, but there was not a great deal between them. His hair was shorn close to his scalp, and here and there punctuation marks of scar tissue evidenced collisions with objects that were harder than his head. A further scar followed a narrow line from behind his right ear and out across his cheek toward his nose. It was thin, no doubt a knife or razor wound, and when Scarapetto smiled, the scar made a fold in his face as neat as a sheet of paper.

"You're new here, right?" Scarapetto asked.

"I am, yes," Michael said.

Scarapetto put his right index finger in his mouth and then proceeded to jab that finger into Michael's breakfast—the egg, the oatmeal, the corn bread.

"And this is your first meal in general, right?"

Michael knew precisely what he was dealing with then. "Looks like it's your meal now," he said.

Scarapetto smiled. "You ain't gonna complain, little man?"

"Not a word," Michael replied. He could see the edges of his own internal shadows, not as if they were moving toward him, but as if he were moving toward them.

"Is that 'cause I scare you?"

"Absolutely," Michael said. "You scare me more than anyone has ever scared me before." His voice was calm, but inside he was truly disturbed. Little more than two weeks earlier, he'd been helping his mother wash dishes. Now he was here, seated across from someone who seemed intent on violently assaulting him while the world looked away.

And then it came, that sense of his father, the certainty of how his father would have dealt with such a situation. But he was not his father. He did not dare rise to the bait.

Scarapetto started to smile, and then he frowned, and then he lunged forward and grabbed Michael's wrists. He pulled Michael forward suddenly, and the edge of the table slammed into Michael's rib cage. Michael exhaled painfully, but he did not look away from Scarapetto.

"You messin' with me, kid?" Scarapetto asked. "You jibin' me, fuckin' with me, playin' smart-mouth with me?"

Michael shook his head ever so slowly. His heart was twice its size, and it thundered uncontrollably in his chest. He could feel the rage building inside him, the desperate need to strike back, to lash out, to destroy. He also knew that whatever happened now, it was going to hurt. Still he did not look away from Scarapetto.

"Well, that's good," Scarapetto said. "That's very good, little man, 'cause you don't wanna get me riled, you know? Folks who get me riled always regret it. They *always* regret it."

Michael was aware then that the surrounding tables were quiet. People were watching him. People were seeing how he dealt with this guy.

Scarapetto released Michael's wrists and leaned back from the table, proud and arrogant now.

He pulled the cuffs of his shirt as if he were checking himself in the mirror at Brooks Brothers, and he smiled a cruel smile that said all that needed to be said. He'd put the new kid in his place. He'd made a mark, scared the little runt, and that was how it should be.

Michael understood then that if he did nothing, he would always be at the bottom of the ladder, right there for anyone to step on if they so wished. He could not fight someone such as Scarapetto. He would not have a prayer. He had to do something decisive, and he had to do it now.

In that moment, Scarapetto turned around to look at the faces that were watching him.

As he did so, Michael Travis took his own life in his hands. He leaned forward slightly and dribbled a mouthful of saliva into the oatmeal on his tray.

When Scarapetto turned back, he was wearing that self-same crooked smile. *Look at me*, it said. *Cock of the walk, I am. Big boss of the hot sauce.*

Scarapetto reached out and slid Michael's tray toward himself. He took a spoon from his pants pocket, breathed on it, polished it on his shirttail as if for effect, and then started eating the oatmeal.

There was silence around that table, but inside the head of every person watching was a *groan* of disgust.

Scarapetto was aware of nothing.

Michael watched him eat the oatmeal, his own expression blank and implacable.

Once Scarapetto was done with the oatmeal, he ate the corn bread, the egg, and then shoved the tray back at Michael.

"I think you finished your breakfast, kid," Scarapetto said.

"Looks like I did," Michael replied.

"Good, was it?"

"Excellent. The best ever."

Scarapetto looked at Michael sideways. Was this kid smart-mouthing him? Was that actually a dig? Better have not been a dig; otherwise . . .

"What's your name?" Michael asked.

"Huh?

"Your name."

"My name is none of your fuckin' business, kid. Why the hell do you want to know my name?"

"Because when someone asks me who's the boss here, I wanna be able to tell 'em."

Scarapetto smiled his sly, paper-cut smile again. "Scarapetto," he said. "Anthony Scarapetto."

"And what do I call you? Do I call you 'Mr. Scarapetto' or 'sir' or what?"

Scarapetto started to nod. "You're a smart kid," he said. "You ain't no fool, is ya? You know how to treat a man with respect, right?"

"I don't know, sir," Michael said. "Seems that if a man deserves respect, then he should get it. Obviously, you know the deal here. I am just a new guy who knows jack shit, and I wouldn't want to upset things. Seems like a new guy would want to make friends with a man like you, someone who could take care of things, show him the ropes in a place like this."

For the first time, Scarapetto seemed to unwind a little. Whatever six-foot steel rod he carried up his ass seemed to give a little, and he nodded his head sagely. "I like you, kid," he said. "You seem like a good kid to me. Why the hell are you in here, anyhow?"

"Because I got no place else to go," Michael said. "My mom killed my dad, and she's in jail and they got no place else to put me."

"Is that so?"

"Yes, sir. That is so."

"Hell, kid, you don't need to be callin' me that. Just call me Tony."

"Really?"

"Sure thing. Tony is just fine. What's your name?"

"Michael. Michael Travis."

Scarapetto reached out his hand. Michael took it and they shook.

"Pleased to make your acquaintance, Tony," Michael said.

"What the fuck is that? Jesus Christ. Who the fuck talks like that? Are you for real, kid? Pleased to make your acquaintance? Seriously, kid, you can't talk like that around here. Folks is gonna think you're a homo or somethin'."

"Are you a homo?" Michael asked.

Scarapetto looked surprised, as if he was now doubting his own ears.

Those seated on the tables within earshot fell silent. That silence seemed to spread out like ink through water.

49

Listen up.

What's happening?

Someone's fucking with Scarapetto. Called him a homo.

No, really?

Really. Now, shut the fuck up, will you?

"What did you say?"

"I asked if you had a home," Michael said. "Why are you here? Don't you have someone to look after you?"

Scarapetto—for a split second—wondered what was happening. He shook his head, just once, like a cartoon character shaking off a damn good whack.

"A home?" Scarapetto asked.

"Sure," Michael said, as nonchalant as anything. "Your folks, right? A home. Everyone has a home, don't they?"

Scarapetto was still frowning. "I thought you asked me..."

The room was silent. Those far away didn't know why they were being silent, but they didn't dare utter a word.

A couple of custodians started down from the far end of the room. Michael could hear the squeak of their shoes on the polished linoleum floor, the metal jangle of keys on their belts. For some reason—inside of himself—Michael felt almost nothing then, as if his real *self* had retreated into some safe internal space, and the *State Welfare Michael*, the one who would survive this, the one who would see him through, was out there facing the world and all it had to offer. The rage had subsided, his blood had stopped boiling, and the shadows had retreated.

"I had a home," Scarapetto said. "A while back. Don't have one no more, as far as I know."

"How long you been here?" Michael asked.

"Three years."

"How much longer you got?"

Scarapetto squinted at Michael. "Why all the questions, buddy?"

"Because that's what friends do," Michael said. "They talk about shit, you know? They ask questions; they answer them. You never had a friend before?"

"Sure I have. I got lots of friends. Everyone likes me, right? Everyone likes Tony Scarapetto."

Michael smiled. "Hey, what's not to like, right?"

Scarapetto smiled back, and then he started laughing. "Right as fuckin' rain, kid. What's not to like?"

There seemed to be a collective sigh of relief. Even the custodians, now within earshot of this exchange, understood that there wasn't going to be a problem here. Scarapetto was smiling, laughing even, and the new kid wasn't gonna get a breakfast tray up his ass. The new kid had balls, that was for sure. Hell, the new kid even spat in his oatmeal before Scarapetto took it off him. If Scarapetto had seen that, they'd be scraping bits of that new kid off the ceiling for a week or more. What's that kid's name? What did he say? Travers? Travis? It was Travis, right?

"So you take care of yourself, kid," Scarapetto said, and got up from the bench. "I'll be seein' you around."

"Sure as shit stinks, my friend."

Scarapetto hesitated once more. Something wasn't clicking somewhere. Something wasn't right with the kid, but then he couldn't put his finger on what was wrong. He shook his head once more, turned his back, and walked away.

As he did so, all eyes followed him, and once he had passed them, those eyes turned back and looked at Michael Travis.

Michael Travis merely picked up the breakfast tray, brushed the crumbs of corn bread off the table onto it, and then rose to his feet. He walked to the end of the hall, the sound of his shoes the only audible noise, and he joined the last of the breakfast stragglers.

"Kinda hungry this morning," he said. "Any chance of some more?"

A greasy-faced teenager with a firestorm of angry spots across his forehead glanced up at one of the custodians.

The custodian nodded once, and Michael Travis was served a second breakfast.

By the time he took his seat again, the hubbub of voices had resumed, just as before, but there was a different timbre and pitch to it. People who had not heard the exchange wanted to know what had taken place. There was very little that remained of the real conversation save two details: The new kid had spitballed his oatmeal before Scarapetto ate it, and then had he actually called him a homo? Really? That was all that remained, for that was what they wanted to believe.

No one explained this version of events to Scarapetto, of course, for no one dared. Scarapetto was a class-A asshole—always had been and always would be—and just because the new kid had bested him didn't mean that Scarapetto couldn't still be as vicious and cruel as ever. The vast majority of kids in State Welfare weren't so eager to start trouble, just to stay out of it.

Michael Travis, however, had somehow avoided a whirlwind of trouble by doing nothing much at all, and he hadn't even realized it.

5

Travis looked to his right. Rourke stood in the open doorway of the McCaffrey Hotel, his hat in his hand.

"Are you ready, Mr. Travis?"

"Yes, Sheriff. Of course."

Again, they took separate cars. There was really no need for Rourke to be present at every interview, but Travis liked the man and felt it would serve him well to include Rourke as much as possible. Rourke was a valuable ally, and he did not want to be disrespectful of his position.

Rourke drove out beyond the town limits, but only for a short while. They were in transit a mere ten minutes, and then the field upon which the carnival had been pitched was evident.

The central marquee was a good fifty or sixty feet high, and from it trailed streams of bunting and a kaleidoscope of tattered and weary pennants. Rourke pulled over, and Travis drew to a halt right behind him. Rourke was out, had already started walking toward the edge of the field, but Travis called him back.

"Hang fire," Travis said. "I just want to take stock of the place."

Rourke returned to his car. Travis surveyed the scene before him, then retrieved his camera from his car and took a number of photographs. He went down onto his haunches and took photographs from all angles, finally walking along the road to look at the field from one end to the other.

Back and to the right, there alongside a bank of trees, were the vehicles that Rourke had mentioned. Travis took out his notebook. Four pickups— a Ranchero, an F-100, an L120 long-bed International Harvester, and a Chevy Stepside with a trailer attached. Behind those was a Chevy Nomad station wagon and a Buick Special. Some way ahead of them was a Westfalia caravan. It was approaching dusk, and there were lights on in the caravan. Even as he looked, Travis saw a silhouette move past the small window.

"That's where the boss man lives," Rourke said. "Edgar Doyle. He and his wife... well, I think it's his wife. Anyway, the pair of them run this show."

"Her name?"

"Valerie, I think. Something like that. Not American. Has an accent."

"That's where we'll start, then," Travis said.

"You need me to introduce you, or you okay?" Rourke asked. "I got things I need to do otherwise."

"You go ahead," Travis replied. "I'll call you through your office if I need anything."

"Good luck," Rourke said, raising his hand as if they were wishing farewell at the train station.

Travis smiled. "I don't believe in luck," he said. "Tried it one time. Total bust."

Edgar Doyle possessed a presence, no doubt about it. He had the caravan door open before Travis even reached the vehicle, and he smiled with such warmth that Travis was somewhat taken aback.

"I imagined someone would be coming," he said, and there was the faintest British accent in his voice. "Sheriff of Seneca Falls he might be, but I didn't imagine Chas Rourke altogether comfortable investigating a murder."

Doyle came down the little wooden steps that had been placed beneath the caravan door and extended his hand.

"Edgar Doyle," he said. "I run the carnival."

"So Sheriff Rourke told me," Travis said, and shook Doyle's hand. "My name is Michael Travis. I am with the Federal Bureau of Investigation."

"A pleasure to make your acquaintance, Special Agent Travis."

Doyle, all of fifty-five or sixty, stood an inch or so taller than Travis. His hair was almost shoulder length, gunmetal gray, close to white at the temples. He was clean shaven but for a small triangle of hair that sat beneath his lower lip and pointed down to the cleft of his chin. He was sharply dressed in a clean white shirt, a deep red tie, a midnight-blue vest and matching pants. Travis's eye was caught by a small enamel badge on the vest's collar, a blue flower, which—if he was not mistaken—was a forget-me-not.

Travis's first impression of Doyle was of a man of considerable confidence. Body language, the hesitancy—or lack of it—with which a person spoke, the ability to maintain eye contact—both while speaking and listening—such things as these had all been part of the many areas that Travis had studied during his time in Kansas City. The unit within which he worked, a unit headed by Section Chief Gale, was still in its infancy, but they had made great progress in identifying the many and varied aspects of the *criminal personality*, as it had been informally labeled. There were other things that Travis observed in Doyle's immediate manner, unsubstantiated

53

as yet, but indicative of some degree of willful contrariness. Though it was merely assumption, the mere fact that Doyle owned and ran a carnival suggested that he was a man of different and unusual values.

"There is something in your accent," Travis said.

"Irish forefathers," Doyle replied. "My family name is Ó Dubhghaill. Means 'dark foreigner,' though there's a little less of the dark in me each year." He smiled and touched his hair.

"I heard that premature aging could be caused by bad whiskey."

"Is that so?" Doyle asked.

"I heard it. I hope you won't be offering me any bad whiskey, Mr. Doyle."

"An Irishman peddling such a thing? I should hope not, Agent Travis." Doyle smiled. "So, you're inviting yourself in for a slug of the good stuff?"

"If you'll have me."

"One way to start a murder investigation, I suppose."

"No need for us to be on anything but friendly terms, Mr. Doyle. As we speak, I have no reason to suspect you of anything. I assume nothing, and I make no guesses. I am just here to look, to listen to see if I can't find out what happened to this nameless victim that lay beneath your carousel."

"Then *mi casa es su casa*, Agent Travis. Please, step inside and we shall share a drink and I will answer your questions as best I can."

The caravan interior was much the same as all such vehicles—a table at the front end, a bench on either side, those benches designed to fold together into a bed. There was a cooker unit, a two-burner hob, a small fridge that looked like a safe, and at the back of the caravan, a further bench, the seat and back of which each moved independently and could be arranged to form a bunk-bed sleeping arrangement if required. For two people it was relatively roomy, all things considered; for four, claustrophobic would have been an understatement. By all appearances, only Edgar Doyle and his partner lived here. If they did in fact use the vehicle to sleep in, then any obvious signs of that had been folded away discreetly. The table was a table, the benches on either side were simply benches, and this is where Doyle directed Travis.

"Please, sit," Doyle said.

Travis sat, and—as Doyle busied himself at the other end of the cara-van—he surveyed the interior. Pieces of seemingly mismatched and incongruous fabric had been pinned to the walls. Over those squares of fabric had been secured posters advertising the Carnival Diablo. Crude in their execution, they nevertheless possessed a sense of gaudy drama. They snatched the eye. They *intrigued* Travis, and the reaction evoked was that here there was something that needed to be seen. Beyond the simple imagery employed—a clown's face, a pyramid of acrobats, in the next, the silhouette of some dark feline creature: a cougar, a puma, something such as this—there were the usual shout lines. *Seeing Is Believing! Not to Be Missed! For Two Nights Only!* But unlike other such posters and advertisements, they also jarred the senses a little. It took a moment for Travis to realize why: The colors chosen were opposites. Red and green, blue and yellow, orange and purple. They had been printed with wildly contrasting hues, and thus viewed indirectly they seemed to move.

Doyle was good to his word. He set a bottle of Irish whiskey and a couple of glasses down on the table, took a seat facing Travis.

"I'm going to take notes," Travis told him, and withdrew his book from his pocket.

"Please, feel free," Doyle replied as he uncorked the bottle and poured.

"What's your full name?"

"Edgar Francis Doyle."

"Your date of birth?"

"July 1, 1897."

"And your wife is with you?"

"Valeria? No, she's not here, and she's not my wife. We have been together for a long time now, but we have never married."

"And her name?"

"Her family name is Mironescu."

"M-I-R-O-N-E-S-C-U?"

"That's right, yes."

"Does she have a middle name?"

"She doesn't, no."

"Her date of birth?"

"She was born in March of 1916. She doesn't know the exact date."

"And she is from where?"

"Originally from Romania."

"But she does live with you here in the caravan?"

"She does, yes."

"And where is she now?"

"She went southwest to a place called Augusta."

"For what reason?"

"She is scouting towns for the next leg of our trip."

Travis paused to raise his glass. Doyle followed suit.

"*Sláinte*," Travis said.

Doyle laughed. "I am impressed, Agent Travis. You even pronounced it correctly. *Sláinte* to you also."

They drank. Doyle refilled the glasses.

"You know I'm going to need you and your people to stay here until my investigation is complete."

"Need, or want?"

"Both, Mr. Doyle."

Doyle shook his head resignedly. "I do understand your position, Agent Travis. However, I have to make a living. There are a good number of people who work in the carnival, and if we don't run the show, we don't make any money. Another few days, and I won't have enough money to feed them all."

"I appreciate that, Mr. Doyle, but—"

"Do you think your Mr. Hoover would be so kind as to foot the bill for feeding all these people until your work is done?"

"That's not quite the way it works, Mr. Doyle."

"So, how does it work, Agent Travis? If we answer all your questions, and you put all those answers in your little book, and you are none the wiser as to who might have killed that man under my carousel, then cannot we wish each other well and go our separate ways?"

Travis felt that Doyle was subtly challenging him.

"How about this?" Travis suggested. "Answer a few questions for me, let's see whether or not this is even a federal matter, and we'll go from there, okay?"

Doyle smiled, and once again there was that tremendous warmth in his eyes, ostensibly an expression of friendliness, but somehow strangely disconcerting. For all Travis's experience in reading people, Doyle was a paradox, at once almost willfully contrary, in the next moment something else entirely.

Doyle withdrew a short-stemmed pipe and a leather tobacco pouch from his vest pocket. He filled the pipe, tamped it neatly, and then proceeded to light it with a long wooden match. The smoke clouded around his face, and when Travis looked up from his notebook, he saw Doyle watching him through that smoke, in his eyes something almost mischievous.

"You have forgotten your questions, Agent Travis?" Doyle asked.

"Not at all, sir," Travis replied. "I wanted to begin with the discovery of the body itself."

"I can imagine Sheriff Rourke has already told you what we reported, and beyond that I have nothing more. A young woman screamed; we rushed to see what had upset her, and there he was under the platform of the carousel. I could tell from the angle of his head that his neck was probably broken, but Sheriff Rourke told me that he had been stabbed."

"That's correct, Mr. Doyle. He had been stabbed. I must ask you how you would know that his neck appeared broken. Do you have experience of such things?"

Doyle smiled. "No experience that would concern you, Agent Travis."

Travis did not push the point, but simply withdrew the photograph of the dead man and placed it on the table between himself and Doyle. He slid it toward Doyle as if this were a game of poker and he was dealing the next card. His hand over the man's face, Travis then uncovered it simply to determine if there was any involuntary or obviously disguised reaction from Doyle. There was nothing. Doyle looked down at the dead man's face and slowly shook his head.

"I have to say that this man is a complete stranger to me. Sheriff Rourke already asked us if we knew him, if any of us had ever seen him before, but no one had. I mean, as you can imagine, we see hundreds of people each weekend, and trying to remember them all would be impossible, but the human mind does have the capacity for recognition, even for a face seen only once. However, I have to say that I honestly cannot recall ever seeing this man before."

Travis believed Doyle. Either that, or Doyle was a masterful and consummate liar. It was true that lying was almost an art form for some, and Travis's training had encompassed aspects of reading through the outer layer of a person. However, no matter the skill of the interrogator, it was now being suggested that a certain element of intuition was required, and intuition—even if there was such a thing—could not be taught. Travis did not concur. It was not that he did not consider the possibility of faculties that extended beyond the primary five senses, it was that such things were unpredictable and uncertain. Travis was of the firm belief that resolute and persistent questioning would ultimately break down all barriers. There was a school of thought that suggested that all people were basically good, even the Dillingers and Clyde Barrows of this world, and that they actually *wanted* to tell the truth. His theory, as yet unfounded, was that the vast majority of criminals made stupid errors and left signs and clues as to their identity so as to ultimately be caught. Why? Simply because they were incapable of restraining themselves from committing crimes and thus needed someone else to stop them.

His instructor had called him an unmitigated optimist, suggested that a little more cynicism and suspicion might serve him well.

As it stood, and in that very moment, Doyle was telling Travis the truth. This was what Travis observed.

"And this?" Travis said, producing the sketch that he had made at the morgue—the sequence of dots that had been tattooed behind the man's knee.

"What is this?" Doyle asked, leaning forward, his expression one of genuine curiosity.

"This is nothing more than what it appears to be," Travis said. "It's a sequence of dots, a pattern. I wondered if it meant anything to you, if it reminded you of anything, if you had ever seen anything like it before."

Doyle studied it for a while and then started shaking his head before he spoke. "Doesn't look familiar," he said, and then he looked up at Travis.

Again that seemingly sincere and ingenuous expression was in the man's eyes.

"So you don't know the victim, are not aware of ever having seen him before, nor does this symbol mean anything to you?" Travis asked.

Doyle smiled. "You ask me that like a man who believes that everyone is fundamentally a liar, Agent Travis. Do you think I am a liar, or is that your naturally suspicious manner making itself known?"

"I consider everyone capable of lying, Mr. Doyle, but I err toward granting people the benefit of the doubt. My inclination is to trust people until they give me reason to distrust them."

"That is quite refreshing, Agent Travis. As you can imagine, in this line of work, everyone considers us crooks and thieves before we even open our mouths."

Travis smiled. "Just as everyone considers agents of the Bureau to be utterly without charm or imagination."

Doyle laughed—it was a natural and infectious sound. "Ha, you have a sense of humor, Agent Travis!" he said. "Try your best not to lose it, eh?"

"I will try my best, Mr. Doyle."

"So, are we finished?"

"For the moment, sir, yes, but I would appreciate your assistance in showing me the carousel itself, the precise location of the body when it was discovered, and I would like to speak to the carousel operator."

"You can do your best, Agent Travis, but he is a mute."

"A mute?"

"Yes. His name is John Ryan. His hearing isn't so good either, but he can lip-read. He can read and write a little, but finds scant use for either."

"And he operates the carousel."

"He does a great deal more than that. He maintains all the vehicles, the arcade games, does general repairs."

"He has been with you long?"

"Since the beginning almost."

"Which was when?"

"Well," Doyle said, "Valeria and I met in France in 1943, and we started the carnival together about three years later. John came to us in about 1947 or '48, as far as I remember."

"And he has been mute since birth?"

"No, Agent Travis. He was suspected of having informed on some criminals, and they took a knife and split his tongue. It could have been repaired, perhaps, but it became infected and had to be removed."

Travis looked at Doyle. Doyle had explained Ryan's inability to speak in such a matter-of-fact and nonchalant manner that it seemed unbelievable.

Travis's reaction must have been evident on his face, for Doyle added, "I think you will find that everyone here has their own unusual story, Agent Travis. John Ryan's is perhaps one of the more interesting, granted, but he is not alone in the... let us say the idiosyncratic uniqueness of his experiences."

"So I would imagine there isn't a great deal that he can add to what you have already told me."

"From what we can gather, he was unaware of the body beneath the carousel until the young woman started screaming. She screamed loud enough for even John to hear her, and he immediately stopped the thing. It was he who went under the carousel and dragged him out, believing perhaps that he was still alive, that he was merely unconscious. Sheriff Rourke explained that it would have been better to leave the victim precisely where he was, thereby preserving the integrity of the crime scene, as he so elegantly put it. Obviously, John thought the man might have fallen from one of the horses and been struck in the head or something, and so immediate medical attention was at the forefront of his mind."

"How would it be possible for someone to fall from a carousel horse and end up beneath the carousel platform?"

"It wouldn't, Agent Travis. Of course not. But we tend not to think altogether rationally in moments of stress and emergency. We don't all think and react like G-men."

Travis did not take the comment as an insult. Doyle's tone did not lead him to believe it had been intended that way.

"Could you show me the carousel now?"

"Absolutely," Doyle replied. He eased out along the bench and stood. Travis followed him from the vehicle and out across the open expanse of land and through the deepening twilight they walked to the main carnival site.

The strings of lights and Japanese lanterns that ran between the tents and awnings were unlit. There was a central marquee, larger than all the others, itself appearing shabby and worn, patched here and there with squares of newer canvas. The popcorn and hot-dog stands stood idle and empty. There was the murmur of voices from people unseen, the scratching of three or four chickens from within a tarpaulin-shrouded cage. The whole arrangement—as Rourke had commented—seemed tired and worn-out, as if the very physical substance of things resented whatever efforts were employed to keep this show on the road. It exuded an air of sadness and dejection, as if here could be found the last of those who rebelled against normality.

Travis, for a moment lost among his own thoughts, became aware that Doyle had stopped walking. He caught himself just in time, yet otherwise would have walked right into the man.

Doyle did not seem to notice Travis's preoccupation and merely indicated the carousel to their right.

"Here," he said, and pointed.

The carousel was larger and more impressive than Travis had anticipated. He had expected a beaten-up, falling-apart wreck of a thing, but what stood before him was quite different.

There were fourteen horses, six composing the inner ring, eight in the outer. Travis counted them as he walked around the perimeter, noticing that they were all in a good state of repair. They were well maintained, their colors bright and fresh, the spiral posts that ran through their saddles and stomachs and held them rigid between the lower and upper platforms were substantial and solid. Travis stepped up onto the platform itself, gripped one of those posts and found it utterly immovable. He stepped between the ranks of horses and then walked anticlockwise between the rows. He proceeded through a seemingly infinite phalanx of animals. He touched each one in turn, ostensibly to check that each was secure, that it was not a hazard to those who rode on it, but in reality for some other reason entirely. He wanted to engage with the physicality of the crime scene. He wanted to be right there in the failing light, right where the body had been found, not as an after-the-fact spectator, but as a real participant, addressing what had really happened, posing questions, determining answers, finding the truth.

Travis felt a hand on his shoulder. It was as if a surge of electricity had shot through him, head to toe.

He turned suddenly, his breath catching in his chest, his eyes wide.

He heard Doyle laughing. "Oh, he made you jump!" Doyle said.

The man who had touched Travis just looked at him. He was old, so very old, and when he raised his eyebrows, it was evident to Travis that this man was asking the reason for Travis's presence.

"Agent Travis, meet John Ryan."

"Mr. Ryan," Travis said. "I am Michael Travis. I am from the Federal Bureau of Investigation. I am here about the man who was found on Saturday night."

Ryan smiled, showed gums that were almost toothless, and his leather face cracked and wrinkled. He turned to Doyle and made a series of gestures and signs with his hands.

Doyle laughed.

"What did he say?" Travis asked.

"I don't think you want to know what he said, Agent Travis," Doyle replied.

"I do, Mr. Doyle. I very much want to know what he said."

"Oh, trust me, what he said bears absolutely no relation to what you want to know," Doyle replied.

"I think I would be the best judge of that, Mr. Doyle."

"Very well, if you insist, Agent Travis. John said—very crudely I might add—that you look like someone put a six-foot pole up your ass. It's his way of saying that you seem a little uptight and edgy."

Travis laughed. He did not feel insulted. He did not feel angry or agitated by the man's wisecrack. However, had he been pressed to describe how he felt, he might have used the word *invaded*, as if someone had looked inside him, as if someone had reached right up inside him and pulled out some private aspect of his life and shown it to the world.

Travis looked at Ryan. "And you, sir, have a face like a saddlebag left out in the rain and then stampeded by buffalo."

Ryan laughed coarsely, and he slapped Travis's shoulder.

"You've got a friend for life now," Doyle said. "You do realize that, don't you, Agent Travis?"

Travis reached out and took Ryan's forearm to get his attention.

"Show me precisely where you were standing when the girl screamed," Travis said. "Exactly where you were and then exactly where the body was."

Ryan nodded and motioned for Travis to follow him. Doyle came up onto the platform and joined them in the center of the carousel.

The central hub of the construct was immobile—a small wooden control booth, windows on each side, within the booth the levers that would start and stop the gears and cogs below, the heavy rubber belt visible beneath their feet, below that the ground.

Ryan stood in the booth, put his hands on the levers, and looked out of the window in front of him in the direction of the tents and vehicles. He nodded.

"He was standing here," Doyle said.

Ryan raised his hand to his ear and then pointed slightly to his left.

"He heard the girl scream and then saw her in that direction."

Ryan made as if to pull the levers sharply down.

"He immediately stopped the carousel. It takes about a minute to come to a complete standstill, but John walked out between the horses and jumped off the carousel to the grass before it had slowed fully."

Ryan then did as Doyle had explained. He fetched out a torch, came out of the booth, walked to the edge of the stationary central hub, and then reached out for one of the posts that ran through a horse. Gripping that post he stepped across the outer platform, now immobile but moving rapidly at the time of the incident, and then weaved his way between the horses, gripping the post in front of him before releasing the post behind him so as to maintain his balance.

He then jumped off the carousel platform to the grass—no more than two feet—and walked to the left, out to where he had seen the screaming girl.

Then Ryan knelt on the ground and looked beneath the carousel. He switched on the torch and directed the beam toward the hub.

Ryan got up again, walked back onto the platform, and started toward Travis and Doyle. Three or four feet from them, he stopped and pointed down.

"The body was under the carousel at this point, just about three or four feet in. It was not so far back as to be completely invisible, but far enough so as to explain why no one had seen it," Doyle said. "Sheriff Rourke also suggested that the sheer number of people around the carousel had obscured any line of sight, and that only at the end of the night when the crowds had dispersed did the body become visible. He also had John take a section of the platform away so he could look for any further indications of what might have happened. He said there was nothing."

"First thing in the morning, I am going to need to look myself," Travis said, "so if you could tell John to do that for me again, it would be appreciated. It's too dark now."

"We would like to open again on Friday evening, Agent Travis," Doyle said. "Do you think that would be possible?"

"I hope so, Mr. Doyle," Travis said. "I have a lot of work to do, a lot of people to speak to, but I intend to work as quickly as I can and hold you up as little as possible. The key is cooperation from everyone, so if you could impress that upon them, it will make everyone's lives a good deal easier."

"So who do you wish to speak with now?" Doyle asked.

"If it is possible to gather everyone together in one place, that would be ideal."

"Everyone?"

"Yes, Mr. Doyle... everyone."

"The central marquee," Doyle said. "I'll have them congregate there."

"Very good," Travis said. He turned to John Ryan. "And thank you, Mr. Ryan." Ryan nodded in acknowledgment. He smiled his gap-toothed smile.

"Fifteen minutes, Agent Travis," Doyle said, and started away from the carousel. "We passed the main marquee as we walked down."

"I saw it," Travis said. "I'll see you there."

Doyle turned and walked away. Travis stood for a while. He felt a little agitated yet didn't know why. He needed to walk perhaps and so started back around the edge of the field. He soon reached a smaller tent, within it the Bonnie and Clyde car that Rourke had spoken of. The bullet holes in the doors were real enough, even the dried blood on the backseat possessed a credibility that was unsettling, and Travis wondered if there wasn't some possibility—some slight and unimaginable possibility—that Doyle had come into possession of the real thing. There was no way. That was a ludicrous idea. That car had been destroyed, surely.

Travis did not know what to make of Doyle and decided not to antici-pate any conclusion. Presumption and preconception were the enemies of successful investigation, and it was the lack of such things that had resulted in Travis's successful identification and location of Anthony Scarapetto back in February of 1953. Had he been told on his first day in general populace that the boy seated across from him, the boy that had challenged him, would be the reason for a personal commendation from FBI Director Edgar Hoover himself, then Travis would never have believed it.

But life unraveled unexpectedly, though possessive of something that implied a sense of predestination. Such things were imaginary, of course. Such things were for folks like Edgar Doyle and his motley crew of gypsies, all of whom were now gathering to meet with Special Agent Michael Travis, the man who killed Tony Scarapetto on a cool Wednesday morning in Stromsburg, Nebraska, in February of 1953.

6

Anthony Scarapetto was not the first man against whom Michael Travis had raised a gun in the line of duty, but he was the first man that Travis shot. That the shot was fatal and that Scarapetto was known to him from Nebraska State Welfare made a difference in the way Travis was viewed by others. More important, it made a difference in the way that Travis viewed himself.

Also, not insignificantly, the manner in which that investigation had occurred and its ultimate result was a contributory factor in Travis being in Seneca Falls in the first place.

So it was that on the same day that Eisenhower turned down a plea for clemency from Julius and Ethel Rosenberg, Special Agent Michael Travis—just twenty-five years old, having been in the Bureau less than three years—was part of a team that staged an armed assault against a known gang hideout in Stromsburg, Nebraska. The gang had five members, one of whom was Scarapetto himself, but Scarapetto was not the central focus of the Bureau's interests. The *prima voce* of this violent and sociopathic little ensemble was one Luke "Smiler" Barrett, so called for the ugly two-inch scar that ran from the corner of his mouth, giving him a perpetual sneer. In the fall of '51, he decided to get a crew together and hit some small-town banks. A couple of the gang—namely Walter Forsythe and William "Wild Bill" Murchison—were a given, and yet it wasn't until Barrett happened upon Anthony Scarapetto and Scarapetto's then-sidekick, Federico de Tonti, that the Barrett Gang realized the collective incarnation and subsequent notoriety for which it would forever be remembered.

Plain and simple, a more cruel and divisive bunch of backstabbing, lying, thieving, gun-slinging hoodlums you could not have wished to happen upon, and from the latter part of 1951, on through 1952 and into the initial weeks of 1953, the Barrett Gang evaded capture and yet robbed more than a dozen banks in the eastern half of Nebraska.

Through Christmas of 1952 and the first weeks of 1953, Bureau attention had been directed even more forcefully to the apprehension of Barrett and his gang. The last reported Barrett Gang robberies had been a week apart, the first in Auburn, Nebraska, the second in Maryville, just fifty miles across the Missouri River into Missouri itself. That robbery, merely eleven hundred and eighty-four dollars from the Maryville First Mercantile Bank, had seen a running gun battle with the sheriff and two of his deputies, and while one of those deputies suffered a shoulder through-and-through, it was here that Francine Pinchbeck, on her way back from school, was shot and killed instantly.

Perhaps understanding that whatever run of luck they might have been enjoying had come to an end, Barrett and the others went to ground. The Barrett Task Force, as it was then known, was stationed in Lincoln, and heading up the Nebraska operation was Special Agent in Charge Rex Farraday. Farraday reported directly to Section Chief Frank Gale and on up through the deputy assistant director to assistant director, then to associate executive assistant director and a further four levels of seniority to the director himself, Mr. Hoover. Mr. Hoover did not like bad press. Mr. Hoover did not like bank robbers. Mr. Hoover, most of all, did not like the fact that a seven-year-old girl had failed to make it home from school. He wanted the Barrett Gang put away, and he wanted them put away yesterday.

The agreed-upon Bureau view as of the last week of January 1953 was that Barrett had fled Nebraska, and would not be returning to Missouri anytime soon either. Bureau offices in Kansas, Oklahoma, Colorado, Arkansas, and Iowa had been placed on full alert.

But Michael Travis did not concur with the agreed-upon opinion. He thought of such people as dogs or hyenas, always in packs, always hunting across the same territory, ever aware that new territories meant new challenges and obstacles. Criminals were—essentially—cowards. No, Travis did not believe the Barrett Gang had fled Nebraska at all. When a dog is scared, it goes home. When an animal is frightened or sick, it heads for the familiar.

And so one evening in early February, staying late to look over a series of reported sightings of Barrett himself and the other gang members, Travis came across something that snagged his curiosity. He knew that Scarapetto was part of the gang, and though he remembered Scarapetto from juvy, he did not feel any great sense of advantage for having previously met him.

The thing that secured Travis's interest was not Scarapetto at all, but someone else entirely. Reading through earlier witness statements of the various bank robberies, he came across a name that caught his attention: Madeline Jarvis. She had been questioned as an eyewitness in the May 1952 robbery in Aurora, Nebraska. She had happened to be in the street as the gunmen fled the bank. Seemingly, she was nothing more than an innocent passerby, and yet her name was again mentioned alongside Barrett's in an unsubstantiated sighting report from York in the first week of January, 1953. That report had come from one Claude Lefevre, a bar owner who knew Madeline Jarvis not only by face but by name.

She was in and out of here numerous times in the last year, he told the interviewing agent. *She's a nice enough girl, a little on the wild side, but I never had reason to throw her out. Just came in, sometimes alone, sometimes with a feller, and she minded her own business*

Claude Lefevre went on to say that Madeline had come in with someone, and it might have been Barrett. Whoever it was, well, he had a scar on the left side of his face. Gave him a mean look, like there was one hell of a nasty streak in there just waiting to get loose.

And that was that. Nothing more was done with the report, because no one had put the two together.

Madeline Jarvis just happened to be a witness to a robbery in Aurora in May of '52, and then she was seen with a man bearing an uncanny resemblance to Luke Barrett in York all of eight months later.

Travis did not believe in coincidences; he believed in facts.

The following morning, Travis submitted a report of his findings to Special Agent in Charge Rex Farraday. Farraday passed that report on to Section Chief Frank Gale. Gale informed the deputy assistant director, who then informed the assistant director, and on up the channels it went until it came to the attention of Executive Assistant Director Bradley Warren. Warren, above all else, was a fair-minded man, too long in the tooth and too experienced to concern himself with currying favor within the hierarchy of the FBI. He was, after all, the executive assistant director, just a few steps down from Mr. Hoover himself, and he had maintained that position by doing what he intended, by saying what he meant, by affording both credit for success and reprimand for failure as each situation required. He wanted to know who Special Agent Michael Travis was. He wanted to know his record, his experience, and his qualifications. When said information had been furnished, he then asked Travis to submit a plan of action based on this supposed connection between Madeline Jarvis and Luke Barrett.

Travis, industrious as always, had already established several facts relating to Madeline Jarvis. A trouble-free good-time girl she might have been, if Claude Lefevre's opinion was anything to go by, but looking further into her history, Travis learned that she was not without her blemishes. She had been arrested twice, once for soliciting, once for shoplifting. She had been fined on both occasions. She did not appear to have a specific address—there were reports of her living in rented accommodation in Osceola, Columbus, Central City, Fullerton, and Schuyler. Three of those locations had seen armed heists perpetrated by the Barrett Gang; two of those locations had seen later sightings of Barrett, one in the presence of Walter Forsythe. The other issue, and this was of great interest to Travis, was that Madeline Jarvis's parents owned a farm in Stromsburg, and Stromsburg sat right in the middle of that network of towns like the hub of a wheel. Madeline's father, Leonard Jarvis, was a farmer. The family possessed a good-sized property with numerous outhouses, adjoining buildings, barns, and grain storage facilities. What better place for Barrett and his compadres to go to ground?

"I think we place a number of surveillance teams around the perimeter of the family property in Stromsburg," Travis told both SAC Farraday and Section Chief Gale in a closed-door meeting on the afternoon of Friday, February 6. "We establish whether this property is being employed as a hideout for the gang, and—if so, and dependent upon the movements and activities of the members—we pick them up individually when they make forays beyond the perimeter, or—if they are holed up—we make an armed raid and secure arrests. If they are in fact there, and I consider this a strong possibility, then there is no question in my mind that we can take the majority of them alive and without Bureau casualties."

"This is good work," Gale told him.

"Agreed," Farraday said. "You picked up on a detail here that could so easily have been overlooked."

Travis nodded in acknowledgment but said nothing.

"I know Mr. Warren is most interested in what now occurs," Gale went on. "He said that if this proves to be as you have suggested, then there might be a place for you in the establishment of a new unit that is being discussed. Tentatively, it deals with the psychology of the criminal mind, a sort of behavioral science, if you will. Still very much in its formative stages, it is nevertheless of great interest to the director. Mr. Farraday here told me what you said about criminals behaving like pack animals, always reverting to safe patterns when under threat. That made a great deal of sense to me and to him. You verbalized something that has been an opinion of mine for some considerable time, young man."

Ultimately, Section Chief Frank Gale's feeling was justified. Surveillance teams were stationed around the perimeter of the Stromsburg farm. Travis himself was assigned as team leader for the unit that watched the Jarvis family home. This was the biggest property, the one where the parents lived, and it was from here that Travis's team took extensive photographs of Madeline Jarvis carrying various and assorted boxes, pots, pans, other such things back and forth to a smaller property behind and to the left of the main house. It was from the windows of this smaller property that lights shone at dusk and into the small hours of the following morning.

And it was from this property that Luke Barrett, Walter Forsythe, Wild Bill Murchison, and Federico de Tonti were seen exiting and reentering on numerous occasions. Only once had Scarapetto been sighted, and there remained the question as to why he did not leave and return to the hideout as the others so frequently did. Unbeknownst to Travis or any of the other agents, Scarapetto had suffered a flesh wound to the left leg during the Maryville First Mercantile shoot-out, nothing too serious, but sufficient to require that he stay horizontal as much as possible.

And so it was that on Monday the ninth of February, Michael Travis was called in to see SAC Farraday, Section Chief Gale, and Executive Assistant Director Bradley Warren, the latter having flown down from Washington to oversee the operation personally. Director Hoover had instructed Warren to come, and with that direction he had also sent a personal message to SA Michael Travis. It read as follows:

Special Agent Travis,
I am actioning a formal commendation for your diligence in this most recent case. However, on a more personal note, I wish to extend my appreciation for your work in this matter. With agents such as yourself in the field, the future of the Bureau is more than secure.
Sincerely,
J. Edgar Hoover
Director

"I've seen no more than a dozen of those in my time," Warren told Travis. "That is quite a privilege, son, and we shall definitely be talking more about your future in this new unit we're putting together."

The planning of the Stromsburg operation consumed the remainder of Monday and all of Tuesday. By nine o'clock on Tuesday evening, the strategy itself, the required teams and their respective leaders, had been established. Travis would, once again, lead a team, and it would be one of the teams that entered the smaller property where Barrett and his gang were holed up. From surveillance, it was rare for anyone to leave the property but Madeline herself, and part of that routine was to prepare breakfast in the main building and then carry it back to the hideout. In the very early hours of Wednesday morning, agents would secure the main property. The parents would be spirited away to immediate safety, their involvement in the harboring of the gang to be established later, and there agents would wait until Madeline came across to the house. Here she would be placed under arrest and then taken from the property to a secure location.

There was no visible telephone line between the two properties. The assumption that no such contact existed between the main house and the smaller one was supported by the number of times that members of the gang moved between the two buildings. Had there been a line, Travis felt sure that these trips would have been unnecessary. It was supposition, but there was a pragmatism and a sense of logic in all he considered. Hence, once Madeline failed to return in the usual time, Travis felt sure that Barrett would send one of the other men over to find out why breakfast was delayed. Barrett would be paranoid, ever watchful, on tenterhooks. Whoever was dispatched to determine her whereabouts would then also be arrested, his detention secured, his removal from the premises immediate.

That would leave only four of the gang in the house, allowing for the fact that Scarapetto was still inside, despite merely one sighting of him.

It would be unlikely that Barrett would send a second man to check on breakfast. Travis insisted on this point quite forcibly, and Warren agreed.

"The fact that Madeline has not returned within the usual time frame and then a second member of the gang doesn't return either . . . well, I have to say that if I were Barrett, already scared, already in hiding, perhaps tense and paranoid, I would be very suspicious indeed. I don't think I would send another man across alone. I think I would come as a group, or not come at all. I honestly feel that once the arrest of the first man has been secured, if in fact a man is dispatched at all, then we go in. As I suggested, with a grain delivery truck coming down from the road along the main route to the house, attention within will be distracted. The primary assault is from the rear, and a secondary assault comes from those within the grain truck."

Warren, Gale, and Farraday agreed. Travis spoke a language they all understood, but there was something different about this young man. He was not a follower. He did not wait to be told. He demonstrated initiative, a sense of measured intuition even, though he respected rank and authority. The raid strategy was ratified. Bradley Warren was on-site, right there alongside Rex Farraday and his unit leaders.

In the early hours of Wednesday, February 11, 1953, Leonard and Edith Jarvis were woken in their beds by agents of the Federal Bureau of Investigation. They were told to swiftly and silently dress, and then they were escorted under cover of darkness to the end of the farm road. Here they were bundled into a waiting car and driven to a hotel in Stromsburg itself. The director himself had instructed that unless there was incontrovertible evidence that they had colluded and conspired to knowingly and actively harbor the Barrett Gang, no charges were to be raised against them. The idea of his G-men safely rescuing a decent, hardworking, yet terrorized Midwestern husband and wife from the manipulative and violent clutches of Luke Barrett appealed to him greatly. It would make excellent press.

With the house secured, it was merely a matter of waiting an hour or so before Madeline Jarvis came across to make breakfast.

And come she did—at 8:05 a.m.

Travis's team of four was stationed in the main house, ready to make their way over to the smaller property where the Barrett Gang were holed up.

When Michael Travis heard Madeline Jarvis coming in through the side kitchen door and calling out to her mother and father, he knew something was wrong.

"Ma! Pa!" she hollered. "I'm in to make breakfast!"

There had been much discussion regarding the Jarvis girl's part in all of this. How involved was she? Had she merely been swept off her feet by the unlikely charms of Luke "Smiler" Barrett, or was she a conniving and mendacious accomplice, ready to sacrifice everything to protect her man and his accomplices? If she was not immediately silenced in that house, would she do all she could to alert Barrett to the presence of the Bureau? Or would she be solely interested in self-preservation?

Travis did not know how Madeline Jarvis would react when faced with half a dozen federal agents; he did not know whether she would lie to save herself, whether she would scream like a fire siren and run to let Barrett know that the FBI were there, or whether she would simply drop into a dead faint from shock.

Though Travis was never one to assume anything, he accepted the strong possibility that Madeline was close to her parents. The parents had given her safe haven, that much at least, and whether they had harbored the Barrett Gang knowingly, or had merely accepted that these dangerous-looking men were "friends", still the more probable likelihood was that their cooperation was born out of love and loyalty to their daughter.

And thus, as Madeline called out a second time to her parents, Travis turned and glanced at Farraday. He raised his hand, indicated that he was going into the kitchen alone. He even set down his gun.

Farraday frowned, furiously shaking his head. This was not the agreed-upon plan. The plan was to silently overwhelm her by sheer numbers.

Travis indicated once again that he was going alone, and he took a step forward.

Farraday grabbed his shoulder, and Travis turned and looked directly at him, and in the young man's eyes there was such a sense of unquestionable certainty that Farraday could do nothing but let him go.

Travis went forward two further steps, and he stood in the doorway of the front room. One step to the left and he would be visible in the hallway. If she looked toward the front of the house, she would see him.

He edged forward again, took two steps into the corridor.

And then he spoke with as calm and reassuring a tone as he could muster.

"Miss Jarvis?"

A moment's silence.

"Miss Jarvis?"

"Who's there?"

"Stay precisely and exactly where you are, Miss Jarvis. Do not move a muscle. Your mother and father are here. We do not wish for any harm to come to them."

Silence again, and it seemed to stretch forever.

"I am walking over to speak with you, Miss Jarvis. My name is Michael. I am here to help you, but whatever you do, you must not move or make a sound. To move or make a sound right now would jeopardize the safety of your parents. Do you understand me?"

"Ye-yes," she said, and Travis could hear the fear and tension in her voice.

Michael took another step, talking as he went.

"I am an agent of the federal government, Miss Jarvis, and I can assure you that your parents will be safe if you do exactly as I say."

"O-okay, okay . . . yes . . . what do you want from me?"

"Can I call you Madeline?"

"Y-yes, sure."

"Okay, Madeline . . . I want you to assure me of something in return."

"What?"

"I want you to assure me that you are not armed, that you have no firearms in your possession, that there are no firearms in the kitchen."

"There is a gun in the kitchen," Madeline said. "I think there might be two."

"Where are they?"

"On top of the cupboard here."

"Is that on the right side or the left side of the kitchen?"

"The right."

"Well, okay. I need you to move as far as you can to the left side of the kitchen, and then I need you to kneel on the floor and lace your fingers behind your head. Can you do that for me, Madeline?"

"Yes, I can, sir. Shall I do that right now?"

"Yes, do that right now, Madeline."

A moment's pause. The sound of movement.

"I'm done, sir."

"Good. I am coming in now, Madeline, and once I am in the kitchen, we are going to talk about some things, okay?"

"Okay."

Michael looked back at Farraday. He indicated for Farraday to follow him with the remaining members of both teams.

And then Michael went forward, one step at a time, slowly and calmly, until he stood in the doorway of the kitchen and looked left.

Madeline Jarvis, twenty-five years old, was kneeling on the floor with her hands behind her head, her expression that of a lost and frightened little girl.

"My ma and pa?" she said.

"Are safe and secure. Do not worry about them. I give you my word they are okay."

The relief was immediately evident, and then she looked frightened once more.

"Luke and the others are in the smaller building behind and to the left of the main house, right?" Michael asked.

It was then that Farraday appeared, behind him six other agents.

Madeline's eyes widened visibly. She knew this was it. World War Three was about to erupt in the house across the road, and her boyfriend was going to die in a hail of government bullets.

"Oh my Lord," she said, the words audible, but the sound of them was more like an exhalation of despair.

"They are all there, right?" Michael asked her. "Luke, Walter, Bill, Anthony, and Federico? They are all in the other house?"

She looked at Travis. "Yes," she said. "They are all there."

And he *knew* she was lying. Fear of what would happen had suddenly overwhelmed any real consideration for anything else, and she had instinctively lied.

"You are lying," Travis said.

Madeline Jarvis looked back at Michael as if he had seen right through her to the very core of her being.

"Who isn't there, Madeline? Who isn't in the house?"

Madeline glanced upward then—an immediate and undeniable reaction.

"Someone's upstairs? Who is upstairs?"

"Tony," she said. "Tony is upstairs. He has a wound in his leg, and my ma was looking after him. They moved him over here yesterday."

"That is not possible," Travis said. "We would have seen that happen."

"It was very late. It was really dark. Luke carried him over on his back with a blanket around him."

Farraday was right beside Travis then.

"He's in the attic room," Madeline continued. "Up there in the roof."

Travis turned to Farraday. "I suggest we act immediately. I don't want to wait for another man to come across from the second house, not with Scarapetto upstairs. I'll take Madeline and one other man. We'll get Scarapetto. You lead the others on the house."

"Agreed," Farraday said.

"You have to take me up there," Travis told Madeline. "I am going to follow you up into the attic, and you are not going to give Scarapetto any indication that I am with you, you understand?"

"Yes," she said. "I promise," perhaps now assured that there was no way out of this, that she was as deep as she could go, that cooperation was perhaps her only route to some degree of mitigation.

And so Farraday took the remaining five agents and briefed them on precisely what they were doing and why. None of them doubted the very real possibility of a gun battle with Barrett and the three men in the house. Scarapetto posed a significant risk as well. All of them would be armed. All of them would be desperate to evade arrest. They would have no doubt that the hangman's noose or the electric chair was awaiting them. To die in a shoot-out with the Feds, perhaps taking a few of the G-men sons of bitches with them, would be far more preferable than rotting in a jail cell and giving J. Edgar Hoover the satisfaction of seeing them executed.

And so it went as planned. Madeline went on up to the attic, Travis behind her, Special Agent Webster behind Travis, and they managed to get into the roof without even waking Scarapetto.

When he did wake, he opened his eyes to the sight of Michael Travis standing over him with a government-issue .45 in his hand, and it was a good ten seconds before the light of realization dawned in Scarapetto's eyes.

"Hey, you don't fucking say," were his words. "Fucknuts Travis. Well, blow me down with a fucking feather."

Madeline Jarvis was silent, standing to the right of Travis.

"She turn us in?" Scarapetto asked. "That bitch was no good. I told him time and again that you never get women involved. Always the fucking weak link."

"No such thing," Travis told Scarapetto. "The only thing Miss Jarvis is responsible for right now is the fact that you are still alive."

Travis took another step forward and aimed his sidearm directly between Scarapetto's eyes. "Where are the firearms?" he said.

"Go fuck yourself, Travis," Scarapetto said. And then he sneered derisively. "You've got to laugh at the irony of this," he went on. "I've been using your name for a good while now. People ask me my name, I tell 'em it's Michael Travis. What do you have to say about that, fucknuts?"

Travis did not respond. He instructed Madeline to kneel on the floor, her hands beneath her calves.

Travis waved Webster over. "Aim your gun at this man's head," Travis said. "If he tries to move, shoot him."

Webster did as he was told, and Scarapetto just lay there as Travis searched the makeshift bed and surrounding area for weapons. He found a pistol beneath the pillow, another gun between Scarapetto's feet.

Travis took them both, emptied them of shells, set them on the floor. He then cuffed Scarapetto, hands in front so Scarapetto could manage the descent from the attic.

Travis motioned for Webster to go down ahead of them.

Travis then sent Madeline down, all the while Webster's gun trained on her from below. Once she was down she was seated against the banister, her arms between the posts, her hands cuffed behind her.

Then Travis sent Scarapetto down, Travis keeping his sidearm trained on him until he was similarly secured with his hands through the banister.

Travis then descended.

At that point, the gunfire began in the second house.

Webster was told to stay with Scarapetto and the Jarvis girl, and Travis went back downstairs.

Returning fire was coming from the upper windows of the rear building. One agent was down. Farraday was directing return fire and a phalanx of additional agents were already making their way down the road from the highway toward the house.

The gun battle would rage for a mere eight minutes further. Two men would be brought out alive yet wounded—Barrett himself and Walter Forsythe. Barrett suffered a gunshot wound to the left shoulder, Forsythe a chest wound that missed his heart and other vital organs by mere inches. William "Wild Bill" Murchison and Federico de Tonti did not survive.

Once Barrett and Forsythe had been handcuffed and placed in the back of separate vehicles, Travis returned to the smaller house to bring Madeline Jarvis and Anthony Scarapetto down. Webster took the girl, and Travis waited for an additional agent—John Langton—to assist him with Scarapetto.

"So now you're the big-shot G-man, eh?" Scarapetto said. He sat there on the floor of the landing, his arms behind him and through the banister. Despite his prone position, he still possessed an attitude of aggressive arrogance and condescension, as if he would never be anything other than the one in charge.

"Michael Fucknuts Travis becomes a big-shot fucking G-man, and now you're gonna get yourself a fucking medal from that faggot Hoover and his faggot boyfriend, Clyde Tolson, and all you faggots gonna have a big fucking homo party and tell each other how fucking great you are, right?"

Travis felt his blood rising. He would not let this man see him riled. He smiled at Scarapetto and stayed silent.

"Oh sure, smile away, fucknuts, 'cause you ain't gonna see me hang for this, you son of a bitch."

Travis again said nothing. The wounded cur dog snaps the loudest when backed into a corner.

Travis released Scarapetto's right hand from the cuffs and reapplied the cuff in order to walk him down the stairs to the kitchen where other agents were ready to take him to a waiting car. Scarapetto went on cursing and yapping while Madeline Jarvis just appeared utterly overwhelmed. From the moment she had left the attic she had not said a word.

Downstairs, Farraday was surveying the situation, the collateral damage, taking stock of all that had occurred in such a short span of time. He had left the second house and returned to the main property once the surviving members of the Barrett Gang had been secured. It was then that events transpired that would later be analyzed step by step, moment by moment, not only to determine why an agent was killed in the line of duty, but also why Michael Travis had acted alone in securing the cooperation of Madeline Jarvis when first she entered the main house. Lastly, questions would be asked and answered about the precise circumstances of the fatal shooting of Anthony Scarapetto.

At the base of the stairwell, seeing agents leaving by the front door, Scarapetto had turned and started running toward the rear of the building. His movements were awkward, as his hands were cuffed, but he was desperate. Travis went after him, followed him out into the yard where Scarapetto was faced with a thirty-yard expanse of scrubbed earth and nothing to shield him from a clean shot.

And here he turned and faced Travis, utterly certain in his belief that Travis did not possess the nerve to shoot him right there in cold blood.

"Stand still, Anthony," Travis told him. "If you move, I will shoot you. Have no doubt about that."

"Screw you, fucknuts," Scarapetto replied. "You ain't got the nerve. You was a faggot wimp when I knew you, and you're a faggot wimp now."

Travis was struck with an image of his father, that single bright blue eye looking back at him from the kitchen table.

Travis held the .45 steady in his right hand. The muzzle was aimed unerringly at Scarapetto's heart.

"On your knees, Scarapetto. You're going in, no two ways about it. Dead or alive, you're going in."

"You go fuck yourself, Travis. You never had any fucking guts, you know that? Even back then you were a pathetic fuck..."

Travis took one step forward and Scarapetto fell silent.

It was a strange conspiracy of emotions that assaulted Travis in that moment. Scarapetto enraged him, a dark edge to that rage, that same desire to obliterate, to hurl himself at the man and tear him apart. And yet there was a calmness in his thoughts. He knew what his father would have done, but he was not his father. And yet he could hear his father, almost as if Anthony Scarapetto now represented everything that he had hated about Jimmy Franklin—the arrogance, the condescending tone, the sneering self-aggrandizement. So it was that one part of himself faced another part of himself, and yet his own identity was lost in the space that sat between them.

"Down on your knees," Travis said, aware of how steady his hand was.

"Go to hell," Scarapetto hissed, and started to turn.

"Jimmy!" Travis heard himself say, and then he pulled the trigger.

There was one shot and one shot only.

The bullet entered Scarapetto's heart.

Nevertheless, Travis believed that Scarapetto was well and truly alive for a good thirty seconds after the bullet hit him. He knew he had been shot, he knew that shot was fatal, and he knew that Michael Travis had indeed possessed the nerve to put him down.

After it was done, Travis stood over him. Looking down at the man's face, and the rage that had filled his chest just seemed to wash away like a bloody cloth beneath running water. He did not understand what he had experienced, and he did not know that he wished to.

Anthony Scarapetto's last dying breath was accompanied by a desperate and pathetic flurry of kicks.

A small cloud of dust rose from the ground around his feet and then settled.

It would be more than a week before Michael Travis met with Executive Assistant Director Bradley Warren. It took place in one of the Lincoln Bureau offices, and no one but Warren and Travis were present.

"I have read and reread the numerous and varied reports of everything that happened that day," he told Travis, "and there are certain questions I have for you, young man. First and foremost, I want to know why you acted alone in securing the cooperation of Madeline Jarvis when she first entered the main building to prepare breakfast for Barrett and his accomplices."

Travis could not answer with anything but the truth. "Because I felt certain how she would best respond, sir," was what he said. "I believed that mention of her parents would engage her attention and cooperation. I also felt very strongly that the surprise appearance of half a dozen unknown men would cause a panic reaction and might thus have served to alert Barrett and the others that she was in trouble."

"You were sufficiently certain of this to modify an approved strategy *in situ*?"

"Yes, sir, I was."

"Well, that doesn't excuse the fact that protocol is protocol, Agent Travis, and even if an agent had not been shot, we would still be conducting this internal inquiry. Other law enforcement bodies might believe themselves excused from such thoroughness if a positive result is achieved, but the Bureau is not just any law enforcement body."

"No, sir."

"Secondly, there is the unresolved matter of why you shot and killed Anthony Scarapetto when he was already handcuffed and unarmed."

"Because he would not cease in his attempt to escape, sir."

"But you could have run him down. I don't believe for a moment that he could have outrun you, Agent Travis. He *was* handcuffed, was he not?"

"Yes, sir."

"So?"

"He would have made it to the road, sir. He would have overpowered the agent in the car by the edge of the upper field. The agent in the car was not an experienced field operative, and he would have hesitated. Scarapetto would not have hesitated, and I believe we would have had a second dead agent."

"You really consider that this would have been the outcome, Agent Travis?"

Travis sat there and just looked at EAD Warren.

Warren, seemingly satisfied with Travis's response, closed the file on the desk before him and leaned back in his chair.

"So, I want to talk to you about this new department that Section Chief Gale is establishing."

"You mentioned it before, sir."

"Mr. Hoover is very interested in the potentials of this new department, and he is keen to staff it with the brightest and the best we have. You do not have family here in Nebraska, do you, son?"

"No, sir."

"I am fully aware of your earlier life and personal circumstances, of course," Warren went on. "Mr. Hoover's only concern is whether or not you feel there is some outstanding psychological difficulty regarding the events surrounding the respective deaths of your father and mother."

"No, sir, there is not."

"You are sure, now? Because Mr. Hoover, though he might be aware of your abilities and potential, does not wish to involve you in a new project such as this if there are going to be any issues with your personal mental and emotional stability."

"There have not been to date, sir, and I can assure you that there will be no issues in the future."

"That is what I understand to be the case, and that is what I was hoping to hear from you. I think we should look further into your suitability for this project and work toward transferring you to Kansas. That is where the new unit will be based for the foreseeable future. Section Chief Gale will be heading it up, and he has already selected a number of experienced and suitable agents."

"I have no problem moving to Kansas, sir."

"Very good. I will make my recommendations, and you will be hearing from me directly."

The meeting ended. Michael Travis remained in the office, aware that there were a number of things that he had chosen not to communicate to Executive Assistant Director Bradley Warren.

The first was the enormous emotional impact he had experienced in returning to question Madeline Jarvis at the State Reformatory for Women in York. He did not believe he would face any difficulty and expressed no concern or reservation regarding this to either Rex Farraday or Frank Gale. It was only when he entered the facility that he felt it. This was where his mother had been held on remand. This is where she had awaited her trial. This is where she had sat alone in a cell and considered the consequences of what she had done.

The second, and perhaps the most important, thing that Travis failed to communicate was the subsequent mental and emotional effect of the Barrett Gang raid. The dreams he suffered had returned with a vengeance, and they had interrupted his sleep every subsequent night for a week following the events of February 11, 1953. The headaches came soon after—intense, like drills being driven though his skull, and yet always brief, short-lived, dissipating as quickly as they had come.

They say the tendency to violence can be hereditary. Was the baton passed, Michael? From father to son, was the baton passed?

Those words went over and over in his mind.

I killed a man. I killed a man in cold blood. I killed a man when no one else would have done so, but I knew I had to kill him.

Perhaps, when all is said and done, I truly am my father's son.

And the images of his dreams remained, stronger than ever, lasting long into each day—the cracked and arid field, the shadow of a man, the sound of the laughing crow—as if those images had been seared into the front of his mind simply to remind him that of all the things he understood, he understood himself the least of all.

These things he did not communicate to Executive Assistant Director Bradley Warren, for these things troubled him, and it seemed that such a sense of internal disquiet was something he needed to hide—not only from himself, but from the world.

7

Michael opened his eyes and looked out through the windshield toward the central marquee of the carnival. There were lights within it, and the silhouettes of the gathering crowd played against the canvas like a shadow show.

He sat for a moment more, and then he opened the door and stepped out of the car. The air had chilled as darkness fell, and he could see his own breath.

Travis already felt a familiar tension in his temples, the warning sign of an oncoming headache. He hoped it would pass. Best answer was to eat well and get some sleep, but there was too much to do, too many questions to ask, too many answers to find.

Travis reached the back of the marquee and started around it. The hubbub of voices within was considerable, and when he appeared in the doorway, it fell quiet.

He stood there for a moment, but that moment seemed to stretch out like elastic and distort. He was faced with the strangest collection of human beings he had ever seen, and he did not know where to look first.

There were perhaps fifteen or twenty people in that marquee. Tables had been arranged, and around those tables were a random collection of mismatched chairs and benches. Those chairs and benches were occupied by the kind of characters that inhabited dreams and nightmares, not reality.

Directly to his right was a group of five men who appeared to be exactly the same. Not only in dress and physical bearing; their faces were identical. Five of them. At the end of the table, visible only from the shoulders up, was a dwarf. Seated at the next table along was a man so unbearably thin it almost hurt to look at him. Travis guessed his height somewhere around five eight or -ten, but he couldn't have weighed more than eighty pounds. Beside the Thin Man sat a dark-haired individual who—at first glance—seemed entirely regular in all aspects. It was only as Travis focused his attention on the man that he became aware of his hands. This was the man of whom Rourke had spoken. He had too many fingers, seven on each hand in fact, and there was something so anomalous about this that Travis felt himself shudder. John Ryan was present, beside him a diminutive Asian woman, and next to her a man of inordinate height and stature. The overall effect was disconcerting beyond belief. Those individuals gathered within the central marquee created an atmosphere by their very presence. Surreal, wholly disturbing, the scene before Travis's eyes seemed to confound and confuse all his preconceptions about the way people *should* be.

Doyle rose, and in his expression Travis could see that he was enjoying himself. Travis felt sure that Doyle was fully aware of the effect created, and yet he was not going to acknowledge it. Perhaps he wanted Travis to feel as though he was the odd one out, the stranger, the misfit.

"Most everyone is here," Doyle said. "Valeria has not yet returned, but I don't believe she will be much longer. Generally, we all eat in here. We have a cook, just like any other Wild West wagon train." He smiled at his own comment. "There are a few absentees. After all, when we are not performing, everyone is free to come and go as they please."

"This is a good start," Travis said. He crossed confidently to the center of the marquee and stood before the assembly. He smiled in as relaxed a manner as he could, and then he cleared his throat.

"Mr. Doyle... if you could introduce me."

"As you wish, Agent Travis," Doyle said, and then he turned to the gathered crowd. "Ladies, gentlemen," he said, raising his voice. "Your attention, please. This is Special Agent Travis of the Federal Bureau of Investigation. He has come down here from Kansas City to look into our murder. He's going to need to speak with some of you individually, and it goes without saying that the more suspicious and dishonest-looking you are, the more intensively you will be questioned—"

There was a susurrus of laughter from the assembly.

"But, just for now, he wants to say a few words to all of us as a group."

Doyle turned, and with a theatrical flourish of his hands, he said, "Ladies and gentlemen, I give you... Special Agent Travis of the FBI."

Travis did not acknowledge Doyle's slightly irreverent manner, just as Doyle had intentionally ignored the effect his carnival people had created on Travis.

Travis stepped forward and spoke directly to those before him.

"Good evening to all of you. Thank you for gathering at such short notice. As Mr. Doyle stated, I wanted to say a few things to the group as a whole, but then I will need to interview each of you individually. That can take place tomorrow and over however many days I stay. I can appreciate that this must have come as a shock, but my first and foremost task is to identify the victim, and then I can better establish whether this is a matter that can be left in Sheriff Rourke's capable hands, or if it does warrant federal intervention. As you know, a man was found dead beneath the carousel on Saturday night. As Mr. Doyle and Sheriff Rourke have already explained, I understand that none of you are aware of this man's identity. However, a further detail has come to light that needs to be considered, and it is concerning this detail that I will be speaking with you on a one-to-one basis. All I can ask is for your utmost cooperation in this matter, and I give you my assurance that I will do everything I can to move this investigation forward to a swift and satisfactory resolution. There is no intention from the Bureau to delay your passage any longer than is absolutely necessary, nor to prevent you from further earning your living."

Travis paused. He still had their attention.

"That is all at this time," he went on. "And unless there are any immediate questions, then I shall wish you a good evening."

"One question."

Travis turned. The man with seven fingers rose to his feet. Everyone looked at him.

"Perhaps it is a foolish question, Agent Travis, but am I to understand that we are all murder suspects?"

"More witnesses than suspects, sir."

"And if the sheriff has asked us what we saw, and we saw nothing, why do we remain potential witnesses?"

Travis smiled. "There are different approaches to such an investigation, sir. The Bureau is responsible for training its agents in a certain way, and the means and methods employed by the Bureau are somewhat different from the Sheriff's Department."

"So are you going to torture us for the truth, or will you merely hypnotize us?"

Again, a low murmur of laughter filled the air.

"Yes, torture will be applied in most cases," Travis said. "We have also found that sleep deprivation can work wonders in assisting people to remember the truth. I tend to prefer teeth-pulling, fingernail removal, and horse-whipping as a general rule, but I am old-school, you see?"

The man seemed surprised by Travis's humorous response. "Seriously, Agent Travis, I am wondering what more you can find out that hasn't already been communicated."

"All I can say is that I've had a great deal of experience in situations such as this and have routinely found that there are things that people do not realize they saw, nor realize that they can in fact remember. By appropriate questioning, those details can sometimes be brought to the fore, and they can be extraordinarily helpful."

"So you can read minds, Agent Travis," the man said.

"What is your name, sir?" Travis asked.

"My name is Slate."

"Well, Mr. Slate, I can assure you that I cannot read minds—"

"Have you ever tried, Agent Travis?"

Travis frowned. "I'm not sure that I understand the point of asking me these questions, Mr. Slate."

"Considering that we are extending sufficient courtesy to answer your questions, it would seem only right that you should extend the same courtesy in return."

"Well, no, I have never tried to read someone's mind, Mr. Slate."

Slate smiled. "Then how do you know it cannot be done?"

Travis smiled patiently. "All I am saying, sir, is that a further detail regarding the possible identity of the murder victim has come to light, and this is something I wish to explore, with your cooperation, of course. I appreciate that you would ordinarily have moved on by now, but until the Bureau and the Sheriff's Department are completely satisfied as to your lack of knowledge or involvement in this murder, then we are going to require your continued presence in Seneca Falls."

Slate smiled once again, and then he placed the palms of his hands together as if to pray. It was as if he were holding a broad fan in front of him, and when he sat down once again, he did so slowly, as if to demonstrate that Travis's answers to his questions had not been answers at all. Travis felt that this had been a somewhat ineffective attempt to manipulate him, as if there was some purpose in making him appear a fool, to appear naive and ignorant.

Doyle was suddenly behind Travis, had leaned in close and was speaking directly into his ear in a hushed voice.

"Ignore him," Doyle said. "He is teasing you. He is simply being mischievous. It is just his nature."

"And not appreciated," Travis said. "This is a serious matter. A man has lost his life."

"No less serious to us, of course," Doyle said, "but for different reasons."

"Different reasons?"

"Not one of us was responsible for that man's death, Agent Travis, and yet here he is, even in death, capable of preventing us from continuing with our lives. Quite selfish, wouldn't you say?"

"Yes, perhaps, Mr. Doyle, but doesn't justice for what was done to him appeal to your basic humanity?"

"The same basic humanity that sees people such as this rejected from society, treated as outcasts? *That* sense of humanity, Agent Travis?"

Travis did not respond. This was becoming a game of words that meant nothing. This was the United States of America. This was the society within which all of those present existed, and irrespective of their chosen walk of life, each citizen had a right to be treated fairly within the standards of the law. Those same expectations then had to be extended to others less fortunate, those who found themselves as victims of crime. A man had been killed. Someone somewhere cared for that man, undoubtedly, and they had a right to know what had happened and why.

"You are simply affording this poor man the same rights as would be afforded any one of us if we found ourselves horribly murdered, aren't you, Agent Travis?"

It was as if Doyle had plucked the very thought right out of his mind.

"Yes, Mr. Doyle," he said, doing all he could to maintain an implacable expression. "That is absolutely what I am doing."

"Truth finds friends in truth, Agent Travis, and lies do not."

"I'm sorry—"

"Do not be sorry, Agent Travis. You are merely doing your job."

"That's not what I meant, Mr. Doyle."

Doyle took Travis's arm and effortlessly steered him toward the doorway of the marquee. Travis felt all eyes were upon him. There was not a sound but for Doyle's voice, and even that was a whisper.

"Do you *know* what you meant, Agent Travis? Do any of us ever really *know* what we mean? Seems to me that the fundamental difficulty in each of us is the inability to say exactly what we mean."

They were outside then, halfway back to Travis's car. Travis was aware of the headache then, more so than before. He instinctively touched his right temple, the point where the pain was most concentrated.

"Your head hurts," Doyle said. "Eat, sleep, we will deal with this tomorrow." He released Travis's arm, stepped back, gave a small bow of his head, and then turned and walked away.

"Mr. Doyle?"

Doyle turned back.

"I have afforded you nothing but respect and patience. I would appreciate the same in return. I will not be spoken to impolitely or discourteously, and I will not be portrayed as anything other than what I am. The truth will come out, sir. I assure you of that. Attempting to make mockery of this investigation will do nothing but incur my anger, and that, I assure you, is not something I would advise that you do. Do I make myself clear?"

Doyle opened his mouth to speak, and then he seemed to think better of it. He smiled sincerely, and then he nodded respectfully and turned away.

Travis waited for the man to disappear into the marquee, and then he returned to the car. It was only as he reached it that he realized his headache had eased, if not dissipated altogether.

Doyle was a showman, and—as with all performers—the face he wore for the world and the reality were very different. If the man believed he could blindside Travis, then he was very much mistaken.

Travis got into the car and started the engine. He put on the headlights, and as he turned toward the road, he saw the silhouettes again within the marquee. People seemed to be dancing. He knew that this was not possible. There was no music. There was no reason for them to dance. Nevertheless, this was the impression he had.

He reached the road and started away toward the center of Seneca Falls.

By the time he reached the McCaffrey Hotel, whatever headache might have been threatening to assault him was nothing but a memory. It was nearing seven thirty, the dinner service was just beginning, and Danny McCaffrey said he had reserved a place for Travis.

"Unless, of course, you'd wish to take dinner in your room, sir," Danny said.

"No, I'd like to eat here," Travis said, and followed Danny through to the dining room.

Travis was served soup, a pot roast, offered a dessert—which he declined—and then he took his coffee upstairs.

For a few minutes he sat in the chair by the window and watched the street below. There were few passersby, two or three couples walking hand in hand, an elderly man with a stooped back and a heavy cane, which he thumped along the sidewalk as he went, a couple of children on bicycles. Seneca Falls and its inhabitants seemed to be going on about their business of being a small and relatively insignificant Midwestern town. Nevertheless, something had happened here that had served to make this place less insignificant, and whether they wished to know what had happened or not, they were soon to find out. That attitude—*If it doesn't directly concern me, then it is of no concern*—did not apply to him. This was a matter of life and death. This was no meaningless detail. This was a cardinal sin, a violation of a commandment, a capital offense. Turn a blind eye to something such as this and you could feel the very foundations of the society start to crack and crumble.

Irrespective of the complacency and indifference of the people of this town, irrespective of the challenging attitude of Mr. Doyle and Mr. Slate, the truth would be found whether they wished it to be found or not. And the Carnival Diablo would stay right where it was until Travis and the

Federal Bureau of Investigation gave them leave to move on. That was all there was to it, and there was nothing else to say.

Travis finished his coffee. He moved to the chair before his typewriter and began his daily report.

8

When Travis awoke, he knew he had dreamed. It was a clear and definitive certainty, unencumbered by any real emotional reaction. It was just there.

He shaved and showered, aware of a dull ache somewhere behind his eyes. He felt sluggish, a little thickheaded, and he wondered whether his dreaming had actually prevented him from resting fully. He got dressed, started to leave the room and head down for breakfast when the report he'd typed the evening before caught his eye.

Methodical and organized in all things, there was yet a sheet of paper in the typewriter. He had typed his report on two sheets, set them down, and had not fed a third sheet into the machine. And yet there it was.

He walked back to the desk and looked down. It was not until he rolled the sheet out from the platen that he saw the word that had been typed.

regulus

Just one word, and one word alone.

He had sleepwalked. There was no other possible explanation for this. He had risen in the night, completely unaware of what he was doing, entered a sheet of paper into his typewriter, and typed a single word. Whether that word possessed any meaning or was utterly nonsensical, he did not know. That was less of an issue right now. The issue was that he had performed an action completely beyond the bounds of his own understanding.

Unless...

Travis hesitated, unwilling to even consider a second possibility... that someone else had entered the room and done this. But how had he not been awoken by them? Perhaps someone had crept in, taken the typewriter away, typed that single word, and then returned it. Even as he considered it, he realized it was a ridiculous notion. What possible reason could someone have for doing such a thing?

That single word stared back at him, almost accusatively.

regulus

Travis went through the process of checking the external door's lock for any telltale signs that the lock had been tampered with, and then he stepped back into the room and surveyed it with as objective an eye as possible. Had anything been moved? Was anything out of place?

Travis saw nothing, and then he stared at the sheet of paper for a good thirty seconds longer, a sense of disorientation creeping through him. Rationality and logic told him that there was some explanation; instinct told him that there was not. He wanted to tear the page into tiny pieces and throw it away, even flush it down the toilet. He did not want to see evidence that he'd done something he could not explain, even that something had happened without his knowledge. But he stayed his hand against the impulse. He placed the sheet of paper right there next to his situation report, and he left the room.

Danny McCaffrey greeted him in the dining room.

"Trust you spelt well, Mr. Travis?"

Travis looked up. "Sorry?"

"I was just wondering if you slept well, sir."

"I thought you said..." Travis frowned. "Slept well. Yes, yes, of course. I slept just fine, Danny. Thank you."

"So what can I get you for breakfast?"

"Danny... did you do as I asked and secure all the additional keys to my room?"

"Yes, Mr. Travis, of course."

"And there hasn't been anyone looking for me? Someone asking if I am in my room?"

Danny seemed confused. "No, no one has asked after you. Are you expecting someone?"

"No, it's okay. I just wanted to check."

"Okay, well, if anyone does ask after you, I'll be sure to let you know. Now, some breakfast. What would you like?"

"Just some coffee would be fine," Travis said. "Actually, a cup of coffee and a piece of toast."

"That's all?" Danny asked. "Breakfast is the most important meal of the day, you know. You don't eat first thing in the morning, you'll be starving when you try to sleep later tonight."

"Just the coffee and toast will be fine, thanks."

Danny acknowledged him and left for the kitchen.

Travis took a seat at the table nearest the window and with his back to the wall. It was early, just before eight, and Seneca Falls had barely awoken. The street was all but empty of people.

His thoughts went back to the sheet of paper.

regulus

Was it even a real word? He needed to check, needed to determine that first of all.

Danny appeared with the coffee and toast.

"You let me know if you need anything else. Can imagine you have quite a day ahead of you."

Travis smiled to himself. Seemed Danny McCaffrey had decided to be his keeper.

"This'll do just fine, Danny," Travis said.

Danny let him be, and Travis drank the coffee and ate the toast without even thinking about what he was doing. His mind was completely elsewhere.

He would need to speak to Rourke about whether there was some kind of teletype facility in the sheriff's office, just in case he needed to get information back to Kansas City in a hurry. It was couple of hours' drive at least, and Travis didn't want to be running back and forth any more times than was necessary. The victim's fingerprints would need to get back to the office so they could begin the slow and laborious task of cross-checking against existing print records. The prospect of returning to Kansas City hat in hand was out of the question. No, this case would end here, and it would end with him. In a way, his entire future depended upon what he did here and now in Seneca Falls.

Trust you spelt well, Mr. Travis?

Travis massaged his temples. This was ludicrous. He was typing things in his sleep, hearing questions that weren't being asked.

Travis left the breakfast room and headed back upstairs. In his room, he placed one of the victim photographs and the fingerprint card in an envelope. He typed out the full name and date of birth of both Doyle and the Mironescu woman, added a note at the bottom of the page that a complete background check was needed, that there would be further checks required in the subsequent twenty-four hours, and placed that in the envelope as well. He addressed it to SSA Tom Bishop. The second photograph and the small drawing of the tattoo he placed in his jacket pocket, along with the outline and prints he had made of the victim's shoes. Travis glanced once more at the single sheet of paper that he had removed from the typewriter, and he shook his head.

It was nothing. Such things happened all the time. Memories had been stirred up by the psychiatrist's interviews; recollections of things he had long ago decided to forget had been brought to the fore; perhaps this word had some meaning from way back when, and people sleepwalked all the time. It was not so uncommon. Was it really any more significant than dreaming? No, in all honesty, it was not.

What Travis told himself as he drove over to the sheriff's office and what he actually believed were not necessarily the same thing, however, for with years of practice behind him, Travis had become quite the master of self-deception.

Rourke was behind his desk. He got up and greeted Travis warmly.

"So, how'd it go out there?"

Travis took a seat. "Interesting people," he said.

"One way of putting it."

Travis held up the envelope. "I need to get this to Kansas City," he said.

"Lester'll take it. 'S only a coupla hours. He ain't got anythin' else goin' on that's more important right now."

"That's much appreciated, Sheriff Rourke."

"And you ain't never gonna call me anything but that, are you?"

Travis shook his head and smiled. "No, Sheriff Rourke, I'm not."

Rourke leaned forward and pressed the intercom buzzer on his desk. "Lester," he said. "Get on in here. Need you to drive something to Kansas for me."

Lester McCaffrey appeared moments later, seemingly eager to be ferrying federal paperwork to the city. Travis gave him the address of the office, said he should ensure that Senior Special Agent Tom Bishop received the material personally.

"And if he's out, mark it for his attention and get someone to put it on his desk, okay?"

"Sure thing, Mr. Travis. It'll be done just how you say."

Lester left the room, and Rourke got up from the desk and walked to the window.

"So what now?" he asked.

"More questions," Travis said. "I want to talk to the Mironescu woman and a few of the others on an immediate basis. I sense a definite resentment among them, as if I am responsible for their not being able to move on. I can see their point of view, but I am sure they would be all too quick to demand our assistance if it was one of their own who'd been murdered."

"Always the way though, ain't it?" Rourke said. "I see a little of it every once in a while, but I'm sure it's a daily routine for cops in someplace like Kansas City. I mean, that kind of ass-backward thinking. We're all a bunch of interfering, no-good busybodies until the shit hits the fan, and then all of a sudden we're the best people in the world." Rourke looked up suddenly, seemingly a little embarrassed. "Excuse the language, Mr. Travis."

"Seems whichever way you word it, Sheriff Rourke, it's the truth. I think it's fair to say that the public as a whole have a love–hate relationship with law enforcement, both local and federal."

"You have such a mighty fine way of putting stuff, Mr. Travis. S'pose that's your college education right there, ain't it?"

"Oh, I think you'd be very surprised to know where I came from, Sheriff Rourke, and why I ended up in the Bureau."

"Well, if you ever want to share a glass or two and tell me that story, I'd be more than happy to hear it."

"Let's get this thing done, and then I might just take you up on that offer." Travis got up. "So I'll be on my way. Thanks for your help so far. It's really appreciated."

"Hey, this is the most excitement we've had here in years," Rourke said.

"Well, if dead people is exciting, let's hope it gets right back to boring very soon, eh?"

"I didn't mean it quite like that, Mr. Travis—"

"It's quite all right, Sheriff Rourke," Travis replied, smiling. "I knew exactly what you meant."

"Well, best o' luck to you," Rourke said.

"Don't believe in it," Travis said, and left the room with a smile.

Valeria Mironescu was an extraordinarily beautiful woman, but her beauty was not immediately obvious in the classically accepted sense. The way in which features were unique, even between twins, the established "rules" regarding the height of eyes compared to ears, the angles of cheekbones, the line of the jaw in relation to the shape of the skull—all these things had been studied by Travis, and studied with a view to better understanding the nature of physicality, physiognomy, the skills of facial recognition. What such studies did not take into consideration was the person themselves. Too many times had he seen the difference between someone alive and someone dead to doubt that *life* played a part in defining someone's appearance. Something inanimate possessed a very different quality than something animated. Skin tone, the reflective quality of the eye, the matter of body language, even the simplest motion of the features—a raised eyebrow, a blink, a slight squint—contributed to an individual's appearance. In death, the body utterly immobile, the facial muscles now redundant, people did not appear at all the same as they had in life.

In this light, and understanding this—at least to a degree—Michael

Travis appreciated that the beauty of Valeria Mironescu was yet something more than her physiology alone occasioned. Her hair was long, almost auburn in color, her eyes perhaps closer to green than anything else, her height no more than five three or four, and yes, she was slim and elegant in her manner, and there was a certain charm in the way she greeted Travis, but the sum of the whole was so much greater than its individual parts.

She wore a long dark dress, cinched tight at the waist with a leather belt, and on her feet she wore boots that would not have been out of place on a Mexican *ranchero*. They were mud-spattered, looked to have seen neither polish nor brush since new, and while they should have appeared incongruous, they did not. If this was how a Romanian gypsy was meant to look, then Valeria Mironescu could not have been a better example.

Travis, for some reason, felt somewhat awkward as he shook her hand, as if he'd approached her in a purely official capacity, intent on demanding answers to questions, and yet her manner indicated a desire to be as helpful as she could be.

"Agent Travis," she said.

"Miss Mironescu," Travis replied.

"Doyle is sleeping," she said. "Let us walk to the tent. I will have someone bring us tea."

She started moving, and Travis could do nothing but follow her.

"I am sorry I wasn't here to see you yesterday," she said. "I was away looking for a further location for the carnival."

"So Mr. Doyle told me."

Valeria laughed. "*Mr.* Doyle? I have never heard him called *Mr.* Doyle. Everyone calls him Doyle, even me. He doesn't even have a first name anymore."

They reached the central marquee, and Valeria took a seat at one of the tables. Travis sat facing her.

She paused to survey Travis for a moment, and then she said, "Doyle told me you were a man of shadows, but he did not say there were so very many."

Travis frowned.

She laughed unaffectedly. "Oh, you must ignore my little comments," she said. "Pay no attention to them."

Travis wanted to ask her what she'd meant—*a man of shadows*. What had Doyle said? What had Doyle seen in Travis that made him comment about it to this woman? Travis withheld his words. He was here on official business, and that was all that needed to concern him.

"As you know, Miss Mironescu, I am here to investigate this terrible business…"

"Terrible business?"

"The man who died."

"Why terrible?"

"The man was murdered, Miss Mironescu. Someone stabbed him in the back of the neck and killed him."

Valeria smiled. "I am from Romania, Mr. Travis. My people, however, are from India, back two thousand years or more. There were Romani long before Christ. We have been killing one another, killing everyone else and being killed the whole time. Romania is a young country, like America, but we used to be part of the Ottoman Empire. And then there's the Transylvanian province, of course, and so we must take into account all the virgins that our vampires have murdered for their blood. So you see, one dead man is not such terrible business, after all. It simply depends upon the context."

Travis smiled, and then he laughed. He had not expected such an answer, and it took him by surprise.

"See, already we are not so serious, eh?"

"In that context, you're right, Miss Mironescu. One man is not such a big deal. However, one man is still one man too many, certainly when it comes to murder. This was not an accident—"

"I am sorry, Agent Travis," Valeria interjected. "I was teasing you, and it was not appropriate. However, it has been said that a serious attitude makes the work that needs to be done all the harder. You seem to be a very serious man, and thus you invite a little teasing."

"I am serious about my work, but never too serious about myself," Travis said. "I do know how to have fun, Miss Mironescu."

"Do you indeed, Agent Travis?"

"Yes, as a matter of fact I do. Why, only six months ago, I left the office five minutes early and took lunch at a diner I'd never been to before."

Valeria laughed, was about to speak when someone appeared with a tray. It was the Asian woman from the night before, the one seated beside the huge man.

"Agent Travis, this is Akiko Mimasuya. Her name means *autumn child*. She is beautiful, no?"

"Good morning, Miss Mimasuya," Travis said.

The girl placed the tray on the table and bowed. She disappeared without responding to Travis's greeting.

"She does not speak to ignorant Americans," Valeria said. "She says they have no culture and they carry the odor of hot dogs."

"She is right. No culture. Stink of hot dogs."

Valeria poured tea, proceeded to place a small cup of seemingly clear hot water in front of Travis. He looked again and saw what appeared to be shreds of leaves and stems in the bottom of the cup.

"Jasmine," Valeria said. "Drink it. It is good for you."

Travis lifted the cup. The aroma was something akin to a flower, very subtle. He sipped and found it refreshing, not altogether unpleasant. "Mr. Doyle gave me Irish whiskey yesterday."

"I don't care for the stuff," Valeria said. "Anyway, tell me what you know about this terrible business."

Travis set down his cup and took the photograph of the dead man from his pocket.

"I have seen this picture before," Valeria said. "I saw the dead man as well. I do not know who he was."

"Does this mean anything to you?" Travis asked. He showed her the diagram he had drawn of the tattoo from the back of the man's knee.

Valeria Mironescu picked up the little diagram and studied it closely. She shook her head. "It means nothing to me. What is it?"

"I am not certain," Travis said. "In fact, I have no idea at all, except that it may help us to identify the dead man."

Valeria returned the diagram to Travis. "I am sorry I cannot help you."

"I know you have already been questioned by Sheriff Rourke, but I need to ask you again. You are sure you had never seen this man before his body was found beneath the carousel?"

"No, I had never seen him before."

"And, to your knowledge, he was not known to anyone else in the carnival?"

"To my knowledge, no."

"And what do you think happened here, Miss Mironescu? Why do you think that a man was killed here on Saturday night?"

Valeria looked away for a moment, and then she looked back at Travis and smiled. It was a pensive smile, almost not there at all. "I don't know," she said. "There must be a hundred thousand ways to kill a person, but there's a very limited number of motives, wouldn't you say? Hate, prejudice, anger, jealousy, greed, fear, vengeance. There can be only so many reasons, can't there? Why this man was killed, and why here, I have no idea."

"Can you think of anything else at all that you feel might have some bearing on this matter, no matter how small, no matter whether you think it's relevant or not?"

Valeria looked unerringly at Travis for a good fifteen seconds, and then she shook her head. "Nothing," she said. "Nothing at all."

"I have a couple of other questions," Travis said. "Your English is remarkably good. I wondered where you learned it."

"I am forty-two years old, Agent Travis. I left Romania many years ago. I knew the war was coming, and I knew that my people would be persecuted again. I met Doyle, and he helped me. I have been in your country for more than a decade."

"And the name of the carnival. Carnival Diablo. Why such a name?"

"Because this is who people think we are, Agent Travis. Anyone different, anyone strange, anyone out of the ordinary falls within such superstitions. As is the case with most people, even yourself, we are simply being who everyone expects us to be."

"I don't think that necessarily applies to me, Miss Mironescu."

"And now you are the one who is teasing me, Agent Travis," she replied.

Travis let it go. Perhaps Valeria Mironescu was attempting to be disarming, but it would not work. Irrespective of whether or not she felt this was a serious matter, it *was* a serious matter. Travis had hoped there would be something in her manner or her body language that told him she knew more than she was saying, but—as yet—there had been nothing. Just as had been the case with Doyle, if she was lying, then she knew more about how to conceal the fact that she was lying than Travis did about reading through such concealments.

"I think that is all for now," Travis said.

"Well, it seems we are here until you allow us to leave," Valeria said. "I don't think that's right, but this is the law, isn't it?"

"Yes, Miss Mironescu. This is a crime scene, and the law applies."

She stood up and extended her hand. Travis rose also.

"A pleasure to meet you, Agent Travis."

"Likewise," Travis said, and she turned and walked away.

Travis sat down again. He looked at the face of the dead man, at the small diagram he had drawn, and he knew that any further meaningful progress would be relatively impossible without accurate identification. He had no reason to suspect that Doyle or Valeria Mironescu were lying when they said they did not know the man. And attempting to connect the dead man with anyone at the carnival was impossible without knowing his identity. This, above and beyond all else, had to be his first order of business. Within three or four hours, he would get word back from Kansas. All they could tell Travis was whether the man was of current significance. His appearance suggested German, Slavic, even Russian. The scars and injuries indicated a military or criminal background. The tattoos? Well, the tattoos, both on the back of the knee and those between the toes, gave credence to possible membership of some unnamed group or organization. Self-applied prison tattoos were not uncommon, both here in the United States and overseas. The Japanese and the Eastern Europeans, in particular, were known to carry hidden tattoos, all of which were of great significance to the initiated, yet utterly meaningless to anyone beyond that circle.

That was the route to take, and of this he felt sure. It made sense to head down to Wichita, no more than fifty miles to the southwest. There would be a field office there, a good-sized library, a university with a foreign studies department, perhaps a division of the mayor's office that dealt with non-nationals, migrant workers, immigrants, and visiting foreigners. Maybe somewhere among all of that he could ascertain the meaning of the tattoos and thus progress this investigation a little further.

Travis headed back to the car and returned to the hotel.

"How's things?" Danny asked him.

"Moving forward, Danny," Travis replied. "I'll be gone for a few hours, more than likely."

"I had my sister make up a lunch for you," Danny said. "I was going to have her bring it down to the carnival for you."

"That's really very thoughtful of you, Danny, but quite unnecessary. You don't need to do that."

"Aw, it ain't nothin'," Danny said. "It's what we do, see? That's just the way we are."

"Well, that is appreciated."

"You go on by the diner as you head off, pick it up from her. Nothin' fancy, mind. Just some sandwiches and a slice of pie."

"Where's the diner?"

Danny gave Travis directions.

"And her name's Laura," Danny called after Travis as he headed out of the foyer and up the stairs to his room.

9

Travis should not have stopped to collect his lunch. He knew that as soon as he saw Laura McCaffrey.

The diner was empty but for an elderly man in a far corner booth, and even as Travis opened the door and started toward the counter, he realized that he could not simply take the proffered package and leave. It would have been impolite, and places such as this were the hub of small communities. The impression with which he left Laura McCaffrey would be the topic of discussion among the regulars, and if he was anything but friendly and courteous, it would not serve him well if wider local cooperation became necessary.

"Hi," Laura McCaffrey said as he reached the counter. She smiled so engagingly that Travis could not help but smile back with a similar degree of enthusiasm.

Laura was a pretty girl—no question about it—but she possessed a delicate sort of awkwardness that made it clear she had no idea of her own attractiveness. Travis guessed she was in her late twenties; she wore no engagement or wedding ring, and from her manner it seemed that she found Travis perhaps a little intimidating.

"You must be Secret Agent Travis," she said.

Travis laughed. "Well, Miss McCaffrey, if you know who I am, then I can't be that secret, can I?"

"Oh my Lord," she said. "I just said that, didn't I? I said *secret* agent, didn't I?"

"Yes, you did."

Laura visibly blushed. "I am so sorry. I don't know what I was thinking. In fact, yes, I do know what I was thinking... at least, well..."

Travis reached over the counter. "Special Agent Travis," he said.

Laura took his hand and they shook.

"I am so sorry," she started once more.

Travis smiled, raised his hand. "Personally, I like it better. In fact, from now on I think I am going to tell people that I am a secret agent."

"You must think me such a fool, Agent Travis."

"Not at all, Miss McCaffrey. Anyway, Danny said that I could pick up some lunch."

"Yes, of course," she said, and passed over the brown paper bag.

"This is really appreciated," Travis said, "and, as I said to Danny, quite unnecessary."

"Oh, it's just nothing at all. The least we can do."

"Well, I am very grateful."

Laura hesitated for a moment and then said, "You have time for a cup of coffee, perhaps?"

"I do, yes," Travis replied. "Just one cup of coffee though, and then I am out to Wichita."

"Oh, I do like Wichita," Laura said. She took two cups from a rack and filled them from the pot to her right. She walked from behind the counter, handed one of the cups to Travis and then took a seat at the closest table.

Travis sat facing her. The coffee was freshly made and good.

"Don't get out there much, what with everything here and the hotel as well, but I do like it."

"The hotel and the diner are in the family?" Travis asked.

"They are, yes. Have been for as long as I remember. We grew up here, all three of us. You've met Lester, right?"

"Yes, of course. He's taking some things to Kansas for me as we speak."

"He's very excited by all of this, you know? I shouldn't say, and it doesn't seem right, seeing as how a man was killed an' all, but Lester says that in all his time in the Sheriff's Department this is the most interesting thing that's ever happened."

"Well, I can appreciate that, Miss McCaffrey, but tell him not to get too excited."

"Have I got him in trouble? You're not going to say something to him, are you?"

Travis laughed. "Nope, not a word. We secret agents are especially good at keeping secrets."

"How dumb must I have sounded?" Laura said. "You're just going to tease me about that forever, aren't you?"

"Absolutely, yes."

"Okay, so now that we've started off our acquaintance on that excellent footing, is there anything else I can get you?"

"No, that's fine, Miss McCaffrey. You and your brother have done more than enough to make me welcome already."

"Well, I presume you're going to be following up on the regulus."

Travis nearly dropped the cup. It slipped a fraction between his fingers, and coffee spilled over the rim onto the table.

"Oh, let me wipe that," Laura said, and started to get up.

"Wait," Travis said. He grabbed her wrist and held it tight.

Laura looked surprised, alarmed even, and she sat down once more.

"What did you say?"

"When?"

"Just then, just a moment ago."

"I said I would wipe that up. I was going to get a cloth and wipe that up—"

"No, before that," Travis said. He looked down at his own hand, the way he was holding her wrist, his knuckles whitening. He released his grip.

"Before?"

"Yes, about following up on something."

"Oh, I was just asking if you would be following up on the rest of us."

"The rest of us?" Travis asked, once again blindsided by something he thought he had heard that now seemed to be something entirely innocuous.

"Yes, the rest of us. Those of us that were there on Saturday night when that man's body was found." Laura paused for a second and then said, "Are you okay, Agent Travis? You do look quite pale."

"Yes," he said. "I am fine. Just fine. Sorry. I thought you said something else."

Laura smiled. "Something dumb, right?"

"No, not at all. I'm sorry. I was just taken by surprise, that's all."

Laura fetched a cloth and wiped the coffee from the table.

"You sure you're okay?" she asked.

Travis looked up at her and forced himself to regain composure. "Yes, everything is just fine." He glanced at his watch. It was a few minutes before noon. "I better be heading out of here," he said.

"Yes, of course. I didn't mean to interrupt your work."

"Well, it was a pleasure to meet you, Miss McCaffrey, and I can imagine we'll be seeing plenty of each other while I'm here."

Laura smiled, a faint rose of color blooming in her cheeks. "Yes, that would be nice," she said. "Until next time, then."

For a moment Travis did not know where to look. He was unsettled, already thrown by what he thought he'd heard, and now was Laura McCaffrey flirting with him?

"Until next time," Travis said, and turned toward the door.

"Your lunch, Agent Travis," Laura said.

Travis turned back. She was standing there with the brown paper bag.

"Ham on rye," she said. "I didn't put any mustard on, 'cause folks either love it or hate it. There's a slice of pie too."

99

"Thank you," Travis said as he took the bag.

He left the diner then, didn't look back even though he knew Laura McCaffrey was watching him, and when he turned the corner and reached his car, he fumbled with his keys before managing to unlock the door.

Travis sat there for a good minute or two.

Well, I presume you're going to be following up on the regulus.

He was unsettled, significantly so. He had a construct, a simple and straightforward reality, and those things that did not fit within that reality were held over to one side until he had time and attention enough to look at them, understand what they were, what part they played in the overall scheme of things.

Seneca Falls, the carnival, Doyle and Mironescu, an unidentified dead man, within a single day, these people, this event, had managed to invade his thoughts to such a degree that he was now sleepwalking, typing words he did not know, hearing things that people hadn't even said.

And this girl, Laura McCaffrey? Had she actually been flirting with him, or was she merely being polite?

If it was the former, then he had to make sure that he gave her absolutely nothing that could be interpreted as a reciprocal interest. He was here for work and work alone. He was a representative of the federal government, and besides... well, besides anything else, there was no way he could ever become involved again. Not now. Not yet. Not after what had happened with Esther.

And then he could see her face, and even though she had been dead for more than eight years, it was as if he had seen her only yesterday.

Travis felt the swelling of emotion in his chest, and he wondered whether he hadn't known when he saw Laura McCaffrey that such a memory might be stirred up. He had tried so hard to forget, to leave it all behind, to make it all disappear, but the simple fact of sitting in that psychologist's office and answering those questions had brought it all to the surface once more. He had responded the way he knew they'd want him to, his manner detached, distant, everything at arm's length. But it wasn't at arm's length, had always been there right beneath the surface, beneath that facade of businesslike pragmatism and efficiency. And now it was all crowded up against him, and the harder he tried not to think of it, the more it threatened to bury him.

Esther Faulkner, the widow of Janette Travis's cousin, the woman who rescued him from Nebraska State.

Dear, sweet Esther, the woman he'd killed with his betrayal.

10

Michael Travis turned sixteen on the tenth of May, 1943. It seemed—for the first time—that the end of the war was in sight. Though Nazi surrender would not come for a further two years, it was a tipping point, and those at State Welfare believed they might not face the choice of serving out their sentence in juvy or signing up for the army.

It was at this time that Michael saw a change in fortune and direction from an unexpected angle. The widow of his mother's cousin, Esther Faulkner, was located in Grand Island, county seat of Hall County. The fact that she was located at all was due to the diligence of one man, a certain Howard Redding, a minor functionary in the Nebraska State Welfare Administration Department. How the unfortunate plight of Michael Travis came to the attention of Howard Redding was simple enough. He read of the mother's case in the *St. Paul Herald*, a newspaper he happened to pick up in the lunchroom one day.

Michael was mentioned in the article, just as an aside, but it piqued Howard's curiosity, and that was sufficient for him to follow up on it. From his professional position, it was easy to find out what had happened to the Travis boy, to locate his current whereabouts, and then to trawl through the city records of the family until he found someone that could perhaps assume guardianship of the boy.

As for the mother, there seemed very little that could be done in the way of mitigation. Not only had she killed her husband in front of the boy, but she had told the attending sheriff, one John Baxter of Flatwater, Nebraska, that she had perpetrated the killing with premeditation and willful intent. There wasn't a jury in the land that would be able to avoid the inevitable verdict and resultant sentence. First-degree murder was first-degree murder. Perhaps it was the simple fact that Howard had no children of his own that appealed to his sense of rectitude and fair play. The boy was not responsible for the mother, yet the mother had been responsible for the boy. From Janette's viewpoint—unbeknownst to Howard Redding—she had taken the greatest responsibility of all, that of sacrificing her own life to protect her son from the Terrible Rage of Jimmy Travis. From Howard Redding's perspective, she had utterly failed as a mother, and yet he did not see that such a failing should result in the punishment of the son. The son, from all appearances, had suffered more than enough already, and he was due a break.

Or so Howard Redding thought.

Howard's first visit to the home of Esther Faulkner did not go as well as he'd expected.

His first impression of Esther was of a woman on the defensive, but about what he did not know. Howard was not a man well versed in the fairer sex, and the fact that she was not only very attractive but a little overbearing made his task all the more arduous. He felt as if he was on the back foot before he even opened his mouth.

"Well, if you think I'm going to take on the responsibility of a teenage kid I've never met, you can go soak your head, mister," was Esther's abrupt and slightly inelegant response.

"But—"

"But nothing, Mr. Busybody," she told Howard Redding from the Nebraska State Welfare Administration Department. "Just because that boy's mother was my husband's cousin, my *ex*-husband's cousin I might add, doesn't mean I have to take one iota of responsibility for him, right?"

"That's right, Mrs. Faulkner," Howard replied.

"Miss," Esther interjected.

"Sorry, *Miss* Faulkner."

"I have yet to revert to my maiden name, but I shall, Mr. Redding. Meanwhile, I prefer to remain a *miss*."

"Of course, yes. Anyway, as I was saying, you have absolutely no responsibility for this matter at all, but considering how you are as close to family as Michael has right now, don't you think that common human decency would allow for a certain sympathy—"

"Well, right there, mister, you got a damned nerve. You think I fell out of the sky yesterday, or what? You think I don't see what you're doing here? You're implying that if I don't take him on, then I lack both common human decency and sympathy—"

"I didn't mean to suggest that, Miss Faulkner."

"Suggest it?" Esther snapped. "You didn't suggest it, mister, you said it loud and clear."

"Well, I apologize, Miss Faulkner—"

"Well, you can darn well apologize till you're blue in the face, it doesn't change the fact that I have no legal obligation to do any of the things you ask me. Am I right or am I right?"

"You are right, Miss Faulkner," Howard replied, feeling once again that small sense of personal defeat that had dogged him his entire life.

He looked around the plainly furnished room, a room where Esther

Faulkner sat alone with her own thoughts much of the time, and he was unaware that—in some strange way—Esther was a kindred spirit, perhaps herself plagued by an unerring sense that life had somehow failed her, or she had failed life, for what she had hoped for and what she was experiencing were about as far from each other as the moon and the sun.

The truth, unknown to Howard Redding, was that Esther Faulkner was nowhere near as tough as she pretended. She was a gentle soul, and her aggressive and domineering tone was merely an affectation. She was gun-shy, sort of *deer-in-the-headlights* when it came to decisions that required responsibility and *doing the right thing*. Scared because she didn't understand what was happening; scared because she was alone; scared because she might find herself obligated to take on a burden with which she could not cope. Her father had been a drinker, had drunk himself into a premature grave, and her mother, Hester, had been a handful and a half of craziness the like of which no daughter should've ever have had to contend. Hester was dead some years now, but the ever-present feeling that she was still being judged for her errors was always around Esther. Her husbands had not served her well, the first one dead, the second one, Kelvin, merely a replacement for her father, himself another drunk no-gooder with more mouth than motivation, more bluff and bravado than backbone. Now she was getting herself talked into another tight corner by some man, and she didn't like the look of it at all.

"If the concern is primarily financial," Howard ventured as a last-ditch attempt to impinge upon the woman's sense of familial conscience, "the state does offer support in that capacity."

There was a heartbeat of silence before Esther responded.

"What does that mean in plain American, mister?"

"It's not a great deal, of course, but the state would assist you financially if you took on the responsibility of the boy, at least until he was eighteen."

Esther looked at Howard Redding very closely. Money *was* an issue, had always been an issue. Her mother had left her a small sum—insufficient to support her exclusively for any length of time, but adequate to subsidize the salaries she acquired from odd months of secretarial and administrative work she undertook.

Esther shifted awkwardly in her chair. "Not that this makes any great deal of difference, but how much are we talking?"

"Well, there isn't a specific amount assigned to each case, but we always gauge it against the cost of keeping someone in a state facility. As far as the State Welfare Institution is concerned, Michael's residence is afforded a monthly stipend of twelve dollars and eighty-five cents."

Esther frowned, as if there was still something she wasn't quite getting.

"So what you're you telling me is that if I take on the responsibility of this boy, the state will give me the best part of thirteen bucks a month?"

"It will more than likely be closer to fifteen or sixteen, Miss Faulkner, as Michael would be required to attend a local school and complete his education, and allowances are made for travel, school clothing, and other such things."

There was an accommodating light in Esther's eyes. "Sixteen bucks, you say."

"Approximately," Howard Redding replied.

"That changes things quite significantly, Mr. Redding," she said. "Not that my primary concern was financial, but that did figure into my reckoning as to how in tarnation I was going to feed a growing boy, a teenager no less, on the money I have to hand, you see?"

"Of course, Miss Faulkner."

The light shone a touch brighter from where Howard Redding was sitting.

He hoped that Miss Esther Faulkner of Grand Island, Hall County, was being honest with him, that her initial and most forceful resistance had merely been due to her concerns as to how she would afford such a responsibility.

"When do you need to know my decision?" she asked, interrupting Howard's doubt-filled thoughts.

"Well, as soon as is possible, Miss Faulkner," he replied. "As far as I am concerned, the nine or ten months that Michael has already spent incarcerated has been far from ideal. I would like to see him released into the care of his family as rapidly as possible."

"I'll do it," Esther said, almost as if it were an involuntary response. "Hell, Mr. Redding, sometimes you just have to go for things, don't you? Sometimes you just have to trust your intuitions and whatever, don't you? Hell, if I'd had a kid in such a predicament as this, then Janette would probably have done the same for me."

Perhaps because he was naturally optimistic, or at least attempted to be, Howard bit his tongue as the question of real motivation floated there at the front of his mind. He knew well enough that Esther Faulkner gave less of a damn for the welfare of Michael Travis than he himself did, that it had merely taken the mention of fifteen or sixteen dollars a month to turn a seemingly uncooperative, unsympathetic woman into a caring and considerate relative.

The reality was actually quite different, and this was where her outward appearance and attitude belied the truth of her sentiments. Like a poorly repaired piece of broken china, the life of Esther Faulkner did not bear anything but the most cursory glance. Any degree of scrutiny revealed the cracks and fissures, and the more you looked, the more obvious they became. She knew she was alone, and she did not like it. In fact, she knew she was *lonely*, and this was a very different thing indeed. She had never been one for sudden change, unexpected occurrences and surprises. Nevertheless, life had been nothing but one of these after another. And yet, here she was, thirty-four years of age, and aside from a string of meaningless jobs, two husbands—one dead, one divorced—she had nothing to show for it. She did not care for her life as it was, and though she would never have admitted such a thing to Mr. Howard "Busybody" Redding from State Welfare, it was the truth. She was running out of time to make something happen, and though the money had been a factor, the thing that had really prompted Esther's change of heart was that taking on Janette Travis's son would mean that her life would not be as it was now. That could *only* be a good thing. At least that's what she wanted to believe. Perhaps she had never done anything really spontaneous and impulsive in her life, but there was something about this situation that had struck a chord. She was alone in a difficult and challenging world, and so was Michael Travis. Perhaps, strangely, this was *meant* to be.

Howard Redding's hope, as he left the Faulkner house in Grand Island, was that regardless of Esther's motivation, Michael Travis could not be worse off here than he was at State Welfare.

It was with this thought that Redding drove back to his office. It was with this thought that he filled out the required paperwork and began the relatively straightforward process of releasing Michael Travis from the custody of Nebraska State to the custody of his mother's cousin.

As for Janette Travis herself, she was still on remand at the State Reformatory for Women. Ten months had passed since the killing of James Travis, and she had yet to stand trial. She had also yet to receive permission to see her son, despite exhaustive written pleas along official channels. Howard was aware of these facts, and yet due process was due process. The wheels of the legal machine ground awful slow, but they ground exceeding fine. As of that moment, his sole concern was the son, not the mother. The law was the law, and if she had taken some time to consider the law instead of putting a table knife through her husband's eye, then her life would not be as it was. Such was the way of things.

And thus it was done. Without consultation, interview, or explanation, Michael Travis was called into the office of the State Welfare Institution warden, Seymour Cordell, he of the strange analogies and childhood cat murder, and informed that he was being released into the care of one Esther Faulkner.

"I'm sorry, sir," Michael responded. "Who?"

"Seems your mother had some sort of cousin, and he was married to

105

this Faulkner woman. He's dead now, but the Faulkner woman isn't, and she lives in Grand Island, right here in Nebraska. You were not aware of this?"

"No, sir, I was not."

"Well, you're aware of it now, son. She ain't a blood relative, but she's the closest you've got right now. You're outta here this afternoon. In fact, you've got about as much time as it takes to get whatever you have into a bag, and then you're gone. Local police are gonna drive you."

Michael Travis did not speak for a moment, and then he shook his head in disbelief. "My mother's dead cousin's widow?"

"Yes, sirree, just like I said. Now git. I got other matters to attend to. Should be grateful, son. Seems you've been given a break."

"Yes, sir," Michael replied, not knowing what to think, not knowing what to feel save a sense of curious detachment. Whatever life this was, it did not appear to be his. Decisions were made without forewarning or knowledge, and he was subject to those decisions whether he cared to be or not. Perhaps a little more of him closed down inside, walled itself up good and sound, for it seemed that since the death of his father, he'd had no more control over his life and circumstances than a fallen leaf in a fast-running stream. Reality seemed vague, indistinct. However hard he was trying to be a realist, reality seemed more unreal than anything else he considered.

Michael Travis did not have anything to pack into a bag. He was given the clothes he'd arrived in, and he changed into them. He turned his denims over to the laundry and was walked back through to the reception building. He saw a woman there, seated alone in a room, seated in such a way as to take up as little room as possible, her purse on her lap, her ankles crossed, her coat pulled around her as tight as it could go. She seemed nervous. It was not something Michael saw, but rather something he sensed. She seemed afraid—not of where she was or what she was doing, but just afraid. Like it was a full-time thing.

The custodian informed him that this was Esther Faulkner, and then he turned and left Michael standing in the corridor alone.

Michael walked to the doorway of the room where Esther was seated.

She looked up as he entered. She visibly flinched.

"Miss Faulkner?" Michael asked.

"Michael?" she replied.

He nodded.

She rose to her feet slowly. She extended her hand, and they shook tentatively.

"We never met before," Michael said. "I'm sorry, this has come as a surprise..."

Esther smiled bravely. "For me too, Michael. And I can't even begin to imagine what you must have gone through these past few months."

Michael looked down at his shoes. He felt something in his chest, his throat, something burning there behind his eyes like the embers of a dying fire. He gritted his teeth, clenched his fists, willed himself not to cry.

He did not know what was happening. Life, like a river, was carrying him somewhere, and he didn't know the destination, if there even *was* a destination.

He looked at Esther, and the expression in her eyes told him that she was perhaps as lost and confused as he.

They stood looking at each other for half a minute or more, and then Michael smiled.

Esther smiled too, and then she started laughing. "We must look like the most foolish of people," she said.

"Foolish. Yes." Michael opened his mouth to say something else, but there was silence.

"I think we just have to give this a go, Michael, and see if we can't make the best of it. What do you say?"

"I think so, yes," Michael replied. He looked into her eyes, looked into *her*, and saw something kind, something decent, something... something he could not define.

It seemed he had no choice but to go with this Esther Faulkner, this widow of his mother's unknown cousin. He would go with her, despite the fact that they did not know each other at all, and he would see what happened.

Maybe this was the way life was supposed to be—a series of unconnected surprises and unrelated events, all strung together with no sense behind them.

Maybe this was a precursor for everything that was yet to come.

Maybe the only predictable thing about life was its innate and inherent unpredictability.

"Shall we go home?" Esther asked, and held out her hand to indicate the door.

Michael could see she was shaking ever so slightly.

"Yes," he said. "That would be fine."

Outside, a police car waited for them. The officer was polite, even opened the door for Michael, and they made their way down the long driveway and away from the building that had been his home for the better part of a year. Looking back over his shoulder, the building seemed so small, so insignificant, disappearing until it was nothing more than a speck of darkness on the horizon.

Michael hoped for one other thing then, as he felt Esther Faulkner's hand close over his and give it a reassuring squeeze. He hoped that the dreams were gone. The headaches too. He hoped that he would no longer be visited by shadows and crows and inhuman laughter. He hoped also that he would no longer feel that sense of anger and violence rising in his blood, would no longer see his father's strangely fearful face each time he tried to sleep, that one cold, blue eye staring back at him, and the sound of blood—*drip-drip-drip*—like some awful metronome that measured his dark and dying heart.

11

As Travis exited the car in Wichita, even now unwilling to really face what had actually happened during his time with Esther, he wondered if he hadn't done himself a disservice by being so dismissive of the Bureau psychologist's interest. If the questions he'd been asked had stirred up so much latent emotion, then wouldn't it have been better to just talk, to just let it go? What was he trying to solve with silence and seriousness? Keeping his job? More than that, it was a matter of not only keeping his job but advancing his career. This was what he wanted right from that moment in a diner in Kearney, Nebraska, in February of 1950. Out of the army, almost drifting, and perhaps fate had once again taken a hand in directing his life. A man had taken a seat beside him, a few words had been shared, and everything had changed. But that was a different story, and it bore no relevance to the reason for his visit.

Travis was in Wichita to determine the significance of the tattoos. That was all. Trusting that identification of its significance would aid in the identification of the man, he did not doubt that he was pursuing the most important line. SSA Bishop and the Kansas office had the deceased's prints. Whether they would make any headway with them was a different issue, and he could not wait to see. The important thing was to keep them updated as accurately as possible. He had not included a copy of the tattoo diagram simply because he did not want to forward a question with no answer. The prints were fine; cross-checking them against the Bureau database was a routine action, but the tattoo was different. This was his puzzle to solve, and his alone; his first case as senior special agent, that case handled rapidly, professionally, and to a good result. That would be ideal. Of course, there was a great deal to do, but if he was systematic and methodical in his approach, then he knew that something somewhere would lead him in a potentially fruitful direction.

Something is better than nothing, his training officer had told him. *Always in such situations, something is better than nothing. A man can be faulted for getting it wrong, of course, but a man cannot be faulted for trying. And use that ability you have, Travis, that ability to reason, to challenge everything, to see logic where logic exists, to reject assumptions and apparent coincidences.*

Now, faced with a real situation—an unidentified dead man, both Edgar Doyle and Valeria Mironescu claiming to know nothing of his identity, and a complete lack of eyewitnesses or forensic clues—what, or more importantly, *who*, could he pursue here?

Keep it simple. Such axioms were drilled into them from day one. *Do what you can do. Do not try to do what you cannot do. Establish a zone of operation, lay down some guidelines, plan out a sequence of actions, and then follow them until what you find forces you to change tack.*

Travis reminded himself of these basic tenets as he made his way up the steps of the Wichita City Library.

Despite assistance from two very interested and eager librarians, there was not a great deal of immediate progress. Travis understood that his official capacity engendered a sense of obligation to help, but the library and its staff did not exist for his use alone. He knew he would keep the librarians' attention only so long and then he would simply become a distraction and an annoyance.

The younger of the two, an intense man by the name of Marcus Briley, recommended Travis speak to a Professor Ralph Saxon.

"If anyone can help you, it'll be him," Briley said.

"Because?"

"Well, he's kind of a walking encyclopedia," Briley explained. "He was a lecturer at the university. He's retired now, but he's been a consultant here for many years."

"And where do I find him?" Travis asked.

"Well, he's here only on Mondays and Fridays, so if you came back in a couple of days, you'd find him here."

"I can't do that," Travis explained. "If he can assist me, then I need to see him today."

"Maybe if you spoke to the chief librarian, she could contact him for you."

"I'll do that," Travis said. "Appreciated."

The chief librarian, though respectful and ostensibly understanding of the situation, wasn't so eager to assist. Her name was Marion Gerrard, and she didn't seem to grasp the urgency of the situation until Travis informed her that it was—in essence—a federal case. Not only that, but concerned the death of a man.

Marion Gerrard's manner changed completely. She was suddenly perturbed. "Oh my," she said. "I feel truly awful, Agent Travis. I am so sorry."

"Please, Ms. Gerrard, don't trouble yourself with the details. If you could simply reach Professor Saxon, I would be most grateful."

"I'll call him at his home this very instant," she said, and reached for the telephone.

Shortly thereafter, following directions that Ms. Gerrard had given him, Travis was dismayed at his own forgetfulness. He had not taken just a few moments to determine whether *regulus* was in fact an actual word. He found it hard to believe that such a thing had slipped his mind. Because he'd wanted it to, perhaps? This was the question he repeatedly asked himself as he crossed town to his next appointment. Why would he *not* want to know if it possessed any meaning? Because it would serve to confirm that his own actions were out of his control? Surely not. And if someone else had typed that word, then what? Was he being directed toward something; even more likely, was he being *mis*directed?

No more than forty minutes later, Travis was standing on the sidewalk in front of a small and unobtrusive house on Cordell Street. Even as he approached the screen, he saw a curtain twitch in a ground-floor window, and the front door was opened before he had reached the top of the steps.

Saxon was an old man, perhaps in his eighties, and yet he seemed to lack no enthusiasm or energy as he greeted Travis. He showed Travis through to a study beside the small kitchen. Here they sat, and though there was no offer of refreshments or anything else, Travis sensed that Saxon was actually thrilled to be consulted in an official capacity by the FBI.

"So, how can I assist?" Saxon asked Travis.

Travis took the small diagram he had made at the morgue from his pocket and handed it over.

"A puzzle," Saxon said. "Might I ask for some details?"

"It's a tattoo," Travis said. "Found on the back of a dead man's knee. It was that pattern as best as I could approximate it, and between the man's toes, there was a series of seven small dots, also tattooed. Not a cluster, but one between each toe."

"Identification," Saxon said. "Tattoos, historically speaking, have often been used to identify membership, even to tell a life story."

"I am familiar with that, yes."

"There is a rule of thumb, for want of a better expression. The more hidden and unobtrusive the tattoo, the more secret the wearer wishes his membership to be."

"And this design?"

Saxon shook his head and smiled. "You need a sociologist or an anthropologist, not a professor of medieval history. I can telephone a friend of mine, if you wish."

"Yes, absolutely. Anything at all that might help would be much appreciated."

Saxon rose and left the room.

Travis sat and waited while Saxon made the call. He looked around the room, the walls of which were crowded with a mismatched selection of various bookshelves, upon them ranging a seemingly endless collection of texts, files, folders, bundles of documents, volumes old and new. If Travis's observation was correct, and he assumed it was, there was no Mrs. Saxon and never had been. Here was a man who had dedicated his entire life to academia.

Saxon returned within a moment. "A wholly disreputable fellow by the name of Marvin Beck is on his way over. He is a retired professor, like me, and we have been colleagues and friends for many years. His specialty is anthropological and social studies, and he will probably be able to shed a brighter light on this than I."

"I am really grateful for your time, Professor," Travis said.

"Oh, think nothing of it, young man. More than happy to help. At our age, a little excitement is all too rare. Now, some tea, perhaps?"

"Please, yes. That would be good."

Saxon made tea, was still making tea when there was a sharp rapping at the front door.

"Go let the old reprobate in, Agent Travis," Saxon called from the kitchen. "Tell him I am under arrest or something."

Travis smiled. He really did like the old man.

Beck, surprisingly, was much the same as Saxon. They were two of a kind, and Travis wondered if there wasn't a network of retired academics and professors, all of them belonging to an unofficial fraternity, all of them doing their utmost to maintain the belief that the sacrifices they'd made—that of children, grandchildren, a horde of descendants—had been worth it for the pursuit of knowledge. Was Travis himself so much different? Would he be the same at their age?

"So, what trouble has he been causing now?" Beck said as he came through the front door. "Saxon, where are you?" he called out.

Saxon was laughing as he entered the room once more. "Mind your manners," he said. "This is Agent Michael Travis of the FBI, and he will no sooner look at you than cart you off to be interrogated about your subversive Communist sympathies. Right, Agent Travis?"

"Absolutely, sir. No question about it."

"Ha!" Beck snorted. "If anyone's the Communist, it's you. Now, get some tea and tell me what's going on here."

Over tea, and holding the small diagram in his hand, Beck's manner changed considerably.

"You say there were tattoos between the toes?" he asked Travis.

"Yes, seven in all. Not a cluster, but one between each toe."

"Such things indicate acts of initiation, sometimes tasks, sometimes penalties," Beck said. "It is a shame I cannot see the body itself, for then I would be able to better determine the age of the tattoos."

"And that would help how?" Travis asked.

"Well, tattoos of this nature are often made at puberty, sometimes even younger. Other times they are made when someone has done things that prove his right to be part of the tribe. But that is more common in the African peoples. This man is white, correct?"

"White, but olive-skinned perhaps. Actually, not so much Mediterranean, more Eastern European."

"And the tattoos themselves, they are small, these dots?"

"Yes, very small."

"And do they seem relatively precise, or do they appear like spots of ink on blotting paper, as if they have spread out beneath the skin?"

"Quite precise," Travis said. "Yes, I would say they were quite defined."

"Which indicates their having been applied in adulthood." Beck nodded slowly, and then he looked over the upper rim of his glasses at Travis.

"I am thinking that they may be as a result of actions performed. I would say that the pattern on the back of the knee is a symbol of membership, whereas the ones between the toes, seven in all, would be more a result of doing something. I think they are earned."

"Earned?"

"Yes," Beck said. "If, as you say, he appears perhaps Eastern European, then I am wondering if he doesn't belong to some kind of gang, some kind of organized-crime network, perhaps. You say he was murdered?"

"Yes."

"Might I ask how?"

"Stabbed in the back of the neck. A blade of some description was pushed upward into the base of his brain."

Beck smiled. "Those who live by the sword shall die by the sword. Not exactly a heart attack or a stroke, eh?"

"No, not exactly."

"Well, from what little I know, and from the manner of his death, I would say that you probably have a killer on your hands, Agent Travis. And now, ironically, he himself has been killed."

"And the tattoo on the back of his knee?"

"I couldn't tell you," Beck replied. "Europe is the wrong continent for me when it comes to anthropological or social rites and rituals." He looked across at Saxon. "What do you think, Ralph?"

"A reversed question mark," Saxon said. "A Cyrillic letter, perhaps Coptic, East Slavic?"

Beck shook his head. "No, none of those. I don't recognize it at all."

"Well, the simple fact is that it could be significant to only those who are part of the organization, if it is actually a mark of membership."

"Perhaps a map of some kind, perhaps the location of something..."

"A constellation?" Travis suggested.

Beck nodded. "As good a guess as anything. Constellations hold great significance in the Middle East and the Africas. A great deal of store is placed in the position of stars at certain times of year. Perhaps it relates to his own birth sign."

"I don't recognize it from the known signs," Saxon said. He looked up and scanned the walls. "I have a text somewhere, I'm sure. The Medieval English sages and soothsayers granted enormous importance to astrological divination."

The text was located, and Travis had to stand on a rickety chair in order to reach it down. The book was heavy, thick with dust, and it was with some awkwardness that the three of them managed to position it in such a way as to survey the endless tables of astrological patterns that were detailed.

When they found it, Travis visibly paled. He felt decidedly nauseous, and Beck asked him if he was all right, if there was something wrong.

"You really don't look well at all, Agent Travis," Saxon said. "Can I get you something?"

Travis could not speak. His mind had stretched awkwardly around a concept that was actually inconceivable, but the evidence for whatever coincidence had taken place here was undeniable.

The word was there, and though he did not believe it and could not explain it, he could not avoid the reality of it.

Regulus.

The constellation that so closely matched the small design he had copied from the back of the victim's knee was called Regulus.

As far as he could recall, he had never seen the word before, and yet here it was. He had actually woken to find it right there on a sheet of paper, and now he was being told that it was the name for this diagram.

He should have made time to research it. He could have so easily consulted a text at the library that morning, but he had not. Had he *really* not wanted to know? Had he actually been scared to find out what it meant?

What could he tell these two old men? What could he even say? It made no sense. None at all.

"Agent Travis?" Beck asked. "You look like someone walked over your grave."

Travis did his best to explain. He had sleepwalked, that was all he could say. He had risen in the night, and unaware of what he was doing, he had typed this very word on a single sheet of paper and left it right there in his typewriter. Or the other possibility... that someone else had done it. He remembered how he had felt that morning, the dull ache in his head, the lack of clarity in his thoughts. And then he considered yet another possibility, something even more disturbing. What if he had been drugged? What if someone had crept into his room and drugged him in order to leave that message on his typewriter?

For a few moments, his mind was utterly quiet.

"I see that this has come as a great shock to you," Saxon said, "but then again, perhaps it is not so much of a surprise."

"More than a shock, Professor Saxon," Travis said. "It's beyond coincidence."

Beck smiled. "We have age and experience on our side, Agent Travis, and perhaps some small understanding of the nature of the human mind, certainly when it comes to the field of education and retention of information."

"I don't understand..."

Beck laughed, almost sardonically. "You said you drove down from Seneca Falls?"

"Yes, I did, this morning."

"A little ironic."

"I'm sorry?"

"The Roman philosopher, Seneca. Didn't he say that luck was nothing more than the coincidence of preparation and opportunity? You seem to have been very lucky in finding us."

"I don't understand," Travis said, still confused, still trying to come to terms with what was happening to his logical thought processes. It felt as if events were conspiring to break him down, to get him to explain something that possessed no rational explanation.

Trust you spelt well...

"Sometimes there are things that can be explained, and sometimes there are not," Beck said. "I guess the nature of your work requires you to be a man of routines and habits, of logic, of concise and complete explanations. I can also see that you are greatly troubled by this. Fortunately, this is one of those situations where an explanation is almost too simple."

"Too simple?"

"Yes, of course. You went to school, did you not?"

"Of course."

"You say that as if going to school is the most ordinary thing in the world. You appreciate that there are a great many more people in this world who do not go to school than those who do?"

"In America—"

"Even in America, Agent Travis, your education depends a great deal upon who you are, where you're from, the color of your skin. However, fortunately you are white and not without some intelligence, and therefore you were able to go to school."

"Yes, I went to school."

"How much information can the human mind absorb and retain, Agent Travis?"

"Well, the brain is—"

"Not the brain, the mind," Beck said. "The brain is a few pounds of hamburger, and I am not sure that I like the idea of my intelligence and character and personality being attributed to a half dozen pounds of hamburger, do you? Just as I do not wish to consider that a muscle in my chest is responsible for who I love."

"The brain, the mind... they are the same thing," Travis said.

"We will agree to differ, Agent Travis. Regardless, the question stands."

"How much information can the human mind retain?"

"Yes."

"I have no idea, Professor Beck."

"A human being can learn ten languages, study music, philosophy, read through a library of books, visit a thousand places, and the capacity of the mind is never even stretched. Wouldn't you agree?"

"Yes, of course," Travis replied.

"Did you ever study astronomy, perhaps? Did you ever take a lesson in the physical sciences where someone spoke of the universe, the stars, the heavens?"

"I never studied astronomy, no, but I studied other things, physical sciences, I'm sure."

"Did any ever speak of Ursa Major, Ursa Minor, Orion, nebulas, asteroids, such things as this?"

"Yes, of course. I have heard of all of those things."

"Well, is it not possible that someone might have shown you some diagrams of the constellations and given their names?"

"Yes, absolutely."

"So there is your answer, Agent Travis. The mind absorbs; it retains.

You think you have forgotten, but you never really forget anything. The only thing you forget is *how* to remember."

Travis paused in consideration of Beck's explanation. "So you're saying there's a possibility that I knew that the diagram was this constellation all along, and it just took some time for that information to surface?"

Saxon leaned forward. "You know, it has been said that if you simply asked for a detail about someone's life every day... if you just asked them once each morning for that same detail, they would eventually remember it. It could be the most precise and specific detail you could ever imagine, something so unimportant there is no way the person could recall it, but it is there, and if you ask for it, you will get it."

"But typing in my sleep?"

"We dream, we walk, we write, we have conversations in our sleep, Agent Travis. The body sleeps, but the mind and the spirit are always awake."

"What you say makes some degree of sense," Travis said. "The fact that I could have remembered that information, but it unsettles me nevertheless."

"And that is because you are a man of logic and pragmatism and evidence and facts. However, a fact is only a fact in relative terms. There is a huge amount about the mind and life that we have never even begun to grasp, let alone understand."

"So now you need to find out what kind of person has a tattoo of a constellation on their body," Beck said. "And if it is Eastern European, then you could do worse than go up to the university and see the head of foreign studies. That would be a point to start, at least."

"I'll do that," Travis said.

"I'll call ahead and tell them you're coming," Saxon added.

And so it was, amid the banter between the old men, interrupted solely as they disagreed about the best route to take to the university, that Travis collected his hat and saw himself out of the house. He sat for a little while in the car, still deeply disturbed about what had happened, though reassured to be perhaps one step closer to identifying the man that lay stiff and cold in the Seneca Falls morgue.

Travis felt disturbed; more than that, he felt *invaded*. That was how he'd felt in the company of both Doyle and the Mironescu woman. It felt to him that each new aspect of this case was testing the very seams of his existence. He was hearing things that were not spoken, remembering things that had long been forgotten, finding that the memories of his own history were seeking him out and cornering him. He knew he would have to remember all of these things, even the very last time he'd seen his mother, the certainty of her death in the room as if another person had indeed been present.

That would come in its own time, but as he drove across to the university, he felt he could no longer avoid the truth of what had happened in Grand Island, a part of his life that would always and forever be Esther's.

12

Michael Travis would not live with Esther Faulkner for much beyond three and a half years, but those three and a half years would influence and affect his view of the world far more than the previous years he'd spent with his parents. What those three and half years would do for Esther, well, that was another story entirely.

The Grand Island house was a small affair by any standard. It needed a lick of paint inside and out, and the wiring was affected by damp from the basement. Odd patches of mildew appeared in the corners of the ceiling when it rained, suggesting holes in the roof and rotten attic timbers, but it had been solidly built and would stand resolute even if nothing was done to improve it. There was a sitting room, a kitchen, and a narrow utility room on the lower floor, whereas upstairs provided two small bedrooms, a bathroom, and a storage space filled with everything that had no official place elsewhere.

It seemed, from what Michael could observe, that Esther had made a real effort to make him welcome. The house was clean, his assigned room had laundered sheets, curtains, a couple of threadbare blankets that had seen better days, and a rug on the floor upon which was some kind of faded seascape. On the wall was a painting of an elderly man with a pipe, the brushwork somehow clumsy and inarticulate, but there was an expression captured that seemed uncannily real.

"That is my grandfather on my father's side," Esther told him. "My mother painted that. Only thing I have of hers."

"So I am related to him, right?" Michael asked.

"Yes, very distantly, I s'pose. Not by blood, of course, but yes, you're related." Esther paused, and then she laughed, and for just a moment Michael saw the girl that she must have once been.

There was no doubt that Esther was a very attractive woman. No doubt at all. Whereas Janette Travis was petite and brunette, almost demure in an understated and fragile way, Esther was altogether bigger, not only physically but in her personality. Esther's hair was a mountain of uncontrollable blond curls that she piled on her head as best she could. Of an evening, she would unpin the whole affair and let it do as it wished. She looked better that way, or at least Michael felt so. Esther wasn't beautiful in a predictable and obvious way, but there was an alluring sexuality in her manner that went much deeper than her skin.

Years later, Michael Travis would sit in a movie theater in Kansas City and watch the first half of *A Streetcar Named Desire*. He saw there on the screen both Janette and Esther, as if each of the significant women in his early life had subsumed some part of Stella, some part of Blanche, and made it their own. He could not bear to watch the entire film, feeling as though something within himself was being twisted painfully tighter and ever tighter. A tourniquet on his heart, his soul perhaps.

But for now, standing there in the room that Esther had made up for him, a thousand unasked questions on his lips, Michael knew nothing of Tennessee Williams, nor of what life would be between that moment and a movie theater in Kansas City, and he closed his eyes and clenched his fists and held his breath for just a moment.

For Esther, something else happened.

From the moment she had seen the young man standing there in the reception offices of the Nebraska State Welfare Institution, she knew it was no longer about the money. The letter she'd received from Howard Redding, the letter that clearly detailed her duties as legal guardian until Michael reached eighteen (. . . *to provide adequate and acceptable shelter and nourishment, provision of medical aid or treatment as required in the event of accident or injury, moral guidance, accessibility to recognized and accepted academic and/or educational tutelage as deemed by law to be appropriate for the child in your care . . .*) had slipped from her mind. Even the addendum included with the letter, the way it nonchalantly informed her that the sum of fifteen dollars and forty-five cents per month had been approved for her care of Michael Travis, seemed irrelevant.

Esther Faulkner had never seen Michael before, and yet there seemed to be something so familiar about him. Whatever was happening, she felt it in her heart, her mind, her soul, right through her body to the tips of her fingers. This was a special thing, and she could not remember ever feeling like it before.

In those few moments as she stood behind Michael—noticing the way he looked at the painting on the wall, the bed beneath, the way he glanced back at her, almost nervous, anticipatory—she wanted to reach out and enclose him with everything she possessed.

She wanted Michael to understand that she would do anything she could to keep him safe, to make things somehow better, to counterbalance the effect of the terrible things he must have already suffered in such a few short years.

Michael took a few tentative steps forward. He reached out and pressed the edge of the mattress, almost as if he were determining its capacity to stand his weight. He turned and sat down.

"You know my mother is in prison, right?" he asked Esther.

Esther nodded. She felt like she was going to cry.

"I haven't seen her."

"I know," Esther replied. "Mr. Redding told me."

"Mr. Redding?"

"He's the man from the State Welfare Department. He's the one who found me and asked me to take you in."

"Can I go and see her?"

"I would think so, yes. I am sure you're allowed to go and see her."

"And I want to go to the house in Flatwater, too," Michael added. "I want to get my things."

"Mr. Redding said you could go there, but you couldn't take anything from the house. He said that everything was the property of the state until the trial was over and the legal process had ended."

"He means that I can't have anything from the house until she's dead, right?"

The sudden rush of emotion was understandable, unavoidable and terrifying. Esther felt as if the world had suddenly filled her chest with all the pain it could muster. Her clenched fist flew to her mouth, and she bit her knuckle to prevent herself from crying out.

Michael, however, just looked at her blankly, as if he had made some comment about the prospect of rain.

"Right?" he echoed.

Esther nodded just once, knowing full well that this—beyond any reasonable doubt—was the fate that awaited Janette Travis. She did not know the full details of the case and did not care to know. Howard Redding had informed her only of those things that he'd felt absolutely necessary. Esther understood that there were those who were inexorably drawn to the morbid details of the dark deeds of others, and then there were those who just simply could not face them. Esther was in the latter category, almost as if such acts of violence and mayhem would serve to remind her that life was raw and angry and possessive of some innate madness in all its aspects and facets. If you went looking for such madness, you were likely to find it, and it was hard enough to cope already. So Howard, gentleman that he was, alluded to the killing of Jimmy Travis as *this most unfortunate incident* and Janette's fate as *the penalty of the law*. It was better that way. It meant that both of them could make believe that they were dealing with something far less threatening and dangerous.

But Michael had not hidden from the reality of what had happened. Michael had been there to see it in all its 3D Technicolor glory. He had seen the knife in his mother's hand. He had seen the handle of it protruding from his father's punctured eye. He had seen the way Jimmy Travis had stared at him, his one and only son, as if—even from the gates of death—Jimmy had looked back from eternity with some sort of unspoken promise on his lips.

Will haunt you forever, kiddo. Gonna be in your dreams, your nightmares, your waking thoughts... always and forever... and though your bitch of a mother might burn in hell for what she did, that won't be enough for me. Wanna see you suffer too, kiddo. Wanna see you suffer if only to make her feel worse...

"R-right," Esther said, and heard her voice crack with grief.

"Will you come with me?" Michael asked, and for one dreadful, petrifying moment, Esther believed that he was asking her to be there when they killed his mother, to watch as they fired a thousand million volts of electricity through her body and burned her to pieces from the inside out.

"Wha—" she started.

"To Flatwater," Michael said. "Will you come with me to Flatwater and to see my mother in the prison?"

"Yes, of course," Esther said without thinking, so utterly, indescribably relieved that he was not asking her what she'd thought he was asking her. It was then that she understood that she could no longer hide from the truth of what had happened. She would have to go and see Janette, and she would have to stand in that house where the terrible thing had happened. She could not backtrack; she could not now decline Michael's request. She had said she would go, and that was that.

Swiftly, as if pushing aside what she was really feeling was something she had practiced too many times, she changed the subject.

"Are you hungry?" she asked.

Michael looked at her, hesitance in his expression.

"Did they institutionalize your stomach, young man?" she asked, smiling. "Here we can eat whenever we like."

"Sure, I could eat something," Michael said.

"So what do you want?"

"Whatever's easiest, Miss Faulkner. I don't want to be any trou—"

He was cut short by her laughter. "Oh, Lordy," she said. "That's gonna have to stop right here and now, Michael Travis. My name is Esther, not Miss Faulkner, just Esther and nothing more nor less than that, okay?"

Michael smiled. It was good to hear someone laughing so unashamedly and not at the expense of someone else's dignity, as had so often been the case at State Welfare. Things had happened there, bad things, wicked things, and he was doing his best not to remember them.

"So, what do you want to eat?"

"You eating too?" he asked.

"Sure am."

"Then I will eat whatever you're having," he said.

"Well, I s'pose that makes things simple," she said. She paused for a moment, just looking at him, thinking to herself that he was really a very good-looking young man, that he would be quite the heartbreaker in his own way, and she felt an odd and awkward stirring among the miasma of emotions that had so vigorously assaulted her since she'd first seen him standing there in the corridor of that terrible, terrible place. Was there guilt there? Some small shadow of guilt for thinking such a thought about such a young man?

"You want to come down and help me?" she asked.

"Sure thing," Michael said, and then—almost as an afterthought, perhaps to begin getting used to something that was sure going to take some getting used to—he added, "Sure thing, Esther."

He rose from the bed and walked toward her. Esther held out her hand and Michael took it. She led him along the hallway, down the stairs, and through to the kitchen.

"I think things are gonna be just swell between us," she said as she opened the refrigerator and took out some cold chicken and a bowl of salad. "I reckon you and I are gonna get along just fine an' dandy."

"I hope so," Michael said. "I want to get along, Esther. I really do. I don't want to be trouble to anyone no more."

She turned then, and she looked at the expression on his face—the way he seemed so innocent, so naive, yet tainted by some deeply disturbing shadow, a shadow so profound and dark that it would hang over him for the rest of his life. How did you even begin to deal with such a thing? Everyone he met, every friend he made, every personal relationship he instigated would find that wound and push its fingers deep inside.

Esther started crying then, and the tears came fast and furious, and for a moment she believed she might just fall to the ground.

Michael was beside her then, and he put his arms around her and pulled her close.

"Hey, hey, hey," he said. "It's okay... It's okay, Esther. It's gonna be fine. We'll cope. We'll do just fine an' dandy, like you said. We're gonna make it..."

And Michael, his heart as hollow as a balloon, paid lip service to consolation and sympathy and wondered if he would ever be able to put into words how truly empty he felt.

Esther's tears soaked through the cotton of his shirt, and he felt their warmth, and he understood what they meant, but there was no connection at all.

If you had something, even something so intangible as an emotion, then life would just take it from you anyway.

Michael had decided to feel nothing, to remain uninvolved, to keep all of life at arm's length and just observe it from the sidelines.

It was safer that way.

Within a matter of days, Michael was enrolled at the closest high school that would take him, and he set himself to catching up the months of study he'd missed while in State Welfare.

Initially, he was treated with a degree of suspicion, as if word of his background had telephoned into something far more threatening and dangerous than it was.

Maybe the kids believed him a criminal, the *juvy* guy, and while they were arranging sleepovers and drive-in trips, Michael was never asked nor included. He was not aware of missing the Saturday-night drive-in showings of *Girl Crazy* with Judy Garland and Mickey Rooney or *The Constant Nymph* with Joan Fontaine, but he was aware of the way in which conversations would drift awkwardly into silence as he passed these clusters of kids—the girls kind of coy, the boys seemingly bluff and defensive—in corridors and outside classes. He did not understand why he was being excluded, nor did he ask.

Within only a couple of weeks, he was called in to see his homeroom teacher, Mr. Julius, for an *informal word*.

"You seem lonely, Michael," he said, easing himself back in his chair and stoking his pipe.

"Lonely, sir?"

"You don't seem to have any real friends, no one you're close to."

"I'm fine, sir. Really."

"Are you, Michael? Are you really fine, or are you just saying that?"

"No, sir. I'm just fine."

"Of course, we would understand perfectly if you were not fine. I mean, taking into consideration the fact that you have had a very difficult start in life—"

"Did someone say I was not fine, sir?"

"Well, not in so many words, Michael, but your teachers have noticed that you spend a great deal of time alone, that you do not mix easily with your contemporaries, that you don't seem to have a girlfriend... or even a male friend, for that matter."

"Is that a crime, sir?"

"No, Michael, of course it's not a crime. I think we're getting off on the wrong foot here. No one has complained about your behavior. In fact, your grades are excellent, and the speed with which you seem to be getting a grip on your work has been truly astonishing. It's just that . . . well, it's just that we are concerned for your mental and emotional welfare, Michael, not just your academic achievements."

"Am I in trouble, sir?"

"No, Michael, of course you're not in trouble."

"Okay."

"Do you have anything to say about this?"

"What can I say, sir? The other kids act like they are scared of me. They don't know why I was in State Welfare. No one has asked me. I haven't told anyone. People believe what they want to believe, and often it's very far from the truth. I can't help it if they are narrow-minded and ignorant."

"I would think that a little harsh, wouldn't you, Michael?"

"Harsh? I think they have been harsh, sir. They call me Juvy Boy and Michael Tragic. They don't know that my mother killed my father and now she is going to be tried and executed."

"Who calls you these things, Michael?"

"It doesn't matter, sir. Really, it doesn't matter at all. I am fine. I am here to get my high school diploma, and I want to go to college if Mr. Redding can arrange it."

"So I do not need to have any concern about you?"

"No, sir, you don't."

"Well, Michael, you certainly seem to be a levelheaded and responsible young man, and I must say that your teachers consider you bright and diligent and well mannered. You are respectful of your elders, and as far as I can see, you have never been in any trouble here at the school."

"No, sir."

"Very well. Off you go now, and if there is anything you wish to talk about, any personal matters, anything that's troubling you, then don't hesitate to come and find me, okay?"

"Yes, sir. Thank you."

And that, as they say, had been that. Or so Michael thought.

Somehow word got out, word regarding the real reason that Michael Travis had been in juvy, and in some strange way that made things worse.

Now he was the son of a killer. Now he was someone who may very well have inherited his mother's homicidal tendencies. Now he was potentially more dangerous than he'd ever been.

Michael, however, had long since decided to stoically weather whatever may have been directed his way, and when those who were attempting to upset him saw that their efforts came to naught, they directed their efforts elsewhere. Michael did not become the cowed and timid victim that they wished him to be, and thus they grew bored. Michael existed as a student, but not as a friend, as a school attendee, not as a participant. He was just there, going on about the business of studying and learning as best he could, and it was only when he returned home that he found some slight degree of solace in the company of Esther Faulkner.

However, things became awkward between Esther and Michael after their first visit to see Janette at the State Reformatory outside of York. Unbeknownst to Michael, Esther had been working with Howard Redding on obtaining visitation rights for Michael and herself. Those rights were granted in the early part of September 1943. York was due west of Grand Island, no more than sixty or seventy miles. Thus, on Friday, September 17, 1943, Michael Travis and Esther Faulkner boarded a bus for the journey to York, Nebraska. Here they would find a car waiting for them, courtesy of Howard Redding of the State Welfare Department, and that car would take them out to the State Reformatory.

Michael had not seen his mother since that fateful day in August of the previous year. The very last words she had uttered to him were still imprinted in his mind: *Now come here and hug me good, and then off with you, boy. You go get Sheriff Baxter and tell him I done killed your daddy with a table knife.*

He did not know what to feel or how to feel it, but as he stepped from the back of that car and walked toward the gate of the reformatory, Esther Faulkner clutching his hand as tight as could be, he knew that this was going to be difficult.

The visit itself lasted no more than thirty minutes. Janette cried a lot, and all the time she cried she was trying desperately not to. Esther cried as well, simply because there was just too much emotion to be borne by Janette and Michael alone.

"I did what I had to do," Janette told Michael. "He was a violent man, Michael, a truly dangerous and violent man, and I just got to the point where I couldn't take it anymore. And the thing that frightened me most... the thing that terrified me more than anything else in the world, was that I knew you couldn't bear to see it, and one day you might just up and kill him. Or maybe he would have killed you. Either that, or you would spend so long listening to his lies and deceptions that your mind would turn. Truth is, I was deeply afraid that you might become like him one day, Michael. I thought that whatever drove him to do the things he did were already inside you, and the more it went on, the more likely..."

She looked down and shook her head. "The truth is, Michael, that I don't know what I thought."

Michael sat and listened, watching his mother as she wept and explained and justified and apologized.

He felt for her, there was no doubt about it, but he struggled to feel for himself. He kept looking at Esther, watching this scenario unfold before her eyes, perhaps trying to imagine how she must have felt, trying to come to terms with how the unpredictable and unrelated action of some distant relative had impacted upon her life in a way that was immeasurable and irreversible.

In a strange way, Michael felt closer to Esther, even though he had known the woman a bare handful of weeks. They were the effect of a common event, an event caused by Janette. Janette would stay behind, whereas he and Esther would walk away together. He and Esther would spend the next weeks and months, perhaps even years, living under the same roof, talking to each other, sharing meals, whereas he would see his mother as and when he was permitted by law.

When they finally parted company, it was to Janette as if her son were being wrenched out of her arms a second time. For Michael, it was different. He did not react in the same way, not immediately. He did not feel the full force of what had happened until he sat at the back of the bus with Esther and they headed out of York toward Grand Island.

It was then that he cried, and he did not simply cry; he sobbed. He sobbed uncontrollably at first, pulling away from Esther and burying his face in the crook of his arm, uncaring as to who saw him or heard him in his grief.

Esther, believing herself unable to do anything to really help him, just sat with her arm around his shoulder. She would listen when he spoke, and that was all she could do. She could not even begin to appreciate what he was experiencing, but she knew that it broke her fragile heart just to hear him.

Finally, the emotional tidal wave spent, he turned to her, and she pulled him closer against her, and they seemed to console each other wordlessly with the simple fact that at least they were not alone.

"Her trial will be soon enough," Esther told him.

"I know."

"Before Christmas, I think," she said.

"Yes, before Christmas."

"Do you want to go?"

Michael was silent for a time. "I don't know," he finally said.

"I don't either," Esther replied.

"I think it will be a short trial."

"Yes. And if you want to go, I will go with you," she said, hoping that he would decide not to.

They did not speak of it again, seated there at the back of the bus, the road spooling out like a black ribbon behind them, holding each other as if each sought nothing but an anchor in this sea of madness.

Esther could not see it, and Michael did not speak of it, but the words his mother had uttered had burned through to the very core of his being.

Truth is, I was deeply afraid that you might become like him one day, Michael. I thought that whatever drove him to do the things he did were already inside you...

That day, that very same Friday, was the day that everything changed between them.

They arrived back at her Grand Island house as evening fell. Michael said he was tired.

"Not physically," he added. "Tired in my mind, I think."

"Take a bath," Esther said. "That will relax you. I will make some dinner for us. Maybe we could have a glass of wine."

Michael went upstairs. He drew the bath. He took off his clothes and stood naked in the bathroom, looking from the small window into the yard behind the house.

The season had turned; the air was crisp and chill, and fall was settling in for the duration. Those few plants and shrubs that Esther managed to maintain in the dry topsoil had conceded defeat until spring of the following year.

Once the bath was full, Michael lay in the water and closed his eyes.

He let the warmth envelop him, and he tried hard not to see his mother's face as she had looked that day. It was not his mother, at least not as he remembered her. She was frail and exhausted and scared. Perhaps, of all things, the greatest difficulty he faced was accepting that he could do nothing to help her. Not now. Not ever. Her fate was sealed, and she had sealed it by killing his father and confessing to the premeditative intent. Perhaps if she had not said that...

"Michael?"

Michael sat up suddenly. Water splashed over the edge of the tub onto the floor. The door was unlocked, and through the two- or three-inch gap between the edge of the door and the jamb, he could see Esther standing in the hallway.

"I'm going out on the veranda to have a glass of wine," she said. "When you're finished, come down and join me."

"Yes, of course," Michael said. "I won't be long."

An awkward silence hung in the space between them for just a moment, and then Esther said, "Good... I'll see you downstairs then..."

Michael did not stay long in the water. He felt a little self-conscious.

There were thoughts in his mind, thoughts that he'd had before, but Esther's presence at the bathroom door had brought them very much to the fore. He got out, dried himself, put on a clean pair of pants and a T-shirt, and then headed downstairs, barefoot, his hair still damp. He found Esther on the back veranda. She was seated in a chair, her back against the wall of the house, a glass of wine in her hand.

"Tough day," she said.

"Yes," Michael said. He walked toward her, perched on the railing facing her.

"How're you doing?"

Michael glanced sideways, a little less awkward now, but still aware of what he was feeling.

"Good as can be," he replied.

"Hurts me to see you so sad."

"Hurts me to be so sad."

"You miss your father, Michael?"

Michael didn't know how to answer the question. He was silent for a time, and then he looked back and smiled at Esther. "I miss the man I thought he was, not the man he was."

"That's a very profound comment."

"I didn't mean it to be."

"I didn't mean that critically," Esther said. "I meant it as it sounded. It's a very profound statement for someone—"

"So young?"

She smiled. "You're not so young, Michael Travis."

"Sixteen is pretty young."

"Well, you might be too young to buy a drink, but you're old enough to deal with one of the most difficult things I ever did hear of."

"Can I ask you a question, Esther?"

"Sure, sweetheart. You go right ahead and ask me whatever you like."

"Why did you take me in?"

That was not the question she'd expected, and she coughed as she swallowed. A drop or two of wine spilled on the front of her housedress.

Gathering her thoughts, she made a fuss of dabbing those spots of wine away with her handkerchief, and even as she was done, she realized that she was not going to get away with anything but the truth. There was something about Michael Travis that made you *want* to tell him the truth. You just had to look into his eyes, and before you knew it, you were talking.

"Honest?" she asked.

Michael smiled. "What else is there, Esther?"

She wondered if he actually believed what he was saying, as if he really believed that there was nothing but the truth.

"At first," she said, "I thought I was agreeing because of the money. Mr. Redding said the state would pay me to feed you and house you, you know? It isn't a fortune, but it isn't peanuts. But then, after I agreed, I realized that I didn't do it because of the money. I was doing it because I wanted to make a change in my life..." She smiled, shook her head as if questioning what she herself was about to say. "It seemed to be—"

"Fate?" Michael asked.

Esther laughed suddenly, almost as if she had been caught out in a fib and there was no denying it.

"Do you believe in fate, Esther?" Michael asked.

"I think that sometimes things happen simply because you believe they will."

"I think you're right," Michael said, and he looked back toward the yard and smiled so artlessly, so sincerely, that she couldn't help but smile back.

"All I know now is that I want to help you," she said. "Having gotten to know you, if they told me they were going to stop giving me that money, it wouldn't matter. I'd want you to stay here."

"I feel like I need to tell you something, Esther," Michael said, and there was a presence, a tension in his voice, that made Esther feel immediately on edge. He looked at her, then turned sideways, almost as if to face her while he was speaking was more than he could stand.

She set down her wineglass on the veranda and steeled herself for whatever was coming.

"I don't know why I have to tell you, but I feel that if I don't tell you, then we might have difficulties between us. I want us to be friends. I want to stay here with you. I don't want to go back to State—"

"And I don't want you to go back—"

Michael looked back at her then, just for second, his eyes unerring. "Let me say what I have to say, Esther, or I might just lose the will to say it."

She nodded. Her heart was beating ever such a little bit faster.

Michael looked away once more.

"I want to stay here with you, Esther, but there is something in my mind, and I don't think it should be there, and it stops me..." He closed his eyes and shook his head. "I think about you, Esther. I think about you a lot."

Esther didn't know where to look. Her heart—beating ever more rapidly—was right there in her chest. She could feel it so strong. Why was it that the heart, the very thing that seemed to represent all that love entailed, was nevertheless most evident when you were afraid? Was she afraid? Was that what she was feeling? Or was it something else entirely?

"I think about you in a way that someone like me shouldn't think about someone like you..."

And then—as if to defy all the laws of rightness and rectitude—Michael turned toward her, and he reached out his hand and touched her arm. His fingertips merely drifted across her skin, but it was as if they possessed a fierce electrical current.

Esther flinched, but she did not withdraw.

She sat there on the chair, all of thirty-four years of age, and felt every joint go weak and useless.

Esther, without looking, reached for her glass. It was right there at her feet, but she misjudged, and the wineglass, now almost empty, toppled over. Miraculously, it did not break, but the last inch of wine spilled out across the plank-board floor. It looked like blood.

Esther reached to set the glass straight, and even as she did, she felt Michael's hand touch her shoulder. She looked up. He rose to his feet, and then he took her hand and brought her to her feet also.

Esther shuddered, both in excitement and trepidation. She did not know where to look, and so she simply held his gaze as he stood there, the expression on his face one of almost unashamed simplicity. Her knees barely held her weight. He raised one hand and touched the side of her face. She believed she would faint.

"No," she said, but she did not shrink back from that touch.

His hand was beneath her chin then, and he somehow drew her toward him without her even being conscious of moving.

Without thinking, she reached up her left hand and placed it on his waist. Michael breathed deeply, and then he dipped his head and kissed her hard on the mouth at first, and then more gently across her cheeks, her eyelids, her forehead.

It was as if everything fell away then—every agreement, every opinion, every *now-I'm-supposed-to*, every accepted rule about how one should behave and why.

Michael was unbuttoning the front of her housedress, and she paused for just a moment before she said, "Not here... Inside..." She took his hand and led him back into the kitchen, to the stairs, and once on the upper landing, she knew there was no going back. She opened her bedroom door; he followed her inside, and they kissed again, fiercely, hungrily, and when he struggled with the clasp of her bra, she simply undid it for him. His hands were on her breasts, her dress was around her waist, and then she felt it just slide to the ground, almost as if gravity itself was telling her that this was inevitable.

Esther stood before him in nothing but her stockings, her garters, and her panties. He smelled so good. He kissed her again, harder, and for a moment she believed she would lose all consciousness. Her head was swimming, and it was merely due to the fact that he was holding her so tight that she did not fall to the floor.

A momentary flash of something made her say, "No, Michael..." But she did not mean it, and it sounded more like a plea for forgiveness rather than a request that he stop.

Michael tugged his T-shirt over his head. Esther unbuttoned his pants; they slid to the ground and he kicked them away.

Her hand moved on his thigh, and before she could think a further thought, he had taken that hand and put it right between his legs.

She closed her eyes and exhaled. She touched him, and he was so hard, and the smell of him, the warmth of his skin, the way it felt as he pressed himself against her...

And then he said, "Oh..." And for a moment there was an awkwardness in his body. He pulled back and glanced down.

Only then was she aware of the sensation on her thigh, that feeling of warmth, the way it trickled down toward her knee.

She smiled awkwardly, almost embarrassed for him, and then she started to laugh and found she couldn't stop, and when Michael realized that she was not in fact laughing at him, he started laughing too.

She took a towel from the dresser and wiped her leg. She undid her suspenders and slipped off her stockings. She turned back to Michael, now dressed in nothing but her panties, and said, "I reckon it's my turn next."

She led him to the bed, and they lay down beside each other. She showed him what to do, how to touch her, how to find the place that needed to be found... slowly... no, even slower than that... yes, that's right, just there, just there...

And afterward, for a while, they just lay there in silence, and when he was ready once more, when she had brought him back to life, she became the first woman that Michael Travis made love to, the woman that took his virginity.

And when they were done, he told her that he loved her, and she said, "You don't love me, Michael Travis. You just fucked me, and now you *think* you love me."

And he said, "No, Esther. I love you."

And Esther Faulkner, wondering what the hell she had done now, did not argue with him.

13

It was midafternoon by the time Travis reached the university. He spoke to a young woman in the reception building, and she made a call.

"Dr. Ebner will be through to see you shortly," Travis was informed. "If you'd like to take a seat."

Travis did as he was asked, waiting for no more than five minutes before another woman appeared in the foyer of the building. She was petite and attractive, perhaps in her late thirties or early forties, and yet wore her hair in a severe style, tied back from her face and captured with a black bow.

"Agent Travis?" she said.

Travis rose and nodded. "Yes," he said.

"If you'd like to come this way."

Travis picked up his hat and followed the woman. She showed him down a corridor on the left side of the building and into an office.

"Take a seat," she said, and Travis did so.

"So, how can I help you?"

"I'm here to see Dr. Ebner," Travis said.

The woman smiled. "Hard though it may be for you to comprehend, I am Dr. Ebner."

Travis's surprise gave him away. "I am sorry, I was—"

"Expecting a man?"

"Well, yes," Travis replied, now feeling awkward.

"Well, I am truly sorry to disappoint you, Agent Travis, but I am Dr. Sarah Ebner, Department of Foreign Studies. If you need foreign studies, then I'm the best that the University of Wichita can offer, certainly as far as mainland Europe is concerned. If you want Asia and the Pacific, then I will direct you elsewhere."

"I really didn't mean—"

"No need to apologize, Agent Travis," Sarah Ebner said, smiling. "As a female academic, especially the head of a department, I am constantly reminded of my basic failure to meet everyone's expectations."

Travis didn't know how to respond, until he saw that Sarah Ebner was withholding herself from laughing.

"I *am* sorry," Travis said. "I was just with Professors Beck and Saxon, and they seem to fit the bill as far as university lecturers are concerned. My own preconceptions, and I apologize for them. You are very young, and not at all what I expected. I thought you were Dr. Ebner's secretary."

"That's because you are a dinosaur and a misogynist, Agent Travis, and when women take over the world, you'll be sorry."

Travis really did feel ignorant. "So, could we please begin again?"

Sarah Ebner smiled. "Tell me what I can do for you," she said.

Travis withdrew the diagram from his pocket and slid it across the table. As he did so, he recalled the moment in the diner with Laura McCaffrey.

Well, I presume you're going to be following up on the regulus . . .

Travis glanced away, cleared his throat. "As far as myself and the professors have been able to ascertain, this is a constellation known as Regulus—"

"And it was tattooed on a man's body?"

Travis looked surprised. "Yes, it was. How did you know?"

"Because, Agent Travis, this is Fekete Kutya."

"Fek—what?"

"Fekete Kutya. It's Hungarian. It means Black Dog, very simply."

"Black Dog."

"Yes."

"And that is?"

"They are a Hungarian criminal organization. They are dangerous people."

"There were other tattoos as well," Travis said. "Seven dots, very small, between his toes."

Dr. Ebner leaned back in her chair. "More than likely, those are his kills."

"Meaning he has killed seven people."

"Yes, exactly. The first eight killings are tattooed between your toes, the next eight between your fingers, and then you do not kill anymore; you just tell others to do the killing."

"And you know of this organization because?"

"Because I am Austrian, because Austria borders Hungary, because I am head of the Department of Foreign Studies, and it is my business—"

"I am sorry, Dr. Ebner. I am being a dinosaur again."

"As I said, I deal with mainland Europe, mostly eighteenth century to modern day, and now . . . well, now we are specializing more and more in texts and treatises on National Socialism and Italian Fascism under Mussolini, but Hungary is also important, certainly more since the civil uprising of 1956. It is fresh in peoples' minds, you see? Other Eastern

European Communist regimes are nervous. They want to understand what it was that prompted this popular revolt. The other issue they appreciate, of course, is that any social instability lends itself perfectly to a marked increase in crime and corruption, and I can tell you that there was a significant upsurge in activity from this Hungarian group just before and during the recent unrest. This, not unsurprisingly, consolidated their position and strengthened them greatly. They are like your Mafia, Agent Travis, but maybe more dangerous and more terrifying."

"And why would someone like this be here in Kansas?" Travis asked.

"I have no idea," Dr. Ebner said.

Travis took back the slip of paper and stared at it. Suddenly, a completely different world had opened up before his eyes. Hungarian organized crime, this Fekete Kutya, and one of their own murdered in Kansas at a carnival? In truth, it possessed an almost surreal quality.

"The more I try to understand, the less I understand it," Travis said, realizing only as the last word had left his lips that this was a thought he'd had no intention of voicing.

"And that is perhaps one of the most valuable lessons a human being can learn," Sarah Ebner said. "What is that old Chinese proverb? A wise man is a man who knows he knows nothing. Something like that."

"I'm sorry," Travis said. "I didn't mean to concern you with the details of this."

"It is quite all right, Agent Travis."

"So what can you tell me about these people?"

"Not a great deal, to be honest. Fekete Kutya is something I am only indirectly acquainted with. One of those things that comes with territory, as opposed to being the territory itself. Historically speaking, they are a very old organization. They go back hundreds of years. They have their roots somewhere in the fifteen hundreds, as far as I know. The history of Hungary is very complicated compared to the history of your country, Agent Travis."

"So who were they, these people? How did this organization begin?"

"From what I understand, it was something to do with the territorial wars of the time," Ebner said. "Hungary was part of the Ottoman Empire. There was a battle in a place called Mohacs in the early fifteen hundreds and the Hungarians were crushed. The king was killed while fleeing from the enemy. The Hungarian nobility was divided, and each camp elected their own king, one called John Zápolya, another called Ferdinand the First. Then Hungary was divided again, and there were three territories, the west and the north under the control of a people called the Habsburgs, the central and southern territories under Ottoman rule. Lastly there was the east. This was called the Eastern Hungarian Kingdom, and it was ruled by the son of John Zápolya. Even later, that part of Hungary became the principality of Transylvania. It was from here that the Black Dog came."

"And they were native Hungarians?"

"Yes, Hungarians loyal to the Zápolya line, and Black Dog was a secret organization committed to regaining control of all of Hungary for Zápolya. They were terrorists, Agent Travis, and they assassinated their enemies, sent spies into other parts of the kingdom, and they did everything they could to overthrow the Ottomans and those loyal to the Habsburgs. Finally, the last of the Black Dog were crushed, and it seemed to disappear. Then, after the First War, it was revived, perhaps only in name, because the Black Dog of today is not the same organization. This is simply a criminal organization, an organization that does not ally itself to any political party. As I said, they are not dissimilar to your Mafia."

"So a man with these tattoos... could be other than Hungarian?"

"No," Ebner said. "Membership is restricted to Hungarian nationals alone. At least it always has been, and I would be very surprised if that condition had changed. Such organizations exist the world over, as you know, Agent Travis. I wouldn't be surprised to find indigenous organized-crime networks and groups for every country on earth. Even the Mafia, ostensibly and historically a Sicilian organization, has become its own offshoot here, but still, even in America, it remains the province of Italians only."

Travis was quiet for a little while, just considering the ramifications of what he had learned. Now he had a nationality, not only a nationality but evidence that the victim from the carnival belonged to an organized-crime network. This information would need to go to Bishop immediately.

"I am really grateful," Travis said. "This has significantly narrowed the playing field for us. However, I have to ask you to maintain complete confidentiality regarding this discussion," he added. "This is an ongoing federal investigation."

"Say no more," Ebner replied.

Travis rose from his chair and extended his hand. "Dr. Ebner," he said.

Ebner took his hand and they shook. "Agent Travis."

"I shall work on my misogyny and general ignorance," he said.

"Good to hear it," Ebner replied, smiling. "Then you may just escape retribution when we take over the world."

Once beyond the confines of the university campus, Travis stopped at a phone booth and called Information. He noted down the address of the Wichita Bureau Office, and he drove over there.

From the lobby, they called down one of the local agents, a young man by the name of Gary Delaney. Delaney said there would be no problem replicating the diagram that Travis showed him and getting a copy of it back to Kansas. Travis wrote a few words of explanation to SSA Bishop, added the fact that the deceased also carried seven tattooed dots between his toes, and waited while Delaney attended to it. He returned after fifteen minutes, handed the original diagram back to Travis, and asked if there was anything else Travis needed.

"No, we're good here," Travis said, and thanked Delaney for his help.

Travis went back to his car. Next step was to return to Seneca Falls and inspect the crime scene itself. He had not seen the specific location of the body's discovery, at least not in daylight, and he would have to get back rapidly if he wished to make his examination before daylight was lost completely. To date, the only person to make an official examination of the site was Rourke. Sheriff he might be, but he was not FBI. Perhaps there was something to be found there that everyone else had missed. Perhaps they had not missed it, merely failed to recognize its import or relevance in this case. Travis had asked that John Ryan remove a section of the carousel so he could see precisely where the dead man had been discovered that night. He knew that Doyle wanted to get the carnival running again; he knew that they wanted to move on as soon as possible; he also knew that he could not commit a graver error than failing to detain the whole carnival until this matter was resolved.

Travis headed away immediately, made good time, and upon arriving, he found the carnival site a seeming hive of activity, the central marquee being the location for some kind of staggered meal service for the employees. Doyle was there, as was Valeria Mironescu. Doyle seemed pleased to see Travis.

"Are we making progress, Agent Travis?" he asked as he rose from one of the benches and crossed the marquee to greet him.

"Please, I don't wish to interrupt your meal," Travis said, "but I need to see the precise location of the body's discovery."

"We already took care of that," Doyle said. "As requested, John removed a number of boards from the carousel's platform so you could more easily see beneath it."

"That is much appreciated, Mr. Doyle."

"Do you need Ryan with you?"

"No, I am sure I'll be fine. Please, continue with your meal."

"Well, go right ahead," Doyle said. "You know where it is. If you need anything, then just head right back here and let me know."

"Thank you," Travis said, and then he glanced at the Mironescu woman—seated just a handful of yards away. She looked at Travis in the precise moment that he looked at her. She did not smile. She did not glance away. She looked at Travis without hesitation or expression— utterly implacable and unflinching. Travis felt a sliver of electricity run through his body. Did he shudder? Did he actually shudder? What on earth was that sensation he felt?

Travis nodded an acknowledgment at the woman, and then she smiled so gently, so sensitively, that he felt once again awkward, just as he had when first they'd met. That smile seemed to express such a sense of kindness, and he could not even define how it made him feel. Not small, not insignificant, nothing like that. It was almost as if she was trying to get him to see something. But what?

We are no different.

"Sorry?" Travis said.

Doyle frowned. "What?"

"Did you say something, Mr. Doyle?"

"Just that you should head on back here if you need anything else, Agent Travis."

"Yes, of course. Thank you," Travis said. He turned and started walking. He glanced back after a few moments. Neither Doyle nor the Mironescu woman were at the table.

Travis knew he'd heard nothing. He tried to give it no further thought. He made his way across the field toward the carousel and stepped up onto the platform. He could clearly see where John Ryan had removed a number of planks from the base of the thing. He maneuvered his way between the horses and knelt at the edge of the aperture. He placed his hands on either side and leaned down to look horizontally along the ground both left and right. The grass was a good two feet beneath him, allowing more than adequate room to crawl beneath the platform and really inspect the area. He would have to do this, of course, as there was no way to determine that the section of platform removed was directly above the precise location of the body.

Travis returned to the car and fetched a flashlight. He took from his jacket pocket the pages upon which he had imprinted both the outline and the sole of the dead man's shoes. He laid his jacket on the backseat, rolled up his shirtsleeves, and tucked his tie between the buttons of his shirt.

Once beneath the carousel, he understood how difficult it would have been for carnival-goers to have seen the body. There was less space than was apparent, and the base of the platform angled down toward its outer edge, so as he crawled away from the hub, the amount of headroom grew progressively less. It was claustrophobic, cold but not damp, and the earth beneath him was firm. Placing a dead man beneath this platform would have been difficult, but evidently not impossible. Someone could have crawled beneath the carousel and then dragged the body in after them, exiting again once the body was in position. Whoever had performed this task would have to have had considerable upper-body strength, but then such a task could have been carried out relatively easily by two people. Travis had inspected the dead man's clothes. There had been no significant quantity of grass stains or skids of dirt. Nothing about the man's clothes suggested a deadweight-drag beneath six or eight feet of wooden platform. Therefore, Travis surmised that the man had been placed on a tarpaulin or something similar, not only significantly facilitating the dragging of the body, but also preventing the staining of the clothes. The victim had not been otherwise wounded. The COD was a single puncture at the base of the neck and upward into the brain. Death would have been immediate. Therefore, just as Jack Farley had concluded, the assault had taken place elsewhere and the victim hidden beneath the carousel some hours later.

Travis surveyed the entire area and yet could not find evidence that a heavy weight had been dragged across the ground. Additionally, there were no drag marks from heels, no clear impressions of footprints, and no signs of an awkward struggle. Of course, placing a man on a tarpaulin and dragging him across the grass would have resulted in surface damage that would easily recover. The body had been found on Saturday night, four days earlier. There was more than sufficient time for the outward signs of such an action to have disappeared.

So, as it stood, the man had been murdered at some point around midnight on Friday, the first of August, the body had then lain undisturbed for a number of hours and then concealed beneath the carousel. Where and why the deceased had been stabbed in the back of the neck was yet to be determined.

Travis scoured the remaining ground beneath the platform and then rolled onto his back and scanned the underside with the flashlight. It was then that he found the shred of fabric, seemingly black in color, snagged by a single protruding nail. He removed it carefully, tucked it into his shirt pocket, and continued looking. There was nothing further, and he crawled out and up through the aperture and back onto the upper side of the platform. He lay on his stomach and leaned through to once again scan the ground. It was here that he identified a blood spill, small enough to be missed by anything but the most perceptive eye. The ground was firmer by the smallest degree, the grass stained almost black.

Travis came down from the carousel and returned to the car. He collected a pair of scissors, two envelopes and his camera from the site kit. Back at the carousel, he cut several blades of bloody grass and placed them inside one of the envelopes, careful not to touch them. He took the fragment of fabric from his pocket and inspected it more closely. It was not black, but a very dark blue, not dissimilar to the standard-issue suit that he and his colleagues were required to wear. Wool, he felt sure, but he was no expert. The fabric also deposited in an envelope, Travis took the camera and walked around the scene. He took numerous shots from numerous angles, knelt once more to take a picture—as best he could—of the carousel's underside. Satisfied that he had sufficient to refer to should he need them, he went back to the car and packed away the equipment.

Intent on heading back to the central marquee and establishing some kind of schedule with Doyle for interviewing other members of the troupe, Travis was preempted by Valeria Mironescu. He saw her walking toward him from the edge of the field, and he waited for her beside the car.

"Agent Travis," she said. "Perhaps you would care to eat with us?"

"I appreciate your hospitality, Miss Mironescu, but no. It wouldn't really be appropriate, though the offer is much appreciated. Besides, I have some sandwiches that were very kindly prepared for me."

"It must be a difficult life, no?"

"A difficult life?"

"Yes, doing what you do. It's almost as if you're obliged to spend your waking hours with the very worst that the world can offer. It must be very exhausting."

"Depends on your viewpoint, Miss Mironescu."

"Oh please, you must stop calling me that. If you must retain some formality, then call me Miss Valeria."

"Very well," Travis replied. "Miss Valeria."

"So tell me your viewpoint, Agent Travis."

"About my job?"

"Yes."

"I am a public servant, first and foremost. My primary concern is the welfare of American citizens—"

Valeria laughed. "So we are undone, then? This ragtag collection of wanderers and fools."

"You are here on American soil, Miss Valeria. As long as you've not committed an act that violates the laws of this land, then your welfare and protection is my concern."

"But still you spend your life with the killers and thieves, no?"

"Maybe you could look at it that way. I don't, to be honest. I consider that without us, the environment would be less safe, that more harm would be done, that more people would be killed."

"You really believe that?"

"Yes, of course. Do you not think this is the case?"

"No, quite the opposite."

"That law enforcement is not necessary?"

"I think that if you forbid something, it makes it all the more likely to happen. We're all children, Agent Travis. If you tell us not to do something, we want to do it even more."

"I wish it were so, Miss Valeria. Then we could simply do away with the police and the Bureau and everyone would be on their best behavior."

"Society would straighten itself out in time, Agent Travis. We'd find ways to deal with the troublemakers."

"I have to say that it's a very nice idea, Miss Valeria, though I believe a little naive and overoptimistic. People have been killing one another for as long as there have been people."

"And are you any closer to identifying the man that was found here?"

"I'm sorry, but I cannot discuss an ongoing case with you."

"I can see that you have made progress, Agent Travis."

"You can?" Travis said, and smiled.

"Of course I can. You are a very intense and serious young man, and I know you will find the truth."

"You do? How so, Miss Valeria?"

"Because you are who you are, Agent Travis. Because you don't let go until you know. Because the real reason you're here is because you have to find out. I think your vocation in life is to learn the truth of all things."

"I don't know about learning the truth of *all* things, Miss Valeria. I think there are some things in life that can never be known."

"Not so," she said. "Truth is everywhere and nowhere. Nothing is a mystery if you look closely enough."

"I wish it were so," Travis said.

"It *is* so, Agent Travis," she replied. "And the more you disagree with your conventions and regulations, the more you will see."

"Conventions and regulations exist for very good reasons, Miss Valeria—"

"Conventions and regulations are created by those who don't want you to look, Agent Travis, and they don't want you to look because they're afraid you'll find out that life is nowhere near as complex and mysterious as you've been led to believe."

"Is that so?" Travis replied, aware that the oblique and ambiguous nature of the conversation was starting to grate on him.

Valeria smiled, and once again Travis was taken aback by the warmth of that smile. "I am not a snake, Agent Travis. I am not trying to upset you. I have no purpose to unsettle your preconceptions about life and people.

I look at you and I see a man in a small white room. I am simply trying to show you that there's a door and that you can leave if you wish."

"Miss Valeria," Travis said, "I appreciate your concern, but you really have no reason to be concerned. I am just fine, thank you. I am doing my job. I am collecting information and evidence, and I assure you that the full weight of the law will be brought to bear upon whoever perpetrated this terrible crime. With this man's identity known, we will be able to determine where he came from, where he was going, and why. Now, my foremost task is to interview as many of the carnival employees as I can. You do not need to worry about me. I will do what I have to do, and then I will be gone."

"Why are you so afraid, Agent Travis?"

"Afraid?"

"You have so much pain in your eyes, and yet you pretend you're not hurting."

"My personal life is just that, Miss Valeria. Personal."

"You know there is a connection between accepting the pain and seeing the truth. I am sure you see that. I am just wondering when you started denying it."

"Denying what, Miss Valeria?"

"That you have a gift, Agent Travis. A gift for the truth."

Travis smiled. "I am a little busy to be playing these games. I really do have work to do. If you could please direct me to Mr. Doyle, I will make arrangements with him to start interviewing the other members of the carnival."

"You know what they say, Agent Travis?"

"What do *they* say, Miss Valeria?"

"They say that sometimes things happen simply because you believe they will."

Travis's eyes widened. He felt for a moment as if someone had punched him in the chest.

"There is a door to the room, Agent Travis. If you try to open it, you'll find that it isn't locked."

And with that, she turned and headed back to the marquee.

Travis watched her for a moment, and then he went after her. By the time he reached the marquee, she was gone. Doyle was there, however, and he approached Travis and stood right there in front of him. He did not see how Valeria could have had time to speak to Doyle, but evidently she had, for Doyle simply said, "Valeria tells me that you want to begin interviewing some of my people."

Travis didn't say anything. He was still somewhat stunned by Valeria Mironescu's final words.

"Has she been teasing you, Agent Travis?" Doyle asked. "She is wicked sometimes. Do not believe a word she says. In fact, do not *listen* to a word she says."

Travis knew he should be agitated, upset even, but he could not muster the energy to feel it. It was as if the conversation with the Mironescu woman had knocked the wind from his sails completely. He gathered his composure as best he could. "I will begin by questioning anyone who was present at the scene on Saturday night," he said. "I need you to inform them that this is a serious matter, that the Bureau has complete authority to investigate this murder, and total cooperation from the Seneca Falls Sheriff's Department. This is not a humorous issue, Mr. Doyle. This is matter of the utmost seriousness, and I would appreciate it if you would afford it the gravity it deserves."

Edgar Doyle's expression was implacable.

"Do you understand what I am saying, sir?" Travis asked.

"I understand precisely what you are saying, Agent Travis. I also understand that there are freedoms and liberties that we—as law-abiding citizens—can take for granted, and you have no authority to inhibit those rights without just cause. Thus far, we have been nothing but accommodating. These people," Doyle continued, indicating the tents and vehicles with a sweep of his arm, "are hardworking people, people trying to make a living, people trying to survive, and whatever might have taken place here should not be reason to threaten them or make them afraid. I speak for myself, Agent Travis, but I speak for all of them as well."

Travis felt angered, but only momentarily. Anger would serve no purpose here. He knew that without Doyle's cooperation, this entire investigation would be twice the work. He paused before speaking, he breathed deeply, and when he spoke again, his tone was measured.

"I have no reason to be here any longer than is absolutely necessary, Mr. Doyle. I want to see a resolution to this matter just as much as you do. I have to return to Kansas. I have other matters to attend to. You have to move on to other towns and cities. I accept that this is difficult for you, and I am not of a mind to make it any more difficult. But these people will listen to you; they will follow your example—"

"I think you are mistaken there, Agent Travis," Doyle interjected. "These people are the very last in the world to follow anyone's example but their own. I understand what you're trying to do, and I know you feel this is the best way to do it, but—believe me—it is not."

"I'm sorry? Are you telling me how to conduct my investigation?"

Doyle looked at the ground for a moment, almost as if he was summoning a little more patience to deal with a stupid and impatient child.

"Agent Travis... listen to me," he said. "You think these people are running away from the world. You think these people are crazy or strange or untrustworthy or out to deceive you with every word they utter. Let me tell you that here you will find some of the most decent and considerate people you could ever hope to meet. People see us and they are afraid. Why? Because we are different? No, not at all. They are afraid because we challenge all their agreements, all the promises they made without understanding what they were promising. We are not the routine job, the new car, the pretty little house in the suburbs with the flower boxes and the shrubbery. We are not the swimming pool or the barbecue or the PTA. We are the children of the devil." He laughed for a moment. "Why did we call it Carnival Diablo? Because that's what people want to believe. That's what people want us to be, and so we will be it for them."

"I don't understand what this has to do with—" Travis said.

"Did you never want to run away to the circus, Michael?" Doyle asked.

Travis—for a moment—was not even aware that Doyle had used his first name.

"Did you not want to do that?" Doyle repeated. "Did you never feel the urge to throw all of this aside and just escape into a world of your own creation?"

"N-no," Travis said hesitantly, but even as he said it, he didn't really know why he hesitated.

"People think we are the ones who have abdicated responsibility. People think we are the ones who have failed in our obligations to society. What society? The society that kills and maims and commits its people to war, the society that sees color as a reason to hate, to persecute? The society that commands obedience from its citizens but hounds them with taxes and laws and a justice system that is flawed and corrupt and diseased from within? That society, Agent Travis?"

Doyle paused for a moment and just looked at Travis.

"People always assume we're running away," he went on. "Always, that we're running away. Like the world didn't want us and we were cast out. You ever think that maybe we didn't want the world?"

Doyle took a slight step forward. "There is no one here who will not talk to you, Agent Travis. No one at all. They will answer your questions as best they can, and I am sure they will tell you the truth as they see it. But they will talk to you because they want to, because they are willing to, not because I ask them to, nor because I set any example. There are no enforced agreements here, Agent Travis. There are no foolish and unfounded laws that we follow blindly, unthinkingly. We are all prisoners. Those who realize they are prisoners at least understand that freedom is possible. When you see that you yourself are just as much a prisoner as the very people you send to Leavenworth and Sing Sing, then perhaps there will be hope for you."

Doyle waited for just a moment, perhaps to see if Travis would respond, perhaps to emphasize the point he was making.

Travis said nothing. He had nothing more to say.

"I suggest you start with Mr. Slate," Doyle said. "His is the caravan over there."

Doyle turned and walked away.

Travis did not feel angry. Travis did not know what he felt. He would begin with Slate, just as Doyle had recommended, but first he would take a few moments alone. He returned to the car, sat in the driver's seat, and closed the door firmly behind him.

The world beyond the vehicle went quiet, and yet the world within started clamoring for attention.

The words that Valeria Mironescu had used had shaken him to the core.

I think that sometimes things happen simply because you believe they will.

It was Esther, still there, still haunting his thoughts, but even more than that, it was the day that they had driven out to Flatwater to collect his few possessions.

The day they returned to the house of his childhood, a place he had not seen since the death of his father.

14

That first night, lying there beside her sixteen-year-old ward, Esther would have imagined herself racked with guilt, her every emotion twisted back upon itself, her sense of self-respect and personal worth just nothing in the fact of this heinous crime she had perpetrated. The age of consent in Nebraska was seventeen. How she knew this, she could not remember, but she did. Most states it was sixteen. Not so in Nebraska. She had broken the law. There was always the possibility of finding herself in jail right beside her cousin—the killer and the child abuser side by side at the State Reformatory for Women.

Nevertheless, she did not feel guilty, nor did she feel ashamed. She felt alive.

She slept that night, Michael breathing softly against her side, the smell of his hair, the excitement of his presence filling her body, her mind, her very *self* with a range of emotions she had long forgotten.

She was not so naive as to believe that she was *in love* with him, not as a woman loves a man, but she loved him nevertheless. Simply stated, she did not want to be denied what she was feeling. She did not want to be elsewhere.

Michael stirred in the early hours, the air still cool, the vaguest light finding its way through the curtains to the right of the bed.

He opened his eyes and found her watching him, a faint smile already on his lips.

His hand strayed across the flat of her stomach. He kissed her shoulder, her neck, and then leaned up to kiss her mouth.

"You slept," she whispered.

"Dreamed," he replied, his voice distant with the vestiges of sleep.

"Of what?"

He shook his head and stretched. "Not of what," he said. "Of who..."

She stroked his fringe from his brow, kissed his forehead and his nose. She turned sideways, pulled him close to her, and he found his way inside her without any help at all. The previous night, hungry, almost starved of real human contact, they had made love in a clumsy, awkward way. Now it was different. Now it was in slow motion, and even as she pulled away, aware that he was climaxing, it felt so right, so perfect. She held his erection in her hand, massaged it slowly until he came, and then leaned close to his ear to whisper.

"We need to get some things," she said.

"Things?" he asked, and then it dawned on him. "Things," he repeated.

There was silence for a time, the pair of them lying beside each other, enjoying the simple fact that they were not alone, and then she asked if he wanted coffee, something to eat perhaps.

"Not yet," he said. "I just want to stay here a while longer. This is the best I have ever felt in my life, and I don't want it to end."

She said it then, even though she didn't want to. She said it because she knew it had to be said.

"It will end, Michael. You know that, don't you?"

Michael smiled so simply, so beautifully, that she wondered why she'd had to utter those words. But it did not matter. He surprised her then, surprised her more than she could ever have believed possible.

"Life is crazy, Esther," he said. He rolled onto his front, leaned up on his elbows. "Life is crazy, and so are most of the people in the world. People think there are rules and regulations for everything. They imagine terrible things will happen if they don't follow those rules and regulations, but it's just not true. Who says we can't just enjoy what we're doing? Who says we have to behave in a certain way? And what will happen if anyone finds out?"

"Well, for a start, Michael, the law..."

"What are you planning to do? Call the cops?"

She laughed, touched his face. "You are too smart for your own good, Michael Travis."

"I don't think that's possible, Mrs. Faulkner."

"Don't call me that, for God's sake!"

"This is what we are doing. I want to do it. I think you want to do it too. Don't you think half the fun comes from knowing that we are the only two people in the world who will ever know how good this is? Makes it all the more exciting when you know it's a secret..."

"To be honest, I don't know if I was the one who seduced you, or you were the one who seduced me."

"We seduced each other, Esther."

She reached up her hands, placed one on each side of his face, and kissed him.

"As long as you understand that this might go horribly wrong," she said.

"I am happier than I have ever been. It might be a terrible mistake, it might go wrong, but until that happens, which I doubt it ever will, let's not wish for it, okay?"

"Okay," she said, and then she shifted sideways and got off the bed. She pulled her robe around herself, stood looking down at him on her bed, and smiled.

"Who would have thought it...?" she said, almost to herself.

It was that afternoon, Saturday the eighteenth, that Michael asked her once again if she would go over to the Flatwater house with him.

"You really want to go?" she asked.

"Yes, I really want to go," Michael replied. "I *need* to go."

"Then we shall go tomorrow," Esther said. "I will call a friend of mine who has a car. He'll take us."

Esther made the call, the friend agreed, and early the following morning, Michael saw a black Studebaker Commander pull up against the curb in front of the house. The man who alighted was sharply dressed, perhaps in his early to mid-fifties, and there was something about his bearing that suggested a military background.

"That's Robert Erickson," Esther said, "an old friend of mine. Was in the army, got himself shot in the leg."

As if to highlight the consequence of being shot in the leg, Erickson came around the side of the car with a cane, leaning heavily on it as he made his way up toward the house. The limp was pronounced, and even the few steps to the front door seemed to require a good deal of concentration.

"Everyone calls him Sarge," she said.

Sarge opened the screen and knocked.

"Come on in!" Esther called.

Esther greeted him with an enthusiastic hug.

"So good of you to do this, Sarge. Really, really appreciated."

"Nothin' at all," Sarge replied.

Michael appeared in the doorway.

"This must be your Mr. Travis," Sarge said. He extended his hand. Michael came forward and they shook.

"Esther told me a good deal about your trials and tribulations, son, and I must say that my heart goes out to you. Terrible bind to be finding yourself in at such a point in your life."

"Thank you, sir," Michael said.

"Oh hell, son, just call me Sarge. Everyone does. Now, we're headed out to Flatwater, right?"

"Yes, that's right."

"And whoever from the Sheriff's Department knows we're coming?"

"Who?" Michael asked.

"It's okay, sweetie," Esther said, and touched his arm. "Seeing as how this is all still going on... with your ma an' all, well there has to be someone there from the Sheriff's Department. You know, to make sure that we don't mess with things that we shouldn't be messing with."

Michael nodded.

"You sure you wanna go out there, son?" Sarge asked, genuine concern in his tone.

"I need to go out there," Michael replied. "It's just something I have to do."

"Well, let's git, then," he said.

Sarge and Esther sat up front, Michael a little cramped in the back. Sarge lit one cigarette after other, and soon the world beyond the windows was obfuscated by a dense fog of smoke.

"You don't mind?" he kept asking, and though Esther seemed not to, the smoke bothered Michael tremendously. He did not feel he could say a word in protest, however. He needed to get out to the house, and Sarge seemed to be the only available way to do it.

The drive was a straight north on 281, a west turn toward Flatwater, a brief stopover to alert Flatwater's deputy sheriff, Harold Fenton, that they had arrived, and then the last couple of miles out to the house itself was in a two-car convoy behind a black-and-white.

The house came up into view like something from a dream.

From a distance, it seemed a mere speck at the side of the road, but as they neared the property, it seemed to grow, not only in real terms, but also in Michael's mind, as if the significance of what had happened here had now afforded the building itself a greater meaning and potency.

The black-and-white pulled to a stop, and it was only when the deputy got out that Michael remembered him from the day his father had died.

This was the man that the sheriff had left behind, the one who had kept an eye on him until the coroner came to take Jimmy Travis away.

Precisely one year and one month had passed since Michael Travis had last seen this house, and yet at once it seemed both yesterday and a thousand years ago.

The Michael that had left and the Michael that had returned were very different people.

Deputy Harold Fenton, all of five seven with an attitude, stood at the foot of the steps leading up the screen and hitched his thumbs through his Sam Browne belt.

"You can enter the house, but aside from your own room, all other areas are out of bounds—"

"Lighten up there, Captain," Sarge interjected. "The kid knows not to touch anything."

"I understand that, sir, but I would be remiss in my duties if—"

Sarge placed a large hand on Fenton's shoulder and squeezed it firmly. "We're both institutional men," he said. "We understand the dos and don'ts just fine, eh, Deputy? Situation such as this affords a touch of humanity, wouldn't you say? Now, why don't we just take a moment over here? Let's have a smoke together. You can tell me some war stories, and we can let the lady and the kid just sort out what needs to be sorted out. There ain't gonna be no monkey business here. What's done is done, and nothin' that the kid might or might not do is gonna change that fact."

Harold Fenton looked a little befuddled, a little off guard, but then he nodded and said, "Sure thing."

"Good 'nough." Sarge nodded at Esther and Michael, and then he turned back to Fenton and said, "So tell me, how many bank robberies you get around these parts? I heard these small-town banks are just heaven for the Dillingers and Barrows of this world."

"Ha," Fenton said. "I'll tell you now, one time we had ourselves a real…"

His voice faded as Sarge walked him back toward the cars.

Michael stood there for a time.

Esther was right beside him, even reached out and took his hand, but he was not aware of it at all.

After a minute, perhaps two, he just started walking. He crossed the dusty yard and started up the steps. The screen catch was flipped. He unhitched it, opened it with a creak and then pushed the front door. It swung inwards soundlessly, and Michael stood in the dim coolness of the hallway without remembering the steps he'd taken to get there. Esther hung back behind him, right there on the other side of the screen.

Everything was strange, and yet everything was too familiar. The hat stand, the rug on the wooden floor, the way the banister turned slightly at the bottom as if inviting you to climb the stairs, the light at the end of the hallway that led down to the kitchen.

To his left was a window that looked out from the side of the house, to his right, the door to the main room of the house. The room where they ate. The room where his father would kick off his shoes, lean back in a chair, listen to a ball game on the wireless. The room from which his voice would echo up the stairs to Michael's room… *Janette, bring me another beer…* or *Michael, get on down here and tell me what in tarnation this mud is doing on the God-darn floor!*

Michael took a step, knowing even as he did so that he would find him.

The board creaked beneath his foot.

He looked back over his shoulder, saw Esther standing there on the steps, her features obscured through the fine mesh of the screen. She said nothing, but he could read her body language.

Shall I come in? Shall I stay right where I am and leave you to deal with this alone?

Michael wanted her beside him, wanted to feel her hand in his, but knew that if she was there, he would not hear what he'd come to hear, would not see what he knew would be waiting for him.

He took another step, and boards that had never creaked now seemed to cry back at him in faint, desperate voices.

His hands were dry, cold even, but his forehead was varnished with sweat. His heart was like a clenched fist, a knot of dark and shadowed muscle deep within his chest, its beating no more evident than the sound of the breeze beyond the walls and windows, as if it wished to have none of this, as if it wished to be elsewhere.

Michael reached the door, and before the table came into view, he closed his eyes tight. He blinked several times then, shook his head as if ridding it of cobwebs, dreams, fragments of imagination that might be precipitated by the surroundings.

Nevertheless, he knew it would do no good.

Michael took one further step, reached the threshold, his right hand on the doorjamb, his left hand down by his side, the calm and measured beating of his heart like a metronome.

Hey, son.

Jimmy Travis sat right where he'd been. That day. That very day. The last day of his life.

He looked directly back at Michael, his right eye open wide, his left eye a bloody socket with a strange glimmer right in the center. It was only when Jimmy smiled and moved his head that Michael saw the knife that was still embedded in his face. Head on, there was merely that dull, gunmetal glint to remind Michael of what his mother had done.

You done fucked the quiff, eh, boy? I seen her a coupla times. Cain't 'member when, but I seen her and figured she'd be good for a party. But you beat me to it, you old dog, and you only sixteen years old. God darn it, boy, you sure as hell is your father's son.

Michael wanted to reply, but even as he opened his mouth, he knew that the words would never be forthcoming.

You just go on thinkin' whatever you wanna think. I can hear you just fine an' dandy.

Michael wondered if he was crazy. He wondered if the trauma of what had happened had turned his mind completely.

You know your problem, kiddo. You always thunk too darn much. That much thinkin' ain't healthy, 'cept maybe for university folks and them that writes books and suchlike. But we ain't those kinda people, kiddo. We ain't those kinda people at all. We's just simple people, the kinda people who can do a fair day's work for a fair wage, mind their own business, you know? All that thinkin' is for college professors and whatnot.

You got what you deserved, Michael thought. It was there, right there at the forefront of his mind and he could not help thinking it.

Did I, now? Is that what you believe, kiddo? That I got what I deserved? Well, let me tell you a few home truths about your darn mother, saint that she was.

I don't want to hear it.

Is that so? Well, it seems to me that you don't have much of a choice, 'cause I happen to be in your head, and that's one thing you ain't never gonna be able to get away from. I'm in your head and I'm in your blood, boy, and blood is somethin' you ain't never gone escape from.

You were the worst, and you know it. You treated her like shit. She deserved better than you, and you know it.

Why you—

Jimmy Travis attempted to move then, gripped the arms of the chair and tried to push himself up. Perhaps there were rules to this game. It seemed that Jimmy could not move, forever consigned to remain there in the moment of his death.

This simple realization gave Michael the nerve he needed to take another step into the room.

Everything was at it had been left. He could see the food on the table, now overgrown with mold, cockroaches scurrying back and forth across the cutlery, the sound of their spindly legs on the ceramic as defined as Jimmy's voice. There was a film of dust covering everything, Jimmy included, and as he moved, that dust lifted and settled, lifted and settled as if the house itself was breathing, and in the vague, tenebrous light from the window behind him, he seemed at once vague and indistinct and then as clear as daylight itself.

You think your mother would be proud of you? You think she'd be proud of you, kiddo? You done fucked her cousin's widder. I didn't do no worse than you're doing right now. Hell, you are a sick kid, you know that? You think you have the right to judge me? You don't have the right to even speak to me, let alone judge me, you self-righteous hypocritical son of a bitch! And I'll tell you now, that ain't never had more meaning than it does right now. Son of a bitch. You are a son of a bitch. Because she was a bitch, kiddo. She was a fucking nasty fucking bitch, and I hope she burns in hell forever...

Enough! Michael thought, shouting inside his own head. That's enough!

Hell, kiddo, I ain't even started.

Well, you're in hell right now! And even if I can see you, I can only see you here. You're stuck here forever, you crazy asshole...

Jimmy started laughing, and as he laughed, his shoulders shook, and the dust that had gathered on his clothes came off in small clouds and floated around his head. The sound of his coarse laughter sent the cockroaches scuttling back beneath the edges of plates and over the table. They dropped to the floor and hurried across the wide pool of dried blood toward the baseboard.

Got you good, kiddo! Got you good. Got you fooled. You liked my little performance there, eh?

Jimmy started to rise from the chair.

Michael watched as his dead father pushed the chair back with his knees and started around the table toward him. He was grinning, and the slack muscles on the left-hand side of his face gave his features the texture of melted wax.

Come give your old pa a big bear hug, kiddo. You knows we's just the same inside, don'tcha? You knows you ain't never gonna get away from your history...?

Michael stepped back, and as Jimmy Travis came within six feet of him, he let out a frightened sound, a sudden exhalation of horror that sounded like a child lost somewhere in the dark and desperately, terrifyingly alone.

"No!" he said out loud. "Don't come anywhere near me!"

"Michael?"

He stopped suddenly. He realized his eyes were closed. He took a deep breath and opened them. Esther was standing right there in the hallway, the expression on her face one of the gravest concern.

"What happened, honey?" she said. She walked forward, reached out her hand and touched the side of his face. "Lord almighty, sweetheart, what happened? I thought I heard you talking to someone? Were you talking to someone? Look at you now... You're deathly cold, and you're shaking like a leaf..."

She held out her arms, and he walked toward her, grateful now for her presence, her warmth.

He knew she could not see anything, and even as she hugged him, even as she held him ever closer, Michael looked back toward the room where he had seen his father.

There was the table, the chair, and the wide bloodstain on the wooden floor. There was the window, the ornaments, the rocker in the far corner, the wireless on the sill, the lamp, the last newspaper his father had read still there on the mantel, but Jimmy Travis was not there. Even the cockroaches had merely been a figment of his imagination.

Michael closed his eyes. He wondered again if he was crazy. He wondered if he would now forever be haunted by the ghost of his father.

I'm in your head and I'm in your blood, boy...

He started again, as if shocked by an electric pulse.

"You are just as jumpy as anything," Esther said. "Come on. Let's get out of here. I'm thinking that maybe this wasn't such a good idea."

"R-right," Michael said.

"You wanna get anything from your room?"

"No, it's okay. I just want to leave," Michael said.

"I think that's best. I don't like this place one bit."

They left together, hand in hand, and when they came through the screen and started down the steps, both Deputy Fenton and Sarge were there to meet them.

"Little shook up," Esther explained. "He'll be okay."

Esther led Michael toward Sarge's Studebaker.

Sarge shook Fenton's hand, thanked him for taking the time to come out, said it was a pleasure talking with him.

Michael paused before he ducked back into the rear seat of the car. He took one more look at the house of his childhood—

Be seein' you, kiddo...

—and then, with an almost imperceptible shudder, he climbed in, pushed himself back into the corner as far as he could, and tugged his jacket around himself.

He could still hear those scuttling cockroach feet over the porcelain plates. He could still see that dull silvery glint in his father's left eye. He could still hear the coarse rasp of Jimmy Travis's voice saying, *God darn it, boy, you sure as hell is your father's son...*

Never, he told himself. Never, never, never.

But the doubt was there. The seed of doubt was there. He felt it stretching its tentative and fragile roots into the earth of his mind, and there was nothing he could do to stop it.

15

There were many things in Michael Travis's life that he did not wish to remember. Some of them were recent, and some of them went right back to the furthest horizon of his memory. For those few minutes, as he sat in his Bureau-assigned late-model Ford Fairlane, he focused his attention on what he had learned, how it could assist him to progress the investigation.

In truth, he had learned very little. The devil was in the detail, however. The connection between Madeline Jarvis and Anthony Scarapetto had been a detail. A dead Hungarian and his connection to this Fekete Kutya was important. Possessive of his nationality, identification was a narrower task, but not a great deal narrower. Maybe Bishop would come back to him with something. Maybe the man was known, already on the run from the federal authorities. As a non-national, there would be records of his entering the country, unless he had entered illegally. Then? Well, then it would be the proverbial needle in a haystack.

So where had this Hungarian come from, where was he going, and why did he stop at the carnival? Had he made arrangements to meet someone in Seneca Falls? From the look of his clothes and personal effects, he was definitely not a wealthy man, but he was not a hobo. Simple and inexpensive his suit and shoes might have been, but they were neither dirty nor worn-out. This—to all intents and purposes—was a man with a life, and that life had ended. However, the mere fact that there was no driver's license, no billfold, no wallet containing business cards, snapshots of kids, a picture of his wife, right down to the fact that manufacturer's labels had been removed from his jacket and pants, was beyond unusual. Either he intended to carry nothing, or everything had been removed from his person before the body was dumped.

It was a mystery, for sure, and that—in and of itself—was sufficient reason to remain.

In essence, what had happened here was an example of why Travis had joined the FBI in the first place. That thirst for knowledge, that *need* to know, just as Valeria Mironescu had pointed out. Those few empty months between Esther's death and Travis's enrollment in the Bureau had perhaps been the strangest of his life. He'd felt as if he'd had no life. That was the only way to describe the sense of purposelessness and mental apathy he'd experienced. What reason had there been to get up? He'd had enough money left over from his army salary to support himself for another six months, another year perhaps, but doing nothing was anathema to him. And why had he chosen the Bureau? Because of the sense of order and predictability it would impose upon his thoughts, his mind, his own personality? The army had demonstrated all too clearly that a disciplined and structured environment best suited him. The ideas he had, the doubts he possessed about himself—who he was, why he was here, what would happen to him, whether he carried some diluted strain of his father's violence in his blood—did not plague his mind when his mind was full. It was in the quiet times, the moments of aloneness when there was nothing specific to consider, that he felt those dark shadows come to life in the back of his mind. Given free rein to truly be himself, who would he be, and of what would he be capable? There were fears there, real fears, but only with the death of his father had they been sufficiently energized to impinge upon him. Was he, in essence, two people? Was he what they called *schizophrenic*? He did not believe so, but even the word unsettled him.

Regardless of rationale, the actual motivation for joining the Bureau, the *force majeure*, happened in a diner in Kearney just three weeks after Esther Franklin's death. Travis had barely gathered his thoughts together after the trauma of that time, the way Esther had faded so inevitably, the words they had shared, those they had not, the certainty that the cancer that had invaded her body would never take her on any other route than to her grave, and all of this while Travis felt so impotent, so insignificant, so meaningless.

Travis was still wrestling with so much when he crossed paths with a man called Donald Gerritty on the afternoon of Thursday, February 23, 1950. Travis did not believe in coincidence, but he did believe in the power of external factors. In actuality, the entire subject of what was now being termed *situational dynamics* was under study in his own Bureau unit. There appeared to be a native and inherent personality in all people, and yet beyond this there were familial, social, environmental, cultural, and educational factors that prompted reactions and responses. What happened in Kearney was an environmental influence, the power of which could not now be underestimated. Indirectly, it was as a result of that occurrence that he was now in Seneca Falls.

Travis had never been to Kearney before, and only as a result of Esther's dying wishes had there been any reason to go. For much of the two weeks following her death, Travis had been involved without pause in the funeral arrangements, the memorial service, attended by a mere handful of those who knew her, the burial, the resolution of Esther's not-insubstantial debts, one of which was to a man in Kearney, just fifty or sixty miles southwest of Grand Island. Esther's house had sold within days, literally, and the proceeds raised, once her overdue mortgage payments had been settled, were barely enough to cover her outstanding liabilities. On the face of it, it had appeared that Esther possessed no money worries at all. In reality, it had been an entirely different story. And so, following instructions that had been left with her lawyer, Michael attended to those matters in a straightforward and businesslike manner, passing on news of her death to those who needed to know, delivering checks and quantities of cash to those who were owed. There was no explanation as to why Esther Franklin owed two hundred and fifty dollars to a man in Kearney, but she did. The man's name was Clarence Brent. Michael had spoken with him on the telephone, arranged a suitable time to visit, and had agreed to bring the money in cash. That Thursday morning, the twenty-third, Michael boarded the bus from Grand Island to Kearney with an understanding that Brent would meet him at the station, the money would exchange hands, and Michael would get on the next bus back to Grand Island. There would be a couple of hours' wait, but the Kearney bus station was right there at the end of the main drag, and Michael could take an early lunch. And so it went as agreed. Michael arrived, met Brent, and handed over the money.

Michael had asked him one question about Esther.

"Did you know her well, sir?"

"Well enough to wait five years to get my money back," was all Brent said, and that was that. He was neither impolite nor brusque, but he did not smile, and it seemed clear that he did not wish to discuss the matter with Michael Travis. After all, Travis was a stranger, and what business was it of his?

The delivery made, Travis left the station and headed up the main drag. He entered the first diner he saw, took a seat at the counter, ordered a cup of coffee and the blue plate special, and sat down with the intention of doing little beyond minding his own business.

Don Gerritty arrived ten minutes later. He arrived at the same time as Travis's food. He asked if the adjacent seat was free, how the special was, ordered the same. He sat in silence, but there was just something about the man that bothered Travis enormously. Travis wouldn't have thought twice about upping and moving to a table, but the diner was full with early lunch traffic, and there was no room. First of all, the man had a Zippo lighter, and he kept opening and snapping it shut. He did not use it to light a cigarette. He just opened it, shut it, opened it, shut

157

it. *Click. Click. Click. Click.* Such things did not ordinarily bother Travis. No, it was not *what* the man was doing, but *how* he was doing it. It was as if he were trying to be as annoying as possible.

Eventually Travis asked him if he wouldn't mind stopping.

"Bothering you?" the man said. "I am so sorry. I wasn't even aware I was doing it. Have a lot on my mind, see? You know how it is."

Travis understood then. The man was soliciting conversation. The man wanted to draw him into something. More than likely a con man. Next would come a line. *Hey, kid, if you don't mind me asking, what line of work you in, and how'd you like to make a few extra bucks?* And then, later, if Travis questioned the motives of the man, he'd say, *But you were the one who started talking to me, kid. I was just minding my own business and you struck up a conversation with me, remember?*

But no, there was no such line. In fact, the man just set down the lighter and went back to his own thoughts.

That, in all honesty, was somehow worse.

"Some difficulty you're in?" Travis asked, unable to restrain himself. There it was again—the *need* to know, the compulsion to find out.

The man smiled, sort of half laughed. "Nothing that should trouble you, son, and certainly nothing you could help with."

The man was perspiring. Travis hadn't noticed that before. His brow was varnished with sweat, and the routine with the lighter had not been simple distraction at all, but nervousness. The man looked at Travis, and there was a real flash of fear in his eyes.

"You sure you're okay, mister?" Travis asked.

The man turned back to the counter as his food arrived. He looked at it as if he couldn't even remember ordering it, and he nodded his head.

"I'm fine, kid. I'm fine. You just go on with your lunch, okay? Don't let me interrupt your meal."

But the meal was interrupted, and there seemed to be no going back to it.

"If there's something you need help with..." Travis said, leaving the statement unfinished.

"Look, kid, I don't know what the deal is here, but there really is nothing you can do. I don't mean to be rude, but this isn't something you should be getting involved in, okay?"

And then whatever anxiety might have been present in the man's face became something akin to abject terror. He appeared frantic and yet unable to move.

A car had pulled up outside the diner, and from it emerged two men, both suited, both wearing hats, and they paused for just a moment before approaching the building.

"Oh no," the man said, and he came down off the stool and headed for the diner restrooms.

The first of the two suited men came through the front door and flashed a badge.

"Please remain calm, ladies and gentlemen. There is no need to panic. We are federal agents, and we are looking for a man who was reported as having entered this building."

Travis stood up.

The first agent looked at him. "You have something to say, sir?"

"Restroom," Michael said.

The first agent nodded, indicated for the second to follow him. As they passed the lunch counter, the first agent asked for Travis's name.

Travis told him.

"I want you to get these people out of here, Michael. You think you can do that?"

"Yes, sir."

"Orderly, calmly, get them all out of here and over to the other side of the street, all right?"

"Yes, sir."

"Good. Get going."

The two agents headed for the corridor that led back down to the restrooms while Travis corralled the diners and directed them out and across the street as quickly and quietly as possible.

He waited with them while the federal agents dealt with the man they were looking for.

It was little more than five minutes before a shot was fired.

It was a single shot, unmistakable as anything else, and the gathered diners started asking Travis questions as if there were something he knew beyond the immediately evident facts.

After another minute, the first agent came out of the diner and waved Travis over.

"Son, I need you to assist the owner of this establishment. I need you to help him bring everyone's coats and hats out of the diner and over to them on the sidewalk. Tell them they will not able to return to their meals."

Travis complied without further questions. He and the owner started gathering up peoples' hats and coats and bags and ferrying them over the street.

On the first trip back, the owner of the diner asked if Travis knew anything about the guy in the restroom.

"No idea," Travis replied.

"He shot himself in the freakin' head in my restroom. Can you believe that?"

"Really?"

"Sure thing. Those two Feds show up, he goes out back, they ask him to come on out, and he shoots himself in the head. Crazy, huh? Wonder what he did."

That was it then.

That was the moment.

Later, years ahead, after his move to Kansas and those first few months of tentative research into a field that was termed behavioral science, they started to use that phrase: *situational dynamics*. Why did one man want to help and another want to harm? Why did two people—ostensibly from almost identical backgrounds and personal circumstances—become wildly different people?

Crazy, huh? Wonder what he did.

After Travis and the owner had returned all the coats and bags and hats and scarves, those same diners did not want to leave. They wanted to know too.

Travis listened to them.

Maybe he was a gangster. Maybe he was on the run. Maybe he killed someone.

To Travis, that nervous and frightened man did not seem to be a gangster at all. He was terrified, and if what the diner owner had said was true, if the man had actually shot himself, then dying right then and there in a restroom must have seemed an awful lot more appealing than whatever fate he believed awaited him at the hands of the Feds.

Travis stayed back across the road and he just observed.

More Feds arrived, then the coroner. At last the dead man was stretchered out and put into the back of the coroner's wagon. The agent who had first spoken to Travis crossed the street and told the hangers-on that it was all over, that there was nothing further to see, that they should all go home.

He did stop to share a few words with Travis and thanked him for his assistance.

"You kept your head," the agent said. "Most people panic in such situations."

"Did a couple of years in the army," Travis said.

"I thought it might be something like that," the agent said.

"So, what was the deal with the guy? I was sat right beside him. He seemed very nervous, and then he got mighty scared when you pulled up outside the diner."

"You'll read about it in the papers tomorrow, I'm sure," the agent said.

160

And with that, he shook Travis's hand, thanked him once more for his assistance, and left.

Travis made a point of finding out what happened the following day.

The man's name was Donald Gerritty. He hailed from Sterling, Colorado. He'd killed his wife. Strangled her and then tried to make it look like she'd hung herself. Soon as questions started being asked by the Sterling Police Department, Donald Gerritty took off. He just got in his car, hit I-76, and headed northeast. The moment he crossed the Nebraska state line at Julesburg, it became a federal matter, and Special Agents Norman Hiscox and Dennis Whyte had taken up the pursuit. Gerritty had made it all of two hundred miles, all the way to Kearney, and whether he was aware of having been followed for all of those two hundred miles was not clear from the small article that the newspaper had afforded his flight. Regardless, Hiscox and Whyte had found him in that diner, and rather than face the consequences of what he had done, Gerritty had decided to end his own life. How he had been in possession of a gun was not reported, but he had shot himself in the restroom of that diner and that was the end of that.

Hiscox knew what had really happened. So did Whyte. Michael Travis did not know which agent was which, and there was no picture of them. There was just a small, grainy monochrome image of Donald Gerritty looking considerably younger and less afraid than he had the day before.

But Travis's curiosity went beyond the immediate whys and wherefores of the death of Gerritty. He wanted to know about the death of the wife. Why had Gerritty killed her? What had been his reasoning? Was it premeditated or spur of the moment? Did he honestly believe he could get away with killing her, or had the murder been nothing more than a sudden and inexplicable response to some stimuli?

On the subsequent Monday morning, February 27, Michael Travis took a bus to Lincoln. He located the FBI office and introduced himself. He said he wished to apply. They took his application, but informed him that the minimum age for acceptance into the training program was twenty-three. He would have to wait until the tenth of May for his answer.

Travis did wait until the tenth of May, and he did receive his answer. It was the answer he'd hoped for, and within a week he had begun a career that had—so far—lasted eight years.

At the start, those first few weeks in the newly established Kansas City unit, there were merely four or five of them, each pulled from different offices across the States. The meetings, the discussions, the initial debates regarding their purpose there, did serve to establish one thing: that the Bureau was looking at something very new.

There were angles and perspectives to all things, and the Bureau's attitude—as expressed by the head of the training program, Section Chief Frank Gale—was that the failure to appreciate every single one of those angles and perspectives was the primary reason for the failure of a case.

Frank Gale was a man of certainty, both in what he said and what he did. Physically, he was no taller than Travis, but he *seemed* taller. He carried himself with authority, and though he smiled often, he nevertheless managed to instill respect and a sense of unquestioning compliance in his charges. Never one to say something unless it needed to be said, Gale was a very experienced Bureau veteran, and immediately Travis had no doubt that he could trust what he said.

"You are here as the devil's advocate, Mr. Travis," Gale said on their first day together. "You are here, very simply, because you challenge everything that is put in front of you, even those things we take for granted, even those things we *know* are true. I know you see yourself as a realist, but you are more the *un*realist."

Travis had not responded, nor asked questions. He believed that everything would unfold in its own good time.

"These men with you," Gale went on. "Perhaps they joined the Bureau for the same reason as yourself, perhaps not. That does not concern us. What concerns us is what we are beginning to call a *situational dynamic*. You have to understand that this is all theoretical, but it is the director's wish that we explore all such areas of the human condition, certainly as it relates to the apprehension of criminals. To best something, you have to understand it, no? Possibly not in every case. One does not need to know the mind of a tiger to shoot it, but knowing the mind of a tiger perhaps gives you an advantage. The way it thinks, where it hunts, how it sees you as a potential threat, how it evades you, the instinctive methods it employs to escape capture. That is what we are looking into, Mr. Travis, and that is why you are here. In fact, when I mentioned the fact that some of you had come to the attention of the director personally, it was you I was talking about."

"The director himself wants me here?" Travis asked, the surprise in his voice all too evident.

"Oh yes," Gale said. "He most definitely wants all of you here. This is being overseen by myself, and even though I might not be running the day-to-day activities of this unit, the reports and findings will all come to me, and then there's only one or two pay grades above me before those reports and findings reach the director himself. As you know, he is a stickler for administrative exactitude, and even though this is a somewhat nebulous and uncharted territory, he feels that an investment of time and resources could be very worthwhile."

"So, can I ask what this unit is called?" Travis asked.

"Simply Unit X. That is our unofficial name. It merely means *experimental*."

"And do we have a mission statement, so to speak?"

Gale smiled knowingly. "You remind me of Clyde Tolson. Same need to know. Same need to put a label on everything. Our mission statement, as you so eloquently put it, Mr. Travis, is to ask every question we can think of, to challenge everything we see, to try to find patterns, seeming coincidences that can then be substantiated, to recognize similarities in motive, intent, decision, and action. Really, we are here to try to discover if there is some way to understand the darkest and most destructive aspects of the human mind."

"And our findings will be studied by the director personally?"

"Of course they will. He was the one who requested this unit be established, and he is quite prepared to fund whatever is required to obtain results."

"And do you know what results he is after?"

"The truth, Mr. Travis. As always, he wants the truth, the whole truth, and nothing but the truth."

And so the work began—work that was continuing even then, work that would perhaps continue for as long as there was a Bureau, as long as there were subjects to interview, crimes to investigate, patterns to follow, lines to pursue.

And Travis had been right there at the forward edge of the thing, though every step of the way he had found himself challenging what he saw, being challenged in return.

Looking back on those initial months, recalling the reports he wrote—knowing all the while that they would ultimately find their way to the desk of Director Hoover himself—he at once recognized the differences between himself and some of the others who were brought on to the team. Travis could divide them into three camps: the hopers, the deniers, the abstainers. The hopers were those who wanted to believe that there were connections through everything, and—as such—every case they studied, every answer they interpreted, every report they wrote simply served to highlight the almost-childlike and naive view that life possessed predictable and quantifiable *reason*. The deniers were the opposite and perhaps feared the possibility that there was reason and rationale behind all things. They did not want to see connections; they did not want to find out that cause resulted in effect, that every decision and action possessed an identifiable and attributable consequence. And then there was Travis, the abstainer, or—as Chief Gale had called him—the devil's advocate. Soon it was evident why Travis was there, for the collected reports of all investigations and studies were brought to him, and his task was to determine where the hopers were hoping too much, where the deniers were denying too much, and how the middle ground might best be navigated.

Travis spent five years in that building, working with an ever-changing cast of characters, directly and indirectly involved in some of the most significant and high-profile investigations that the Bureau had undertaken. Travis was among those who interviewed the bank robbers, the killers, the terrorists, the political subversives, the reactionaries and would-be revolutionaries. From individuals connected to the Hollow Nickel Case to the Brink's Robbery, from Baby Face Nelson's compadres to Gerhard Puff and George Heroux, Travis had crisscrossed the country with his notebook, his tape recorder, his unquenchable thirst for answers. He had interviewed Angelo LaMarca in the fall of 1956 after LaMarca's conviction for the kidnapping and murder of the Weinberger baby. Had he not been there in Seneca Falls, he would have been down in Nassau, Florida, for LaMarca was due to be executed the very next day. In his stead, there would be some other member of the X Unit, asking questions, trying to establish some further understanding from LaMarca about what had happened, his motives, his rationale, the thought processes that took place, the reason he believed that the opportunist kidnapping of a baby and a request for two thousand dollars in ransom money would have solved any problems at all.

In January of 1957, Hoover came to visit. It was Friday the eleventh, the day of Jack Graham's execution in Colorado for the November '55 sabotage of United Airlines Flight 629. With twenty-five sticks of dynamite, a blasting cap, a sixty-minute "off-type" timing device and a battery, Graham had blown a DC-6B out of the sky above Longmont, Colorado. He had killed forty-four people, five of them United Airlines crew members, one of them a baby. Travis had interviewed Graham at Colorado State Penitentiary just three months earlier, once again stringing together some semblance of a biography, trying to get to grips with how Graham had become the person he was. Had the man been born with a destructive impulse, an impulse that drove him relentlessly toward some preordained and unalterable conclusion, or had there been factors—familial, environmental, social, cultural, even pathological—that had contributed to such an end?

Where were their exhaustive investigations taking them? What was Unit X learning, and how could it contribute to a more effective Bureau? This was what Hoover wanted to know, and this was what he asked Special Agent Michael Travis when they were introduced.

Hoover's manner was as Travis had expected. Despite his immediate proximity, the director seemed to be ever distant. Even as he shook Travis's hand, Travis felt as if he was being surveyed, inspected, weighed. Hoover's notorious unpredictability, his severity, his ability to make a snap decision about someone's character that could then never be reversed, was legend, but Travis did not fear meeting the director. In truth, he welcomed it.

Travis stood in the presence of a man he had long respected and admired and yet felt unnerved by his presence. His loyalty to Hoover was unquestioning, and yet even as Hoover spoke to him, Travis felt a degree of suspicion in Hoover's manner. He could have been wrong, but Travis felt as if Hoover was looking for some reason not to like him, as if Hoover wanted to justify some sort of basic and inherent distrust of all men.

"As you know," Hoover explained in the brief conversation they shared, "I established the Bureau laboratory in 1932, all of twenty-five years ago. It has served its purpose, no doubt, but its purpose is very specific, very tangible, very functional. It does not matter how many bullets or knives or dead bodies we look at, such things do not help us to understand the mind. Hence we now have this unit, Unit X, which I believe might ultimately be called the Behavioral Science Division. You are a new viewpoint, young man, a new, fresh, vital viewpoint required to keep us right there at the cutting edge of law enforcement."

Travis listened but did not speak. It was customary, certainly with Hoover, not to speak unless specifically invited to do so.

"I have read some of the summaries and reports you have written, Special Agent Travis, as has Mr. Tolson, and we have been impressed with your precision and directness. However, you lack an element of imagination. You lack the degree of foresight that would make so much of what we are doing here so much more real and applicable. Do you understand what I mean?"

"Yes, sir," Travis replied.

"What I hope to accomplish, young man, is a view into the criminal mind, you see? I want to see behind the eyes of the criminal. I want to understand why the murderer kills, why the bank robber is incapable of any constructive contribution to society, why the subversive Communist sees reason in the most unreasonable political ideology. I want to know what they are going to do before they do it."

"I understand, sir."

"But do you believe it is possible, Special Agent Travis?" Hoover asked.

"Yes, sir," Travis lied. "I believe everything is possible."

"Now, is that a well meant but meaningless aphorism designed to placate me, Agent Travis, or is that what you really think?"

Travis looked at Hoover directly. "I am a realist by nature, sir, and I do not believe that my nature will ever fundamentally change. I do not need to believe in something to make it happen, nor do I need to believe in something to have it be true. There are many things I do not understand, and there are many things I do not *need* to understand. I know what questions need to be asked, and I know what you are looking for. My every waking moment is dedicated to giving you as much useful and usable information as can be isolated and documented. I am here to challenge everything, and I will continue to challenge it."

"You would do well on Capitol Hill, young man," Hoover said with a careful smile. "I shall have to keep an eye on you."

Hoover looked at Travis unerringly for one moment, and then he smiled once more, this time in a somewhat forced fashion, as if friendliness was as much a stranger to him as Communist sympathy, and then he left the room. Travis was left with the feeling that he had somehow said the wrong thing, but then wondered if everyone felt that way around J. Edgar Hoover.

Later, Chief Gale came to see him.

"You impressed the director," he said, "but he feels that you need to expand your tolerances."

Travis frowned.

"Too rigid," he said. "His exact words? New ideas were never discovered by men with preconceptions. That's what he said, Agent Travis."

"I cannot change who I am," Travis replied.

"You don't need to change who you are," Gale replied. "You just need to change the way you see everyone else."

It was that comment, that specific comment, that came to mind as Travis sat there in his car. And just as had been the case with Donald Gerritty, both the killing of his wife and his own suicide, so it now was with this current investigation. Hungary. Fekete Kutya. A killer had been killed.

Michael looked out toward Slate's caravan. It was now almost dark. There was a light within the caravan and a silhouette within.

Shadow play, Travis thought, and smiled to himself. Enough with Doyle and the Mironescu woman. Enough of their games.

Travis locked the car and started across to the caravan, feeling already that familiar tension in his temples.

16

Slate's caravan was a little smaller than the Westfalia and set back beneath the trees. Travis did not see how he could have missed it when surveying the line of vehicles the day before.

"Agent Travis."

Travis looked up. Mr. Slate stood on the upper step of the caravan entrance. Travis had seen him the day before when he'd spoken to the collective group, but now he was arm's length away and appeared quite different. His features were aquiline, well defined, and his hair was cut a little longer than average. There was something altogether precise about his demeanor, as if someone had taken time to outline him with a fine black pen. Slate extended his hand then, and when Travis took it, he was aware of his own change of expression. Had he been focusing, he would have been less likely to react.

"Always gets 'em," Slate said, and laughed. "Throws people off completely when they shake a hand with too many fingers."

Travis didn't know what to say.

"You don't need to say anything," Slate said, as if he'd heard the thought. "I am completely oblivious to anything anyone does or says, believe me. Come on in. You look like a man who needs a strong cup of coffee."

"Thank you," Travis said. "That would be good."

Slate turned and entered the caravan, ducking his head as he went back through the doorway. Travis followed him, was surprised by the seeming spaciousness within the vehicle. Slate lived alone, evidently, for the bed at the far end was no wider than a shelf, and the accoutrements and utensils that Travis could see were suited to a bachelor, not a husband.

"We've not been introduced," Travis said. "At least not formally."

"I know who you are," Slate said, "and I know why you're here. My name is Slate, and I am a cardsharp, a conjurer, a magician, and a liar."

"A liar?"

"It is all lies, Agent Travis. All of this. The carnival, the people who work here, everything. We make magic, we create illusions, we deceive and misdirect, and then we fleece the innocent, unthinking public for their dimes and dollars."

"I think that's perhaps a little harsh, don't you?"

"I am not being serious, Agent Travis. We are here to entertain. We provide distraction from the trials and tribulations of everyday life, and then we are gone."

Slate held out his right hand and then brought all seven of his fingers together as if snatching something from the air.

"Here," he said, and then opened his fingers suddenly and blew into his palm, "and then gone..."

Out of nowhere, a white feather drifted up and then down toward the floor.

"Very impressive, Mr. Slate."

Slate caught the feather before it touched down and handed it to Travis. Travis reached out to take it and then found himself touching nothing. The feather had gone, disappeared even as he was looking at it.

"Where did it go?" Travis asked, smiling.

"Perhaps it was never there, Agent Travis."

Slate paused for effect and then indicated the table. "Please sit," he said, "and I will fulfill my promise of a cup of strong coffee."

Travis sat, found himself glancing around for any sign of the white feather. Slate had secreted it about his person somehow, but how he had done that, Travis could not guess. That was the skill of a sleight-of-hand artiste, however, a skill learned and then practiced again and again until it was seamless.

Travis did not sense the same degree of challenge from Slate. First impressions were of someone quite unassuming, despite the theatrics. Slate's body language did not suggest resistance.

"Cream, no sugar," Slate said, "strong enough to start a dead man's heart." He turned then and looked over his shoulder at Travis. "Perhaps not the best thing to say under the circumstances. I apologize."

"No concern," Travis said. "We so often deal with death with a sense of humor. It's a natural defense mechanism."

Slate busied himself with making coffee, and soon the smell of it filled the caravan.

"Tell me about Saturday night," Travis said as Slate brought cups to the table.

"Saturday night was the busiest night we've seen for weeks." Slate held Travis's gaze for a moment and added, "Every once in a while, the stars are in our favor. The weather is good, the word of mouth spreads, there is a distinct absence of local preachers advocating temperance and sobriety, and the carnival is barely able to cope with the numbers that appear, and seemingly from nowhere. They just flood in by the carload and spend a small fortune."

"And when the body was found?"

"Well, it was late. Perhaps eleven or thereabouts. I remember hearing the girl scream, and I wondered whether it was just someone playing a prank. Then there was all manner of confusion, and I went over there and saw John Ryan crawling beneath the platform to reach him."

Travis took the photograph of the dead man from his jacket pocket and put it on the table.

"This is him, isn't it?" Slate asked.

"Yes, that's him."

Slate picked up the photo and looked at it for a good while. "Not a clue," he said. "I can't say that I've never seen him before because in this line of work you see thousands of different people in a month, but he's not familiar to me."

Travis took the diagram of the tattoo and showed Slate.

"And this?" he asked.

"What is this?"

"It's a diagram of a design found on the man's body," Travis explained, alert for any indication in Slate's manner that he recognized it. "I wondered if you had ever seen anything like this before, this pattern, or if you had any idea why someone might have it tattooed on their body."

"A tattoo, you say?"

"Yes, Mr. Slate, behind his right knee."

"Fascinating," Slate said, and took the piece of paper from Travis. "The design means nothing to me," he said, his body language indicative of nothing but his own simple curiosity, "but tattoos are often used to indicate membership of some group, some organization, you know? In the Far East it's very common."

"You have been to the Far East?"

"I have been everywhere, Agent Travis," Slate replied. "The Far East, Arabia, Mexico, England, Italy, Spain, France, Holland, South America. I am, as they say, a well-traveled man."

"Might I ask how old you are, Mr. Slate?"

"I am fifty-one. In human years, at least."

Travis frowned.

Slate smiled, gave a little laugh. "I am joking, Agent Travis. It is my nature to try to lighten everything a little. Please pay no mind to it."

"You appear younger than you are," Travis said.

"The penalty of wickedness is perhaps the appearance of youth. No one ever takes me seriously, you see?"

"Wickedness?" Travis asked.

"Perhaps too strong a word. Mischievousness. A general unwillingness to grow up, you know? Being an adult always seemed so insufferably dull to me."

Travis smiled and sipped his coffee. The man might have been a little left of center, as seemed to be everyone he had thus far met, but his coffee was very good indeed.

"It is, isn't it?" Slate said.

"Sorry?"

"The coffee. Good."

"Er, yes," Travis replied. "How did you know I just thought that?"

"I didn't," Slate said. "You tasted the coffee; your features relaxed a little. When something is good, we relax; when something isn't, we become more tense. It is just observation, Agent Travis, not mind-reading... though if you want me to read your mind, I could have a go."

"That won't be necessary," Travis replied. "So, back to the matter at hand."

"The tattoo," Slate said. "I have no idea at all. Sorry I can't help."

"That's quite all right," Travis said. "I appreciate your time and cooperation. This man's death has an explanation, and I will find it."

"Are you sure of that, Agent Travis?"

"Sure that I will find an explanation? Of course I am sure. Everything has an explanation."

"Aha, that is where you appear to possess a great deal more certainty than I," Slate said. "I have found quite the reverse, to be honest. The older I get, the more I see, the more people I meet, the more questions I have. And no, I do not believe that *everything* has an explanation."

"I am not talking about the eternal questions, Mr. Slate. I am not talking about whether or not there is a God, or why we are here, or where we are going—"

"Oh, I have no problem with those questions," Slate said. "Those are the easiest of all. I am talking about the difficult questions, the ones that no one seems to have been able to answer in all the eons of time."

"Such as?"

"What is really happening in the minds of women. There's one to begin with. That's a question that will never be answered, wouldn't you say?"

Suddenly Travis was presented with an image of his mother's face. It was there, right there in front of him, almost as if she were seated before him instead of Slate.

It was the night before she died, those few moments where he seemed to make some sort of *connection* through the distance that existed between them. It was his mother, the woman he remembered, the woman who had given birth to him, who had raised him, the woman who had taken a table knife and driven it through his father's eye...

Will haunt you forever, kiddo. Gonna be in your dreams, your nightmares, your waking thoughts... always and forever...

"Agent Travis?"

Travis looked at Slate.

"Are you all right, Agent Travis?"

Travis felt as if there were no air at all in the caravan.

"I need to step outside for a moment," he said.

Travis got up, knocked over his coffee cup, and the last inch of coffee spread across the table. He looked down at it. He saw red wine on the floor of Esther's veranda. And then he saw blood on the wooden floor of the Flatwater house...

"I'm so-sorry," he stuttered.

"It's all right," Slate said. "It's nothing. Go... step outside. Get some air."

Travis headed for the door, opened it, narrowly missed striking his head on the upper frame, and then almost lost his footing down the narrow steps to the grass.

He stood there for a moment, a real sense of tension in his head, his throat, his chest. He looked out toward the central marquee, now lit within, and there, before his eyes, he saw the Asian girl from the day before.

She was on a platform no more than three or four feet high. She was dressed in a skintight silver outfit, somehow bent over backward and yet looking at him from between her own legs. She was smiling directly at him, no doubt about it, this image of utter impossibility, as if she had somehow been broken in half and put together incorrectly.

He remembered her name. *Akiko*. Autumn Child.

Travis turned back toward the caravan as Slate came down the steps after him.

"Are you all right, Agent Travis?" he asked.

"Ye-yes," he said. He breathed again, felt the cool air fill his lungs. "I am okay. Just a little dizzy, I think."

"Is there anything else I can help you with, or are we done?"

"I think we're done, Mr. Slate. At least for now."

Slate came forward, handed Travis the picture and the diagram.

"I hope you find the answers you're looking for, Agent Travis," Slate said. "So few of us ever do."

Travis said nothing in response. He walked away, and only when he reached the edge of the road did he turn back.

Slate stood there, his hands down by his sides, but palms turned toward

Travis. His expression was guileless and sincere, as if he were saying, *There is nothing else to see here, Agent Travis, nothing but what you see already.*

Travis reached his car. He fumbled with his keys and dropped them. He snatched them from the ground, opened the door, and got in. Only when he'd slammed the door shut behind him and Slate had gone back into his caravan did he feel that he could think straight. He wondered if he wasn't sick with something. He felt troubled; a sense of unease ran right through him like a virus, like some airborne infection that had somehow penetrated his skin and gotten inside.

He shuddered, tried to close his eyes. The sense of disorientation increased, and he opened them once more. He was surrounded by the ever-present feeling of being watched and yet had no rational explanation for such a feeling.

Whatever it was, it was not good, and to close his eyes to it—both physically and figuratively—would be to fail to see what was coming. For something was coming—of this he was sure—and somehow he knew it would not be good.

17

Travis did not wish to speak to Edgar Doyle. He did not wish to speak to anyone.

He drove back to Seneca Falls and parked outside the hotel. Inside he found the reception area empty. He turned to the stairwell and heard his name called. Looking back, he saw Laura McCaffrey in the hallway that led to the dining room.

"Agent Travis," she said.

"Miss McCaffrey, good evening."

"Danny said you might be back. Have you had dinner?"

"No, I haven't. I'm not all that hungry, to be honest."

"A sandwich, then?" she said. "You must eat something."

Travis headed back down the stairs, simply because Laura McCaffrey—in that moment—seemed to be the first truly normal person he'd seen that day.

"Thank you," Travis said. "That would be good."

"Come on through to the kitchen," Laura said. "I've made some coffee too."

Laura McCaffrey told Travis to sit at a small table near the stove. She said little as she prepared his sandwich. She set it in front of him and then took a seat facing him, her elbows on the table, her hands around her own coffee cup, and she smiled at him with such sincerity that he found it hard to look away from her.

He ate half the sandwich without even being aware of eating it, and his coffee cup was refilled twice. He felt as if he were dreaming.

"So how was your day, Secret Agent Travis?" Laura eventually asked him.

Travis smiled, had to contain his laughter for fear of losing a mouthful of coffee. This was what he needed. He needed someone like Laura McCaffrey to remind him that the world was not full of crazies and carnival freaks.

"It was okay, Miss McCaffrey," Travis said.

"Would it be such hard work for you to call me Laura?" she asked.

"No, not such hard work," Travis said. "Laura it is."

"So, did you find out who the dead guy was?"

"Not yet, no."

"Hell of a thing, that carnival, you know?" Laura went on. "I was there Friday night, the night it opened. Never seen anything like it before."

Travis looked at her closely. There was a sense of surprise in her tone, as if she was recalling something that was puzzling even to herself.

"What do you mean?" he asked.

"Well, I've seen those sorts of things before, you know. We all have. County fair comes down here, even the circus one time or other, and you see these folks with the tricks and whatever. But these people are different. There's something not right about them." She shook her head, smiled a little nervously. "I'm talkin' out of turn, Agent Travis. I'm sorry. I didn't mean to say anything." She started to get up from the table.

"Hold up a minute," Travis said. "What do you mean?"

Laura sat down again. She leaned forward a little, as if now this was something she didn't wish anyone to overhear.

"I saw that man, you know, the one who looks like he'd just blow away in a strong breeze..."

"The Thin Man?" Travis asked.

"Yes... and then there's the other one with too many fingers." She shuddered involuntarily. "Creepy as hell, he was, you know? But then he did some things that I have never seen before, and I just cannot get them out of my mind. They have been puzzlin' the hell out of me ever since, you know?"

Travis leaned back. He was curious now.

Laura smiled nervously. "I'm sorry. It was just thinking about those things, and I was suddenly back there. They had that music an' every-thing, that carousel music, you know?"

"Calliope."

"What?"

"That's what it's called. That kind of music. Fairground music, music for carousels and the like. Calliope."

"Oh right, yes. Whatever it is, it was going the whole time, and I went into that tent where that man was doing tricks..."

She looked up at Travis, was silent for a moment.

"Did you see something that troubled you, Laura?" Travis asked.

"Well, you see people do tricks and whatever, and you think, oh, he's got a card up his sleeve, or he had that coin in his hand all along. Hell, I even learned one time how to do that thing for the kids where you make it look like you took a dime out of their ear and then you give it to them, right?"

"Yes, sure," Travis said, his mind immediately going back to the white feather that was there and then gone.

"But this was different, Mr. Travis. I mean, he was good, real good... like *too* good, if you know what I mean."

"*Too* good?"

"You ever see someone make a card change color in front of your eyes?"

"Change color?"

"You know, like he has an ace of hearts in his hand. It's an ace of hearts. That heart is right there, red like blood, and then he gives you the card and asks you to hold it facedown on your knee, right. He has the card, he shows it to you, he gives it to you, you put it facedown on your knee, and then he says something and you turn the card over and it's black."

"The ace of spades."

"No, sir, the ace of hearts, but it's black. He made the heart go black."

"Surely he just gave you another card, one that was already black."

"No, it wasn't possible. You should see him do it. And that wasn't the only thing I saw him do that I couldn't explain. I mean, you expect them to be good, don't you? You expect them to do things that make you go *Wow* an' all, but you think about it afterward and you can see how it might have been done. Some of the things he did are still puzzling the crap out of me—"

Laura stopped midsentence. "Oh, I'm sorry. I didn't mean to say that."

Travis smiled. "It's quite all right, Laura. I've heard a great deal worse, believe me."

He saw she was quite embarrassed, and so he just prompted her again. "So, what else happened that night?"

"I can't even begin to remember now, Mr. Travis. The more I think about it, the harder it seems to recall anything specific. It wasn't just the things I saw, it was the whole way that place made me feel. I mean, I've been up to that field a hundred times in my life. Hell, we used to play there when we were kids. I know that place like my own backyard. I saw them puttin' them tents up, all raggedy and fallin' apart it seemed, but when me an' Danny went up there Friday night, it was almost magical." She paused, looked directly at Travis. "It's real hard to describe a feeling sometimes, Mr. Travis, but there was a feelin' around that place that sort of spooked me even before I saw anythin'. I mean, don't get me wrong, there was nothin' right there in front of me, and the kids were havin' an absolute hoot an' all, but when I heard that some guy had been found dead out there the next night..."

Laura McCaffrey closed her eyes for a second. She took a deep breath.

Travis stayed silent; he knew well enough not to interrupt that internal line, the little monologue now continuing that would stop in its tracks if he made his presence felt.

"I heard that a man was killed up there... and it sort of..." She shook her head. "I have to say that it didn't surprise me as much as it should have, Mr. Travis. Almost as though if someone was going to die in Seneca Falls that night, then that was the only place it could have happened..."

She looked away toward the window. "Danny says I have a gift, you know?"

"A gift?" Travis asked, even now aware of the fact that there was something utterly charming about Laura McCaffrey, a sense of unprepossessing innocence that was nevertheless truly engaging. Listening to her just talk was the exact thing he needed right now.

"Like sometimes when you know something will happen, right?"

Laura hesitated, looked at Travis as if waiting for confirmation.

"Yes," Travis said, uncertain of what he was being asked, but concerned only that she didn't stop talking. She made him feel calmer somehow, and it was not something that he even questioned.

"Little things mostly," Laura went on. "Like when someone comes into the diner and you know they don't have two red cents in their pocket, but they order up a blue plate special and a slice of pie an' everything. You know they're gonna eat everything and then run off without payin'. That's happened twice here. I knew they weren't gonna pay, and I told Danny, and he said that that was just not the way things were done. You don't ask people to pay for things 'fore they had them. Anyways, I was right and he was wrong. Two times it happened, and two times those fellers just took off outta here and ran off down the street."

Laura reached out and touched the edge of the coffeepot.

Travis watched her hand, her delicate fingers, the seeming grace with which she moved. She seemed so relaxed. Travis wondered how it would feel to be so at ease.

"Danny said it was just my imagination the first time. I said that there was nothing wrong with using your imagination, as long as you didn't use it for bad things, right? Second time he didn't say anything much at all, but sometimes he calls me a witch. Just for a joke, you know?"

She looked at Travis.

Travis smiled. He sensed her reaction. He held her gaze, and she looked away.

"Anyways, when the thing happened with Monty Finch's boy an' all, well, Danny said that maybe I did have a little bit of the gift. I think it scared him some, to be honest."

"Monty Finch?"

"He's dead now, been dead two years. He was old; his heart gave out.

What happened was that Monty Finch got robbed in his own home. Someone came into his house with a pillowcase over their head, eyeholes cut in it an' all, damned near scared him to death right then and there. I spoke to the doctor after Monty died, and he said that a shock like that might very well have weakened the old man's heart. Anyways, this person came into Monty's house late in the evening, he's wavin' a gun, got this pillowcase on his head like he's one o' them Klan fellers down south, and he robs the old man blind. Takes off with more than a hundred bucks that the old man has saved. Anyways, it's all the news the next day. Old man Finch is okay. He's shaken up some, as anyone would be, but him bein' so old, it's really knocked him sideways. He comes on down to the diner for breakfast just the way he's done for as long as I can remember, and while he's sat there eatin', I look at him and I knew. I *knew*, Mr. Travis."

"Knew what, Laura?"

"I just *knew* that he was robbed by someone who knew him, someone close. I told Danny. He told Lester. Lester told Sheriff Rourke, and they go see old man Finch and they find out that he had a son. Hell, no one even knew he had a son. Son was a crook all right, had just come out of prison, and they did some checking up on him and found him holed up in a motel just a dozen or so miles from here." Laura McCaffrey smiled a little awkwardly. "Word was that he was in there drunk with a prostitute."

"So the son had robbed his father."

"He had indeed. They even found the pillowcase right there in the room with the holes cut in it an' all."

"So you were right?"

"I was."

"And this relates to what happened on Saturday night because?"

"Yes, sorry. I was just tellin' you that so you knew I wasn't just some crazy lady gone mad in a small town in Kansas 'cause she's got no one to talk to."

Travis smiled, again sensed something, an unspoken response to his change of expression. "Never even crossed my mind, Laura."

"So yes, Saturday night. Well, Friday night, actually, 'cause I was only up there on the Friday. Like I said, I saw some things up there that I couldn't explain. That would have been okay, all by itself, and I am sure it would never have entered my mind again had that man not been found dead. I mean, when it comes to stuff like that, there's always gonna be stuff that doesn't make sense, right? What kind of magician have you got if everything he does you can see right through, eh?"

"What did you see, Laura?"

"I'm sidetrackin' again, aren't I? I'm sorry. That's just how I am. Danny says I could work for the tire company just talkin' enough hot air to fill all their tires. So, Friday night, yes. Well, Mr. Travis, I have to say that it wasn't anything to do with what I saw. What I saw was just whatever it was. No, it was more to do with how I *felt*."

"How you felt?" Travis asked, and the slightly elevated sense of expectation deflated as quickly as it had risen. He'd thought that Laura McCaffrey was going to give him something, that there would be some small fact that she had failed to mention. She had seen something that had given her pause, in and of itself meaningless to anyone but Travis, but he—with his ever-questioning attitude, with his training, with what he knew of evidence, both probative and circumstantial— would see it as something else entirely. Something that would give him reason to suspect collusion and conspiracy among those in the carnival.

"How I felt, yes," Laura echoed. "Like I said, there are some feelings you can't easily describe, but whatever might be going on up there, there's *definitely* something strange about those people. It's like the folks who come in here without any money, or what happened with old Monty Finch. Sometimes you just *know* when something's wrong, even when you don't know exactly what it is. And that, Mr. Travis, you can take to the bank, if you know what I mean."

Travis smiled, finding it hard to hide his disappointment.

Laura McCaffrey believed she had given him something of great value, and Travis had no mind to let her think otherwise.

"Thank you for your time," he said. "It really has been useful, Laura."

"I said that to Danny, Mr. Travis. I said that I should perhaps come to see you, that I should tell you what I thought. Danny said that it was none of my business and I should stay out of it. I think he was just afraid that you'd think his sister was as mad as a box of crackers."

"No, not at all. Quite the contrary. Like I said, it's been very helpful."

Laura McCaffrey refilled Travis's cup once more. "Is there anything else I can get you? A slice of pie, perhaps?"

"I'm good, Laura, but thank you."

"I'll leave you alone now," she said. "I am sure you've got plenty of things to be getting on with."

"Would you stay just a little longer?" Travis asked. "Unless you have someplace else you need to be?"

Laura frowned, a little puzzled by the request. "I don't have anyplace else to be," she said. "Did you have some more questions?"

"No, Laura. No more questions. I have to be completely honest and say that I have spent the whole day dealing with . . . well, with matters of business. If you don't have to rush away, why not just sit a while longer and talk to me?"

"If you like, Agent Travis."

"Michael," Travis said. "Out of hours, I am Michael."

"Very well, *Michael*." Laura blushed a little and nervously touched her bangs.

"So, tell me about the McCaffreys," Travis said.

"What's to tell?" Laura asked, and then she paused. "Oh, wait a minute. I could tell you about my great-grandfather on my mother's side. He was a bootlegger, and a good one at that."

"That'll do for starters," Travis said. "Tell me all about the bootlegger."

18

Thursday morning, and Travis drove out to the carnival site before Danny McCaffrey had even begun the breakfast service.

The evening before, he had stayed and talked with Laura McCaffrey far longer than he'd planned, and afterward had felt no wish to do anything but write his daily report and get some sleep. Though his body was not tired, his mind was, and the rest had served him well. He felt sharp and alert, all too eager to push this thing ever forward to resolution.

Seated in his car, waiting for the first signs of life among the trucks and caravans, he was interrupted in his thoughts. Alone and contemplative, Travis was suddenly startled as someone struck the window beside him.

He turned and looked up at the smiling face of Edgar Doyle.

"Why are you sat out here in this car?" Doyle asked.

Travis wound down the window. "Good morning, Mr. Doyle. I am here to resume my interviews. I am ready to speak to whoever else might be available."

"Might I ask to what end, Agent Travis? Haven't you already established that your dead man was a stranger to us, that we have no idea where he came from, why he was here, or what happened to him?"

"No, I have not established that, Mr. Doyle."

Travis wound up the window and started to open the door.

Doyle stepped back. "Am I right in understanding that the carousel, as the location of the body, is the only area of this carnival that is an official crime scene, to use your phrase?"

"At this stage, yes, though other areas may become relevant as I look them over."

"So, how about this? How about I take you on a guided tour of every vehicle, every tent, every corner of our little world, and if you give it the all clear, then we open the carnival again tomorrow evening? Everything save the carousel, that is."

Travis could see no immediate reason to decline such a proposal, and so he said so. "But," he added, "if I suspect that any attempt is being made to obscure anything from me, then I reserve the right to retract my authorization for the carnival to reopen."

"Agreed," Doyle said, and extended his hand.

Travis took the man's hand and they shook.

"Very well," Doyle said. "Let us begin the guided tour, then. I will introduce you to everyone and show you where they sleep, where they practice, where they stow their personal effects and equipment. You go ahead and ask me anything you like, and I will do my best to answer it. But first, we go to my caravan and I will give you the cast of this little drama."

Valeria was absent, and for some reason Travis was disappointed.

"She has gone to Marion," Doyle said.

"I beg your pardon?"

"You saw that Valeria was not here, and you looked a little down."

Travis looked askance at Doyle. This was the second time this had happened, the very real and unsettling feeling that someone could see inside his head.

"I am not reading your thoughts, Agent Travis," Doyle said, as if— once again—answering a question that had not even been voiced. "I am observing what is there to see and interpreting it. I am doing what I am sure you do every day of your life. We all make assumptions, of course, and often we are wrong, but this time I was right, yes?"

Travis nodded. "Yes."

"Very good!" Doyle clapped his hands together. "Then I shall continue to do this, and you will believe me to be a strange and remarkable man of mystery."

"I would prefer it, Mr. Doyle, if we maintained a purely professional relationship here."

"So no games, then?"

"Precisely. No games."

"Oh, how dull your life must be, Agent Travis. To live a life without games and dreams and imagination must be so unbearably routine. I can't even begin to imagine the effort required to keep all those walls around. It must be exhausting."

"I am just fine, sir. Now, to the personnel of the carnival."

Travis withdrew his notebook and walked to the table where he had previously sat with Doyle.

"There is yourself, Miss Mironescu, Mr. Slate, John Ryan and Akiko—"

Travis flipped through a couple of pages and checked her surname.

"Akiko Mimasuya."

"Names, yes. I would have thought you would have appreciated something of their background, perhaps?"

"Only if it is relevant to this case, Mr. Doyle."

"How could it not be? These are, after all, the very people you are investigating, are they not? Investigating as potential suspects, accomplices, at the very least material witnesses to a homicide. I would have imagined that the more you knew of them, the more relevant and valuable their responses to your questions would be." Doyle leaned forward and placed his hands flat on the table. "If, for example, I told you that Mr. Slate's name was not Slate at all, that he was once convicted of perjury, that he has been living under an assumed name for the last twelve years, and that his father was a very well-known counterfeiter... would that change your perspective on the discussion you had with him this morning?"

"What you are telling me is true?"

"No, Agent Travis... well, at least not all of it. I was just making a point."

"Is his name Slate?"

"No, his name is not Slate."

"What is his name?"

"You did not ask him?"

"I asked him what he knew of the events of Saturday evening."

"His name is Harold Lamb. He is from Minnesota, and his father was not a famous counterfeiter at all. In fact, I have absolutely no idea who his father was, though I do know that his mother was a prostitute from Cedar Rapids, Iowa." Doyle smiled. "And now, Mr. Slate, being the bastard child of an Iowan whore, appears to be a very different man indeed, does he not, Agent Travis?"

Travis said nothing.

"And then we have the acrobatic troupe, the Italian brothers, all five of them. In order of descending age, they are Antonio, Giulio, Maurizio, Giancarlo and Gianluigi. Their family name is Bellanca, and yes, they all look the same. They are quintuplets, you see? You see one, you see them all. You see them all, you see just one. I have worked with them for more than five years, and still I am not certain which is which. Then there is our human skeleton, Oscar Haynes. All of seventy-five or eighty pounds, hails out of Chicago, hell of a poker player. Next, you have our resident giant and strongman, six feet eight inches tall, maybe three hundred and twenty pounds. You can't miss him. He's from Budapest, and his name is Gabor Benedek."

"Gabor Benedek is Hungarian?" Travis asked, thinking immediately of Fekete Kutya and the information Dr. Ebner had given him. Even as he wrote Benedek's name in his book he underlined it.

"He is indeed Hungarian," Doyle said. "He has not been with us long. Just a year or so. He was in Hungary in October and November of 1956, during the uprising. His brother was one of the first people shot by Soviet troops outside the Radio Budapest building. His sister was killed by the State Security Police. Gabor was among the two hundred thousand refugees who fled Hungary during that time, and he found his way to America."

"We gave him political asylum, I presume?"

"Why? Are you going to call the authorities, Agent Travis? Are you going to find out if he is here illegally and have him deported?"

"Such an issue is none of my concern at this juncture," Travis said. "If, however, Mr. Benedek is in any way involved in this case, then his nationality and political status will obviously be taken into consideration."

"You are a careful man, Agent Travis. You are well-practiced in saying something without saying anything at all."

"Please go on, Mr. Doyle."

"We have a dwarf. He is four feet and two inches tall, and his name is Chester Greene. He and Gabor work together often. They perform together, often travel in the same car, and sometimes when we have to walk long distances, Gabor will carry Chester in a bag on his back, and if you think I am joking, then I can assure you I am not."

"And Miss Mimasuya?"

"Is Japanese, and I believe has a double-jointed capacity in every limb of her body. You may have seen her practicing."

"I did, yes. It was slightly disconcerting."

"She is made of elastic, it seems, and has performed as a contortionist for much of her life. I think, even as a child, she was working as an acrobat alongside her parents."

"And her parents are still alive?"

"Her parents were killed during the war, Agent Travis. Killed by Americans."

"And John Ryan lost the ability to speak when his tongue became infected, if I remember correctly?"

"Yes, that's right."

Travis leaned back in the seat. "Seems to me that there is a great deal of history here, Mr. Doyle. A great deal of loss and tragedy among such a small number of people."

"Well, I told you earlier that I was not reading your mind, Agent Travis. I can't do that. I have no such ability. Valeria, however... well, she cannot read minds, but she is certainly very perceptive and attuned to the presence of some people. She tells me that you are a man who has also suffered greatly in such a short number of years."

"As I said, Mr. Doyle, I am just fine, thank you very much. My personal life has absolutely no bearing on what I am doing here."

"Oh, I beg to differ, Agent Travis. Your personal life is precisely the reason you are here. Had you not been significantly influenced by your own past experiences, then you would never have taken this job. Everyone does what they do for a reason. Everyone finds their vocation, one way or another, and this—this investigation, this enforcement of the law—appears to be yours. We either choose our jobs, Agent Travis, or our jobs choose us. I think you'll find that holds true in the majority of cases."

"And you, Mr. Doyle? What brought you here? Why are you traveling across America with a carnival?"

Doyle leaned forward until his face was merely a foot from Travis's. "Because I am the devil, you see? I am the devil after whom this carnival is named, and I am on a mission to collect lost souls such as you and bring them to hell."

"Devil or not, sir, you are quite the showman. I asked you the question in all sincerity, Mr. Doyle. Why are you doing this?"

"Does this bear any real relevance to your case, Agent Travis?"

"I don't suppose it does, Mr. Doyle. Not specifically."

"And yet you are interested?"

"I am, yes."

"Very well, then I shall make you a deal. I will tell you my story, or at least as much of it as I am prepared to share with you, and in return you will tell me a little of yours."

"Well, I'm not so sure about that," Travis said.

"What harm can there be in it? We are merely talking, nothing more nor less, and just as you have no guarantee that I will tell you the truth, I have no guarantee that you will tell the truth either."

"Save our word," Travis said.

"And a man is only as good as his word, right?"

"Right."

"So, what's to lose?"

"Very well," Travis said. "You tell me a little of yourself, and I will reciprocate."

"And I shall make some tea," Doyle said, and rose from the bench.

He talked as he busied himself with the pot and cups, as he filled a pan and set it on the stove.

"I am from the south of Ireland," he started. "And that's a place that's seen its fair share of troubles. Religious wars and political divisions for hundreds of years, and yet we have weathered it stoically, somehow managing to retain not only our thirst for a good whiskey, but also our sense of humor." Doyle turned and looked at Travis. "It's a nation of differences, and this last war was something that highlighted the differences. You know that we are two countries, right?"

"Yes, of course," Travis replied, immediately aware that something in Doyle had changed. His voice was more animated, his body language also. Perhaps vanity, perhaps a natural raconteur, he seemed in his element.

"Well, that division, in a land mass that covers about one third of the state of Kansas, has been there since the early 1920s. Unionists, nationalists, the Irish Republican Brotherhood, Sinn Féin, all of them seeing the second war as a means by which their own political goals could be achieved. Those who plotted against the British knew that a rebellion would best be undertaken while the war was actually going on. They hoped to incite a popular uprising, and the greatest support for that, understandably, came from Germany..."

Travis continued to watch Doyle as he spoke. In some strange way, it reminded him of being read to as a child, the way his mother would bring characters to life, the way she would make the voices, the way she would keep Michael hanging off every word that left her lips.

Travis was aware then, for no apparent reason, of how much he missed her.

Doyle brought the teacups to the table and set them down. He took his seat once more and continued talking.

"And so it happened. Brotherhood volunteers and members of the Irish Citizens Army marched into buildings and offices right across Dublin, pronouncing as they went that this was a peoples' uprising, and they demanded freedom from British rule. The British were fierce and uncompromising. Within a week, the rebellion was smashed, much of central Dublin was flattened, and there were more than five hundred deaths. All the key figures of the IRB were arrested, fourteen of them were executed, and though the rebellion itself had failed, it was nevertheless a moment of great significance for the Irish people and their homeland. Those who had been executed became martyrs, and there is nothing more vital for a cause than a martyr. A dead leader can be so much more powerful than a living one, you know?"

"Yes, I can see that," Travis said.

"I was just twenty years old in October of 1917, but I already knew things were changing. Sinn Féin was taken over by a man called Éamon de Valera, the only surviving commander of the 1916 uprising. Britain was in trouble. What would happen throughout the empire if Britain failed to control this small island on its own doorstep? Sinn Féin wanted an independent Irish Republic. Britain was not prepared to give it up. So began a war between the Irish guerrilla forces and the British army that would last until the middle of 1921."

Doyle paused to drink his tea, and Travis—realizing that he had completely forgotten his own—drank also.

"This is all so much history now," Doyle said, "but finally a partition was drawn between the six counties in the northeast and the twenty-six in the south. I was in the north when Germany invaded Czechoslovakia and immediately understood that the south of Ireland would be of great interest to Hitler. There it was, right on the doorstep of the only country that presented an immediate threat to his domination of Europe, and the population could perhaps be seduced by propaganda, made to believe that allegiance to Nazi Germany would give them the freedom they had sought for so long."

Doyle stood and crossed the narrow confine of the caravan to bring the teapot to the table. He refilled Travis's cup, then his own. Before he started speaking again, he lit a cigarette.

"And it was into that cauldron that I was hurled in the early part of 1940, Agent Travis. Finally, we get to the point! I know we Irish have a reputation for talking too much, but sometimes I even surprise myself!"

"Go on," Travis said. "I am honestly fascinated."

"You remember the deal, though?" Doyle said, smiling. "A story for a story was the agreement, was it not?"

"Of course, yes," Travis said. "Please... continue."

"My job, though to call it a job was stretching the term considerably, was to keep the British informed of pro-Nazi allegiances and sympathies in the south. My family came from the west, a town called Kilfenora in County Clare. We descended from a famous line of drunkards and troublemakers, you see? Everyone knew the Kilfenora Doyles, and that was part of the reason the British sent me back." Doyle shook his head and sighed. "People died for reasons; people died for no reason at all. It was a dreadful period of history, and had it not been for you fellows, then it might all have come to nothing."

"I had no idea," Travis said.

"About the war?"

"About you, Mr. Doyle."

"Well, why would you have any idea? I have told you very little about myself, my family..." Doyle paused and smiled wryly. "Case in point, you know nothing at all about my errant and troublesome stepbrother, and that, believe me, is a saga all its own."

"I suppose it's preconceptions," Travis said. "You think you know people. You think you have some idea of who they are, what kind of life they have led, and you learn some small truth and it changes your preconceptions completely."

"Oh, we were busy enough through the whole war," Doyle said. "I investigated the relationship between Francis Stuart and a German intelligence operative called Helmut Clissmann. Clissmann's cover was the German Academic Exchange Commission, arranging cultural exchanges between Irish and German teachers and students, but in reality he was establishing intelligence lines into Ireland, the IRA itself, and Stuart helped him. Stuart even toured Germany, lecturing and teaching, used that position to carry messages to the Abwehr from the IRA's chief of staff, Stephen Hayes."

Doyle smiled, lit another cigarette.

"And so it went on, the lies, the deceptions, the espionage, the aborted planning for an Irish invasion by the Nazis... and I stayed right in the middle of all of it until the war was over. I was sent into France in mid-1943 as well," Doyle added, "but that was for something entirely different."

He paused for a moment, his mind seemingly elsewhere, and his fingers touched the small enamel flower on the collar of his vest. "And that was where I met Valeria. At the time she was all of twenty-seven years old, fierce and passionate and breathtakingly beautiful. She was working with the French-Canadian Resistance team organized and led by Renaud Larouche and Gaston Lepage. They were legendary men, both of them, and I had the great honor of working with them later. However, at that time, I was in France for just a few weeks, but Valeria and I had already begun a relationship before I left. I didn't then see her for another two and a half years. We were actually reunited in England in January of 1946, and that—of all things—was the strangest coincidence you could ever imagine. There had been no communication between us during that time, and I had no idea whether she was even still alive. I *felt* she was. That's all I can tell you. I felt she was still alive, and she believed I was still alive, and there was such a strong connection between us that we knew we would keep on looking for as long as it took."

"So if you were only in France for a few weeks, where did you go then? What did you do for the last two years of the war?"

"Numerous and varied things, and I worked again with Larouche and Lepage, as I said."

"Doing what, exactly?"

Doyle smiled. "Enough questions, Agent Travis."

"At least tell me how was it that you managed to meet Valeria again in London?"

"She can tell that story so much better than I," Doyle replied, "and I feel I have said more than enough to fulfill my end of the bargain."

"Okay, Mr. Doyle. Perhaps one other smaller question... not about your past, but just to satisfy a little curiosity I have."

"Which is?"

"The badge on your lapel," Travis said. "What is that for?"

"That has a significance only I would understand, Agent Travis."

"It's a forget-me-not, isn't it?"

"It is, yes."

"And it has some sentimental value? I don't think I have ever seen you without it."

"You are observant. Let us just say this. Let us say that it is my shield against all ills. It is the thing that makes me invincible."

"I'm sorry?"

"Like your dead man, perhaps. He carried a badge as well, did he not? Perhaps a little more permanent, but a badge all the same."

"You mean the tattoo? So you wear the badge because you are a member of something?"

"Really, that is it for questions, Agent Travis. I am humoring you out of courtesy, not duty or legal obligation. It is now time for a little part of your life to be shared with the world, don't you think?"

"I promise that there is nothing from my life that could even compare to what you've told me."

"I know that that's not true," Doyle said. "You are a man of shadows, are you not?"

"You said that before. Miss Valeria said that as well. What does that even mean?"

"You know what it means, Agent Travis. We see right through you. You are as transparent as a pane of glass. Everyone has a life, and its significance and importance cannot be compared to that of another. They are not connected, and they are not related. The force with which one person is affected by an event is not comparable to the force with which someone else would experience the same event. Does that make sense?"

"Of course it does, yes. We are even discussing such things in our work at the Bureau."

"I would imagine that you are," Doyle said. "Everyone is unique. Everyone responds differently to stimuli. The mental and emotional effect experienced by two people from the same source is entirely different, is it not?"

"Yes, I would agree."

"So, there we have it. Just because you consider it slight or unimportant does not change the fact that I might consider it earth-shattering in its significance."

"Agreed."

"So, tell me something that is of no consequence, Agent Travis, and we will see whether it is actually of no consequence."

"What do you want to know, Mr. Doyle?"

"Whatever you wish me to know, Agent Travis. Sometimes the first thing that comes to mind is the most important, you know? Sometimes you just have to be willing to say what's on your mind..."

19

"The dreams have come back."

Those were the words that left Michael Travis's lips, and even as he heard them, he did not understand why.

"I had them as a teenager," he went on. "Just before I joined the army. I had them then, and then they stopped for a while, but I have always been afraid that they would come back."

Travis paused and looked at Edgar Doyle.

"But they have, and it worries me."

"Because?" Doyle asked.

"Because I do not understand them."

"Do they need to be understood, Agent Travis?"

Travis smiled, waved his hand in a dismissive fashion. "Of course they need to be understood, Mr. Doyle. Everything in life needs to be understood."

"And what of those things that can never be understood?"

"Such as?"

"Déjà vu," Doyle said. "Have you ever experienced déjà vu to such a degree that it is almost religious in its intensity?"

"Yes, I have, as a matter of fact. I don't know that I would use the word *religious*, but I understand what you mean."

"Religion just means a belief, Agent Travis. It doesn't mean church or God or praying or anything else. It just means a belief. When I say religious in its intensity, I just mean that it's almost impossible to believe that you have not been to this place before, that you cannot understand where such a feeling could come from. You know what I'm talking about, right?"

"I do, yes."

"So where does that come from? Why would a human being feel such a thing in a place they had never seen before?"

"I do not know, Mr. Doyle."

"And yet even the term itself—*déjà vu*—means *already seen*. What causes that, Agent Travis? What causes a human being to feel such a thing?"

Travis shook his head. "As I said, I do not know."

Doyle smiled. "Valeria says it is our previous lives reminding us that we are immortal."

Travis laughed, but Doyle did not laugh with him.

"Go on, Agent Travis. Tell me about the dreams."

Travis cleared his throat. "I am in a field," he said. "It is cracked and arid, dried out. There are fissures in the ground. I can see a shadow. At first I thought it was someone else, but now I am starting to think that it might be my own shadow. And I can hear a bird, perhaps a crow. The sound it makes is like someone laughing. And that is all. It comes to me periodically, always vivid, always so very clear in my mind when I wake, and I have no explanation for it at all."

"And it started when you were a teenager?" Doyle asked.

"Yes," Travis replied. "I was thinking of it as you were speaking of your own experiences in the war. You said you went to France in the middle of 1943."

"That's right, yes."

"In November of that year, my mother was sentenced to death for killing my father. That's what I remember most about 1943, Mr. Doyle... that my mother was sentenced to death for murdering my father."

Travis expected some reaction from Doyle—an expression of shock, surprise, a few words of sympathy, condolence perhaps. Something. Anything.

Doyle returned his gaze unerringly, almost without any flicker of recognition in his eyes, almost as if Travis had made some innocuous comment about the weather.

"In August of 1942, when I was fifteen years old," Travis went on, "my mother stabbed my father through the eye with a table knife, Mr. Doyle. She killed him instantly, and then she sent me to fetch the sheriff. She confessed to it as a premeditated act of murder, and so she was tried and sentenced to death. She was executed in August of 1947 in Nebraska State Penitentiary. I saw her the night before she died, and for all but a brief moment, she didn't even know who I was. She killed my father, Mr. Doyle. She killed my father and then she lost her mind completely."

Travis caught himself as his fists clenched and his knuckles whitened. He did not feel good. He experienced a sudden sensation of disorientation and instability. The tension within him was like a hot coal in his chest. He was losing control of his emotions, and he did not like it at all. And then—for just a split second—it was as if he were looking down on himself and Edgar Doyle, as if he were right there against the ceiling of that tiny caravan, a caravan that now seemed inordinately vast, and he was looking down at himself talking to the man who sat facing him.

Then the strangest thing happened, for Doyle looked up *at* him, directed his eyes to the ceiling, and said, "Tell me what happened after your father died, Michael," and even though Travis knew that he was seated on the bench, even though he could feel the bench beneath him, it felt as if he were in both places simultaneously.

And with that question, the simple fact that Doyle used his first name, Travis was suddenly facing the man again.

There was a sensation in his ears, similar to that experienced when taking off or descending in an aircraft. The pressure was there, and then it was gone.

Travis took a sudden deep breath and held it.

Doyle, again implacable, merely watched him for a while and then said, "Whenever you're ready, Agent Travis."

"There are headaches," Travis said. "When I have the dream, I get headaches. Sometimes before, sometimes after." He laughed nervously. "I don't even know why I am telling you this."

Travis hesitated. He felt like a child—somehow fragile, vulnerable. It was not a feeling with which he was familiar, nor a feeling that he liked.

"A long time ago... 1943 again, September, I went back to the house of my childhood, where my father was murdered, and I saw him there. He'd been dead for more than a year, but I saw him sitting right there at the table where he'd died. He spoke to me, Mr. Doyle."

You done fucked the quiff, eh, boy? I seen her a coupla times. Cain't 'member when, but I seen her and figured she'd be good for a party. But you beat me to it, you old dog, and you only sixteen years old.

"What did he tell you?" Doyle asked.

God darn it, boy, you sure as hell is your father's son.

"Agent Travis?"

You know your problem, kiddo. You always thunk too darn much.

Doyle reached out and touched Travis's arm.

Travis snapped to, as if from a reverie. "He told me that I spent too much time thinking," he replied, for some reason completely unable to express the first memory that had come to mind. "He told me what he thought of my mother. He told me that he was inside my head and that I would never be able to get rid of him."

"And did you believe him?"

"Believe him?" he said. "How could I believe him or not believe him? He was a figment of my imagination, Mr. Doyle."

"Imagination is sometimes more powerful than reality, Agent Travis," Doyle said. And then, with a crooked smile, he added, "Or so I have been told."

192

"You're not the first person to tell me that I lack imagination, Mr. Doyle," Travis said.

"Who said that, then? One of your superiors at the Bureau?"

"Mr. Hoover himself."

"Is that so?"

"Yes, it was Mr. Hoover."

"And there's a man with an imagination, if ever there was one," Doyle replied.

"Why do you say that?"

"To create something, you have to imagine it first, do you not?" Doyle replied. "Your Mr. Hoover has been very busy. He has imagined himself to be the conscience of the nation, perhaps the world. He has imagined that he can discover everyone's secrets and hold them secure in his vaults and archives. He has files, Agent Travis. That's what Mr. Hoover has. He has files about you and me and Valeria and Sheriff Rourke and the townspeople of Seneca Falls. Anyone who interests him earns a file, do they not?"

"He believes that the law cannot be enforced without a real appreciation of each individual, and that appreciation comes about as a result of accurate information."

"He is a paranoiac, Agent Travis. Little more than a spy. He has allowed his personal curiosity to become a psychotic obsession."

"I am not able to comment, Mr. Doyle, and I won't."

"Now, if you report my comments to Mr. Hoover, then I might earn myself some more pages in a file, yes? I might even be tempted to have you do that. It sounds exciting. It appeals to me, being a subversive, perhaps even a Communist."

"Now you are the one with the imagination, Mr. Doyle."

"Perhaps it will be contagious, Agent Travis, and perhaps a little contagion of imagination might help you solve this case that is so troubling you."

"Why do you say that? Do I give the impression that it troubles me?"

Doyle laughed suddenly, brazenly. "You wear it like a heavy coat, my friend," he said. "What is the relevance of this case? Why is it so important to find out who this dead man is?"

"If you knew him . . . if he were a friend of yours, even a relative, wouldn't you want to know what happened to him?"

"Perhaps, yes."

"Perhaps?"

"Bodies are frail, Agent Travis. They break very easily. Who knows what happened to him, or why. We die when we die, and usually we die because we deserve it. Either that, or we feel that we have reached the end of our game and we want a new one to play."

"That is a strange viewpoint, Mr. Doyle."

"Strange? I would think that your viewpoint is far stranger, Agent Travis."

"Mine?"

"That a man is just his body. That a man is nothing more than a collection of fat and muscle and bone and chemicals with a street value of about two dollars. That his intelligence, his creativity, his imagination, his vision, his dreams, his ideas come from a few pounds of hamburger inside his skull. That seems to me to be the most far-fetched and ludicrous idea of all, wouldn't you say?"

"It depends..."

"On what, Agent Travis? On what you believe?"

"Yes, I suppose it does depend upon what you believe."

"Oh no, and there lies the rub! It does not depend on what you believe, Agent Travis, but more upon what you *permit* yourself to believe. And permitting yourself to believe that there might be a past and a future for every human being on this planet is entirely dependent upon being willing to experience the fear that comes with such a possibility."

"The fear?"

Doyle nodded sagely, seriously. "Yes, my friend. The fear."

"Fear of what?"

"That there might be some life that you have lived before. That when your body dies, you might discover that your body was nothing more than a shell, a vehicle, an envelope for a message, you know? That there is a future, and that future carries with it the responsibility and consequence of what you have done in the past."

"Reincarnation," Travis said. "Is that what you're talking about?"

Doyle waved aside the question dismissively. "A name. It doesn't have to have a name, Agent Travis. Not everything needs to carry a label, you know? Call it whatever you like; it makes no difference. Just because a table is called a table doesn't make it any more or less of a table."

"But things have order, Mr. Doyle. There is order and disorder—"

"And it seems to me that the crux of many of your own problems have come about as a result of your unwillingness to tolerate the magic of disorder."

"I don't even know what that means," Travis said.

"Oh yes, you do, Agent Travis. You know precisely what that means. Everything in your life is packed up neat and tidy in a little box. The box has been stowed somewhere safe, somewhere where it can be found if needed, and each box has a label. The problem here is that you never want to open the boxes, do you? You never want to go back down the corridor of your past and look inside those boxes. Well, there are some people who will look, and they have been looking for a long, long time. The five senses, Agent Travis, depicted as five horses drawing the chariot of the body, the mind being the chariot's driver. Katha Upanishad, sixth century BC. The Tamil text, Tolkāppiyam, third century, speaking of the sixth sense of *mind*. Āyatana, and the *sense sphere* of the human mind. The Greco-Romans cults, the Eleusinian Mysteries, the history of Esoteric Christianity, Clement of Alexandria and the *disciplina arcane*, Origen's belief in the preexistence of the human soul, alchemy, astrology, theurgy, the demonic magic of *goetia*, the Kabbalah, Rosicrucianism, the Behemenists, and then, as advocated by our dear friend and savior, Mr. Hoover, the supposed benefits of Freemasonry, the *craft* and all it proposes, its history going back to Hiram Abiff, the architect of the Temple of Solomon."

Doyle leaned forward and took Travis's hands. "The good, the bad, the crazy, the brave, the brilliant, and the deranged, my friend. They have been looking for a very long time, and no matter their intention or motivation, they have all wanted answers to the same questions… Who are we? Where did we come from? Why are we here? Where are we going? This is a history so much longer than you and I can even imagine… and what we have here, this ragtag band of troublemakers and subversives, is just another echo of that same song."

Doyle's eyes were alight. Travis was unnerved, but he could not look away.

"Too scary to even contemplate, eh?" Doyle asked. "What if we stepped outside the box and took a walk, Agent Travis? What would happen if we just took a walk beyond the borders?"

"I—I don't know…"

Doyle smiled. He squeezed Travis's hands reassuringly and then released them. He rose to his feet suddenly. He looked at his watch and then smiled enthusiastically.

"It is past lunchtime. Valeria has not returned. We have both been talking for some considerable time. I don't know about you, but I am starving. In fact, there should be some food in the marquee. We could perhaps go and eat with everyone else?"

Travis's chest felt hollow, like a fairground balloon. He was suddenly aware of how hungry he was.

"Very well," Travis said. "I will come and eat with you, and then I can perhaps speak with some of the other personnel."

"Personnel? Really? I would think that they are the most unlikely kind of people to be referred to as *personnel*."

"I am who I am, Mr. Doyle," Travis said, somewhat defensively. "My manner is my manner, and if it appears too formal, then I am sorry. This is just the way I am, and for a short while, you will have to tolerate it."

"Oh, I don't tolerate a great deal, Agent Travis," Doyle replied. "In fact, I would say that my personal philosophy of life compels me to take all those things I find intolerable and change them for the better."

"Well, you will have to exclude me from your philosophy, Mr. Doyle. I am more than happy with who I am, and I have no desire to change."

"Is that so?"

"Yes, Mr. Doyle. That is so."

"Well, perhaps we might be able to stretch your imagination a touch, Agent Travis. After all, even Mr. Hoover himself has requested that much of you."

Doyle led the way out of the caravan and across the field toward the marquee. Already the sound of voices was audible from within, and across the field came the aroma of something that served only to heighten Travis's hunger.

"Aha," Doyle said. "Gabor has been cooking. That, if I am not mistaken, is the smell of *porkolt*. Maybe he will have made dumplings as well. Most excellent."

"*Porkolt.*"

"It is like a stew, perhaps. Beef, maybe chicken. Whichever, it will be good. And you have to drink a glass of wine with it, Agent Travis. If you refuse, you will offend Gabor, and he is six foot eight and three hundred pounds! I am not suggesting you get drunk and dance for us, Agent Travis, merely that you share a small glass of wine with your meal. If nothing else, it will perhaps make these people feel a little less threatened by your presence."

"Perhaps one glass, then," Travis said, "for courtesy's sake."

"For courtesy," Doyle said. "Another gentlemanly quality."

Together they entered the tent, and Doyle greeted Gabor Benedek warmly.

"*Porkolt*, I believe," Doyle said.

The giant nodded.

"Agent Travis will be eating with us, Gabor, and he has yet to experience the wonders of Hungarian cuisine."

"Welcome, Agent Travis," Benedek said, and extended a hand twice the size of Travis's.

Travis's hand was swallowed, crushed, and then returned. Even as they exchanged pleasantries, Travis thought of Fekete Kutya, whether Benedek would know anything of this organization, whether he actually knew something of his dead countryman.

"Get a plate," Benedek said, and indicated crockery and cutlery beside the large pot of stew.

Travis did so, Doyle followed suit, and soon there was a line of people behind them, all waiting to be fed.

20

The return of Valeria Mironescu changed the atmosphere within the central marquee immediately.

No more than five minutes had passed since Travis and Doyle had sat together at one of the tables before she appeared. She was alone, dressed in jeans, a chambray shirt, a suede jacket, and boots.

Doyle rose to take her hand, kissed her on the cheek, asked her to sit. She did so, and Doyle left to get food for her.

"Bring wine!" she called after him.

"Was it a successful trip?" Travis asked.

"Always the little adventure," she said. "Despite their seeming similarity, each town has its own unique identity. Kansas is very different from Colorado, which is very different from Texas or Alabama or... where is it you are from?"

"Nebraska, originally."

"Nebraska, yes. They are all so very different. Each state seems to be its own little country."

"I suppose so, yes."

"How is your *porkolt*?"

"Excellent, really excellent."

"Of course. Gabor only uses the best horse meat."

Travis near-choked, and Valeria started laughing.

"I am teasing you, Agent Travis."

"No horse, then?"

"No, of course not. How could we afford horse meat? He uses only the tiredest old donkeys for the stew."

"I thought it was a little different from the usual," Doyle said. He had reached the table, and he set down a plate before Valeria. He had also brought a bottle of wine and three coffee cups.

"I didn't want to ask Gabor in case he crushed my head like a grape."

Doyle poured wine. He passed the cups around.

"Excuse the absence of glasses," he said.

Travis took the cup tentatively. He felt he should not drink with these people, but he wanted to. A couple of mouthfuls would not hurt, and—as

Doyle had said—such a gesture might ingratiate Travis into their community a little.

Doyle raised his cup for a toast. "To new friends," he said.

"New friends," both Valeria and Travis echoed.

They drank. The wine was good. It reminded him of evenings with Esther, the months before he lost her.

"Where did you go?" Valeria asked.

Travis looked up at her. "Am I so easy to read?" he said.

"One of the easiest, I believe, Agent Travis."

"I was remembering someone."

"You lost them?"

"They died."

"I am sorry to hear it."

"What was her name?"

Travis smiled. "What makes you think it was a girl?"

"Because men never look like that save when they are thinking of lost loves, Agent Travis."

"Her name was Esther. She got very sick, and then she died."

Valeria raised her cup, as did Doyle. "To Esther," she said.

Travis looked at the strange pair facing him—the crazy Irishman, his Romanian *wife*—and it felt for a moment that there, right there and then, that a more heartfelt and sincere acknowledgment was being made for the loss he had suffered than any funeral or memorial service back in Grand Island.

"Yes," he said, his voice a broken whisper. "To Esther." And then he drank from the cup and the cup was empty, and before he knew it, Doyle had refilled the cup and Travis did not protest.

"Eat," Doyle said. "Eat your *porkolt*, some dumplings, drink some wine, and we will talk of other, less difficult matters."

And so Travis ate, and there was nothing for a while but the hubbub and laughter of gathered people, and as he looked around at the adjacent tables—at Akiko Mimasuya and Oscar Haynes, at Harold Lamb from Minnesota whose mother was a prostitute, at Gabor Benedek and the five identical Bellanca brothers, as each of them caught his eye and nodded, smiled, raised a cup in his direction—he felt somehow strangely comforted by their collective presence. He did not know why, and he did not understand it, and it did not matter.

Travis went back to his meal, and when he was done, he looked up at Doyle and Valeria Mironescu and he smiled.

"Thank you for sharing your meal with me," he said. "That was the best meal I have had for some considerable time."

"Tell Gabor," Valeria said, and nodded toward the giant.

Travis looked at Benedek, caught his attention.

"A wonderful *porkolt*, Mr. Benedek," he said. "Truly wonderful."

Benedek smiled, raised his cup. Travis raised his cup also, found it empty, and Doyle refilled it for the third time.

Travis drank.

"So, I left you two alone and what trouble did you cause?" Valeria asked.

"We shared a little history," Doyle said.

"Did he bore you to death with his war stories, what a hero he was, how many lives he saved?"

"A little of the war, Miss Valeria. And I understand you fought with the Resistance in France?"

"I have been fighting my whole life, Agent Travis," she said. "Against the Communists, against the Nazis, against the imperialists, the fascists, and now against mediocrity, banality, ignorance, stupidity, against all the preconceptions that people have about one another. Some of us are born to fight, Agent Travis. Some of us will even start a battle in order to have something to fight for."

"And Agent Travis told me a little of his own life," Doyle interjected. "You were right, my dear. He is indeed a man of many shadows."

Travis waved Doyle's comment aside.

"And how is your case progressing, Agent Travis?" Valeria asked.

"Beyond ascertaining the significance of the design I found on the dead man's body, there is very little else."

"And you know what it means?"

"I do, yes."

"You can tell us, perhaps?" Doyle asked.

Travis saw no reason not to divulge some small part of the information he had gleaned. "The dead man was part of a Hungarian criminal organization known as Fekete Kutya, or Black Dog."

"Is that so?" Valeria asked. She turned and called out to Benedek. "Gabor, come here a minute."

Benedek joined them at the table. Seated facing him, Travis felt like a child.

"You know of an organization called... what was it?"

"*Fekete*—"

"Fekete Kutya," Benedek interjected. "Yes, I know of them, but I am surprised to hear that name here."

"Apparently, the dead man was part of this group," Valeria explained.

Benedek was visibly surprised.

"What do you know of this?" Travis asked.

"Not a great amount," Benedek explained. "I know *of* them. They are criminals and killers. I have no personal history with them."

"But you know of them because..."

"Because everyone knows of them, Agent Travis. There are stories about them, the things they have done, the influence they have over the police in Budapest. That is all."

"You have not been here long, have you, Mr. Benedek?"

"Not long, no."

"And yet your English is excellent."

"I left Hungary in January of last year. My father was a professor of literature at the University of Budapest, and we spoke English at home, even as children. My father's brother came to America in the twenties and raised his family in a place called Aurora in Illinois. He owns a restaurant there. That's where I went after the uprising. I was with my uncle for some weeks, and then I met Edgar and Valeria in a town called De Kalb, and I decided to travel with them. Like Valeria, I have the Eastern European gypsy in my blood, and I cannot get rid of him." He smiled, his expression somehow pensive. "Every time I stop moving, he starts to scratch at my soul."

"And your own parents... they are still alive?"

Benedek shook his head. "No, Agent Travis, they are dead. My family is Jewish, and he and my mother were murdered in Auschwitz in June of 1944."

"The Holocaust," Travis said.

"Indeed, the Holocaust. My grandparents also, several aunts, uncles, cousins... In fact, when the war ended, there were very few of us Benedeks left at all. My brother and my sister both survived, but my brother was shot by the Soviets and my sister was killed by the State Security Police."

Travis shook his head in disbelief. "Is there no end to the tragedy in your life, Mr. Benedek?"

"My life is no better or worse than anyone's here, Agent Travis. There are some who say it is our lot to suffer in this life and that we will be rewarded in the next."

"Do you believe that?" Travis asked.

"I *want* to believe it," Benedek said, "if not for me, then for my parents and the rest of my family who are dead."

Travis reached out and placed his hand on Benedek's forearm.

"I did not mean to cause you any upset, Mr. Benedek. I am sorry if recounting these events has troubled you."

Benedek gripped Travis's shoulder with a huge hand. "If you had upset me, I would have just crushed your head like an apple!" He laughed, lifted the wine bottle, and refilled the cups on the table.

"I think I've had more than enough wine," Travis said.

Benedek looked stony-faced and then raised his hand over Travis's head.

"Drink," he said, "or your head will be crushed!"

They laughed, all of them, and they drank the wine, and then Benedek rose from the bench and started clearing away plates and cups from the other tables.

"Can I help you?" Travis said.

"It is good. You should go about your business, Agent Travis. You have a dead Hungarian killer to identify, and that is far more important than washing plates."

"And I have matters to attend to also," Doyle said as he rose from the bench.

Travis rose also, watched Doyle and Valeria Mironescu leave the marquee and head back toward the Westfalia.

Within less than a minute Travis was alone, and he looked out through the doorway at the landscape before him. All of a sudden, it seemed bleak and desolate, as if there were nothing at all for him beyond the canvas walls of this tent.

He sat down again, drained the cup before him, and then he reached for the bottle of wine.

21

Travis sat at the small table in his room. The typewriter before him remained silent. It was Thursday evening, and here he was trying to type a report that should have been completed the previous day. He remembered leaving the marquee alone and walking back to his car. Then he must have fallen asleep. That would have been the only explanation, for the next thing he recalled was the fact that it was almost dark and he was very cold. He had drank perhaps half a bottle of wine, and he had passed out. That was the truth. There was no excusing such lack of professionalism. He did not feel so much guilty as slightly ashamed of himself.

Travis knew he had to straighten things out, get things back on an even keel. Permitting himself to be drawn into any kind of personal relationship with these people could do nothing but compromise the integrity of the investigation.

Travis tried to focus on the report, but his mind was elsewhere.

The fact that his attention was also drawn to the single sheet of paper beside his typewriter, upon it the word *regulus*, was no help. He still struggled with the explanation he had been given by Saxon and Beck. He was still haunted by the possibility that someone had done this, that there had been no instance of sleepwalking, that it had been a direct effort to influence the direction of his investigation.

Travis turned the page over. He could not think about it. He had to focus on what was real, what lay there within the borders of the probative and credible.

The simple fact that Doyle, Mironescu, and Benedek had all possessed some direct or indirect connection to military or paramilitary activities had no bearing on the case, save to recognize the fact that they were all familiar—to a greater or lesser degree—with the very physical aspect of war. What did that suggest? That they were all capable of killing a man? Perhaps, perhaps not. Again, so much hinged on the identity of the man, and that identification was paramount. Travis believed himself sufficiently divorced from the *personality* of this case to be able to let go if it were determined to be of nonfederal interest. If he was recalled to

Kansas, would it concern him? No, not at all, except if his recall were in some way a reflection of his failure to fulfill his duty. That could not be allowed to happen. Today would be different. Today would be a model day.

Travis looked over his notes. He was interested to speak next with the Thin Man, Oscar Haynes. Then there was the dwarf, Chester Greene, the contortionist, Akiko Mimasuya, and the five Bellanca brothers. Harold Lamb, aka Mr. Slate, would need another visit, but not as yet.

Travis left the report undone; it could wait until later, and then he would summarize the results of both days' interviews.

Downstairs, he asked Danny McCaffrey for the use of a private phone line.

"There's one back in the kitchen," he told Travis.

Alone, Travis called the Kansas office, asked for Tom Bishop.

"Travis," Bishop said. "About time we heard from you. Got the information you sent through, and yes, looks like your dead guy belongs to some crime gang."

"They're called the Fekete Kutya," Travis interjected. "It means Black Dog. From what I have been able to establish, they are a Hungarian crime organization."

"Good work, Travis. That's more than we had. We were simply able to establish that this kind of tattooing is employed to denote membership of certain Eastern European gangs. So where are we with this now? We any further forward on finding out who he was?"

"No, sir," Travis replied. "I am going to have to ask for assistance on that. I sent through the prints, and I am wondering if they can be run on the system."

Bishop paused before replying. "It hasn't yet been confirmed as a federal matter, Agent Travis. Until that is done, I do not see it's possible to utilize Bureau resources."

"But my concern is that without Bureau resources, we will not be able to identify the deceased. Without accurate and confirmed identification, there will be little chance of determining where he came from, why he was here, where he was going. That will inhibit determination of—"

"Agent Travis?"

"Yes, sir?"

"Stop talking for a moment, and listen."

Travis held his tongue. Bishop's tone had changed ever so slightly.

"Have you stopped for just a second and asked yourself why Section Chief Gale assigned you to this case? Not only to this case specifically, but alone, and as a senior special agent?"

Travis said nothing, knowing that he could very easily answer the question incorrectly. Better not to take the risk.

"You are a good agent, Travis, no doubt about it. You follow the rules, you color inside the lines, and you follow protocol and Bureau procedure to the letter. However, it has to be said that despite all the best advice, all the rules and regulations, no advancement in investigative technique was ever brought about by those who did precisely what they were told and only what they were told. Are you following me?"

"Yes, sir, of course."

"You recall meeting Mr. Hoover?"

"I do, sir, yes," In truth, Travis could remember it word for word.

"Something about lacking imagination, remember?"

"Yes, sir."

"What did he mean, Travis? What did the director mean when he said that?"

"I'm sure that—"

"I'll tell you, Agent Travis. I'll tell you what he meant. He meant that you possessed potential, that he saw a great future for you, yet such a future would perhaps be inhibited by your routine and predictable approach—"

"But, sir, I—"

"You remember the Scarapetto case, Travis?"

"Yes, sir."

"We followed your lead on that one, Travis. You stepped outside of your fixed ideas for just a moment, and you found the Jarvis woman. You made a decision in that kitchen that could have resulted... well, let's just say that it might not have turned out as well as it did. That specific case is one of the reasons you are out there in Seneca Falls, Agent Travis, and that is one of the reasons I will not be able to assist you with federal resources until *you* determine that this is a federal case. If I do not operate in this way, then anyone might as well come along here and utilize federal resources and appropriations to find lost cats and dogs."

Travis did not reply; he could hear Bishop breathing.

"Are we clear on this, Agent Travis?"

"It's a test, sir."

"It's a murder investigation, Agent Travis."

"Yes, sir, but from what you've said— "

"I have advised you to use your imagination, Agent Travis. Sometimes, the use of one's imagination allows for the possibility that you do not communicate everything undertaken in the field to determine the truth."

Travis opened his mouth to ask another question and then decided against it. He had the message loud and clear. This *was* a test. This was his trial by fire. If he did this, if he actually conducted and concluded this investigation alone, then who knew what he would be offered? It unnerved him a little, but it also excited him.

"So, are we done asking questions, Agent Travis?"

"Yes, sir. We're done."

"Good. I am glad to hear that. So, let me tell you what I want from you. I want you to vigorously investigate this homicide. I want you to vigorously investigate the people that were present when this body was found. I want you to submit one final report. I do not want daily situation reports. I do not want interview transcripts. I want you to spend your time as an investigator, not as an office boy. I want you to act alone. I want you to use whatever resources you deem fit to employ, but they cannot include this office, nor the office in Wichita. Expenses will be met by the Bureau, within reason, of course, and we want to see this matter addressed and resolved with the greatest expediency."

"Yes, sir," Travis said.

"Good. So, let's get out there and solve a murder, Agent Travis."

"Yes, sir."

The line went dead.

Travis sat there at Danny McCaffrey's kitchen table with the receiver in his hand. He stood up, replaced it in the cradle on the wall, and then walked to the window. From there he could see out into a small yard behind the hotel.

He knew what was going on now. He smiled to himself. He would have done better to ask no questions at all, but if this was what it had taken to level the playing field, then so be it.

He was being given free rein to run this case as he saw fit. Bishop, as his supervisor, Gale as his section chief, perhaps even the director himself, wanted to see what Michael Travis was capable of when he was let off the leash.

Nevertheless, the forward progress of this investigation was almost exclusively dependent upon the identification of the dead man. It seemed realistic to now move forward on the basis that he was indeed Hungarian, that he did belong to this organization, Fekete Kutya, that he had himself murdered seven people.

Travis went upstairs to his room. He sat on the edge of the bed. He knew that he possessed nothing of any real worth. Doyle and Mironescu had said nothing to either incriminate or absolve themselves, nor Slate, nor Benedek. In fact, the only striking thing about any of their testimony, for want of a better word, was the simple lack of reaction to this situation. These people ran a carnival. The carnival traveled the United

States. A dead man had been found beneath a carousel, stabbed in the back of the neck, and there had been no uproar, no drama, nothing. It was almost as if they were taking the whole thing in their collective stride. Maybe that was down to the simple fact that each of them had come from backgrounds where such things as unexplained deaths were really not that noteworthy. There had been talk of Nazis in Ireland, the French Resistance movement, Auschwitz, the Hungarian uprising. It was as if each of these people had come rushing out of some hot cauldron of violence and mayhem, and one more dead body was of no significance at all.

No, there was too little that made sense and too much that confounded Travis for him to pass off their lack of reaction as anything other than complicity or collusion. These people knew *something*, and they were hiding it well.

He had no choice now but to continue his questioning. Oscar Haynes, the human skeleton, was next. Travis was curious to see what he had to say for himself, whether he too hailed out of some terrible past, whether he too was running away from a history of violence and drama.

There was a time for thought, and there was a time for action.

Travis got up and put on his jacket.

22

Despite the lateness of the evening, Oscar Haynes had been all too willing to accede to Travis's request for an interview. Travis met with him in the marquee.

"So what is it that you want to know?" Oscar Haynes asked.

"You were here when the body was found, Mr. Haynes."

"Yes, I was," Haynes replied. "I was not near the carousel, but I heard the commotion and came over. I hung around until the sheriff turned up, and I saw them bring the body out. I know it was akin to rubbernecking as you pass a car crash, but you sort of can't help it, can you? Natural human curiosity wins over every time." He smiled sardonically, and with a sweeping gesture of his hand, he added, "And that's the reason people keep coming to things like this."

"Meaning?"

"They want to know if we are real, Agent Travis."

"If you are *real*?"

"We have been doing this for centuries. We are the caravan of lost souls and castaways. We are the ones who float at the edge of society and are viewed with equal amounts of suspicion and curiosity."

"Can I ask about your own background, Mr. Haynes?"

"You can ask, for sure. Whether or not I tell you the truth depends upon whether or not you give me cause for concern."

"I am sorry."

Haynes leaned forward. As he did so, not only did he place his hands on the table between them, but he further exposed his wrists. They were so very thin, almost painfully so, and Travis reacted visibly.

"We upset you, don't we? Me and Mr. Slate with his fourteen fingers, and Akiko when she turns herself inside out. But all of that is nothing compared to the way Doyle and his crazy woman seem to see inside your mind."

"Crazy woman?"

Haynes laughed and looked directly at Travis, and there was something altogether disturbing in his expression. His face was a skull, near as damn it, and his eyes were shadowed and sunken. Haynes was right;

these people did unnerve Travis, but not in the way that they believed. Each of them, for no explicable reason, made him feel transparent. They did indeed play his own insecurities against him, and that was the reason he had so easily been taken in by Doyle's charms. That's why he had shared food and wine with them. They made him feel as though he had to earn their cooperation. They were legally bound to cooperate. The law was the law, and they were obligated to uphold and abide by that law as much as anyone else. He—Michael Travis—was the Bureau representative here, and he would dictate the terms of play.

"So why have they sent you, Agent Travis? Tell me that much at least."

"I am surprised you are asking me. You already know why I am here."

"Apparency and reality are not necessarily the same. Why you think you are here and why you are actually here might not be similar at all." Haynes nodded his head. "I know who you are, Agent Travis. Well, I say I *know* who you are, and that is not entirely true. I know of you. I have heard your name before."

"You have?"

"I am from Chicago, Agent Travis. I ran with a certain crowd. I floated around the edges of that scene for a while, and then I got out."

"What scene, Mr. Haynes?"

"The Chicago scene. The hoodlums and bootleggers and button men. I knew all of them—Capone, Bugs Moran, McErlane, Shorty Egan, and Morrie Keane. Hell, I did a handful of years in Menard Correctional, occupied the same cell that van Meter had occupied back in twenty-four. I even met Dillinger one time, a year or so before he was killed."

"And you know of me because?"

"Because I heard about what happened to Tony Scarapetto…"

A brief flash in Travis's mind. Standing there in the backyard behind the Jarvis farm. Gun in his hand. That sense of rage and injustice boiling inside his chest, how he could do nothing but pull the trigger.

God darn it, boy, you sure as hell is your father's son.

Travis flinched, as if shocked by a current of electricity.

"You were the one who killed him, right?"

Travis focused on Haynes's face, corralled his thoughts. "I did, yes."

"I remember hearing about it, remember your name, not so different from Melvin Purvis, you see? You ever meet Melvin Purvis?"

"I did not, no," Travis said, feeling his heart beating just a little faster.

"Hardheaded son of a bitch. No sense of humor. You'd think, wouldn't you, that after killing Dillinger, after actually getting Public Enemy Number One, he'd lighten up, right? No, sirree, he was just as much of a ball breaker after that as he was before."

"Why did you go to Menard, Mr. Haynes?" Travis asked, wishing to steer the conversation away from Tony Scarapetto.

"I was a smuggler, Agent Travis. Pure and simple. I drove those trucks down from the Canadian border into Chicago for more than ten years."

"And you were caught?"

"In a manner of speaking, yes."

"Meaning what?"

"I got tired of the life. I gave it up. I had to give it up. I saw too many dead guys, too much blood, and it started to make no sense."

"So you gave yourself up?"

"I allowed myself to be caught for something dumb, but it got me out of the loop. You don't get out of that racket unless you get killed or go to jail, Agent Travis. I got myself busted on a seven-to-ten beef, did five years in Menard, got paroled, and stayed the hell out of Chicago until I was cleared to leave the state. Then I just traveled a while until I met this crowd of hobos and dropouts. I've been here ever since."

"And you earn a living by being—"

"The skinny guy?" Haynes laughed. "Oh no, the skinny thing is just for effect, you know? That's just to charm the ladies, right? No, sir. I am the illusionist. I am the one who draws a veil of disbelief and wonderment around you and will not let you go."

"You do tricks?"

Haynes smiled at Travis as if he were a child. There was something almost *disappointed* in that expression. "Yes, Agent Travis. I do tricks."

"I didn't intend for that to sound derogatory, Mr. Haynes. I am just not quite sure what you mean."

"Edgar tells me that you are considering permitting us to open the carnival again tomorrow night."

"I am considering it, yes."

"Well, you should let us do that, Agent Travis. You should come and see the show for yourself. It is quite a thing, let me tell you."

"I will make a decision, Mr. Haynes, and I will let Mr. Doyle know that decision as soon as it has been made."

"I think you might be surprised, Agent Travis, but then you might see some of what you have been looking for all along."

"What do you mean by that, Mr. Haynes? I might see something that relates to the death of this man last Saturday?"

"Is that why you are here, Agent Travis? To find out who killed that man? I heard from Gabor that he was part of some foreign crime gang."

"That may well be the case, yes. Can you please explain what you mean, Mr. Haynes? You say that if I allow the carnival to run on Friday night, I will see some of what I have been looking for. You also seem to be questioning whether my presence here is solely for the purpose of investigating this homicide. What are you trying to say?"

"I am not trying to say anything, Agent Travis."

"You are implying something, Mr. Haynes—"

"Did you never tire of it, Agent Travis?"

"Tire of what?"

"The lies, the falsehoods, the pretense, the bullshit."

"I'm sorry. I don't understand, sir."

"No need to be sorry, Agent Travis. Sorry is the very last thing you have to be here."

Haynes looked away for a moment, as if his attention had been distracted by something, and then he turned back to Travis.

"Do you see a pattern here, Agent Travis?" he asked. "Do you see a common thread weaving its way through all of this? These people," he went on, indicating beyond the tent with a wave of his hand. "These strange, crazy, inexplicable people. Do you not see the thread that ties all of us together?"

"I see a similarity in their background, perhaps," Travis replied.

"The violence, right? The brutality of their lives. Gabor's family, the things that Edgar and Valeria did during the war. The history I left behind in Chicago. You're talking about these things, right?"

"Yes."

"Those things might have been the catalyst, Agent Travis. The *force majeure*, if you will. Bodies at rest and in motion, right?"

"Explain what you mean, Mr. Haynes."

"We take a path, Agent Travis. This road you are on, this career, this life you are living, did you ever stop to think why?"

"Yes, of course. We all think about why we do things."

"That, sir, is where I beg to differ. I would say that the vast majority of people just sleepwalk through the entirety of their lives, following the rules and regulations that have been laid down for them, abiding by the consensus of opinion, never once challenging the way of things. What life is, and what people are fooled into believing that life is, are not the same thing at all, Agent Travis."

"I don't see what this has to do with the man who was killed," Travis said, feeling a sense of exasperation clouding his thoughts.

"Oh, I disagree," Haynes replied. "I think this has everything to do with the man who was killed. Who was he? Where did he come from? Where was he going? What external factor influenced his life to such a degree that his life was brought to an end?"

"Those are the precise questions that I am trying to get an answer to,

Mr. Haynes, and that, whether you think it or not, is the precise reason I am here."

Haynes smiled. "Of course it is."

"Once again, simply by the tone of your response, you are suggesting that what I am saying is not true."

"Quite the contrary, Agent Travis. I am doing no such thing. I have never once questioned what you are saying. You believe it is the truth, and there we have it. We all live the same way."

"We are getting off the point, Mr. Haynes," Travis interjected.

"If you say so."

"So, here it is, a simple question, Mr. Haynes. Are you—or have you ever been—familiar with the deceased?"

"No, sir, I have not."

"Had you ever seen him before?"

"No, sir."

"Did you see him on Saturday night before he was found dead?"

"No, sir, I did not."

"Before Mr. Benedek mentioned it to you, had you ever heard of this Hungarian criminal organization known as Fekete Kutya?"

"No, Agent Travis, I had not."

"Has anyone said anything to you before or since this incident that leads you to believe that they know something of the origins of this man, where he came from or what he was doing here?"

"No, sir, they have not."

"Do you possess any suspicion, substantiated or otherwise, that indicates that anyone within this community is aware of some fact relating to this case that they have not communicated?"

"No, not at all."

Travis nodded. "Okay, Mr. Haynes. Those are the questions I wanted to ask you."

"Really?"

"Yes, sir."

"You do not want to know what I think?"

"If it bears relevance to this case, yes, of course."

"Perhaps it does not bear an immediate relevance to this case, Agent Travis, but I believe it bears relevance."

"Very well. What is it that you think?"

"Actually," Haynes said, "now that I consider it, it might be a whole lot better for you to see what I think."

"You have something to show me?"

"Oh, I think we all have something to show you, Agent Travis."

"Mr. Haynes, whatever you have to say, just say it."

"Let the carnival run tomorrow night, sir, and I think certain things might become a great deal clearer."

"Meaning what, exactly?"

"I am saying that if you allow us to show you what the carnival is, then you might have a change of viewpoint that will allow you to see things differently. I believe that the Carnival Diablo might just light a fire among the last dying embers of your imagination."

Haynes smiled. "And now, if there are no more immediate questions, I shall go." He rose from the bench and walked toward the marquee doorway. "Perhaps you would like for me to send Chester Greene to speak with you?"

Travis looked up. "Yes," he said. "Mr. Greene. That would be most appreciated."

"I shall tell him now," Haynes said, and then there was a knowing expression in his eyes, as if he knew very well that Travis was lost for words.

23

Despite his diminutive stature, Chester Greene possessed a strangely disarming charisma.

He took a seat facing Travis and waited patiently for Travis to speak, as if he possessed not a single concern in the world.

"This is just routine procedure, Mr. Greene," Travis began. "I need to speak to everyone who was working at the carnival on Saturday night."

"Ask away, Agent Travis."

"Where are you from?"

"Originally? Originally, I'm from Oklahoma City. Wasn't there long, however. My father had me shipped off as soon as he could get someone to take me. My mother was a dwarf, had worked in circuses most of her life. She got pregnant, my father stuck by her, but once she was gone, he didn't want the problem."

"They were not married?"

"No, sir, they were not."

"And how old were you when your mother died?"

"Is this really necessary, Agent Travis? What does my personal history have to do with the fact that there was a dead man under the carousel?"

"Nothing, to be honest. I was merely interested, Mr. Greene. I am sorry if I have offended you."

"Offended? Good God, no! It would take a great deal more than a few questions to offend me, Agent Travis. Besides, it's only fair. I understand that you talked to Edgar, and you were willing to discuss a little of your own personal history."

"But I spoke with him in confidence—"

"Hey, what you gonna do? Get a lawyer? Nothing is in confidence here, Agent Travis. They want to play their games, then they can go ahead. Let's not let them in, eh? Best way to keep them out is to have no secrets inside, right?"

"I have no idea what you're talking about, Mr. Greene."

"Pay no mind to me, Agent Travis. Most of what I say is nonsense, and you really shouldn't take it seriously."

"Well, okay. Now to Saturday night."

"Hell of a thing, eh?"

"You had never seen him before? Not that night, or perhaps some other night earlier in the week?"

"No."

"And nothing's been said by anyone that suggests what he was doing here?"

"Oh, I think it's pretty obvious what he was doing here, Agent Travis."

"It is?"

"He was the reason, was he not?"

"The reason for what?"

"The reason for you being here."

"I am sorry, Mr. Greene. Once again I seem to find myself taking part in a conversation that seems to be some other conversation entirely."

"You'll figure it out, Agent Travis, I'm sure. You just need to use your imagination."

Travis inhaled slowly. The very worst thing he could do was let these people see that they were getting to him. Yesterday he had been willing to grant them the benefit of the doubt. But now the rules of this game had changed. They knew something. Perhaps not all of the truth, but some of it.

"You try my patience, Mr. Greene."

"And you try ours, Agent Travis. We are not responsible for the death of this stranger. He came here to do harm, perhaps. He came here en route to somewhere else. Who knows? Certainly no one here. We are citizens of the United States of America, just as you are. We have livelihoods to maintain. You are preventing us from going on about our business because of something that does not matter—"

"You think a human life does not matter, Mr. Greene?"

"I think your dead man believed that, yes. Gabor told me that this man belonged to an organization that thought nothing of taking human life. In fact, his membership alone required that he be a murderer. Is that not so?"

"If what Mr. Benedek says is true of this organization, then yes, there is a good possibility that the dead man was a killer."

"An eye for an eye, was it not? It's been said that a man dies when he's meant to die. Some say that Dillinger would've died outside the Biograph Theater irrespective of whether Melvin Purvis or Sam Cowley had been there to meet him. They say he would've been hit by a truck as he crossed the street. Maybe a piano would have fallen from the sky and crushed him like a bug. Oscar Haynes told me that he met Dillinger one time. Said that if ever there was a man carrying a bullet with his own name on it, then it was John Dillinger. Perhaps your carousel man had a rendezvous with fate, Agent Travis, and we were just the sideshow attraction."

"I appreciate such a possibility, Mr. Greene, of course. Man has believed such things for as long as man has been around, but—"

"You don't believe in destiny, then, Agent Travis?"

"I believe in the destiny that a man creates for himself."

"Well, perhaps your Hungarian knew his time was up. Perhaps he finally saw the error of his ways and knew that the only way to curtail his own homicidal tendencies was to end his life."

"He did not commit suicide, Mr. Greene. He was murdered."

"A suicide can be a murder, Agent Travis, and a murder can be a suicide. People do allow themselves to be murdered, right? People do find ways and means to make others responsible for the most terrible things, simply to make them then carry that burden of guilt for the rest of their lives."

"The only thing you need to assure me of, Mr. Greene, is that you have no information that would be of assistance in resolving this homicide."

"I don't know that for sure, sir."

"Meaning what?"

"I have some ideas of what might have happened, though whether or not they bear any connection to the reality of what happened I do not know."

"You have a theory."

"Several, Agent Travis."

"And are any of these so-called theories possessive of substantive or provable evidence, even a fragment perhaps?"

"I think we'd agree that hypothesis is the mother of invention, Agent Travis, not necessity. I would say that hypothesis is the mother and bravery is the father, wouldn't you? Be brave with one's hypotheses, and one might find the truth."

"And that would be?"

"I don't know. It is not my investigation, Agent Travis, and I don't know what you are trying to learn here."

"The identity of a dead man, Mr. Greene, and who might have been responsible for his murder."

"That would be of no concern to me. I would want to know why fate brought him here."

Chester Greene smiled, again without the slightest sense of sarcasm, and he maneuvered himself off the bench and stood up. He was no taller on his feet than he had been when he was seated. That, in itself, was disconcerting. Travis suddenly felt like a bully, as if he had taken advantage of the man's stature and tried to overwhelm him. He had done no such thing, of course, but he couldn't help but feel that way.

"I might be small," Greene said, once again giving Travis the impression that his innermost thoughts were being divined, "but I have a big mind. Bigger than most people, I have to say. My mind encompasses what has happened, what is happening, sometimes what I believe *will* happen. If that's what you want to know, then there it is. What you imagine is true, Agent Travis, though you are afraid to let yourself believe it. Come to the carnival. Let it open. Let us regale you, and then you can go away and think about it in a different light."

"I am of a mind to disallow the carnival to open tomorrow night, I have to say, Mr. Greene. I have found your responses, and those of Mr. Haynes, to be obtuse, unhelpful and, as far as I can see, intentionally confusing—"

"Let it go, why don't you? You're not the first who's tried this, and I am sure you won't be the last—"

"Tried what, Mr. Greene?"

"To get at the truth, Agent Travis."

"Of the dead man? What are you talking about?"

"The dead man? No, of course not! Open your eyes, Agent Travis. Open your eyes wide, and you might just see how far beyond one dead Hungarian this really goes. This is nothing more than a charade, a theater within which we are all appearing. It is very modern, perhaps, because none of us have been given lines nor character names. Perhaps we are all supposed to play ourselves. What do you think, Agent Travis?"

"I think, sir, that you are talking about something of which I have absolutely no understanding."

Greene stepped forward. He grabbed Travis's hand. His grip was firm and unyielding, and though Travis could have wrested free he did not feel the impulse to.

"Say that again, Agent Travis. Look at me directly and say that again."

"Say what?"

"What you just said."

Travis stared back at Greene. He did not even blink. "I said that you were talking about something of which I have absolutely no understanding."

Greene did not respond for a moment. He simply continued to look right back at Travis.

Finally he nodded, released Travis's hand, and smiled.

"I believe you," Greene said. "Though that does not necessarily mean that this will be any easier for you to deal with."

"Deal with what?"

"The truth, Agent Travis. Isn't that what we are all looking for?"

"Yes, indeed. The Hungarian—"

"You still think this is about him? Seriously, Agent Travis, you really are very limited in your appreciation of what is actually happening here, aren't you?"

"We are not here being friendly, Mr. Greene. We are here to talk about how someone's life came to a brutal end at your carnival—"

"I think not, sir," Greene said.

"You are saying that he did not die at the carnival?"

"That's right."

"How do you know that?"

"Am I right?"

"I am not disagreeing with your statement, Mr. Greene, but I want to know why you think he died elsewhere."

"Because I understand some of the rules of how these things work."

"Explain what you mean."

"Not yet."

"Mr. Greene—"

"If you're asking me to tell you where he died, I have not the faintest clue."

"I have no wish for further games, Mr. Greene. Not now, not later, not ever. I want you to tell me the truth of what you know. I want you to explain to me how you are so certain that this man did not die at the carnival."

"I am not *so* certain, as you say, Agent Travis. I have a suspicion, and that suspicion is based on some considerable experience of what has been done to people like us."

"People like you?"

"We are the outsiders, Agent Travis. We are the ones nobody wants because we cannot be explained. Society is compelled to label everything, and yet we not only cannot be labeled, we refuse to be. They cannot let us be. They see something here that scares them, but they see in it some kind of potential to use it to their advantage. And if you wish for further explanation, then do what I asked of you, and you will see."

"Let you open the carnival again tomorrow night."

"Yes, Agent Travis. Let us open the carnival."

"And if I do, then what?"

"Then we will give you a show you will never forget, Agent Travis."

"Is that so?"

"I believe it is."

"And is there anything you can give me in return for my permission to do this?"

"You have had a hard life. It shows in everything you do, everything you say, everything you are. I am sorry you had such a hard life. Not for

218

how you feel, Agent Travis, but for how it has limited what you permit yourself to feel. You are so closed, so narrow in your view, so limited in your perspective. You trust your eyes, your eyes, your certainties. I understand it completely, you know? I might not sound like I do, but I do. But sometimes what you see is an illusion, and illusions can be quite as convincing as any reality."

"What are you willing to give me, Mr. Greene? If I let you open the carnival, what will you give me?"

Greene reached out and took Travis's hand once more. There was a sense of electricity that seemed to emanate from his skin, and Travis shuddered.

"I will give you this, Agent Travis," Greene said. His voice was low, and he leaned forward in such a way that Travis could do nothing but lean further toward him.

"You are not your father's son, Michael Travis. What you most fear does not run in the blood, my friend. That is a myth. You are not him, and he is not you. You are free to be yourself."

Travis snatched his hand away from Greene, almost as if he had been electrocuted.

"Wha—"

Greene stepped back.

Travis fell silent. There were no words to express what he felt.

Greene's expression was implacable. "We are inviting you to the carnival, Agent Travis. In fact, you are the guest of honor. It will start at seven precisely. Don't be late."

Greene left him sitting there—speechless, almost without thought. Something had happened. Something he could not explain. Something he did not *want* to explain. He believed that if he allowed himself to, he would just cry. He did not dare, because he knew that it was out of his control, and he might just go on crying forever.

All he could see was his mother's face—the way she looked back at him on the day before she died. That moment—that single, simple moment— when he made a connection to her, when the madness somehow released its grip for just a second and she became the mother he remembered and loved.

The pain was not physical. It was mental, emotional, and somehow even spiritual. It was as if there were two Michael Travises: the real one and the ghost of the past. The ghost of the past was nothing more than some representation of who he might have become had everything been different. His father had been good and kind and decent and he did not drink and fuck other women, and he loved his wife and treated her well, and Michael had grown up in a house where the things that mattered

219

the most were kindness and decency and trust. He had gone to school, to college, and he had worked hard and gotten good grades, and he had never gone to the army or to the Bureau, and now he was married with children of his own, and he had a job someplace that mattered. He had a job that did not entail looking into the deepest and darkest recesses of the human condition, there to find the worst thing that human beings could do to one another. He did not know murderers and serial killers; he did not know sociopathic bank robbers and child abductors; he did not know thieves and liars and rapists and those who would stab you through the heart for a handful of dollars and never give you a second thought.

He did not know these people, and he had no desire to know them.

But the past was all that it was, and it could not be changed. The past belonged to his mother, his father, to Esther and everyone else he had left behind.

The past was a different country, and he could no longer speak their language.

Michael Travis took a deep breath and exhaled slowly.

He rose from the bench and left the marquee. He crossed the field to his car and got inside. He started the engine and pulled away toward the road.

He wanted to get away from here. That was all he knew. Everything else had vanished—every certainty, every thought, every feeling.

Perhaps for the first time in his life, he just wished to be completely and utterly alone.

24

He dreams of Japanese lanterns.

They are strung together from the back porch of the Flatwater house, and they travel as far as the eye can see. It is dusk, and it must be summertime because he can hear the cicadas and they breathe their own strange and unearthly susurrus.

Michael is watching snaps of heat thunder unfold along the horizon, like exclamation marks jumping down from the belly of the clouds, almost too fast for the eye to see.

He can see the shadows in the fields, and they seem to reflect the shadow within himself, the shadow that was always there, will always be there, and within that shadow lies the certain knowledge that not only will there forever be things that he does not understand, but that he himself will never be understood.

His mother calls his name.

He does not want to go back there because he knows she is dead.

His father calls his name also.

And he does not want to see his father, because he will stand there with a knife in his eye and he will tell Michael things that he does not want to hear.

But—for some reason—he knows these things are not true.

You are not your father's son, Michael Travis.

He prays for it, even though he does not believe in prayer.

What you most fear does not run in the blood, my friend.

For you cannot believe in something that you cannot see.

That is a myth.

But how can that be true, when he sees his mother—even now—walking toward him, walking out to the back of the house, coming to get him for dinner?

And then she is standing there, and the smile on her face is calm and kind and gentle, and there are no signs of death about her, and her hair is not shorn and blackened, and her eyes have not burst with the fifty thousand volts of electricity they drove through her, and her arms do not hang limply by her side, unable now to reach, to touch, to feel...

You are free to be yourself.

Michael takes one last look at the darkening horizon, and then he turns and follows her into the house.

As he moves, his shadow drifts unnoticed across the cracked and arid field, and from somewhere close at hand, he hears the sound of a crow.

And then he is elsewhere. He does not recognize this place, and then he begins to understand that this is perhaps the place into which he has retreated. Here is the place he has hidden from the world. It is quiet. Nothing moves, and the only sound seems to be that of his own heart, perhaps the blood in his veins, the air in his lungs.

He is not afraid. He moves slowly, and he can see the edges between sleeping and waking, the way in which daylight has begun to invade his senses, the sounds around him now, the noises above and beneath.

And then he wakes.

Michael Travis lies there in his narrow bed in the McCaffrey Hotel and knows that something within himself has changed.

He does not know what, and he does not wish to look, but he knows that he will have to.

It is inevitable.

25

"Mr. Travis?"

Travis looked up suddenly.

Danny McCaffrey was beside the table, coffeepot in hand.

"You all right, Mr. Travis?"

"Yes, of course. Why do you ask?"

"We were just in the middle of a conversation, and you disappeared."

"I'm sorry, Danny. I think I had a short night's sleep."

"The bed isn't good?"

"The bed is fine, Danny. The room is just fine. I have a lot on my mind."

"Yes, of course."

"So, what were we talking about?"

"Oh, nothing important. Just that my sister said that you were a very decent man, very polite an' all."

"And your sister is very pretty and charming, Danny."

"How the hell she is still single, I do not know. I tell her that she's got to get herself settled down. She says she's not found the right man yet. Anyway, she said that you're letting the carnival open up again tonight. Is that right?"

"Where did she hear that, Danny?"

"No idea, Mr. Travis, but she's busy asking her friends and all manner of people to come on over and see it."

"She must have been very impressed by it when she saw it last week."

"Oh, that's just Laura. She's into all that hocus-pocus stuff, you know? That fortune-tellin' and palm-reading and tarot and whatnot. I seen and heard a great deal of that stuff, but I gotta tell you that there's a guy down there does some stuff that I can't even begin to understand."

"Which guy?"

"The little guy. The dwarf."

Travis recalled the final moments of his meeting with Chester Greene.

"And then there's the guy with seven fingers. Now *he* is a magician, making stuff disappear and whatever. But I'll tell you now, that little guy is some kind of mind reader."

"Well, it's evidently a trick, Danny, because it's not possible for one person to read another's mind."

"You go tell that to Larry Youngman."

"Who?"

"Larry Youngman. Owns the tavern down there. You can't miss it because it's called the Tavern. Two bars in Seneca, Larry's place and the Travelers' Rest, which is owned by Hank Dietz's widow. Larry'll be down there now, cleaning up before things get crazy. Folks'll have put out the word that the carnival's on tonight, and Seneca Falls will be as busy as New York City by five o'clock, I guarantee it."

"So what happened with Mr. Youngman?"

Danny gave a wry smile. "Oh, you go ask him, Mr. Travis. He'll tell it a great deal better than I ever could."

"I'll do that, Danny."

"Oh, and one other thing, Mr. Travis."

"Yes, Danny."

"Be obliged if you wouldn't be flirting any more with my sister, okay?"

Travis was stunned. "I can assure you, Danny, that I was not—"

Danny McCaffrey suddenly burst out laughing. "Oh my, you shoulda seen your face, Mr. Travis! I am sorry. I just had to do that. Laura said you were such a polite man and so well mannered, a real gentleman, she said. She said to play a joke on you. It was her idea, I swear."

Travis got up from the table, and for a brief moment he was genuinely amused. "Yes, well, very funny, Danny. Tell her that it was much appreciated."

"She said to tell you to lighten up some. I told her I should never say such a thing to a man from the Federal Bureau of Investigation, that more 'an likely I'd get myself arrested. Anyway, she put me up to it. No offense intended, Mr. Travis."

"And none taken, Danny."

"Well, she just won a buck off of me, that's for sure."

"How so?"

"She bet me you would smile, and I said you wouldn't, and I seen you smile, Mr. Travis, no denyin' it!"

"Well, I am sure she will find a good use for that dollar tonight, eh?"

"Oh, I'm sure she will."

"I'll be away to see Mr. Youngman, then," Travis said.

"Tell him 'Hi' from me, would you?"

"I will, Danny."

Travis left the dining room and crossed through reception to the front door. He paused for a moment, wondered whether he should head back to his room for his overcoat. He looked out. The day was bright and fresh. The sky was cloudless. Looked like it would be fine weather for the carnival.

He shook his head. He'd not given his permission, at least not directly. An assumption had been made by Doyle that Travis would have no disagreement, and Doyle had been right. He himself wanted to see what all this fuss was about.

But there was something else as well. He could not explain it, and he did not wish to explain it, but what Chester Greene had said to him—how he was not his father's son, that what he feared most was *not* in his blood—had... had what? All Travis knew was that since Greene had uttered those words, he'd felt somehow different. It was subtle, completely intangible, and yet it had eased him. He felt somehow less afraid. Of what, he did not know, and for some reason it did not matter.

Travis did not look inward. He did not seek out the edges of the shadows. He did not prod the sleeping wolf with a pointed stick. He let it be.

Travis did not return for his overcoat. He left to see if Larry Youngman could help him better understand what he had found in Seneca Falls.

The Tavern was as it sounded, all wood and worn-out leather and an open fire that Larry Youngman was cleaning even as Travis arrived.

"Not open, son," Youngman said. "Not for another hour or two... and I have to tell you that if you'd be lookin' for a drink at this time o' the mornin' then you don't need me, you need a doctor."

Travis smiled. "My name is Michael Travis. I am from the Federal Bureau of Investigation."

Youngman got up off his knees and set down the brush he'd been using to clean out the ash trap beneath the fire. Travis figured him for late fifties, early sixties, and he was a big man, a good head taller than Travis.

"Ah, our own Melvin Purvis," Youngman said. "Word was around last night that you were handy with the old sidearm there. You done shot some gangsters an' all."

"A couple, yes. But that's not why I'm here."

"I should think not. Closest we got to a gangster in Seneca Falls was Hank Dietz, charging five cents more than me for a glass of beer. He's dead now anyway, and his wife is runnin' the place into nothing."

"I came to talk to you about what happened at the carnival last Friday night."

Youngman smiled and then shook his head. His back was bowed, his hands filthy with soot, a streak of gray on his cheek, and the way he stood there, hands hanging by his sides, his brow furrowed, his eyes peering out at Travis from within heavy shadows, he seemed like something out of history, some shambling woodsman emerging from a medieval forest.

225

"Who's been talking?"

"I was speaking with Danny McCaffrey down at the hotel. He said that something happened on Friday night, the night before the body was found."

"Not easy for folks, is it?"

"What isn't?"

"Leaving things alone. Everyone's got to be up in everyone else's business." Youngman shook his head resignedly. "Ah well, I suppose that's the downside of livin' in a place such as this. Everyone knows your business, and they're always very keen to be discussin' it with one another."

"What happened, Mr. Youngman?"

Youngman walked to the bar and eased himself up onto a stool. He indicated for Travis to take the next stool, and then he turned and faced the bar itself. Travis just sat silent and waited for Youngman to start talking.

"You ever lose someone, Mr. Travis?"

"Yes, Mr. Youngman, I have."

"Someone close?"

"Yes."

"You ever feel afterward, you know . . . after they were gone, that you would have wished for one minute, thirty seconds even, just a few moments more to say what you always should have said when they were alive?"

"Yes, Mr. Youngman, I have. I don't think there's anyone who hasn't felt that at some point in their life."

" 'Cept those lucky ones who never lost someone important. That does happen, you know? Some folks go all their lives and it never really hits them. Even when folks lose their parents, they somehow take it in their stride and deal with it. Maybe that's because you've always somehow managed to anticipate that. That never comes as a shock, does it? Rare is it that a child dies before the parent, right?"

"Yes, for sure."

Youngman shook his head. "Not so rare here."

"You lost a child, Mr. Youngman?"

"Sure did, clumsy that I was." He smiled ironically and then sighed.

"What happened?"

"It's somewhat of a long story, but I can give you the short version. Had a wife. Not the current one, but the one before. Been married three times, Mr. Travis. First wife left me because of the drink, second wife because of the gambling, and the third wife rescued me from an early grave. Second wife and I had a boy. Her name was Marilyn, the boy's name was David. Hell of a kid, even if I say so myself. Lord knows where he got his looks from, because they sure as hell didn't come from me. Anyway, off he went to school one day, eleven years old, wintertime, never a second thought about it. Never came home. Got a visit from the then-sheriff, Dan Warner, to say that David had been hit by a car or a truck or something. They'd found his body at the side of the road no more than half a mile from home. Looked like someone had just plowed right into him, broke him apart, and then drove off. Left him there at the side of the road in the snow."

"That is truly terrible, Mr. Youngman. I cannot even begin to understand how you must feel."

"You get over it, Mr. Travis. That was all of twenty years ago. He'd have been a grown man by now, probably more trouble than he was worth, never calling, never visiting 'cept when he needed me to bail him out of some hole he'd dug for himself. Don't matter how old they get; they're always gonna be your kids, and they're always gonna be in trouble."

"Did they ever find out who the driver was?"

"Nope, never did, and never really will."

"There's always a chance—"

"The man who killed my son is dead, Mr. Travis."

"But I thought you said—"

"I don't know who it was, 'cept he was from Colorado and he done killed himself a year later."

"I don't understand, Mr. Youngman."

"What I said was one thing, Mr. Travis. What that little feller told me Friday night was quite another."

"Chester Greene?"

"That'd be his name, yes. He told me what happened."

"But how?"

"Don't know, sir, and—to be honest—I don't want to know. All I know is that the man who killed my son was so burdened with guilt, he done killed hisself too. He put a pistol in his mouth and he blowed his own darn fool head off."

"But I don't understand why you would believe such a thing."

"Well, I do know it, sir. I know that's the truth just like that little feller knew my son's name, knew what date he died, knew my second wife's name and that she left me."

"He told you these things?"

"Yes, he did. Clear as daylight, he told me those things."

"Well, there must be an explanation for it, Mr. Youngman. There has to be. He must have found out about you before you went to the carnival."

"Well, maybe he did, sir, but if he did, then he's even cleverer than I thought. I was living in Brandenburg, Kentucky, at the time, Mr. Travis, and I came here more than ten years ago and have never spoken of that to a living soul. My second wife is dead too, so she never spoke to no carnival dwarf neither. There's no way in the world that that little feller could have known about what happened unless he has some kind of a gift."

"Well, okay, it would be easy enough to find out if a man committed suicide a year after this happened—"

"I ain't gonna go lookin', Mr. Travis. I'm fine just knowing as much as I know right now, and I don't want to know any more. That whole thing has been put to rest for me now, and if nothing else, I am grateful to that little guy for telling me what happened. Tell you the truth, I was haunted by that. Haunted by some sort of idea that I would never find out the truth. That might not sound very likely, seein' as how twenty years have passed and I ain't done nothin' about it, but a man can still be haunted by an idea, Mr. Travis, even if he don't raise a finger to do anything about it. Truth is, I feel different. I feel like a weight has been lifted off of me. It weren't never right nor fair that my boy got killed, but at least I know that the man who did it didn't escape justice. Far as I know, he's roastin' his heels in hellfire even as we speak."

"Do you not want to know what really happened, Mr. Youngman? Don't you want to prove it?"

Youngman smiled. "I'm not from the Federal Bureau of Investigation, Mr. Travis. I ain't preparin' anything for a trial here. That little feller put my mind at rest. He told me what happened, and he told me that my boy is safe and well, and that he done moved on and he's someone else's son now and he's bein' looked after just fine an' dandy. He says that my son don't feel no bitterness toward me, nor his ma, and he didn't lay the blame on anyone but hisself and that darn fool driver for not lookin' where he was going."

"And you believe this, Mr. Youngman?"

"Sure I do."

"And if it's not true?"

"Hell, Mr. Travis, if it ain't true, then so be it. I *feel* it's true. Gotta say that I *know* it's true, and that's good enough for me."

"And how much did this information cost you?"

"Cost me? Cost me all of ten cents to step inside that tent, Mr. Travis."

Travis shook his head in disbelief.

"Crazy stuff, eh?" Youngman said.

"Sounds crazy, absolutely."

"Well, maybe there isn't an answer for everything in this world, Mr. Travis. All I know is that I don't feel like my boy is waiting for me anymore, you know? I feel better. I feel lighter. I feel like I can move on, and after twenty years, that sure as hell comes as a relief to me, I have to say."

Youngman glanced at his watch. "You want a drink with me, Mr. Travis?"

Travis smiled. "I will, Mr. Youngman. Just a small one, please."

"A small one?" Youngman frowned and shook his head. "I wouldn't know what that was even if I seen it, Mr. Travis."

Travis did have just one drink, and he did not stay long at the Tavern. When he left, he was pensive. He walked back to the McCaffrey Hotel, but instead of going inside, he sat in his car for a while. He asked himself if there was something here that he did not wish to know about. He also thought of the question Larry Youngman had asked him, whether he himself had lost someone, and that it had been neither his mother nor his father that had come to mind, but Esther. The Bureau psychologist had asked him about Esther, and—as always—he'd skirted around the question. But it was there now, and it could not be avoided.

The deterioration of his relationship with Esther—perhaps inevitable due to their respective ages, the inherent difference in their attitudes, the simple fact that they could not, by definition, enjoy many of those public aspects of togetherness that seem such a necessary part of an intimate relationship—seemed to accelerate most noticeably once Travis had resumed his education. He had wanted to study beyond a college graduation, but there seemed to be reasons upon reasons to prevent this Money initially and then a seeming lack of support from the Nebraska State Welfare Department. Howard Redding—he who had been so diligent in his efforts to locate a guardian for Michael—died suddenly and unexpectedly at his desk on a warm Tuesday in the spring of 1944. Howard Redding was forty-one years of age, and something just burst in his brain. Technically, it was known as a subarachnoid aneurysm. Howard had been suffering from mild headaches for a while, and on the morning of Tuesday, May ninth, he sensed a strange weakness in the right side of his face. He attributed it to tiredness, the fact that he had been working long hours, but it was not tiredness at all. A few minutes after eleven a.m., the aneurysm ruptured and leaked blood into a membrane that covered Howard Redding's brain and spinal canal. On the same day that the Soviet army finally captured Sebastopol, ushering in the final year of the Second World War, Howard Redding passed away quietly and without drama at his desk. It was two hours before anyone found him.

Howard's replacement, a younger man by the name of Christopher Macklin, was all too keen to follow the rules, color inside the lines, dot the *i*'s and cross the *t*'s. Cutbacks were the order of the day, some due to the war effort, impinging now even on the mighty and seemingly infinite resources of the United States, others due to the fact that Nebraska governor Dwight Griswold's first term was coming to an end, and his reelection campaign was focusing on economy and full employment. Less money was available for fewer things, and somewhere near the very bottom of the list of priorities was the funding of an education for delinquents.

So Travis had been home a great deal. He found work—odd jobs in construction and munitions production, but he was not happy, not by any stretch of the imagination.

Just three days after General Alfred Jodl signed the instrument of unconditional surrender in a small red schoolhouse in Rheims, Travis turned eighteen years of age. Esther Faulkner was three months shy of thirty-six. Their relationship had become strained and tense, something that both of them had noticed during the previous months. They still slept together, they still ate together, but that sense of indivisibility, that sense of unity that the world could not impinge upon or influence, had become as fragile as an egg. Perhaps this *affaire de corps et coeur* had been a lie from the start, but neither of them would have believed such a thing. Perhaps, for Travis, it had been nothing more than the firework display of first love, his virginity swept away by a woman of experience. Perhaps, for Esther, it had been the last desperate grasp at a youth now passed by, a wholehearted and yet futile chance to find something truly special in an otherwise mundane and ordinary life. Whatever the reason for its inception, whatever the reasons for its demise, it was suffering a slow and agonizingly awkward death in that small Grand Island house through the latter part of 1945 and the early months of the subsequent year.

In June of '46, Michael told Esther he was leaving. It was a Tuesday evening, and she was seated in the kitchen when he returned from work.

"I have to go," he said, his tone so matter-of-fact and unremarkable.

"I know you do," she said, and there in her eyes was some sense of philosophical resignation. She uttered those four words as though they had been on the very tip of her tongue for as long as she could remember and yet had not found the right moment to express them. This seemed inevitable, almost as if some complicit agreement had been made for such an eventuality, and yet it had taken this much time to bring it to its natural and inescapable conclusion.

"I have found a room," Michael said.

"Yes."

"Not far, a few miles away. I have enough money saved to be able to rent it for a while. I don't know what I'm going to do, but I think you'll be happier without me around."

"Yes," Esther replied, but she did not necessarily believe this.

Michael sat down across from Esther. He reached out and took her hand.

"Do you think what we did was a mistake?" she asked him.

"No. Do you?"

A tear emerged in slow motion from her eye and rolled lazily down her cheek. "I don't believe in mistakes," she said. "Mistakes are for other people."

"I don't want to remember this with sadness, Esther."

"Then don't."

"I don't want you to remember it with sadness, either."

"I won't," she said. "I will remember it for what it was."

"And what was it, Esther?"

"Probably the last real love affair I will ever have."

"I don't believe that. You are young, and you like people too much to be alone."

"My mind is old," she said. "My heart is old. I am tired of forgiving people for the stupid things they do."

"You will find someone," Michael said. "Or someone will find you."

"Go," she said. "The sooner the better. I knew this would happen. I don't blame you, and I don't blame myself, and there's no use trying to figure out who did what or who was wrong. It just is."

Michael squeezed her hand. "I will always love you, Esther."

"And I will always love you, Michael," she replied, and she closed her eyes and did not open them until he had left the room.

Travis packed up his things and departed that evening. The house was empty when he finally closed the door and walked down into the street. Esther had already left. She had gotten dressed up in her finest and taken a bus to Hastings. She found a bar on Wintergreen Street and drank herself into a hotel room with a stranger called Eugene. When she woke the following morning, her head like a cracked gourd, Eugene was gone. She could barely recall his face, and she had never known his surname. Again, as with her first sexual encounter with Michael, she did not feel cheap or disgraceful or ashamed. She felt lost, a little confused, and a great deal uncertain. It had been a bad day, but there had been worse in her life, and she had recovered from them. How much of herself she would now recover she did not know and could not predict. She seemed to be losing small fragments of her identity with each passing year. This was perhaps just the nature of things. Perhaps you ended as you began—with nothing at all.

Travis existed in solitude but for the day-to-day requirements of work. It was then that he enlisted in the army, perhaps to give his life some structure, some sense and purpose. Perhaps it was merely to have his mind filled with something other than questions. He did not believe in fate, but he believed in the errant and fickle nature of life. Life could not be predicted and controlled, not as people believed. What you felt one day was not what you felt the next. He did not doubt that he loved Esther, would always love her, but something vital and intrinsic and personal had changed. Was this growing older? Was this what becoming a man was all about? Learning not how to love, but how to love less? Learning not how to feel, to emote, to engage, to connect with people, but how to withdraw, disconnect, retreat into a reality that made sense to oneself, irrespective of whether or not such a reality made sense to anyone else? To accept what one was, well, that seemed to be the hardest task of all. To stop pretending that you were something you were not took courage and a degree of honesty that most people did not possess.

In those few final weeks between leaving Esther and boarding the bus for Fort Benning, Georgia, the dreams returned with a vengeance. The shadow, the cracked and arid field, the crow that laughed. And now the dreams were followed by headaches, and the headaches seemed strong enough to burst his head like an overripe melon. He experienced three or four such dreams, maybe even more before he finally left Grand Island, and they always followed the same theme. The overriding emotion within them was fear. This was no nail-biting, sweating, terrified fear; this was no screaming from the room; no abject horror; no frantic escape from some nightmarish vision of desperate evil. No, nothing like that at all. This was a creeping, insidious, malevolent sense of possession that seemed to pervade and permeate everything he thought, everything he felt, everything he was. This was a fear that came not from without, but from within. And thus he knew, if nothing else, that this was a fear from which he could not escape.

More than anything, he hoped that the deep and inescapable sense of emptiness that existed within him, an emptiness occasioned by his separation from Esther, would somehow subside and disappear with time. As if that decision was now the precedent against which all future decisions would be made—those to leave instead of staying, those of distance instead of closeness, those to stay silent instead of speaking—and he, Michael Travis, a man with no real country, would somehow and forever be a stranger to the world.

Esther had been the only one to really understand what had happened to Janette Travis. She had been the only one there at the end. And if Michael had stayed, if he had been brave enough to understand what she

232

had done, then his life might have been something completely different altogether.

Such was the burden of the one left behind.

Seated in the car outside the McCaffrey, it was these things that occupied his mind, as if the seams between past and present were somehow disappearing.

Even as he saw Slate turning the corner at the end of the road, he thought of the letter Esther had left for him, tucked there inside *The Grapes of Wrath* on his bookshelf in Olathe.

He knew—perhaps more than anyone—that he was here in Seneca Falls because of Esther Faulkner.

He also knew that when he returned, he would have to take that letter and read it.

26

Travis did not get out of the car as Slate approached the McCaffrey Hotel from the direction of the bank. He merely watched as a procession of people followed him—Chester Greene, Gabor Benedek, the Bellanca brothers and Akiko Mimasuya. The Bellanca brothers were dressed identically, and—even as he watched—Benedek hoisted Chester Greene up onto his shoulders. They were passing out flyers, and people were taking them, and folks were coming out of stores to fetch handfuls of the things. Those handbills were even being tucked behind the wipers of parked cars.

The little procession went on, and though there was something small-town and provincial about it, Travis was aware of another thing entirely. There was a sense of anticipation surrounding these strange, anachronistic people, as if how they looked was nothing to do with *who* they were.

Travis watched them head off down the main drag. To his knowledge, they did not know he was there, and no one looked back. He opened the door and stepped out.

"Good for the town."

Travis turned to see Sheriff Rourke standing there with the flyer in his hand.

"Brings people here, gets them spending money, and we can always use people coming here and spending money. And folks are appreciative that you gave them permission to open up again tonight." Rourke took off his hat and walked around to the side of the car where Travis was standing.

"So," he said, "how goes it with your dead feller? Any the wiser as to who he was and what the hell happened?"

"Not a great deal," Travis replied.

"Heard he was some sort of foreign killer, maybe?"

"The telephone game, Sheriff."

"So he wasn't no killer, then?"

"We cannot be sure as yet."

"Heard he had the names of all of his victims tattooed all over his body in some secret language."

234

"You saw the body, Sheriff Rourke. There were no names tattooed on it, and there is no secret language."

"Idle minds are the devil's playground, right?"

"Yes, indeed."

"So I'll let you get on, then."

"Well, that's why you requested our assistance, Sheriff Rourke."

Rourke frowned. "I didn't request any federal assistance, Agent Travis."

"I'm sorry?" Travis asked, frowning.

Rourke shook his head. "That's why I figured you guys for being so sharp, so on the ball, you know? I didn't make any official request. I guessed you'd heard about it through the grapevine, so to speak. Or maybe one of the other sheriffs had informed you... those that I sent the photo of your dead guy to."

"So you didn't file anything? You didn't call anyone?"

"No, sir, I did not."

Travis paused. His first reaction was to call Bishop, but he stayed his hand. If an official request had not been put in, he wouldn't have been there in the first place. It was a simple communication breakdown, in and of itself of no great significance. Perhaps Rourke was right with his second assumption, that one of the other sheriffs had asked for help. Or perhaps...

"So you'll be coming to see them do their show tonight, I hope," Rourke said, interrupting Travis's train of thought.

"Wouldn't miss it for the world," Travis said.

"Good 'nough, Agent Travis. Well, I best be gettin' on. Places to go, people to see an' all that. You have a good day now."

"The same to you, Sheriff Rourke."

Rourke left him standing there beside the car and headed off down the street toward the Tavern.

Travis half-expected Edgar Doyle and Valeria Mironescu to appear, but there was no sign of them. He considered driving out to the carnival site, to make his presence known, to share a few words with Doyle about Doyle's assumption regarding the reopening of the carnival, but he decided against it. In some instances, maintaining a degree of distance contributed more to one's sense of jurisdictional control than wading in and interfering. He would let Doyle believe what he wished to believe, and if it became necessary to assert his authority once more, then he would do so without hesitation.

The fact of the matter was that he wanted to see these people at work; he wanted to see what it was that had the people of Seneca Falls in a state of electrified expectation.

Travis crossed the street to the hotel, and as he reached the sidewalk,

Doyle appeared from the reception area. He was alone, and he wore a knee-length black velvet cape, a wide-brimmed hat, and in his hand he carried a twisted wooden cane.

"Agent Travis," he said matter-of-factly. "I have come with a personal invitation to our little performance this evening, and then afterward, if it suits you, a little dinner with myself and Valeria."

"I will be at the carnival," Travis said. "However, I will be there in an official capacity, Mr. Doyle, as would be expected under the circumstances, and though I am appreciative of your invitation to dinner, I am going to decline. I am sure you understand why and that it will not be taken as a personal slight."

"Not at all, Agent Travis, not at all."

Doyle did not move on. He stood there looking at Travis, his expression neither one thing nor another.

"Was there something else, Mr. Doyle?"

"Did you ever hear of a man called Harold Blauer, spelled B-L-A-U-E-R?"

"I can't say I have, Mr. Doyle. Who was he?"

"Oh, he was just a tennis player. No one special. I just wondered if you knew of him."

"No, I am not so much the sports enthusiast, Mr. Doyle."

"Oh, I wasn't asking you in reference to the fact that he was a tennis player, Agent Travis."

"So, why ask?"

Doyle opened his mouth to speak and then glanced back as Valeria Mironescu appeared from the entranceway of the hotel.

"Ah, my dear. Agent Travis and I were just passing the time of day."

"Agent Travis," she said, smiling. "A pleasure to see you, as always."

"And you, Miss Valeria."

"Well, we have a great deal of work to do," Doyle said, "as I am sure you do, Agent Travis. We shall see you later this evening, then."

"You shall. Mr. Doyle," he added, nodding politely, "and Miss Valeria."

"Bring your round head this evening," Valeria said, and winked. "Leave your square head behind." She laughed, almost mischievously, and then the pair of them walked away, arm in arm, across the street and past Travis's Fairlane.

Travis watched them go, uncertain as to what she was implying by her final comment.

Travis went on up to his room, took a shower and put on a clean shirt. He made a note of the name Doyle had mentioned. Harold Blauer. Where had he heard that name before?

He considered taking some time out to begin his report, the single report that would be filed with Bishop when the case was finally closed.

When was the operative word, not *if*. And when he did write that report, everything needed to be cut and dried, every *i* dotted, every *t* crossed, and perhaps that report would find itself on Mr. Hoover's desk. If not the director himself, then possibly Mr. Tolson.

This evening would be nothing more than an opportunity to see these individuals in their own environment and was not altogether invalid in better understanding how they thought, how they operated, how they behaved. You wish to catch a wild animal, then you better understand its natural habitat. That was the entire ethos of the work he had been undertaking with Unit X in Kansas. Get inside the mind of the criminal, and the criminal becomes an understandable and predictable creature.

Perhaps Doyle believed Travis naive, unschooled and unfamiliar with the vagaries and idiosyncrasies of the human condition. Well, if that was the case, then Doyle was in for a surprise. He had to be alert for everything, for this was where Doyle and his people would show the faces that they wore for the world. Perhaps one of them would let something slip. Perhaps Travis would see something that opened up a further line of investigation. Close to four days, and he had nothing but a tattooed Hungarian killer with no past, no present, and most definitely no future.

Hoover, Tolson, Warren, Bishop, Section Chief Gale aside, Travis himself could not let this investigation die a quiet and lonely death in the middle of nowhere.

27

The sounds and smells of the carnival came up to meet him as Travis parked his car and started down toward the edge of the field. He had seen the lights and heard the calliope music within a quarter mile of the place, and along the edges of the road it seemed that all of Seneca Falls and a half a dozen towns beyond had made plans to be there.

The atmosphere was one of excited anticipation, evident in the wide eyes and enthusiastic smiles of both adults and children alike.

Travis saw Larry Youngman on the other side of the road, ahead of him a gaggle of kids, and—glancing back over his shoulder—he saw Danny McCaffrey get out of a car with his sister, Laura, both dressed as if for a city restaurant. Travis was aware of the lift he felt in his sprits when he saw her, and he did not ignore it.

By the time Travis reached the field itself, he was somehow caught up in the atmosphere, as if something contagious was in the air, absorbed through the pores perhaps, something that made it almost impossible to resist the ambience created by the presence of these people.

At the makeshift gateway to the field stood the five Bellanca brothers, dressed from head to foot in white, their faces white but for dark circles around their eyes. They should have appeared strangely frightening, but they did not. They did not speak, but they mimed some sort of running joke, slapping one another on the back, laughing silently, handing out balloons and candy skeletons to the kids as their moms and dads paid the entry fee and passed under the archway of Japanese lanterns.

Travis was waved through with no charge, but he insisted on dropping a handful of coins into the bucket. He did not want to be granted any special dispensation, however slight it may have been. One of the Bellancas gave a graceful bow and smiled widely through the skull-like apparition of his features. Travis smiled back. He could not help himself.

Already the place was crowded. The music was loud, and it swelled against his ears and seemed to resonate inside him. He had never experienced anything quite like it. The shabby marquee and the scatterings of tired tents had become something altogether different. Shapes and symbols he had not noticed before, painted there upon the canvas, were now visible from the glow of lamps and lanterns within. In one tent, someone he could only assume to be Akiko Mimasuya, performed acrobatic contortions before a light source. She was visible only as a silhouette, and—as a result—the effect was even more disorientating and unsettling than when he had seen her in rehearsal. She seemed able to bend her body in ways that were not physically possible—at once crouching like a panther, in the next moment unwinding like a snake, and then suddenly she was some other creature that Travis had never seen before. It was then that he understood the crude image on the poster in Doyle's caravan. It had not been that of an animal at all, but of Akiko.

A smaller tent contained the Bonnie and Clyde car, now strangely illuminated, seeming even more real than when he had first seen it. Beside the tent was a range of curious sideshow attractions—the Fiji mermaid, the Giant Rat of Sumatra, the skeleton of a two-headed dog. Farther down, there were stands selling hot dogs, popcorn, and soda floats.

People seemed transfixed every which way Travis looked. Children, eyes bright, devoured handheld clouds of cotton candy. Their parents seemed captivated in an equal degree of wonderment. Travis saw the McCaffreys again, Laura even waved enthusiastically at him, and for a moment it was as if he was watching them as children.

Travis raised his hand in acknowledgment, once again felt a twinge of something, an emotional reaction to her enthusiastic greeting, and then she vanished into the sea of people once more.

The hubbub of voices was present beneath the music, and Travis heard words and half sentences as he moved through the crowd.

Look, Ma! It's a man with—

Oh my Lord, I have to say I never saw such—

You come right back here now, young man. How many times have I told you—

Pa! Pa! Pa!

But I want some now—

It was strangely reassuring to find himself surrounded by real people with real lives. That's how it felt. He had been here no time at all and yet had somehow seen so many slight shifts in his own viewpoint. The people he had interviewed—each in turn—had somehow tilted the axis of his perception. Perhaps they had not intended to do such a thing, but nevertheless it had been done.

For whatever reason, and how it had come about, Travis believed himself to be a different man from the man that had left Kansas City only a handful of days before. That sense of ever-present anxiety had diminished somewhat, the knot that sat in his lower gut had somehow loosened, and the feeling of caution and suspicion with which he had viewed the world for as long as he could remember seemed somehow unjustified here.

And then he remembered *why* he was here.

"Agent Travis!"

Travis turned at the sound of his name and was confronted by the towering presence of Gabor Benedek. On his shoulders sat Chester Greene. Greene was dressed in a black pants, a black shirt, and a top hat adorned with peacock feathers. Benedek himself wore a white guinea tee, white pants, and a multicolored sash was tied around his waist.

"It is good to see you!" Greene shouted above the noise all around them. "Hope you enjoy the show!"

"Thank you, Mr. Greene," Travis replied.

"You should have a hot dog," Benedek said. "They are very good."

"I will," Travis replied. "I am hungry, yes."

Benedek pointed to the hot-dog stand, back in the right-hand corner of the field. There were two people manning it, neither of whom Travis recognized. He bade farewell to Benedek and Greene and made his way over there.

Travis stood in line behind a half-dozen other people, and when it came to his turn, he was greeted by a young couple, all enthusiastic smiles and heartfelt welcomes.

"What'll you have?" the girl asked. She was in her mid-twenties at a guess, and Travis wanted to know who these people were. They had not been present at any of the meetings or meals in the central marquee.

He said he'd have a hot dog with everything on it—onions, cheese, sauerkraut, ketchup, mustard.

"Who are you?" he asked as he handed over his money and took the dog.

"You're the FBI man, right?" the young man asked him.

"I am, yes."

"Name's Ben Littleton," the man said. "This here is my wife, Sue-Anne."

"Pleased to meet you, sir," Sue-Anne said.

"Likewise," Travis replied. "You don't work for these people, do you?"

"Oh no," Ben said. "We just came down here, and Mr. Doyle asked us if we wouldn't mind helping out some. More than happy to, of course. It's a fun place. You should see that man with his tricks. The one with all the fingers. Spooky!"

"No, it's the Thin Man who does all them tricks," Sue-Anne interjected. "Makes you see things that ain't even there," she added, and laughed.

"Hell, they all do something wild and wonderful," Ben said. "You just have to see all the shows."

Travis stepped a little closer to the hot-dog stand. "Were you here last Saturday night?"

"Oh, look out, sir," Ben said. "We got a queue backing up behind you. Can't keep these hungry folks waiting!"

Travis stepped to the side, saw a line of people behind him, and all of a sudden both Ben and Sue-Anne Littleton were serving customers. Travis was forgotten. He walked away, ate his hot dog—which *was* very good indeed—and he made a mental note to go back to speak with the Littletons about anything they might have seen or heard on the night the body had been discovered. He also thought of Frances Brady, that he had intended to track her down, to speak with her as well, and how it had slipped his mind entirely.

Travis made his way back toward the central marquee. Within it, a low stage had been erected, the remainder of the space cleared of tables and chairs. Strings of lights hung from the inner roof, giving an impression of a multitude of stars. The effect was surprisingly good, and Travis was impressed with the ability of Doyle and his people to create such an environment in so brief a time. It did feel as if the real world ended at the makeshift gateway to this field, and here there was something else going on, something that tapped into everyone's wish to escape the humdrum, the routine, the predictable. That was all it was, after all—an illusion. There was no real magic here. Real magic did not exist. Sleight of hand and misdirection was all it took to deceive the less discerning eye. Travis believed himself quite capable of explaining everything that he might see this evening, and yet he was more than content to let Doyle and his people engage his attention and entertain him. It was an opportunity to see them working within their own zone of familiarity, and in such a zone they might relax their caution, and in relaxing their caution they might give him something that would assist the investigation.

Travis made to leave the marquee when his eye was caught by Mr. Slate.

"Mr. Slate," he said, approaching the man as he appeared from the left side of the stage.

"Agent Travis," Slate replied. "A good evening to you. You have come to see my show?"

"It begins soon?"

"In a few minutes. If you want to see the spectacle up close, then you better stay. It can get pretty crowded in here."

"I am sure I will be able to see all I need to see, Mr. Slate."

"Oh, up close and personal is better, Agent Travis. That way you can see all the tricks of the trade, so to speak."

"Then I shall stay right here," Travis said, his attention caught by the sound of voices as people started entering the marquee.

Slate carried a small table to the center of the stage and set it down.

"I must go," he said. "A few last-minute details to attend to."

"Of course, Mr. Slate."

Travis moved to the side of the stage and looked back toward the entranceway. He saw a few familiar faces from Seneca Falls, but the vast majority were strangers. He tried to count them, but once past fifty he lost track. Slate had been right—the marquee became crowded, so crowded as to see Travis backing up to the side wall adjacent to the stage. He could still see clearly, very clearly indeed, but he felt somehow claustrophobic amid the jam of bodies. It was hot in the tent, and he loosened his tie. He was relieved not to have brought his hat and overcoat from the car.

Without warning, a silence fell on the crowd. There was still the faint murmur of voices, but this was punctuated by *Sssshhh* and *Quiet now; it's starting.*

The calliope music had faded. Perhaps it was still playing, Travis wasn't sure, but then it was overtaken by the sound of classical strings coming from somewhere behind the stage. A gramophone, no doubt, playing something with which Travis was unfamiliar. It was beautiful, nonetheless, and Travis felt a certain sense of nostalgia overtake him. Where that had come from, and why, he had no idea. He had no reason to feel this way. And then he remembered. Esther, oftentimes, would listen to such music on her own record player, those days she sometimes spent in her pajamas, caring not to get dressed, caring to do nothing but lie on the sofa, perhaps watch television, perhaps drink some wine. Sometimes he would find her still there in the evening; he would frown at her, and she would merely laugh.

"Lighten up, Mr. Serious," she would say. "Sometimes you need a Sunday even when a Sunday isn't scheduled."

He could see her face then, as real as if she were standing right in front of him, and he felt a sharp pain—not physical, but emotional—run right through his body.

Why had he deserted her? Did she get sick because of his departure? Did he in some way contribute to that?

"Ladies and gentlemen!"

Travis looked back to the stage.

Edgar Doyle stood there, dressed in his suit and cape as he had been earlier, in his hand the twisted cane, beside him Valeria Mironescu, stunningly beautiful in a long black dress embroidered with bloodred roses. Her hair was tied away from her face, and a multicolored waterfall of ribbons flowed down her back.

"We welcome you to the Carnival Diablo!"

Travis edged forward. He wanted to see Doyle and the woman more clearly, but his view was partially obscured by a tall man in a heavy overcoat.

Doyle raised his cane and swept it from left to right. "Watch in wonder!" he said. "Be amazed, astounded, stupefied, stunned, and staggered by the wondrous magic of Mr. Slate!"

There was riotous applause, and Doyle and Valeria Mironescu left the stage.

Slate appeared at the rear of the stage center, dressed now as Chester Greene had been—black pants and a black shirt. He wore no hat, however, and when he walked forward toward the audience, there was a hushed sense of anticipation.

Slate held out his right hand, and from the center of his palm a flower slowly appeared, white and pale like an orchid. Travis smiled. There was nowhere for that flower to come from besides Slate's shirtsleeve, and the smoothness with which he performed that seemingly effortless trick was quite impressive. Slate took the flower from his right hand with his left, and then he held it flat against his palm. His seven fingers closed around that bloom, and he closed his eyes.

The music continued, softer now, almost inaudible but nevertheless very much present.

Slate opened his eyes suddenly, then his hand, and there was a second bloom, a third, a fourth, and he tossed those flowers into the audience. Travis watched as those flowers were snatched from the air by the spectators, and when the flowers were gone, there was a substantial thunder of applause for Mr. Slate.

Slate drew the small table toward him. From it he took a pack of cards. He fanned them, showed the audience. It was a regular pack of cards, by all appearances. Slate closed the fan, held out the fan for a nearby child to take one at random.

The child took it, held it up, was instructed to show it to the audience without Slate seeing it.

The seven of spades.

The child returned the card, facedown, and then Slate held the pack against his forehead for just a second.

He then tossed that pack of cards out into the audience. Again, hands snatched upward and retrieved them. Every single one of them was the seven of spades. Another round of applause.

Slate then asked for a volunteer. Unsurprisingly to Travis, Laura McCaffrey hurried on up to the stage. The crowd applauded her.

Travis could see Danny right there, beaming from ear to ear. The man was proud of his sister in every way possible, and for a moment Travis felt... felt what? He did not know, and he put such thoughts out of his mind and watched as Slate presented his next trick.

"We have never met, have we?" Slate asked Laura McCaffrey.

"No, sir."

"Your name, my dear?"

"Laura. Laura McCaffrey."

"Good evening, Laura. A pleasure to make your acquaintance."

"Likewise, I'm sure," she said. She gave a small curtsy.

"I wondered if you would be so good as to help with me with my next presentation."

"Ooh, yes please," she said, and she laughed nervously. She glanced down at her brother, gave him a little wave. Danny McCaffrey waved back. It was then that she made eye contact with Travis. She did not raise her hand to acknowledge him, but she looked at him so directly, so pointedly, that Travis was almost stunned. It was only as she turned her attention back to Mr. Slate that Travis realized he had stopped breathing.

Slate produced a blindfold from his back pocket, another set of cards from the table.

He held up the blindfold, had Laura inspect it, cover her eyes with it, and pronounce that she could see nothing through it at all.

"Very good," Slate said. "Now, if you don't mind..."

He turned her away from him, and then he tied the blindfold, ensuring that it was not too tight, and yet she could still see nothing.

Laura held her hands out and waved them a little. "Where am I?" she said, and the audience laughed.

"We will need complete silence," Slate said. "*Complete* silence."

Laura stood there.

Slate took a pack of cards from the small table and showed them to the audience.

"Ordinary cards," he said. "Regular cards." He handed them to a man standing near the stage so he could inspect them. The man did so and returned them forthwith. Slate put them back on the table.

Slate turned to Laura. "Now, my dear, this is very simple. I too will apply a blindfold. I will then place my right hand on the top of your head. I will then pick a card and show it to the audience. I will not see it, and nor will you, of course. You will then tell them what card I am holding up."

There was a moment's hesitancy, and then Laura said, "But I *won't* see it, will I? I have this blindfold on."

A murmur of uneasy laughter threaded its way from those near the stage and out into the audience.

For some reason, Travis felt a knot of concern in his gut. Butterflies.

That was the sensation. Like when he was a child and he knew his father had been drinking. Like the world was made of eggshells.

"Don't worry, my dear," Slate said, his voice soothing, almost avuncular. "Just tell me the first card that comes to mind when I say the word *Now*. You understand?"

"I think so, yes."

"Very good. Once again, ladies and gentlemen, I need *complete* silence."

Slate set the table to his left and slightly behind him. He produced a second blindfold and applied it. He felt for the edge of the table, the cards he'd positioned there, and then he raised his right hand and placed it on Laura McCaffrey's head.

Did Travis see her flinch? Did that just happen?

Slate took the first card and held it aloft.

It was the five of hearts.

Even if his own blindfold was superficially applied, even if the fabric was sufficiently transparent for him to see the card he had taken, there was no way Laura McCaffrey would know what he was holding. Unless…

"Now," Slate said.

Laura flinched again. Travis felt sure of it.

"I don't know," she said. "I don't know which card it is."

Sounds from the audience.

"The first thing that comes to mind, Laura," Slate said, his voice gentle, almost persuasive.

"Hearts," she said, the word snapped from her lips like a threat.

A collective *Oooh* among the audience.

"I don't know," she said. "I think it's hearts."

Slate dropped the card to the stage.

"We try again," he said, and he took another card and held it up for the audience to see.

The nine of clubs.

"Now," he said.

"Nine," Laura said. "Of spades?"

The sound from the audience was one of slight disappointment. Close, but no cigar.

"Don't question what you see," Slate said. "The first thing that comes to mind, okay?"

"Okay," Laura said, and then she added, "I think I need to pee."

There was an unsteady laughter from some in the audience.

Travis looked at Danny McCaffrey. The smile was gone. He looked simply concerned.

Slate took a third card, held it up.

The eight of hearts.

"Now," he said.

"Eight," Laura said. "Hearts."

The audience started to clap.

"Silence!" Slate said.

He dropped the eight of hearts and took another card.

The four of spades.

"Now," he said.

"Four of spades," she said.

There was no applause, just a strange uneasiness that emanated from the stage and spread out among the spectators.

Slate took another card.

The seven of clubs.

"Now," he said, this time his voice barely a whisper.

"The seven of clubs," Laura said.

Slate dropped the card.

Another one, and yet another, each time Laura McCaffrey giving the correct number, the correct suit, each time Slate allowing the card to fall to the stage at his feet.

And then they were done and Slate took off his own blindfold, also that of Laura, and they stood there together, Slate holding her hand in his, she smiling, looking somehow proud of herself even though she seemed not to understand what had happened, and Slate's face was varnished with sweat, and his eyes seemed to look back at the audience from some place that was not the tent, was not that small stage, was not some field in Seneca Falls, Kansas.

Something had happened here. Travis had watched the entire thing, and he could not even begin to explain how Slate had done this.

Akiko Mimasuya appeared to the left of the stage. She held a huge bouquet of flowers, those same white flowers that Travis had seen appear from Slate's hands.

Slate took the flowers from Akiko, presented them with a flourish to Laura, and then he took her hand and assisted her as she stepped down from the stage.

Danny grabbed her like he'd believed she would wander off alone if left unattended, and Laura McCaffrey just looked back at him with a sort of distant vacancy. She looked exhausted. She looked utterly exhausted.

The crowd were still applauding and whistling. Whatever had happened here, it had impressed them greatly.

Travis, however, was very definitely unsettled. He elbowed his way as quickly as he could through the throng and found the exit. Then he stepped out into the cool night air and took several deep breaths.

"He's good, wouldn't you say?"

Travis turned.

Doyle stood there, a sly smile on his face.

"But it's just a trick, of course, Agent Travis," Doyle replied. "Nothing more nor less than a trick." He touched the brim of his hat with the head of his cane, and then he walked away into the shadows.

28

Travis headed for his car. Still people thronged toward the carnival, chattering, laughing, excited.

It was like fighting against an incoming tide, and—unable to resist—Travis felt himself being turned back the way he'd come. He went with it, still disoriented, still trying to address his own reaction to what he had seen. Somehow, some way, Slate had managed to get Laura McCaffrey to *see* the cards—cards that even Slate had not been able to see. At least that was the appearance of what had happened. Doyle had said it was a trick. But what kind of trick was this?

Back toward the main marquee the crowd went, and Travis found himself at the doorway once more, this time amid a crowd of excited children.

"See the magnificent Bellanca brothers!" Chester Greene was shouting. "See the magnificent Bellanca brothers!"

Travis searched for money, but before he had a chance to pay the entry fee, he was inside the tent. The stage was still there, but all signs of Slate's presentation had gone. The vast majority of those in attendance were children, and Travis found himself at the rear of the marquee with a handful of adults.

The Bellancas appeared, all of them dressed identically, their faces white, their costumes striped in black-and-white vertical lines, and they began by tumbling and gamboling and catching one another and holding each other aloft and then letting go in ways that drew gasps of surprise and wonder from the audience.

Travis found himself barely able to watch at one point—one of them, held vertically aloft by the linked hands of another two, and then a fourth and a fifth climbing higher and higher until there was a black-and-white human column that turned and turned, faster and faster, the two on the ground growing ever quicker as they spun. Those above held their arms out to their sides, and Travis watched as those black-and-white stripes blurred into an indistinct gray, faster and faster and faster.

And then Akiko Mimasuya appeared, and with half a dozen swift steps, she had scaled the human column. She was upside down at the very pinnacle, and then her feet were held, and she was spinning also, but horizontally, her arms out to her sides, colored scarves unfurling from her fingers. Still the column turned ever quicker, and with the bursts of color at the top, it was like watching some kind of human firework display. It was all Travis could do to keep his mouth closed. It wasn't until he experienced a fainting sensation that he realized he was once again holding his breath.

And then the column was slowing, and Akiko came down, climbing gracefully, like some sort of spider, and lay on the ground.

The brothers were around her, and they seemed to be pushing her with their feet.

Akiko responded by folding in her elbows, her knees, tucking her head down, and then it seemed as if she was curled into a ball, almost fetal, and one of the brothers lifted her and put her on his shoulder. Like Atlas bearing the weight of the world, save there seemed to be no weight in her at all. She stayed there—immobile—and then the brothers were each bowing their backs, leaning forward and making a circle. They stood with their feet apart, each the same height, and with their arms raised upward and then crooked so each held the elbows of the one adjacent, they created what could only be described as a fence, and within that fence of upright arms, Akiko was contained. She started to roll then, head over heels, across the bowed backs of the Bellanca brothers, her sideways fall prevented by their arms. Again, a strange and surreal thing to witness, for it became almost *un*human, like something that defied the very nature of human physicality. Suddenly, Akiko seemed to unfold like a flower, and she was up on her hands and feet, running around the narrow circle like some kind of caged feline thing, and then she was on her feet, and she seemed almost to fly across those bowed backs, her feet barely touching them, again the multicolored scarves billowing from her hands.

The children were utterly captivated, and—looking sideways—the adults each held that same expression of disbelief.

Whoever these people were, they were just unbelievably good at what they were doing. Akiko Mimasuya then appeared to fold up like human origami, and wherever she stepped, wherever she extended a leg, wherever some means was required to prevent her falling or tumbling to the ground, there was an arm or a hand there to stop her in the precise moment it was required.

And then the brothers were down on their knees, again forming a circle, their foreheads to the ground, Akiko in the middle of them, lying on her side with her arms over her head, her knees tucked up into her chest.

Travis was uncertain as to whether there had been music previously, but in that moment, he became aware of music. Very aware indeed. It was Oriental, no doubt, but there was something altogether hypnotic about the specific intonation, perhaps the rhythm, the sequence of notes and chords that were being played. He watched in silence, almost unable to move, as Akiko performed a dance within that circle of prostrate men. Akiko Mimasuya was a green shoot emerging from frozen ground, a flower opening in spring, a bird taking flight, a preening swan, a slender tree bowing deferentially before the might of the wind. She was…

Travis was enchanted, transfixed, staring in wonder, unable to blink, unable to avert his gaze or consider any thought at all but for that which was happening in front of his very eyes.

Akiko Mimasuya ceased to belong to any realm of physicality or tangibility that he understood. Akiko Mimasuya became something other than a delicate and laconic Japanese woman; she was not the daughter of people killed in the Pacific conflict; she did not belong to the Carnival Diablo; she did not serve tea or smile politely or watch Michael Travis with an air of distance and a lack of comprehension. She was someone else entirely. She was some*thing* else entirely. Travis felt his misconceptions and preconceptions slip away unchallenged. He wanted to speak to her. He wanted to ask her… Ask her what? He did not even know what he would say if she gave him a moment to open his mouth.

And then her dance was complete, and once more she folded down into nothing, and the Bellanca brothers lifted her between them and carried her away and out of the marquee as if she weighed nothing at all.

The audience erupted in applause, and the children were all dancing themselves, trying to copy what they had seen.

Doyle appeared then, and the children fell silent. He held his cane aloft, and he waved it back and forth above the host of bright and eager upturned faces.

"The Thin Man is coming," Doyle said. "Go now! Run, children! Go get your folks! Tell them the Thin Man is coming!"

There were squeals of excitement, and the children went in all directions, bursting out through the doorway of the marquee in a rush of noise and uncontainable energy.

Travis was left there at the back, alone, he believed, though he seemed unable to turn either left or right to determine whether there were other adults still present.

Doyle looked at him.

"Enjoying the show, Agent Travis?" he asked, and then he smiled, once more touching the brim of his hat with the head of his cane, and—without waiting for a response—he was gone.

Travis wanted to leave but could not. He needed some air. He wanted to see the sky, to feel his feet on solid ground. The performance had impressed him, no question about it, but it had also unsettled him, just as had been the case with Slate and Laura McCaffrey. His parameters were moving. That was the only way he could describe it. His understanding of what human beings were capable of was somehow shifting. There were things here that he was struggling to understand, struggling to explain, and he did not like it. This flew in the face of things that he *knew* to be possible, things he knew to be impossible, and though there had to be a rational and understandable explanation, he was damned if he could see it.

He looked toward the doorway, knew that any attempt to escape would see him trampled underfoot by the incoming flood of people. He stayed back at the side of the marquee, close enough to the stage to see what was happening yet sufficiently shrouded in shadow so as not to draw attention to himself. The marquee filled up quickly, and there were children running back and forth between the legs of the adults. They'd heard the Thin Man was coming, and the Thin Man was evidently someone they wished to see. This was Oscar Haynes, born and raised in Chicago, a man who had walked around the edges of that world within which Travis himself had been involved so many times, the world of hoodlums and gangsters and racketeers and bootleggers.

The music began. The crowd fell silent. Every once in a while a child erupted in laughter and an adult was heard to *Ssshhh* them. The music was ponderous and dramatic, and when Oscar Haynes appeared on the stage there was a collective gasp of something that fell between wonder and horror.

Oscar Haynes was a walking skeleton. His clothing was skintight, and on it was painted the human frame, seemingly every bone and joint, and his face was painted white, his eyes heavily shadowed, and on his *skull* he wore a top hat, from the band a festoon of short and brightly colored feathers. He moved awkwardly, like some sort of zombie, and the children screamed excitedly, both terrified and transfixed. The effect was startling to say the least, and Travis stepped forward to better see what Oscar Haynes was going to do.

This was no two-bit hustle for dimes and quarters. Everything Travis had seen thus far was remarkable in its own way. Laura McCaffrey, Danny, Sheriff Rourke—all those who had commented on the carnival, that it had to be seen, that it was impressive and special—had been right. Travis was without words. He really was without words.

But the Thin Man was something different. This was a spectacle that possessed a sense of the grim and macabre, and yet the children did not seem afraid.

Haynes stood for a while in silence, and then—as that same silence filled the marquee—another record was placed on the gramophone. This was lighter altogether, even playful—just a simple piano melody accompanied by a few strings. It changed the mood in the tent, and the skeleton on the stage became almost cartoonlike. Due to the skintight nature of Haynes's costume, it was impossible to see how he could conceal anything, but suddenly his hands were full of flower petals. He tossed them into the audience, and a great red cloud hovered over the heads of the spectators for a second. Hands reached to snatch them from the air, but—even as fingers touched them—they were gone.

A gasp of amazement filled the air.

Haynes held his stomach and mimed laughter.

Again, Travis experienced that rush of awkwardness, as if his own skin could not contain him. It was an illusion, no doubt about it, but how had Haynes created that illusion? Was this some kind of mass hypnotism? It could not have been, for there was no such thing. Surely it was not possible to make everyone see the same thing at the same time? Travis did not have a moment to question it further. Haynes was at the edge of the stage, within arm's reach of those at the front of the crowd. He started to turn then, just around and around, and as he turned, he appeared to shrink down toward the ground. Faster and faster he went, and with each revolution, he grew smaller and smaller, somehow contracting his limbs until he was little more than three feet tall, and yet he was entirely proportioned, and he did not seem to have bent his legs, and he could not have been kneeling, for Travis could see the man's feet. Oscar Haynes was the same height as Travis, perhaps taller, and then he was half that height, and still turning, turning, growing in height again, yet again, until he was once again as tall as he'd been when he'd begun.

Haynes slowed to a halt, and as he stopped, Travis could see that he held three or four scarlet balls in each hand, each of them the same size, no bigger than a golf ball. Where had they come from? How had he created the appearance of shrinking in size, and—even as he returned to his normal height—obtained six or eight red balls?

Haynes started to juggle those balls, and Travis watched, his eyes wide, as those balls flew ever faster and higher. There were six or eight and then there were ten, then twelve, and then it was as if there was a constant stream of scarlet red balls flowing from one hand to the other in an uninterrupted sequence. Again a gasp of wonder and disbelief issued from the gathering, and Travis stepped forward again to see more closely what was before him. His mind was fighting what was in front of his eyes, and yet he knew this was no hallucination, no delusion. This *was* an illusion—it *had* to be—but it was unlike anything he had ever seen before.

And then the balls were disappearing, seemingly being absorbed into Haynes's hands, for there was an endless stream of them, and then they seemed to be intermittent, and then Travis believed there were few enough of them for him to count, and then there was four, then two, then none.

The balls were gone—every single one of them—and there was no place into which they could have possibly vanished.

The crowd erupted into spontaneous cheers and clapping and whistling. The sound was close to deafening.

Travis clapped with them, involuntarily perhaps, for his mind was elsewhere, still trying to fathom this, still trying to make sense of something that made absolutely no sense at all.

Haynes looked at him then. Travis knew it. He *felt* it. That skull looked right at him, and did Haynes wink at him? Was that some sly and knowing glance of *acknowledgment?*

Got you now, haven't I? it said. *Go figure this one out, Agent Travis.*

Or was it merely Travis's imagination?

He stepped back, trying perhaps to be invisible, to go unnoticed, but he knew that Haynes was fully aware of his presence.

"Two volunteers!" Haynes shouted.

It seemed that everyone in the tent but Travis wanted to volunteer, but Haynes plucked two children from the front row, neither of them more than ten or twelve years old. He positioned them facing each other and at right angles to audience, Haynes himself behind them and facing the crowd.

"Silence please, ladies and gentlemen," Haynes said.

The crowd hushed, as silent as a funeral.

Haynes raised the hands of the child to his right, turned their palms upward, and then had the second child do the same. Their fingertips were perhaps two or three feet apart.

Haynes stepped back again, and then he raised his hands.

Before either child could do or say anything, a fine white line seemed to materialize between their outstretched fingertips, spanning that gap between them, and as it grew brighter, it seemed to solidify, until it was as if a rope of light tied their hands together. The light moved, no doubt. It seemed alive and real and as tangible as daylight itself. The crowd gasped. The children's faces were animated and dreamlike, full of amazement, seemingly unperturbed by what was happening between them.

Haynes clicked his fingers and the light changed color. White to blue.

Again, another click of the fingers. Blue to scorching red. Red to yellow. Yellow to white once more. And then he was waving his hands over that rope of light, and the color changed again and again, faster and faster, until there was a pulsing rainbow between those children.

The crowd was stunned into silence.

And then the light went out. It snapped almost audibly, like a distant crack of thunder, and it was gone.

The children stood there, and their hands were filled with candies, almost too many for them to hold. Simultaneously, seemingly without prompt, they both turned toward the audience and tossed those handfuls of candies toward the spectators. The children grabbed those candies from the air. The kids on the stage were laughing, and as they stepped down and were received by their parents, Travis could see an expression in those adults' faces. It was almost gratitude, as if their children had been selected to receive some special gift, as if they had been chosen above all others to experience something truly meaningful and profound.

Haynes took his bows, and then he left the stage.

The tent started to empty out, the hubbub of excitement and chatter dying down, and Travis was one of the very last to leave.

He took some steps toward the stage, scanned the ground for the petals that Haynes had thrown into the audience; he saw nothing but trampled grass and muddy footprints.

He heard someone behind him, knew it was Doyle, had a question on his lips even as he turned.

"Not yet, Agent Travis," Doyle said, preempting anything Travis might have asked.

"But—"

"The show isn't over yet," Doyle said. "You have yet to see Mr. Greene weave his . . . his—what shall we call it?—his *mind magic*. Then, and only then, will I answer your question."

Travis had already forgotten the question he'd intended to ask.

"Walk. Breathe. Look at the sky for a while, Agent Travis. Come back to earth, as they say." Doyle smiled, and there was something so sincere in his expression that Travis felt completely undone. He felt as if the stitching that held all his seams together had loosened considerably, and all of a sudden he would fall right out of his body and never be able to return.

"All I will say," Doyle whispered, "is that people sometimes see just exactly what they want to see. The mind is powerful, Michael. Too powerful to put in a box. Too powerful to hide away from. Too powerful to do anything but accept that it has unknown and unlimited capabilities, and we haven't even scratched the surface. As you know all too well, sometimes things happen simply because we believe they will."

Doyle reached out and touched Travis's arm.

"It gets easier, Michael," he said, "just as long as you don't fight it."

29

Travis did not fight it, not because he didn't wish to, but because he possessed neither the will nor the strength.

Somewhere within himself something was faltering, as if some slow and relentless wave of self-doubt was eating away at the foundation of his certainties. He did not feel good. Nor did he feel bad. He did not know how he felt, and thus he was unsure of what to think. He knew that these people had done something to him, but he did not know what. He knew that they were doing something to the people of Seneca Falls, to all the carnival's visitors, but he could not identify what it was that was happening. Some kind of mass hypnotism. Some kind of mind invasion perhaps. Some kind of mental intervention that created a collective experience, a collective appearance. But such things were not possible. Travis knew that such things were utterly impossible, and yet he possessed no other explanation.

Travis then did as Doyle had suggested. He walked out of the tent and crossed to the edge of the field. This time he was not turned back by crowds of people. He held on to the wooden fence and he looked out toward the horizon. The air was chill, the sky clear, and visible as if within arm's reach were not only the lights of Seneca Falls, but also the stars above his head. They seemed equidistant, as if one were merely an earthbound reflection of the other, and somewhere out there, somewhere farther than his eyes could see, the sky and the earth were stitched together by some invisible hand.

"Mr. Travis?"

Travis turned at the sound of the voice.

Laura McCaffrey stood there, her brothers Danny and Lester nowhere to be seen. She seemed almost embarrassed.

"Laura," Travis said, wishing he could remain alone, wishing he could just have these few moments to gather his thoughts together.

"I was just wondering if you..." She looked away, as if consulting some unseen person on how best to ask whatever she wished to ask.

"If I?" Travis prompted.

"Well, Danny and Lester and I . . . we just wondered whether you would like to come to dinner at our house on Sunday."

She paused for a moment. "We are at church in the morning," she went on, "but we always have a Sunday dinner afterward, and you don't know anyone here, and you spend all your time working, and we just wondered if you—"

"That is very much appreciated, Laura, of course, but Bureau protocol . . ."

Laura nodded understandingly. "I thought that would be the case," she interjected. "Nevertheless, the invitation is there. I wanted to ask you, and I've done so. I am sorry you can't come, and I'm sure Danny will be sorry too. He does so admire you, you know?"

"I'm sorry?"

"Well, he always had his heart set on being in the Sheriff's Department like his brother, but he was sick when he was a child, and he has some kind of weakness in his heart you see? It's not life-threatening or anything like that, but he is limited when it comes to heavily exerting himself. He can't run very far. He tries not to lift things that are too heavy. That's all, really. However, it meant that he couldn't be a sheriff, and I know that is always going to be a disappointment for him." She smiled coyly. "You, however, are from the Federal Bureau of Investigation." She laughed briefly. "He calls you the G-man. I know from the way he talks about you that he admires what you do, and he kind of wishes he could do the same."

"Well, for what it's worth, I am sure Danny would make the most excellent G-man."

"Oh, you should tell him that, Agent Travis. That would just make his day. You have absolutely no idea."

"I'll be sure to do that, Laura."

Laura McCaffrey hesitated for a moment, and then she said, "Are you not allowed to have any friends, Agent Travis?"

Travis looked at her. A frown creased his brow.

"I'm sorry," she said. "That was very rude of me. I didn't mean—"

Travis raised his hand and she fell silent. "No offense taken. I understood what you meant just perfectly."

"Well, yes, and I am sure you have just a wealth of friends back in Kansas, right?"

"Yes, Laura. A wealth of friends."

"I have to be getting back," she said. "I want to see the little man again. What he did on Friday was just remarkable, and I have to see him do it again."

"You're speaking of Chester Greene, right?"

257

"If he's the little man, then yes, that's him."

"And what is it that he did on Friday?" Travis asked.

"Oh, he can see right into your mind, Agent Travis," she said. Her eyes lit up like Roman candles. "Right into your mind. The most remarkable thing I ever saw. It just has to be seen to be believed."

"Well, I wouldn't miss it for the world, then," Travis said.

"Okay," Laura said. "Well, the invitation for dinner is still open if you decide we're no longer murder suspects."

"Appreciated," Travis said.

Laura stepped forward and started to reach out her hand. She hesitated, merely grazed the sleeve of his jacket with her fingertips, and it seemed that there was just a world of unspoken words in her eyes.

"If you ever feel like you need another friend," she said. "I mean, I know you have so many back home, but if you ever…" She looked away, embarrassed again, but there was such kindness in her eyes that Travis felt his heart would burst.

"It was nice speaking with you, Laura," he said.

She touched his sleeve once more, and then she turned suddenly and hurried away.

Travis watched her go, his breath caught in his chest, and then he looked upward to the sky, down again to the lights of Seneca Falls, and he inhaled deeply.

He knew then that he was tired of fighting the world, but he knew he dared not stop. If he stopped, then what would he do? Who would he be? What would become of him?

Michael Travis gripped the fence and bowed his head.

He counted to ten, and then he headed back to the marquee to see a dwarf from Oklahoma City perform *mind magic*.

30

Travis was not late, but he did enter the marquee to find the place jammed from side to side. There must have been three hundred people in there. Scanning faces, he recognized almost no one. It seemed that each time he looked, there were new people to see, all of them strangers, all of them wearing that self-same expression of transfixed anticipation. There *was* something in the atmosphere. There was no denying it. Travis did not like it, nor could he determine what it was that he did not like.

The stage was empty but for a single wooden chair. It was the folding kind, the kind one might put in the back of the car for a picnic. There was no sign of Doyle or Valeria Mironescu, nor Slate or Benedek or Akiko Mimasuya. He could not see Laura or the McCaffrey brothers, nor Larry Youngman or Sheriff Rourke. Travis felt even more alone than ever before.

It was a little while before Travis became aware of the music. If he was not mistaken, it was Stravinsky's *The Firebird*, again something he knew solely because of Esther's interest in such music. It created an ominous feeling perhaps, something altogether uneasy and unsettling, and when Chester Greene finally walked onto the little makeshift stage, as the music swelled and then quietened, the crowd of spectators seemed to hold their breath in unison.

Greene stood center stage, and for such a tiny man, he seemed to not only command the attention of everyone present, but also project a charismatic aura that reached the very back of the tent with ease.

He smiled, winked at the audience.

"Lighten up," he said quietly. "I ain't gonna bite."

There was a moment's hesitation, and then a ripple of laughter spread through the tent. There seemed to be a collective exhalation, and a sense of strange relief filled Travis's body. He did not know what he had been expecting, but the feeling had been that it would be the worst. Now that was gone, gone altogether, and he was merely standing there watching a small man from Oklahoma start his carnival routine.

Greene nudged his hat back on his head. He stood with one hand on his hip, the other on the back of the chair.

"Tell you something now, you menfolk. What's the best way to remember your wife's birthday?"

Greene paused for a second.

"Forget it once!"

A smattering of laughs throughout the crowd.

"I have a friend called Lionel. He's Jewish, like me. Nice guy. Has a wife called Frieda. Took Frieda to the doctor for a checkup. Doctor did a full examination. He comes out to see Lionel in the waiting room, says, 'Lionel, I'm sorry, but I've got some bad news. I've done a full examination of your wife, and I don't like what I'm seeing.' Lionel, he looks at the doctor, and he says, 'Hey, Doc, no need to get personal. I seem to remember your wife ain't no oil painting neither.'"

The crowd was laughing then, the earlier sense of unease now completely gone.

Greene tipped his hat and winked again.

"Another friend," he went on. "Name's Moshe. Went to see his psychiatrist. Moshe says to the psychiatrist, 'I had a strange dream recently. I saw my mother in the dream, but then I noticed she had your face. I found this so worrying that I immediately awoke and couldn't get back to sleep. I just stayed there thinking about it until seven a.m. I got up, made myself a slice of toast and some coffee, and came straight here. Can you please help me explain the meaning of my dream?' The psychiatrist kept silent for some time, then said, 'One slice of toast and coffee? You call that a breakfast?'"

Even Travis smiled, found himself resisting the desire to laugh, and then he let it go. The man was funny, no doubt about it.

Greene took a step forward, put his hands on his hips. "A businessman boards a plane and sits next to an elegant woman wearing the largest diamond ring he's ever seen. He asks her about it. 'This is the Egoheimer diamond,' the woman says. 'It's beautiful, but there is a terrible curse that goes with it.' The businessman is curious. He asks her what the curse is. The woman shakes her head, looks very serious. 'It's called Mr. Egoheimer.'"

There is barely a breath before the crowd erupts with laughter.

Greene was in his element. He took a bow.

"Too kind, too kind, too kind," he said.

The audience settled.

"But we digress," Greene said, and with that he took off his hat and put it under the chair. He sat down, his hands on his knees, his knees together, and he smiled at the crowd. He said nothing at all for a good thirty seconds. He just sat there and smiled, and instead of unnerving them, it seemed to do the opposite. People seemed to just relax, to settle down, to ready themselves for whatever was coming next.

"There are ways and means," Greene said quietly. "For everything, there are ways and means. Some we understand, some we don't. Some make sense, and some seem to possess no sense at all. Sometimes people tell you that what you don't know can't hurt you, but it's the other way around, folks. If you know something, well, you can do something about it, right? If you understand something, well, you can work it out, rationalize it, fix it good and proper so it's not a problem anymore. Seems to me that the thing we should all fear the most is ignorance. Most of the troubles we see in the world are born out of ignorance. Ignorance leads to impatience and intolerance and hatred. Just look at the way the colored folks get treated sometimes. Look at the way the Jewish people were persecuted in the war. All out of ignorance."

Greene leaned forward, his elbows on his knees, his fingers steepled together. "So, I always say it's better to know than to not know. Better to see than to be blind. Better to find out than leave it all covered up and hidden. If you hide a light under a bushel, well, it doesn't change the fact that the light is still there."

There was a murmur of consent in the crowd. All of a sudden it started to feel more like a revivalist meeting than a carnival act. Greene had their attention, no question about it, and for a moment Travis wondered whether this monologue was the precursor to some further sort of collective hypnosis. Was he—even now—lulling them all into some false sense of security?

Trust me, people. Listen to my voice. It is calming, it is soothing, and you can believe every word I say. Look at me now. Do I look like the kind of guy who would sell you a bill of goods?

Wasn't this the point of such a pretense, to make people feel that Chester Greene—the funny Jewish dwarf—was incapable of anything but the truth?

Travis felt that sense of instinctive suspicion, as if to build a wall around his mind, refusing to allow himself to be duped into seeing or hearing something that was anything but real and tangible.

"Erasmus once said that man's mind was formed in such a way as to be far more susceptible to falsehood than truth. Tonight, ladies and gentlemen, we shall try to redress the balance a little. We shall try to return a little truth into the grander scheme of things. However, there are some things that are more easily done than said, so I am not going to try to explain what happens here tonight."

Greene smiled at the audience, and then he took a deep breath.

"And so . . . we begin with the small matter of a broken promise."

Greene scanned the audience, and then his attention appeared to be fixed somewhere over to Travis's left. The stage was lit, the audience in semidarkness, and Travis could not see who Greene might have been looking at.

"She made a vow," Greene continued, "and she made it with the best intention in the world, and—in all honesty—it wasn't even possible to keep that vow. Not really. Not if she had been truthful to herself and to her mother. But she made the vow, as we often do, and then the time came when the vow was broken, and ever since that time, she's been holding on to it like she did the very worst thing in the world, and for all the world to see, she is unhappy and burdened and will never find a way to smile again."

There was a breathless silence in that tent.

Greene echoed that silence for a moment, and then he shook his head. "Promises to those who are dying are sometimes the best way to kill those who are left behind, my dear."

There was a stifled sob from somewhere within the audience.

People moved, and right before Travis's eyes, the crowd parted, and a man and a woman came into view. The woman was crying, no doubt about it, and the man beside her held her as if she were deadweight.

Greene was good. Travis had to grant him that. What could have been more likely than someone in the audience burdened beneath a promise to a dying person that they then failed to keep?

"When someone you love dies," Greene said, "it feels like a little of you dies as well. The more you loved them, the more it feels like your life will never be the same. They went, that's understood, but you are left behind, and you still have to live your own life the best you can."

The woman held the handkerchief to her face. The man beside her looked at Greene as if he were administering some kind of emotional resuscitation.

"You are Alice, aren't you?" Greene said, no absence of certainty in his voice.

The woman stifled a painful sob and nodded in the affirmative.

The plant, Travis thought. He would bet his life on the fact that this woman was not from Seneca Falls. This was an outsider, brought in to play the part, to get the audience going.

The impulse was to call out, to make some comment, to at least make his protest and disagreement heard. This kind of thing was outrageous, not only from the viewpoint of tricking the public out of their money, but also the fact that it was tantamount to fraud. Lord only knew what would be going on in the minds of the others present. Watching this kind of thing, *believing* this kind of thing, gave people false hope. It gave them ideas that things could be understood that could and would *never* be understood.

Greene shook his head sagely. "It's time now, Alice," he said. "It's time to let her go, to let her be. The longer you hold on to it, the longer you will stay upset, and that's doing nobody any good."

Greene looked up at the roof of the tent. "She holds on for you, Alice. You know that? She's right here."

The audience gasped in collective wonder.

"She's held on for you all this time. She loves you so very much, and she can't bear to see you unhappy, and if you'll just let her go now, if you'll just wish her well and let her go, then she can move on. Until you do that, well, she is just caught here in our world, and she cannot move on to where she needs to be."

"Alice" started sobbing more pronouncedly. Whoever she was, she was also good. The "husband" played his part with stoicism.

"So, that's what you need to do, Alice, and though this is more for her than for you, I am sure you will feel an awful lot better."

Chester Greene leaned forward. "Let go, my dear. Just let go. You won't drown; you won't die. It will all come out right in the end. I promise."

The "husband" started toward the stage with "Alice," and when they reached it, he held out his hand.

The crowd held their breath.

Greene reached back, and for a moment their fingers touched.

"Thank you," the "husband" said, his voice cracking with emotion. "Thank you *so* much, Mr. Greene."

The couple turned, and then applause started. People touched them as they walked, hands to their shoulders as if acknowledging them for some commitment to faith.

There was a sense of fervor and enthusiasm surrounding the whole performance that just seemed so very wrong to Travis.

He felt at first contemptuous of Greene, of Doyle, of all of them, and then a growing sense of disgust invaded his thoughts. What would happen now? "Alice" and her "husband" would be seen to offer some financial contribution as they left? Was that how it worked? Would they hand over five bucks, and thus prompt others to start emptying their pockets?

Travis swallowed his sense of shame at what he was witnessing, and then he wondered whether the dead Hungarian had been here too, whether he had seen what was happening, whether he'd started to make noises about the kind of confidence trick that was being perpetrated. Was that why he had been killed, for suggesting that he would expose their scams and have them investigated by the authorities? Was this nothing more than a simple case of murder for profit? Murder committed to prevent the exposure of a lucrative scheme founded in lies?

The applause died down.

Greene rose from the chair and walked back and forth across the front of the stage.

"My mind is filled with happiness," he said. "Where are you? The ones with the child?"

There was a brief exclamation of surprise from somewhere in the shadows. People stepped away, and a young couple came forward.

"You learned today?" Greene asked the woman.

The woman nodded, smiling from ear to ear.

"They are going to have a baby!" Greene said.

The crowd applauded.

"Congratulations to you both," Greene went on. "A truly wondrous and wonderful thing!" He winked, smiled at them both. "And don't worry," he added. "When your mother finds out, she'll stop nagging at your husband about finding a better job!"

The woman looked stunned, the husband started laughing, and then the crowd was laughing too. The earlier sense of despondency and sadness had been completely dispelled. The crowd were animated, wholly engaged by Greene's performance, and he was milking it for all it was worth.

"The boxes are there, folks," Greene said. "Sometimes you just gotta face that fact and take a look. As has been said so many times before, many of life's problems can be solved with just twenty seconds of courage. And you know what else? Time doesn't heal. No, sirree. Old Man Time is the Great Pretender, you know?"

Greene took a seat. He lit a cigarette, and the smoke rose above his head in hieroglyphics. There were shapes and faces among those arabesques and garlands, hanging there like ghosts, and then they folded away into nothing.

"Time doesn't mend a broken heart. Time doesn't bring back those we have lost. Time merely dulls the sharp edge of memory, but those memories can often return sharper than ever and cut you just as deep." He shook his head and smiled sardonically. "And if anyone would know the truth of that, then it's me."

Greene dropped the half-smoked cigarette and extinguished it. He rose from the chair and walked to the edge of the low stage. He raised his right hand and held it with his palm facing the crowd. He closed his eyes, and then he started to breathe more heavily.

The crowd fell quiet.

"Sometimes people decide to die," Greene said. "And it doesn't matter what you say or do; they are going to die. This is not fate or destiny. This is the power of the mind over the body."

Greene leaned forward. "Do you know that there are certain Native American Indians who possess the capability of stopping their own hearts? They can do that, you know? When they get old and they believe it is time to move on to the happy hunting ground, they can simply sit down, lean against a tree, close their eyes, and stop their own heart. Someone will come by later and find them, and there is such an air of peace and tranquillity about them. Remarkable, you might think, but all of us possess such capabilities. There is nothing one human being can do that another can't. All that we were once capable of doing, we can do again. All that we have forgotten, we can once again remember. We can see the past, the present, the future. We can learn from history but remain unaffected by it. There are answers there, the answers to every question you might ever have asked, and yet we are afraid to open our eyes and ears to those answers." Greene paused. He scanned the crowd, and then he seemed to identify someone in the shadows to the right.

"The truth, my dear, is that there was nothing you could have done. That is what I am saying. Some people make a decision to die. Some people have grown tired of the game, and they want a new game, a better game, and the unknown future presents a possibility so much more appealing than the present. And when it comes to suicide... well, this person has simply reached a point where even they themselves believe that the world would be better off without them. That is the truth they see. A sad truth, granted, but nevertheless a truth they believe. And it is all too easy to ask yourself what you could have done or said that would have made it different. The fact of the matter is that there was nothing you could have done or said that would have made the slightest bit of difference. He decided it was time, and that was that."

Travis looked closely, and—just as before—the people around Greene's *target* seemed to step away.

A woman came forward, perhaps late thirties or early forties, and yet Travis suspected she might have been younger. She carried age before her time, it seemed. Why he felt this to be the case, he did not know. It was just something he sensed.

"Your brother was a good man," Greene said.

The woman looked visibly shaken. She took a handkerchief from her skirt pocket and clutched it as if it were a lifeline somehow capable of rescuing her from the emotional tidal wave there on the horizon of her thoughts.

"He was a good man, but he carried his ghosts well, Miss Petersen."

The woman gasped audibly.

"Ron Petersen carried his ghosts through childhood, through his teenage years, all the way into adulthood, you see, and there was no one who could have alleviated him of that burden. Sometimes we are born with ghosts, bringing them into our current life from some past existence perhaps. Sometimes those ghosts are just waiting for us when we arrive, and they attach themselves to us, they become part of us, and unless you learn where they come from, they will always haunt you. This is why the truth of life is so important. This is why we have to look in order to see, to listen in order to hear. This is why we have to ask questions, and we have to keep on asking those questions until we find an answer that makes us feel better. The truth might hurt, but the truth will always heal. It is not time that will heal, but the truth over time. That is the difference, friends and neighbors."

Miss Petersen stepped forward. She was now just a few feet from the edge of the stage.

"I—I lo-loved him," she said, her voice frail but clearly audible.

"I know you loved him, Miss Petersen," Greene said, "and he knows that you loved him, and he also knows that you would have done anything for him. However, the truth is that there really was nothing you could have done. Your brother had a rendezvous with death, and there was nothing that was going to prevent him from meeting it."

Miss Petersen started crying, but it was not some overwhelming display of grief. There was a sense of unburdening about her, as if some weight was being lifted from her shoulders.

"And so," Greene continued, "it is time for you to forgive yourself, my dear. It is time for you to stop the endless questions about whether you could have done this or that or the other. He has been dead for six years, and you have been dead as well. At least some part of you went with him, and it is time to take it back. There is a man who loves you, and he needs you to be well and happy. He wants to spend his whole life with you, but he does not want to live with your dead brother as well. Your brother has gone, and yet you keep trying to get him back. Let him go. The past is the past. Do not hide from it, of course. It will always be right where it is. You can see it, but you do not need to keep pulling it up into the present, and it certainly has no place in the future."

Miss Petersen took a further step forward, and she held out her hand toward Chester Greene.

What was this? Travis wondered. Was this *now* where she led the field, the first to hand over money, and the crowd would follow? But there was no money. There was just Miss Petersen's hand reaching out toward Chester Greene, and Chester came forward himself and took her hand, and she held on to him for just a second. Their eyes were level, for Chester was standing on the stage, and for a moment it seemed as if there were no one else in the tent.

"Thank you," she said, her voice all but a whisper, but it was heard by everyone in that tent.

"Live," Greene said. "Stop dying, my dear. It's not your time, and it won't be your time for a great many years to come."

Miss Petersen gripped Chester Greene's hand once more, and then she turned and disappeared into the crowd.

"And now ... now it is perhaps time for a little housecleaning, eh?" Greene said. He returned to the chair and sat down. He leaned back and crossed his legs. The audience seemed to edge closer, as if he was going to share something of a more personal nature with them.

"The mind," Greene said, "is like an attic. It is up here ..." He tapped his forehead with his index finger. "It is up here, and we know it's there, but we sort of ignore it. It goes about its business on a day-to-day basis, and while we take the time to tidy up and clean every other room in our lives, we often forget this one altogether." Greene smiled knowingly. "But this, dear friends and neighbors, is where we find the past. Of course, there are good times and bad times. That is life. That is what being human is all about. And I'm not talking about the good things, people, I am talking about the stuff that hurts. The good stuff we keep, you see? The good stuff doesn't go in the attic. That's what we put on display. That's what we carry around with us that we want our friends and family to see. However ..." Greene uncrossed his legs and leaned forward. The audience seemed to lean right on back at him. "And this is a big *however* ... the things we don't want, the things we hide away from the world, well, this is where we find the trouble. These things are like little weights, like little anchors, and we find ourselves slowing down. Every day we get older, and every day we add a little more weight, a little more unnecessary baggage, and life becomes harder, and we become more bitter, and after a while we find ourselves resenting the youth and happiness of others. We don't like to admit it, but it's true. We are alone, and we see a young couple so in love, and we hate them just a little bit. We have no job, we are struggling, and we see someone heading off to work, and we hate them just a little bit. Of course, we don't hate them really, but we hate the idea of how they make us feel. Because we should know better, and we know we're not bad people, but then why do we react in such a way?"

The crowd murmured.

Even Travis felt that there was little of what Greene was saying with which he could find disagreement. How many times had he seen couples together and thought of times he'd spent with Esther? Hadn't that even happened, albeit subconsciously, when he'd first met Edgar

Doyle and Valeria Mironescu? Hadn't that happened when he'd taken time to comment—even if only to himself—regarding how attractive Laura McCaffrey was?

"But the past is a different country," Greene continued. "The past is a different country, and sometimes we forget that in this country they speak a different language. We forget that tongue, and we forget part of our own life, and though it may not seem to be the case, that part of our life is vitally, vitally important. Why? Because that's the attic, my friends. Because that's where you find all those damp and dusty boxes. Because within those boxes are the memories you don't want to remember, and sometimes you just have to steel yourself, you have to roll up your sleeves, you have to climb that ladder into the roof of your house and start opening those boxes once more."

Greene placed his hands together palm to palm and smiled with great sincerity.

"Now, I am not a preacher," Greene went on. "I am not a man of the Lord. Heaven knows, I have done enough in my life to earn myself a special hot place down there..."

Greene nodded at the ground. There was a ripple of uncomfortable laughter from the audience, due perhaps more to the self-same recognition in the congregation than anything else. Weren't we all our own worst judges? Didn't we deem our own crimes, however small, worthy of a far more severe sentence than that which would be granted by others? Of course we did. That, once again, was simply human nature.

"But perhaps I won't find myself there, folks. And I'll tell you why. Because we always tell ourselves it was worse than it was."

Travis looked at Greene. Hadn't Travis just considered that same exact thought?

"We always tell ourselves that what we did was far more serious than it really was, you know? We do that. We all do that. That's just part of human nature."

Again, a murmur of consent from the audience.

"So, if we learn nothing, we have to learn how to forgive ourselves. We have to remember that others will never be as harsh as we are with ourselves—"

"I want to speak!"

The crowd turned in unison.

Sheriff Rourke stood forward. The people around him stepped away. There was no mistaking who he was. He was standing right there in front of everyone, and irrespective of the fact that he was out of uniform, there would have been few people who didn't know who he was, even among the out-of-towners.

Rourke stood for a moment in silence, and then he held out his hands at his sides, palms forward, as if saying, *Here I am. This is me, and I am ready for everyone to hear what I have to say.*

"You want to say something?" Greene asked.

"I just want to say something, Mr. Greene."

Travis was impressed with Rourke. He was the local representative for law and order, and now he was going to impress his authority on these proceedings. Despite asking everyone to call him Chas, despite his easygoing and avuncular manner, he was going to tell Chester Greene and the rest of these people exactly what he thought of them.

Rourke cleared his throat. "Well, in truth," he said, "I want to tender an apology, actually. I spoke badly of you and your people when you came here. I really did. I said some harsh things. I used words that it was not right to use, and I wanted to say I was sorry."

Travis was stunned. He couldn't believe what he was hearing.

There was a small ripple of applause, and before it had a chance to grow, Greene raised his hand and silenced it.

"We were received no better or worse here than anywhere else, Sheriff Rourke. I am sure what you said was not so bad, and certainly no worse than the things that are routinely said to my face, but I appreciate the sentiment, and I acknowledge your apology. However, I do not believe that this was really what you wanted to say, was it?"

Travis wondered whether now was the time to speak up, to elbow his way to the front of the crowd and demand that they stop this charade immediately. Something within himself prevented him, yet had he been asked he would not have known how to describe it. Fear? Surely not. Perhaps some concern that the crowd would turn on him, that their belief in whatever it was that Greene was doing was far greater than their belief in Travis's right to uphold the law?

Greene stood up and walked to the front of the stage.

Rourke took a single step back, but it was so clear that he was withdrawing from whatever it was that he was confronting.

"I know it was a long time ago, Sheriff Rourke, but sometimes those things that happened in childhood are the most dangerous. The mind is impressionable. Everything seems so much more important to a child. Everything seems so much more significant. And those memories, the distant ones, are the ones that have had the longest time to fester and grow more bitter. And remember what I said... we judge ourselves ever more severely than others will judge us. It was an accident, perhaps?"

Rourke's eyes widened. He looked at Greene, and then he turned and looked at the faces around him.

The sense of anticipation was almost physical. Travis could sense that the air itself had changed. It seemed harder to breathe. There was a constrictive sensation in his chest. His hands were sweating, and he found himself willing Rourke to speak. He wanted to know what had happened. He *needed* to know what had happened.

"W-we were just ch-children, you understand?" Rourke said. "We were just little kids, and we didn't think..." He lowered his head for a moment. His chest rose and fell as if he was suppressing some huge wave of emotion. "We didn't think," he said. "That was the problem right there, wasn't it? We just didn't think about what we were doing, what we were saying, and this has haunted me all of my life. I try so hard to forget, and weeks, sometimes months will go by, and I won't even think of it, but it's always there..."

He looked up at Greene and smiled in recognition. "In the attic, Mr. Greene. Right up there in the attic, isn't it?"

Greene nodded, but did not speak.

"We chased that kid every day," Rourke went on, his voice hurried. "We called him names. We threw stones. We pushed him into puddles of dirty water. One time we pushed him off the bridge into the river, and he was damned near swept away. Hell, he could have died, you know? That poor defenseless, dumb son of a bitch could have died, and we would have murdered him, wouldn't we? We would have been murderers; at ten or eleven years of age, we would have been responsible for taking the life of another child."

All of a sudden Rourke was not alone. Another man stood beside him, his hand on Rourke's shoulder. A gesture of support, of understanding. It took a moment for Travis to realize that it was Larry Youngman. Rourke reached up and gripped that consoling hand, and the two of them continued to stand there together as Rourke went on.

"His name was Bobby, and he was a Jew." Rourke looked up at stage. "Which, considering present company, makes it seem all the worse, Mr. Greene."

Greene waved his hand dismissively.

"He was just a regular kid. He didn't look no different, and he didn't sound no different, but he was a Jew. That made him different. That made him a target for our name-calling and baiting, our... our mental torture. Because that's what we did to him, you see? We tortured him. I mean, it was before all this stuff came out about what happened during the war, the way the Jews were persecuted and murdered. We didn't know about that, you know? That's not why we chased him and bullied him. We chased him and bullied him because he was different, that was all... And when you people came into town, when I saw you for the first time, I was reminded of this so terribly. It was such a strong memory, Mr. Greene, and it's been preying on my mind ever since you arrived, and I just knew I had to say something…"

Rourke lowered his head.

"Thank you for opening the box, Sheriff Rourke," Greene said. "And I can tell you right now that Bobby is just fine."

Rourke looked up, his eyes wide.

Greene smiled. "Believe me or not, Bobby Alberstein is fine and well. He got married, has three kids, and runs a successful chain of convenience stores in the Midwest."

Rourke stepped back. Youngman stepped aside.

"But… but… his name? How did you know his name?"

Greene shook his head. "You opened the box, Sheriff Rourke… I just had a moment to look inside."

Travis looked at Chester Greene, this Jewish dwarf from Oklahoma City, and then he turned and looked at Sheriff Charles Rourke of Seneca Falls, Kansas. Had they really staged this? Had they planned this together? And, if so, was he somehow involved in the death of the Hungarian man? Surely not.

Rourke's reaction to this revelation seemed genuine enough, but perhaps Rourke was as skilled an actor as he was a liar. Perhaps the friendly and cooperative small-town sheriff persona that he seemed to wear so effortlessly was nothing more than a facade.

Travis was confused. Here was something that ran far deeper than he'd at first believed. Either that, or…

The other possibility seemed too ludicrous and surreal to consider.

"He's o-okay?" Rourke asked.

"He sure is, Sheriff Rourke," Greene said. "In fact, he tells his friends that the bullying and harassment he received as a child toughened him up. He tells them that had he not been bullied, he would never have had the courage to ask his wife to marry him, and he would have been too indecisive and nervous to take a punt on his own business. He even mentions you by name. Chas Rourke, he says. That asshole made me the man I am today."

The audience erupted into laughter. Rourke stood there for a moment, and then he started laughing too, crying as well, and Larry Youngman stepped forward once more and put his arm around Rourke's shoulder. Rourke's entire body seemed to shake with emotion. Travis had never seen anything quite like it. If this was an act…

The crowd seemed to swallow Sheriff Rourke. There were hands on his shoulders, people hugging him, and then—after a minute or two—the audience settled down.

Greene stood there in silence for a little while, and then he smiled and nodded his head. "And now I am tired," he said. "I am very tired."

One person started clapping, and then two, three, ten, twenty, and soon the tent was bursting with riotous applause. There were whoops and screams and whistles, and Travis watched in wonder as the entire congregation closed up toward the edge of the stage, reaching out to the little man, trying to touch him, as if merely making contact would somehow realize some supernatural effect on themselves and their lives. Travis had never seen anything like this outside of evangelical gatherings. Greene had taken on the mantle of preacher, confessor, savior. It was almost religious in its enthusiasm, and Travis was both appalled and transfixed.

Greene received their enthusiasm, but he did not stay long. He was gone within a minute or two, and the people were left talking animatedly among themselves, little crowds assembling around Sheriff Rourke, Miss Petersen, the young pregnant woman and her husband.

Travis was sweating profusely beneath his shirt. He had not realized how hot it was inside. He knew that he couldn't absorb any more. His emotions wrestled with his certainties, his suspicions with his convictions, and he had to get away. He walked around the back of the gathering, along the edge of the tent itself, until he came to the doorway. He passed out into the cool night air unnoticed, and he stood there—once again looking at the sky—and his body felt like a thousand pounds of darkness, so much blacker than the sky, so much heavier than the earth beneath his feet.

He breathed deeply—in, out, in, out—and he felt the vista before his eyes waver just a little. The horizon seemed to disappear, and then it was right back where it was supposed to be. He felt as if he were hallucinating, as if someone had perhaps put a drug in his coffee, and now he was seeing and feeling things that were not even real. He wondered if he had been drugged... if he had actually been drugged before, that night when someone crept into his room and typed a single word on a sheet of paper...

"Good, eh?"

Travis turned to see Doyle standing no more than six feet away. He was smoking a pipe.

Travis just started at Doyle, momentarily incapable of speech.

"Is your head still square, Agent Travis?"

"I-if th-that question is designed to elicit some reaction from me, Mr. Doyle, then I am afraid it will not. I believe I understand what you are asking me, and I will not play the game."

"Which is answer enough," Doyle said. "Such a shame."

"A shame? What's a shame, Mr. Doyle? That I am not fooled by such performances? Granted, they are very impressive, both Mr. Slate and Mr. Greene. Extraordinary talents for sleight of hand, even sleight of mind, might we say, but the truth of that matter is that I have not seen anything that has proven beyond a reasonable doubt—"

"Proven what, Agent Travis? What do you think anyone is trying to prove here?"

"That you can read people's minds, Mr. Doyle. That you can see into the past. That you can know things about people that they don't even know themselves. This kind of thing has been going on for hundreds of years. You people set yourselves up somewhere, you make people believe that you are capable of something, that you possess some kind of ability or power that is beyond the parameters of human capability, and then you fleece them for all you can get—"

Doyle raised his hand. "I am not of a mind to argue with you, Agent Travis, nor am I of a mind to counter your accusations, all of which, I might add, are utterly unfounded and entirely without substance. What happened in there tonight was what happened. How people reacted to it was how they reacted to it. Some people feel better. In fact, I would go so far as to say that the vast majority of people who were present tonight have gone home feeling better than when they arrived. Everyone but you, Agent Travis. Perhaps it touched a raw nerve; perhaps it made you feel vulnerable or exposed or afraid. I don't know, and I don't know that I care to know. What I see, what I hear, what I feel is what I see and hear and feel, and I do not need anyone to agree with me to know that it is true."

Doyle looked away toward the horizon, and then he looked back at Travis with a knowing smile.

"I will bid you good night, sir, with the hope that you sleep well, that you do not dream, that you wake refreshed and content. Personally, I cannot even begin to imagine the claustrophobic sense of isolation you must feel each and every day of your life. To have no faith, to have no belief, to have no magic? Oh, that must be the worst hell of all."

Travis opened his mouth to speak, to give some sharp rebuttal, but he had nothing.

By the time he realized he had nothing, Doyle was gone.

31

That night the dream returned, almost as if Doyle's words had been a premonition.

The shadow of a man, the cracked and arid field, the laughing crow.

This time, however, Travis was aware of other aspects of the dream that he had not previously noticed. Somewhere in the background was the sound of calliope music—distant and almost inaudible but definitely there. Every once in a while he believed he heard the sound of child calling his name. Far to his right, there along the horizon, was a disappearing line of telegraph poles, the wire between them black with grackles and other birds he did not recognize. And there between the telegraph poles the ground was blanketed with endless forget-me-nots.

And then the footsteps came, and they were slow and labored, and each time he sensed from which direction they were coming, he would turn, and there would be nothing there but more distance, the horizon beyond, a deep and profound sense of being alone. And yet the feeling of being watched. The *certainty* that he was being watched.

Travis did not like this feeling at all. It slipped beneath his skin and enveloped his nerves.

Even as he dreamed, he knew he was dreaming. He knew he was sleeping, right there in the McCaffrey Hotel in Seneca Falls, but he could not bring himself awake.

Over and over in his mind, he turned the events of the evening—the things he had seen and felt, the things he had witnessed in others, the fact that however much he wrestled with his conscience and his rationality, he could not explain what had happened. He *knew* there was an explanation—he *knew* this without doubt—and yet he could not find it. The death of Ron Petersen, the story from Sheriff Rourke about Bobby Alberstein, the fact that such things had happened when the carnival had gathered before.

It was with that thought that Travis woke.

And he lay there for half an hour, his throat as parched as the arid field, still the echo of the laughing crow, the grackles on the telegraph wire, the sound of the footsteps that yet never reached him.

Eventually he rose and took a drink of water from the glass beside his bed. He walked to the window, drew back the curtain a handful of inches, and looked out into the cool blue of nascent dawn. It was a little before five, and already the light was rapidly peeling back the shadows.

He knew in which direction the carnival lay, and though his first instinct was to dress, to walk back out there, to look at this place in daylight once more—but with a different eye, a different state of mind, a different scale of perceptions—he withheld himself. A calm and measured state of mind was required. But it seemed as if his own past, his present, even his future were being undermined. Travis walked back to the bed and sat down. Most everything had been objective. Most everything had been studied, right back to college, the things he had learned in the army, everything he had been taught in Bureau training, everything he had recorded, annotated, and transcribed while working with Unit X in Kansas City. Academic, always maintaining a *safe distance*, and yet who were they fooling with their reports and documents, their detailed summaries and color-coordinated filing systems? Life was not paperwork. Life was not observing, analyzing and documenting. Life was living. Life was losing his parents, losing Esther. Life was hurtling through an obstacle course while flash charges deafened you, some drill sergeant screaming obscenities at you, finding yourself waist deep in mud, your rifle buried beyond reach in the filth beneath you. Life was the Scarapetto raid, the certainty that you had killed a man. Life was standing in a morgue and questioning the presence of inexplicable tattoos on the unidentified body of a murdered Hungarian. Life was seeing a woman like Laura McCaffrey and knowing that a girl like that could never love the kind of man that you were.

And was this him? This dry and humorless man? Was he this way because of what had happened, or would he have been this way regardless of the circumstances of his childhood and teenage years? These were the very questions with which he had been challenged by the Bureau psychologist in Kansas, the very questions that they had focused on within Unit X. Was a man born with identity intact, or was he a product of his environment? That was as much a question for himself as it was a question for any of the unit's subjects.

But now, the past aside, it was the present that needed explanation. Things had happened—strange things—and Travis knew that their explanation would somehow relate to the resolution of the homicide. They had to be connected. Understand one, and he would understand the other.

Some of those answers had to lie with Chester Greene. All of those answers had to lie with Edgar Doyle and Valeria Mironescu. This was their creation. Everything that had happened here, everything that was happening right now, lay within the province of their understanding. The half answers, the inferences and innuendos, the ever-present sense that they themselves were intentionally keeping him at arm's length, was something of which he was certain.

It was then that Travis noticed the sheet of paper upon which he had written the name Harold Blauer. Doyle had given him that name almost as an aside, almost nonchalantly, as if it meant nothing at all. And yet Travis did not believe Doyle to be a man who did anything unless he intended it. That name had been forwarded for a reason. That name possessed significance. Bishop had told him that he was not to involve other Bureau offices in his investigation, but this now seemed ludicrous. The very least he could do was drive out to Wichita and see if this Blauer existed somewhere within the Bureau system. Travis was then struck by another thought. Was the dead man Harold Blauer? Was this whose body was found beneath the carousel, the body still residing in the Seneca Falls morgue? Blauer did not seem to be a Hungarian name, but perhaps the man had used an alias. If he was in fact some kind of assassin, then it would be routine to operate under an alias.

Travis looked at the bedside clock. It was quarter past six. He showered, dressed, was out of the hotel by seven and on the road to Wichita. He would arrive before eight, take breakfast in a local diner, and be at the office as it opened. It would take no time at all to locate Blauer on the system, if he was in fact there, and he could be back in Seneca Falls before ten to track down Doyle and Valeria.

The drive was uneventful, the highway clear of traffic, and Travis was there early. The office was unmanned as yet, so Travis walked a block and a half and found a diner. He took coffee, ate a piece of French toast and a few mouthfuls of scrambled egg.

Travis retraced his steps, waited merely a handful of minutes before Gary Delaney appeared. Delaney seemed surprised to see him again.

"I have to tell you that I received a message from Supervisor Bishop," Delaney told him as he opened up the office.

"Advising you that I was to be afforded no significant assistance in this investigation, right?"

Delaney looked awkward. "Not in those words, exactly, but that was the basic idea, yes."

"Well, I am not here to ask for your assistance as such, Agent Delaney. I just need to access some information that may or may not be on the system."

"Well, we have Receive Only Model 28, so I would have to call in your request."

"Which is what I am going to ask you to do, Agent Delaney."

There were a few seconds of awkward silence.

"I am not so sure, Agent Travis. The message from Supervisor Bishop—"

"I am a senior special agent," Travis said, his voice calm and unhurried. "I am pulling rank on you. I am giving you a direct and legal order. Supervisor Bishop's message did not say that you had permission to ignore or countermand an order, did it?"

"No, sir, it didn't."

"So, there we are then. I am giving you an order. You are complying with that order. If it then comes back to you... well, it won't come back to you, will it? It will be my responsibility and my responsibility alone."

"Yes, if you put it that way."

"And it's a really simple thing, Agent Delaney. A request for some information regarding one person, and that's all."

"Their name?"

"Harold Blauer," Travis replied.

"B-L-A-U-E-R?"

"That's right, yes."

"And do you know anything about him?"

"My understanding is that he was a tennis player."

"A tennis player?"

"Yes."

Delaney hesitated once again. "I'm sorry, Agent Travis, but there's something about this that seems awful strange. I was puzzled when I received that message from Supervisor Bishop, and now you're here in person asking me to assist you when I have been asked not to do so."

Travis smiled, trying his best to put Delaney's mind at ease. The man was doing his job, coloring inside the lines, so to speak, and was concerned that he might incur the displeasure of his seniors. How easily Travis could see himself in this man.

"I appreciate the dilemma, Agent Delaney," Travis said. "I really do. The simple truth is that this is a test case."

"A test case?"

"In essence, yes. I received a promotion to senior special agent, you see, and along with that increase in responsibility comes an assignment where you are required to pursue the case without external office assistance. Now, I can wait until the City Library is open and go trawl through their newspaper archives, but here we are dealing with a homicide investigation. Irrespective of whatever else might or might not be going on, we are still dealing with a homicide, and the perpetrator of that murder is unknown and on the run. Not only as a federal law enforcement official, but also as a good citizen, it seems nothing less than irresponsible not to break a little rule in order to expedite the case and bring a felon to justice."

"Yes, I can see that, Agent Travis, and that is why I am fighting with this," Delaney replied, and there was a look in his eyes as if he was beginning to reconcile himself to the situation.

"But I really don't want you to compromise your integrity on this point, Agent Delaney—"

"It is not a matter of integrity, Agent Travis," Delaney replied, "but a matter of which is for the greater good, and I cannot see how assisting you in this small matter could be anything but positive. I understand that this case might be a test for you, but it is still a case, and—as you say—a man's life has been taken and someone is responsible. You think that this Blauer might be involved?"

"I have no idea," Travis said. "It is just a name that has come up in the course of the investigation, and I want to rule him in or out, one way or the other."

"Then I'll do it," Delaney said. "To hell with the consequences. It doesn't seem right to me that a federal officer should be prevented from using Bureau resources."

"That's very much appreciated, Agent Delaney."

Delaney started toward an office at the rear of the building. "I'll send the request now. It's early, and we might be lucky. Catch them before the full day's workload starts. Usually it takes a while to get a reply, but we'll see, eh?"

Delaney left the room, and Travis walked to the front window of the office. He looked down the street both ways. There was very little foot or vehicle traffic, but it was Saturday, and the vast majority of citizens would be home with family. He looked at the absence then—as clear as daylight—and it struck him with some force. He had his room at the McCaffrey, not for long, but it was home until this case was complete. And once complete, he would return to Kansas, there to find his sparsely furnished apartment, his books, his neatly arranged provisions, a single houseplant on the windowsill—a cactus, simply because such a plant required no real attention or care. What was he doing now? Was he questioning the existence he had created for himself? Was he actually challenging the rationale of his own life?

Travis turned at the sound of Delaney returning from the back office.

"Seems we're out of luck," Delaney said.

"I beg your pardon?"

"Classified," Delaney said.

"Seriously?"

Delaney handed Travis a sheet of teletype paper. Across the top was printed the date, the call sign of the Wichita office, and beneath it a few lines stating that the information request could not be fulfilled due to the fact that Delaney possessed an insufficiently senior authorization grade.

"Let me use it," Travis said.

"You're sure?" Delaney asked.

"Not a hundred percent, but I'm going to try anyway."

Delaney—once again visibly uncertain—showed Travis through to the back office. Travis keyed in his ID and repeated the request. As an afterthought, and to satisfy another small curiosity, he requested any information on organizations that employed a forget-me-not design as a membership symbol.

"We just have to wait," Delaney said. "No way to tell how long it will be."

"I understand," Travis said. "Same system in every office. I know how it works."

"Of course you do," Delaney said. "I'm sorry. This just makes me a little nervous."

"Don't worry," Travis said. "No one's going to be losing their job over this."

They returned to the front of the office. Delaney suggested he go out and get coffee.

"Good idea," Travis said. "Black, no sugar."

"You want anything else?"

"I'm good."

Delaney left, was gone a good fifteen minutes, returned just as the teleprinter started chugging away in the back.

Travis walked on through. The information request had been authorized and fulfilled. There was not a great deal of text, but at least there was something.

Travis tore off the pages and sat down. Delaney brought the coffee, set it there on the desk, and though he was obviously tempted to hang over Travis's shoulder and find out who this Harold Blauer was, he did not. He made himself scarce, and Travis appreciated this.

The brief report made no real sense to Travis.

The earliest note of Harold Blauer was in December of 1952 when Blauer—apparently depressed after a divorce—voluntarily admitted himself to the New York State Psychiatric Institute for treatment. What happened then seemed like something out of a sensationalistic dime-store novel. Blauer—seemingly consensually—agreed to be part of an experimental research program being undertaken by the US Army Chemical Corps into an untried depression medication. In fact, these medications were chemical warfare agents, and Blauer was administered a series of four injections. He protested any further injections, citing the adverse effects that he was experiencing, but he was convinced to continue, the threat of committal to Bellevue Hospital hanging over him. The fifth injection was many, many times stronger than any previous injection. Blauer suffered a series of adverse effects ranging from a stiffening of the musculature to oral foaming. Oxygen, glucose, even sodium amytal did nothing. This continued for two hours, and then Blauer lapsed into a coma and died. The certificate of death stated COD as *coronary arteriosclerosis; sudden death after intravenous injection of an undisclosed substance.* It appeared that all records of this event were then moved out of state by the army, despite a court order requiring the production of those documents. The report went on to state that Blauer's last and fatal injection had been four hundred and fifty milligrams of an experimental mescaline derivative code-named EA-1298. As of that moment, the case remained closed and no further investigation into Blauer's death was scheduled.

On the final page, merely a couple of lines, Travis read that the forget-me-not had been chosen by the 1938 annual Nazi party Winterhilfswerk, a charitable foundation charged with the responsibility of collecting donations so that other state funds could be released and employed for rearmaments.

That, in essence, was the sum total of the report in Travis's hands, and though he found the material disconcerting, if not almost un-believable, he had no further understanding of why Edgar Doyle would have mentioned Blauer's name, nor why he wore a badge that indicated membership of a pro-Nazi foundation. Was that what he had been doing for the last two years of the war, raising money for the Nazis? What had he said about that badge? That it was his shield against all ills, the thing that made him invincible? What could he have meant?

These were questions that could be answered by Doyle alone, and so Travis folded the report, tucked it into his pocket, thanked Delaney once again for his assistance, and left the Bureau office.

32

Arriving back in Seneca Falls, Travis drove straight to the carnival site. Even as he approached the location of the previous evening's experiences, he realized that he'd done all he could to blanch his mind of what he'd seen and heard. There was no immediate explanation for Oscar Haynes's ability to *see* cards through the eyes of another human being, and there was most definitely no explanation for Chester Greene's ability to know what he did about peoples' lives and past circumstances. If it was not collusion and prior arrangement with the subjects in question, then it challenged most of what Travis understood about the human mind. Perhaps it was only natural that Travis blocked these thoughts from his immediate consciousness. But what was really certain? And where was the dividing line between what was real and what was not? In fact, was there a dividing line at all?

With these questions at the forefront of his mind, he exited the Fairlane and walked to Doyle's caravan. It was a little after eleven, and he doubted that even Doyle would still be asleep so late in the morning.

Before he reached the vehicle, the door opened. Valeria Mironescu appeared in her robe. Her feet were bare, but she seemed not the slightest bit self-conscious.

"Agent Travis," she said, and smiled in her most engaging way.

"Miss Valeria," Travis replied.

"You are looking for Edgar," she said, more a statement than a question.

"I am."

"He is here. We are just having some coffee if you would like to join us. Do you like Turkish coffee?"

"I can't say that I have ever had it."

"Well, then, you must try it." She leaned back into the caravan and called out to Doyle. "Edgar, put some clothes on. We have company."

"You rise late," Travis said.

"Not so late if you live a predominantly nocturnal existence," she said. She winked. "Vampires, you see, Agent Travis. Perhaps half vampires, eh? We can take the daylight, but only from lunchtime onward."

Doyle appeared behind Valeria. He smiled at Travis, seemingly pleased to see him.

"Agent Travis," he said. "I have been expecting you. Please, just give me a moment to throw some clothes on, and then join us for coffee, why don't you?"

"I will, thank you," Travis said. "I have some questions for you, if you have time."

"Always," Doyle replied. "I always have time for questions, Agent Travis."

Doyle and Valeria Mironescu disappeared into the caravan. The door was closed behind them, and Travis waited no more than five minutes before it opened again and Doyle stepped out. He was lighting his pipe as he came, and then he stopped and extended his hand.

"Good morning, Agent Travis," he said.

Travis shook the man's hand. "Good morning, Mr. Doyle."

"Did you come with your square head again?"

"Of course, Mr. Doyle. Can you not tell? I am beginning to believe it's the only one that works."

Doyle looked at Travis with an expression of patience, as if now explaining something for the second or third time to a slightly backward child. "Do you even understand what I mean when I say your square head, Agent Travis?"

"Miss Valeria made the same comment, Mr. Doyle, and yes, I know what you mean."

"Tell me."

"You are implying that I can look at what is happening here with all my preconceived ideas and personal certainties intact, or I can allow myself a certain degree of flexibility."

"Complete flexibility. Complete freedom of thought. Complete absence of fixed ideas and preconceptions. That's what I am advising, Agent Travis. When you walk down the road, you can look at your own feet, the road beneath, or you can look at the surroundings, the sky, the trees, the scenery as it unfolds, and you can trust your feet to continue taking you in the direction you're headed."

"I appreciate directness, Mr. Doyle. The equivocal answers, the allusions, the inferences, the open-ended statements are all so much a waste of time—"

"Well, that's where you and I have to perhaps agree to differ once again, Agent Travis," Doyle said. "Come. Let's go inside, and we shall continue this overdue conversation."

"Overdue?"

"Oh, don't you think it's overdue?" Doyle said, and then he walked to the caravan without waiting for a response from Travis.

Once inside, Doyle directed Travis to sit. Valeria Mironescu brought a metal coffee pot and the smallest cups Travis had ever seen.

"It is strong and bitter, and you may need sugar," she said. "It is perhaps an acquired taste, but you cannot acquire the taste unless you try it, right?"

She poured the coffee. Doyle added a heaped spoonful of sugar into his cup, and Travis did the same. He tasted it. It was quite dreadful, and there were coffee grounds in his mouth.

"Too quick," Valeria said. "You need to let the grounds settle at the bottom."

Travis set the cup aside.

"So?" Doyle asked.

"So, tell me why you consider this a game, Mr. Doyle. I don't see it that way at all, as I am sure you know."

"I am not trying to be evasive, Agent Travis, and I am not interested in provoking any kind of response in you aside from a willingness to step outside the lines."

"I have no difficulty stepping outside of any line, just so long as it gives me a satisfactory explanation."

"And if there isn't one?"

For a moment there was silence, a sense of tension, and then Valeria sat beside Doyle. The pair of them looked at Travis as if he were an exhibit in a gallery. He felt unnerved by such a focus of attention, and he spoke quickly, if only to distract their attention, to make them stop looking at him that way.

"There is always an explanation," he said.

"Always?" Doyle asked.

"Yes, always. Everything has an explanation, Mr. Doyle."

"I don't disagree with that statement. At least, not in principle. Let us say that everything *does* have an explanation, but some of the explanations require that you look at things in a very different way."

"And again, you are being circumspect and guarded. You seem to have an infinite capacity to answer questions without ever really answering the question."

"I shall take that as a compliment, Agent Travis."

"It was not intended to be."

"I was joking."

"I was not."

"I think you're both idiots," Valeria Mironescu interjected. "It's like listening to squabbling children. I think you both need to grow up, frankly."

Doyle laughed. He put an arm around her shoulder, pulled her close, and kissed her forehead. "See, this is what we all need, Agent Travis. A grounded and level-headed woman to tell us when we are behaving like children."

Travis did not laugh. He did not smile. "I don't see it as a game. You cannot even begin to comprehend how significant this investigation is, not just to the Bureau, but to me personally."

"It is your test, is it not, Agent Travis?" Doyle asked. "They sent you on your own. That is not Bureau protocol."

"I don't think you're in a position to explain Bureau protocol to me, Mr. Doyle."

"I might just surprise you there, Agent Travis," Doyle said. "From what I understand, it is not entirely usual for the Federal Bureau of Investigation to dispatch a man alone. That aside, I do not understand why additional officers have not already arrived to assist you. You have been here for four days, and you are none the wiser as to the identity of the dead man, let alone the identity of whoever might have been responsible for his murder. It appears to me that you have been thrown in at the deep end in anticipation of your bringing this matter to an acceptable resolution by yourself."

"That may very well be the case, Mr. Doyle."

Doyle leaned forward. "So let me ask you a question for once, Agent Travis."

"Go ahead."

"What if the murder of a man is not the real investigation here?"

"If it is not, then what is?"

"I mentioned a name to you, Agent Travis. Do you remember?"

"Harold Blauer."

"Yes, Harold Blauer. Did you find the time to learn something of his fate?"

"I did, yes, and that is one of the reasons I am here now, to ask you about this man. Why did you mention that name to me? Does he have some connection to what is happening here?"

"Would you indulge me, Agent Travis? Would you let me tell you about the fate of another man who has some connection to this?"

"So you *are* saying that Blauer is connected to this case, even though he died six years ago?"

"I am, and it was a very unnecessary tragedy. However, he was not the only one, and that is why I want you to hear the story of a man called Frank Olson."

"Is that the name of the man who was found here?"

"No, Agent Travis. I do not know the name of the man who died here."

"So who is this Olson, and what does he have to do with this case?"

"Frank Olson was a doctor. In fact, he was a US Army scientist and one of their top researchers into the field of germ warfare. He was administered a drug without his knowledge. Actually, he was shut in a New York City hotel and given that drug repeatedly over a nine-day period. Olson fell into a deep depression as a result of that drug. In truth, he lost his mind, and the army feared that not only would he talk about what had been done to him, but that such revelations might compromise their continued research into germ warfare. He had a minder with him at all times, a man called Robert Lashbrook. Lashbrook worked for an organization right there in the heart of the American intelligence community. Anyway, Lashbrook didn't do such a good job of keeping an eye on Dr. Olson, for Olson jumped, or—as many people believe—was thrown, from the thirteenth-floor window of that hotel. What little remained of him was there on the sidewalk, and the army and Lashbrook's employers worked furiously to cover up the circumstances that led to the death of Dr. Olson. Whether or not there will ever be an investigation into that death is doubtful, but Frank Olson died, just like Harold Blauer died, and it is unlikely that anyone will ever do anything about it."

"And these people, Olson and Blauer... you are telling me this because?"

"Because you need to know who you are working for, Agent Travis, and I think it is only fair that you have some kind of understanding of the real reason for your presence in Seneca Falls."

"The people I work for? What are you telling me, that this Robert Lashbrook worked for the Bureau?"

"No, he didn't, as a matter of fact. He might as well have, for there is little difference between the FBI and the organization that he did work for, but no, he was not a G-man."

Travis frowned. "I am confused."

"Don't be," Doyle said. "That is their intention in such cases, to throw as much misinformation at you as possible, and it leaves you with a sense of disorientation. Even Goebbels made such a reference, didn't he? Something to the effect that if you told a big enough lie and kept repeating it, then eventually people would come to believe it. Even Socrates commented on the fact that if you want to make a lie work, then you need to attach a small element of truth to it. Truth, or at least the promise of truth, holds us like glue. Is it not the case that our natural human reaction is to reject those things that we don't understand, the things that trouble us the most, just because we don't want to believe that other human beings can be that evil and corrupt? Is it not true that if a man acted in the same way that most of the world's governments act, then we would have him arrested, tried, convicted, and executed before he could do any further damage?"

"Are you telling me that the Federal Bureau of Investigation was in some way involved in the deaths of Harold Blauer and Frank Olson? Is that what you are saying, Mr. Doyle?"

"No, sir, I am not. I do not think that they were directly involved in *those* deaths."

"Meaning?"

"What do you think I mean, Agent Travis?"

"I think you are implying that the FBI is in some way involved in the death of the man that was found here in Seneca Falls."

Doyle smiled, looked at Valeria Mironescu, and winked. "Give the man a Kewpie doll."

"This is utterly outrageous. Mr. Doyle. How can you possibly think that the Bureau had anything to do with this homicide?"

"I am permitted to think what I wish, Agent Travis. In fact, not only am I permitted to think what I wish to think, I am also permitted to say what I think without fear of reprisal, attack, censure, or penalty. Doesn't the Constitution say as much?"

"I think there is a difference between freedom of expression, Mr. Doyle, and unfounded allegations and accusations against one of the most important and powerful law enforcement organizations in the world."

"And there lies the rub, Agent Travis. The bigger the organization, the more easily it hides its identity. The bigger the organization, the more easily it not only obscures its intent, but also the consequences of its actions."

Travis felt the indignation and rage rising in his chest. For Travis, the Bureau stood for integrity, honesty, the maintenance of law and order, everything without which the society could not possibly hope to survive.

"Every once in a while, we reach a watershed," Valeria Mironescu said. She reached out and touched Travis's hand.

He withdrew it sharply. "You people are unbelievable," he said. "I come here as a representative of the federal government. As far as you are both concerned, I am the law. I am here to investigate and expose the truth regarding a man's death. With a single phone call, I can have fifty agents here, a hundred if I wish, and we can turn every single one of you inside out."

"And if we knew something, Agent Travis? If we really knew something and we didn't tell you?"

"Then you would be charged with obstruction of justice, that at the very least. If found guilty, you would serve a jail sentence, and in some instances, I am sure that the possibility of extradition out of the United States might be considered."

"Always the little people ground to dust in the teeth of the mighty machine," Valeria said.

"Little people who lie and withhold the truth," Travis replied.

"No, sir," Doyle said, "Little people who tell the truth and thus fill the graveyards of this nation, I am afraid."

"What is this? A game of contradiction?"

"I don't want to say that you are naive, Agent Travis," Doyle said, "but you *are* naive. You have allowed yourself to believe those things that make you feel safe. You have allowed yourself to ask only those questions that can be answered without challenging your own concept of how life works. Well, life does not work that way, at least not any life that could be worth living."

Travis stared at Doyle. "Don't you turn this back on me, Doyle. You have no right to—"

"To what, Agent Travis? I have no right to what? To tell you my opinion? To tell you what you don't want to hear? I think you'll find that as long as I am not breaking your very precious and sacred laws, then I am home free. You cannot go on pretending to yourself, Agent Travis. You are too smart. You are too perceptive. You have solved certain personal problems by closing down your mind and your heart to some fundamental truths. That is all too obvious. The question is why. Why would a man—a decent man, a good man, an aware man—force himself to forget the past, force himself to never look back, to never confront the things that had happened in his life? Why would he do that? Is it because he is afraid of maintaining his sanity? Perhaps, but then the sanity that he is trying to maintain is itself a kind of *in*sanity, wouldn't you say? How does it feel to be so wound up, Agent Travis? How does it feel to never once confront the fact that your mother killed for you, that she went to her own death in the firm belief that she was doing the right thing for her son?"

"Stop right there, Doyle!" Travis said. "This is now too, too much."

"I think it is not enough," Doyle replied.

Once again, Valeria leaned forward and grasped Travis's hand. "Listen to him, Michael," she urged. "Just stop for a moment and listen to what he is telling you. He is trying to help you. He is trying to get you to see what has happened to you, what is happening to you right now, and what lies ahead if you keep going in this direction. The people you work for—"

"Enough about the people I work for," Travis said, and snatched back his hand.

"The people you work for are not good people, Agent Travis," Doyle said. "Are you not able to see even a little of the reasoning behind why you are here?"

"I am here to investigate a murder," Travis said. "Plain and simple."

"I am sorry to say that this murder, as you call it, is anything but plain and simple. You are not here to identify a dead man. You are not here to even determine who might have killed him or why. You are here for a very different reason altogether."

"You people are deluded. You people believe your own fantasies. What happened last night... what I saw here, those kinds of fantasies and deceptions, are not real life. That is not the world in which we live, Mr. Doyle. That is magic and trickery and illusion, and it does not translate well to the harsh light of day. Under the colored lights of the circus, the carnival, the traveling sideshows yes, but out here in the world in which I live, it is as much use as... well, I don't know that it serves any purpose at all."

"It gives people truth where they had none, Agent Travis," Doyle said. "It allows people to find some meaning and sense in amid all the madness. It makes people happy. It eases their burdens and anxieties. And though you consider it an illusion, a trick, a deception, I can assure you that it is not."

"More lies, Mr. Doyle, and I am growing tired of listening to them. If you want a truth, then there is the truth as I see it right now. You are a liar and a charlatan, and though I am intrigued by how you create these illusions, I am not here to address that. I am here to address the death of an unknown man and whatever web of deceit you attempt to weave around it, I know that someone here knows what happened, and I will be damned if I am going to leave Seneca Falls without the truth."

Doyle's expression was neither condescending nor patronizing. It seemed sincere, almost sympathetic to the dilemma that faced Travis.

"I am sorry for your loss, Agent Travis," he said quietly.

"My loss?"

"The loss of your belief in humanity. The loss of your faith in people. The loss of your trust in yourself. The loss of your innocence, your willingness to be open-minded, your empathy, your curiosity, your courage—"

"My courage?"

"The courage we sometimes need to hear things that we don't wish to hear, to accept the fact that we might not know everything that there is to know about the mind and the soul, about people. That seems to me to be the greatest loss of all, wouldn't you say? The loss of our belief in possibilities."

"And now you sound like some evangelical preacher, Mr. Doyle," Travis said, his tone almost derisive. "Now you sound like you're trying to convert me to some—"

"Enough now, Agent Travis," Valeria Mironescu said. "The pair of you are now beginning to sound ridiculous. Whatever Edgar says, you contradict, and that is not even a discussion. That is just people contradicting one another. Even a child can do that, and you are no longer children."

"Sadly," Doyle said, and laughed.

The tone changed then—suddenly, almost imperceptibly—but Travis felt his sense of anger dissipate. He looked at Valeria Mironescu, at Edgar Doyle, and there seemed to be nothing there, as if the tension and resistance he'd felt so strongly no longer possessed any substance at all.

"I think we are of very different viewpoints," Travis said. "I am not here to contradict you, nor to argue with you, Mr. Doyle. I can appreciate that you have certain ideas and beliefs, and though I do not agree with them, that does not mean that I am unable to accept them."

"I think accepting my ideas and beliefs is the very last thing you are willing to do, Agent Travis. That is the whole point of bringing you here and showing you what we are doing."

"Meaning the things that I saw last night."

"That, yes, among other things."

"And now what? Now you are telling me that Chester Greene can read people's minds, that he can see things about people's past experiences, that he can just look inside peoples' heads and tell them things that they didn't even know themselves? Is that what you are telling me?"

Doyle nodded. "In a word, yes. And, to be honest, Mr. Greene is not the only one who possesses such a faculty."

Travis smiled, and then he started laughing. "Okay, Mr. Doyle, then I am willing to acknowledge that I do not accept all of your ideas and beliefs."

Doyle leaned forward. "And you want to know something else, Agent Travis?"

"Yes, of course, Mr. Doyle. Please tell me something else."

"Chester, that fat little dwarf from Oklahoma, said very emphatically that of all the people in that tent last night, of all the people that he could have read, you were the very strongest. He said that your thoughts, whatever was going on in your mind, was the strongest perception he was receiving. I would agree with him on that point. People who possess this gift are like radio antennae, you see? They are like an antenna, and they just pick up on the wavelengths that people emanate, and they can read them as easily as you would read a newspaper."

"Oh, he said that, did he? Well, that seems to be very convenient, considering the conversation that we're having, wouldn't you say?"

"You want to know something else?" Doyle asked.

"You go on and tell me whatever else you care to tell me, Mr. Doyle," Travis said.

"I can tell you that those who hide from their pasts the most are also those who transmit the strongest images and emotions."

"Oh, is that so?"

"Yes, Agent Travis, that is so."

"And would you like to expand a little on that theory, Mr. Doyle? Would you be able to give me anything other than a completely unprovable and unsubstantiated flight of fancy?"

"I would, yes."

There was silence for a moment.

Travis raised his eyebrows. "And so?"

Valeria shook her head. "You are sure, Agent Travis?"

"Sure of what?"

"Sure that you want to open Pandora's box?"

"Hit me with it," Travis said, and leaned back.

Valeria looked at Doyle. "Edgar—"

Doyle raised his hand. Valeria fell silent.

"I am now risking my life," Doyle said. "Also that of Valeria here, most definitely that of Chester Greene and Mr. Slate. In fact, I am risking the lives of everyone here. I want you to appreciate what I am putting on the line here, Agent Travis."

Travis said nothing.

"Do you understand what I am saying, Agent Travis?"

"No, sir, I do not. I have heard nothing but theory and supposition. I have heard nothing that leads me to believe that you are anything but a dreamer, Mr. Doyle."

"Even after last night, Agent Travis? Even after what Chester said to you about your father?"

"I will give you that one, Mr. Doyle. That was very astute of him. A little wild, a little off-the-cuff, but I have to admit that he took me by surprise."

"I don't know that I have ever seen anyone fight something so hard," Doyle said. "You really are terrified of what might happen if you open your eyes, aren't you?"

"I think you believe me to be someone else, Mr. Doyle. I am not terrified of anything you might say or do, I can assure you."

"Very well," Doyle said, matter-of-factly. "So we shall open the box."

"Open away, Mr. Doyle. Let's see what's inside, shall we?"

Travis leaned back. He put his hands on the table. He felt utterly calm, utterly relaxed, not the slightest bit concerned about whatever Doyle might say next.

Doyle looked at him closely, and then he closed his eyes.

The voice that came from Doyle's lips was unmistakably that of Doyle, but there was an undertone, an edge, a harshness to it that was unsettling.

"Don't even open your freakin' mouth," Doyle said.

Travis frowned. Who was he talking to?

And then—out of no place at all—a vague memory began to stir.

"Long day, dumbass workers, problems you could not even comprehend, and the last thing I need is to hear some bullshit whiny freakin' bitch going on at me about how I'm late."

Travis's intake of breath was clearly audible. His fists clenched involuntarily. He looked at Doyle; still his eyes were closed. Then he looked at the woman beside him. She was smiling in that same way that Doyle had done earlier—somehow sincere, somehow patient, somehow sympathetic, as if here she was the bearer of unfortunate news.

Doyle opened his eyes and looked directly at Travis. "And I don't need to see you sharing sideways fucking glances with her like you think you're better than me. Don't think I don't know what you say about me, you pair together like snakes in a freakin' basket. Get my dinner, get me a drink, and leave me the hell alone, all right?"

Travis found his voice. "Enough!" he barked.

"Tray and cup, fucknuts," Doyle said, and Travis could see the face of the teenage Tony Scarapetto right there in front of him.

"You done fucked the quiff, eh, boy?" Doyle went on. "I seen her a coupla times. Cain't 'member when, but I seen her and figured she'd be good for a party. But you beat me to it, you old dog, and you only sixteen years old. God darn it, boy, you sure as hell is your father's son."

"No! Enough!" Travis said.

Doyle sneered, but it was not Doyle at all. It was as if there was a second face behind Doyle's and it was that face that Travis could somehow see.

"You think your mother would be proud of you? You think she'd be proud of you, kiddo? You done fucked her cousin's widder. I didn't do no worse than you're doing right now. Hell, you are a sick kid, you know that? You think you have the right to judge me? You don't have the right to even speak to me, let alone judge me, you self-righteous hypocritical son of a bitch! And I'll tell you now, that ain't never had more meaning than it does right now. Son of a bitch. You are a son of a bitch. Because she was a bitch, kiddo. She was a fucking nasty fucking bitch, and I hope she burns in hell forever..."

Travis snatched a cup from the table and slammed it down. It shattered into a dozen pieces, one of which punctured his palm. The flow of blood was sudden and significant. It ran from his hand and started spreading across the linen tablecloth.

Doyle snapped to, as if jerked back from reverie, and he just looked at Travis with a weary and somewhat saddened expression in his eyes. "You are your own shadow," he said quietly. "The shadow you see in that field is you, and there is no crow, Michael. That's the sound of you laughing at yourself... something you forgot to do a long, long time ago."

Valeria turned and looked at Doyle, then reached out her hand and touched the side of his face.

Travis tried to stand, but dizziness overcame him.

"You stay right there," Valeria said. "I will fix your hand."

Travis did as he was told, unable then to look at either of them.

Valeria went to the small sink and fetched a cloth. She pressed it against the wound in Travis's hand, now evidently shallow, almost superficial, but still bleeding profusely.

"W-w-what is ha-happening to m-me?" Travis stuttered.

"You opened the box, Michael," Valeria said. "That was all. You just opened the box."

Travis turned and looked up at her.

"Don't be afraid," she said, her voice somehow soothing. "Better to know than not to know, however hard the truth might be. That's what we always say, right, Edgar?"

Edgar Doyle nodded his head. "Right," he said, his voice tired. "Better to know than not to know."

Travis felt his emotions unravel. He wanted to cry, but he dared not.

"Do it," Doyle said. "Just let it go."

And Travis did. He leaned forward, rested his forehead on the crook of his arm, and he just wept.

33

After a while, he did not care that they were there, watching him as he fell to pieces. For that's how it felt, as if he were being pulled apart at the seams, and every carefully constructed rationale and reason for being the way he was seemed to count for nothing in the face of what he was experiencing.

And the tears seemed to run out and the feeling of tension in his chest, his throat, in every muscle of his body seemed to ease, and he felt a sense of balance and composure returning. But he was different. He knew that. It was not easy to determine how he was different, but he was.

Both Edgar Doyle and Valeria Mironescu seemed entirely calm. The look in their eyes was one of reconciliation, as if they had expected nothing less than this, as if this had been their intention all along.

Travis looked at Doyle.

Doyle smiled and shook his head. "No," he said.

"No what?"

"The answer to your question. You were going to ask me whether or not I could hear every thought you had. The answer is no. No one can do that. At least not in my experience."

"But—"

"Like that old expression, how people can wear their heart on their sleeve. People carry their past around with them, the things they've forgotten, especially the things they think they're no longer affected by. I would even go so far as to say that the things that cause the most trouble for people are the things that are buried the deepest. That seems to be the way we are put together."

"I feel strange," Travis said. "I feel transparent."

"I know."

"I don't like it. I don't like this feeling at all."

"It is just new," Doyle said. "You know, you are perhaps one of the most tightly wound people I have ever met, Agent Travis. The most suspicious—"

"Not suspicious," Valeria interjected. "I don't think Agent Travis is suspicious. Guarded perhaps, even cautious, but not suspicious."

"You're right," Doyle said. "Suspicious is not the right word. You are very grounded in reality, but the reality you have chosen as your anchor is perhaps the most fragile and insubstantial of all."

Travis shook his head.

"An idea is more powerful than anything," Doyle said. "Without an idea, nothing could exist. A building is a building, but without the idea for the building, there would be no building. The building is tangible, real, present, but the idea is stronger."

"I don't know what this has to do with what is happening here," Travis said. "I don't even understand why you are telling me this."

"Because we have to trust someone," Valeria said, "and we have chosen you."

Travis tried to stand again, but he was unable to find a sufficient sense of balance to make it to his feet.

"Just sit there for a while," she said. "Listen to what Edgar is telling you. What harm can it do to listen?"

"Emotion," Doyle said. "There's another one for you. Which is stronger, the situation itself or the emotion it provokes? I'd say the emotion. You forget the details of location, time, even people, but it's almost impossible to forget the emotion."

Travis closed his eyes. He could see his mother's face, he could see Esther's, and a wave of anguish swelled and receded inside of him.

"You question everything," Doyle said, "and the way you question things, the fact that you demand evidence that can satisfy your immediate senses... well, that is the reason that man is dead. You have to ask the question, why *you*, Agent Travis? Why you, specifically, and why alone, why not with a partner, as is ordinarily the case? Why did the FBI send Special Agent Michael Travis down to Seneca Falls to investigate this murder?"

"Because that is my job, Mr. Doyle. Because that is what we do."

"No, sir," Doyle said. "This is not what you do. Not in this case. This case is something else entirely, and if you really want to know the truth, then you have to understand that this man is dead *because* of you."

"What on earth does that mean, that he is dead because of me?"

"Well, I'm sure he would have wound up dead sooner or later," Doyle said. "But let us say that he died a little prematurely, perhaps. And he did not die here, Agent Travis. I can imagine that whatever postmortem might have been undertaken has confirmed that point. I am sure he was considered the most deserving of sacrifice for this experiment, and his body was brought here so Special Agent Michael Travis could come and investigate."

"Sacrifice? Experiment? What on earth are you talking about?" Travis looked at Valeria. "Are you hearing what he is saying? Does this make even the slightest bit of sense to you?"

"It makes sense, Agent Travis," she said. "I don't want it to make sense, but the facts are the facts, and I know how much you like to deal with facts."

"That man was murdered, Agent Travis," Doyle said. "He was executed, to be exact, and his body was brought here. From where, I don't know. Perhaps he was in custody. Perhaps he was already part of some grand scheme that had been discussed and agreed at the highest levels. All I know is that you were sent here, not to investigate the death of an unidentified man, but to investigate us."

"What possible reason could there be for me to investigate you?"

"The world always wants what it cannot have," Doyle said. "Even when something is free, people want to own it, control it, dictate how it can and cannot be used. But you cannot own an idea, and you cannot put an emotion in a box, no matter how hard you try. The human mind and the human soul are not the property of the federal government, Agent Travis, regardless of what they might think. And the federal governments of this world have been trying to do this to people like us for as long as civilization has existed, and I use the word *civilization* in its loosest sense. You cannot kill the truth, and people will always find the truth even when the greatest efforts are made to hide it."

'The federal government has not murdered anyone," Travis said. "There are executions, of course, but that is the law of the land, and the judicial system affords a protocol and a system to establish guilt beyond reasonable doubt, and then a jury of peers will make the decision as to whether a man should be put to death for his crimes—"

"Stop listening to what you have been told, and start listening to yourself," Doyle interjected. "Seriously, you have no idea how ridiculous you sound. The world as you see it is not the world as it is. The world you see is built of lies and misdirections. You are being fooled and deceived on a daily basis, and have been for the whole of your life, Agent Travis. For some people, this is a game, but for people like us, people who are trying to exist, trying to go on about our business with nothing but the very best intention toward our fellow man, this has gone far beyond a matter of principle and has become a matter of freedom, a matter of life and death. You think that you are the first person that has been sent here? You think you are the first one to investigate who we are and what we are doing? You are not the first, and I am sure that if you do not give your superiors the answers they want, then you will not be the last. There is a difference this time, however, because they have never gone to such lengths before. There has always been some slight degree of subtlety, no matter how obvious their efforts might have seemed to us, but this time they have become desperate. This time they were prepared to kill a man in order to get you here."

"I am afraid for your sanity, Mr. Doyle," Travis said.

"I am afraid for yours, Agent Travis."

"I am not rambling about some incoherent and preposterous conspiracy theory."

"And nor am I," Doyle replied. "You keep on fighting, don't you? You really are one stubborn son of a bitch."

"Enough now," Travis said. "I will be making arrangements for further agents to attend this case. I will make one phone call, and they will be here within hours."

"Somehow I doubt that," Doyle said.

"You know nothing."

"I know enough to know that you're on your own, Michael. You make as many calls as you like; you're going to get the same answer. There's not going to be any more agents. There's not going to be any backup or support or anything else. This is your baby, as they say."

Travis was angry beyond words, but he knew that losing his temper would merely disadvantage him.

"You ever wonder how many people actually know you're here?" Doyle asked. "I don't mean us, of course. I mean those within your very special Bureau. How many people did you speak to? How many people wished you success in your investigation? How many people have contacted you since your arrival to ask for progress reports, updates, leads you are pursuing, suspects you have identified? Four days, Agent Travis. Four days and you don't even know the name of that dead man. What little you do know came from your own industry and work. But what do you have? That he was Hungarian? That he worked for this Black Dog organization? That is all you have, and it is not a great deal, is it?"

"You are beyond insane, Doyle," Travis said.

"So you keep reminding me." Doyle looked down at the table, then sideways at Valeria Mironescu. "What do we do with him, my dear? What on earth are we supposed to do with such a stubborn and mule-headed individual? You think they could at least have sent us someone with a fragment of imagination."

Valeria smiled. "But surely they sent him here for that very reason? Because he possesses no imagination at all?"

"How could I know about things that have never been spoken of, never been discussed, never even been verbalized outside your own mind, Agent Travis?" Doyle asked him. "Who else knows what your dead father said to you in that house in Flatwater? It was Flatwater, right? That's where you were born, and that's where your mother killed your father, isn't it? How could I know such things unless I am telling you the truth about who we are and what we are capable of?"

"I have no answer for you, Mr. Doyle," Travis said. He realized he was clenching his fists, his knuckles visibly whitening.

"Because you *really* don't know, or because you are afraid to acknowledge what is right there in front of you, as real as this caravan, as real as this field, as real as the entire town of Seneca Falls, and yet utterly intangible, utterly invisible, utterly inexplicable? Which one is it, Agent Travis? Which one is it?"

"I am not answerable to you, Doyle. I am not answerable to anyone but myself and the people I work for—"

"And did you ever stop to wonder about the motives and intentions of the people you work for? Did you ever take a moment to look behind the curtain, eh? You are having the rug pulled out from under you, as they say, and it is a most unsettling feeling."

"You are not saying anything that unstabilizes my certainty, Mr. Doyle—"

"I doubt that is an entirely accurate statement, Mr. Travis. For someone so hell-bent on establishing the truth, it seems a little ironic that the individual to whom you lie the most is yourself."

"A man is tested by the opinions he hears in life, Mr. Doyle. The more you challenge what I know to be real, the more I believe in my own interpretation of reality."

"As is the case with most people, Agent Travis, and what desperately dull lives they lead. Fear of the unknown is the greatest fear of all. The humdrum banality of everyday life is far less threatening than the possibility of something beyond what we see and hear and touch and experience with our five senses. There are worlds beyond worlds out there, each as real as the next, and yet we decide to imprison ourselves in this safety net of assumption and caution, and why? Because we are afraid, right? Afraid to think, afraid to question, afraid to feel, afraid to look. And then, just as we die, we finally have some small glimpse of what we have missed; we see how blind we have been..."

Doyle leaned forward, and he spoke with urgency and insistence. "I cannot ask you to throw away all your preconceptions and misconceptions, Agent Travis, but I can ask you to open your eyes, perhaps your mind as well. See what has happened to you. See what you have become. And then see who we really are. Ask yourself whether what you saw last night had anything but a positive effect. Who was hurt, Agent Travis? Ask yourself that question, my friend. It is not always enough to judge people by what they do, but also by the consequences of what they do."

"You test my patience, Mr. Doyle," Travis said. "You test my patience and my ethics and my integrity, and I do not appreciate it. I do not know what it is that you are trying to achieve, but I do not believe it is good. I think you are the one with negative intentions here, *my friend*. I think you have ulterior motives and undisclosed agendas, and I am going to do everything I can to find out the truth. What gives you the right to challenge me?"

"Ha!" Doyle exclaimed. "The very same thing that gives you the right to challenge me, Agent Travis!"

"I have the law on my side, Mr. Doyle, as you seem too able to forget."

"The law?" Doyle asked. "The law? Seriously? The law counts for nothing here, Agent Travis. The *law* is perhaps guilty of far greater crimes than all the criminals it has ever tried to convict. The crimes committed in the offices of lawyers, in the courts, in judges' chambers, in the House of Representatives, the Senate, even the office of the President of the United States, far outweigh anything that might even have been conceived by your ever-so-precious list of public enemies. Go ask Chester Greene. He knew most of those who brewed and bootlegged and smuggled the liquor that was served to America during Prohibition. The congressmen and police captains, the ATF agents, the FBI were all taking their own slice of the pie. And Prohibition was merely a sideshow to the main performance, as they say. What about bribery, corruption, political influence in the corridors of power? What about the legal system? What about the banks, the industrial-military complex? What about drugs, prostitution, assassination, the very way in which laws are made and passed within our own governments, all of it corrupt, all of it fueled by lies and slander? What about the newspapers, what about your own commander in chief, the great and mighty J. Edgar Hoover, outlawing this and that, making pronouncements like he is some kind of Roman emperor, telling people how they can and cannot behave, what they can and cannot do, and yet behind closed doors, he wears his mother's clothes and—"

Travis brought his hand down on the small table. The sound was deafening within the confines of the caravan.

"Enough!"

Doyle fell silent, and yet there was something in his eyes that seemed satisfied, as if this kind of forceful reaction was precisely the thing he had wished to see.

"How dare you?" Travis said. "You honestly believe that you can challenge me in this way, Mr. Doyle? You honestly think I will stand for this kind of thing?" He looked at Doyle with disgust. "You think you have the right to say just whatever you wish? Well, you don't. This is tantamount to slander. I know exactly what it is that you're trying to do. I see through you, Mr. Doyle. I see right through and I do not like what I see. This is not a game, sir. The Bureau has the right to take whatever action it feels is necessary to—"

"To what, Agent Travis? To serve its own ends and—"

"You say one more word, Mr. Doyle, and I am arresting you."

"For what, might I ask?"

"Complicity in murder, Mr. Doyle."

"Prove it."

"I will."

"Then do it, Agent Travis. If you can prove that he was murdered here, then I will turn myself in to the sheriff of Seneca Falls, and I will make a full and detailed confession of how I killed him."

"I have one further question for you, Mr. Doyle."

"Fire away, G-man."

"What was it that you did in the final two years of the war?"

Doyle frowned. "And this possesses relevance because?"

"Because I want to know, Mr. Doyle. Because I am asking you. Tell me that you were not in Germany."

"I was in Germany, Agent Travis."

"As I thought."

"And that is all you want to know?"

"For now, yes." Travis stood up. "You people are unbelievable," he said.

"I would hope so," Doyle replied.

Travis shook his head resignedly, and then he walked to the door.

34

Travis did not think. He got in his car and drove out to the Greenwood County Morgue. He wanted to see the dead man again. The dead man was a single anchor in this storm of insanity, and he needed a clear and uncertain reminder of why he was even here in this godforsaken place.

There were so many things he could have said to Edgar Doyle, but he knew that they would count for nothing. The man possessed a viewpoint all his own. The man was a subversive, more than likely a Communist, and precisely the kind of individual that was undermining the very stability of the society that good and decent people like himself were trying to create and maintain. A few questions before the House Un-American Activities Commission would not go amiss on Doyle and his freak show. As for whatever he might have been involved in during the final years of the war, well, that would be another line to vigorously pursue once the immediate investigation was complete.

Travis pulled up before the low building outside of Seneca Falls. Wolf was nowhere to be seen, and the place looked deserted. He knocked on the door repeatedly, remembering that Jack Farley was somewhat deaf, and that last time he and Rourke had visited he had not heard them. There was no answer, the door was firmly locked, and even at the back of the building there was no sign that anyone was present.

Travis headed back into town, went directly to the sheriff's office, and there he found Rourke.

"Sheriff Rourke, good afternoon," Travis said as he was shown into Rourke's office.

Rourke rose from his desk, shook Travis's hand. "So, what can I do for you this afternoon?"

"I need to speak with Jack Farley."

"On the phone or in person?"

"In person, preferably. I want to see the corpse again."

"Good enough," Rourke said. He took a piece of paper from a scratch pad on his desk and scribbled down the address. "It's not far," he said. "Down here to the right, take your first left, keep going on past the convenience store, and then second on the right beyond that you'll find a large white house on the corner of Elm and Warren. That's Farley's place."

"One other thing," Travis said.

"Sure."

"Last night..."

Rourke grinned. "That sure was something, wasn't it? Hell of thing, that. Near as damnit gave me a heart attack when he mentioned that name. Have thought of that kid I don't know how many times." Rourke shook his head, seemingly still bemused. "Bobby Alberstein, of all people. Absolutely amazing."

"Who did you tell about what happened between you and this Alberstein boy?"

"How do you mean, who did I tell?"

"Well, your friends, you know? Members of your family. Who did you discuss those events with prior to last night?"

Rourke seemed puzzled. "I didn't discuss them with anyone, Agent Travis. To be completely honest, I didn't even want to remember it myself. I was such an asshole to that kid. Looking back on it now, I was an asshole to a good number of kids, but he was by far and away the worst. Couldn't even imagine what was inside of me to want to behave like that toward someone."

"So you never spoke of it?"

"Well, all I can say, Agent Travis, is that sometimes you do things you're ashamed of, and the last thing you're gonna do is talk about them."

"You're absolutely sure you never mentioned it to anyone?"

"Sure as daylight is daylight, I never said a word to anyone. Why? You think there was some kind of trick going on there?"

Travis looked at Rourke with an expression of slight disbelief. "Well, there had to be a trick, didn't there, Sheriff Rourke? I mean, it's not possible for someone to be able to look inside someone's head and determine what they're thinking, is it?"

"Well, before last night I would have agreed with you, Agent Travis. But... well, it goes without saying that I was the most shocked of all when that little man said Bobby Alberstein's name. Never in a million years did I expect that to happen."

"I can appreciate that," Travis replied. "Well, let me ask you this. How do you feel about it? Do you not feel as though this was an invasion of your privacy, that your rights as a private citizen were somehow violated?"

"Hell, no," Rourke said, smiling. "To be frank, I feel like I have taken a load off. It was like I hid that all the way down deep inside of me, and to have it brought out into the open like that, to find out that the guy was actually okay, that he even remembers me, that he talks about me like I did him some kind of favor… well, I have to say that I feel a good deal better about myself."

"Are you going to make any effort to find out if Greene was telling the truth?"

"Not a hope, Agent Travis. What purpose would it serve? The fact that Greene even knew about it tells me all I need to know. If he knew the guy's name, if he knew what I did back then, then there's no reason for me to question what he says about where he is now."

"You're just going to trust his word on this?"

"He didn't need to tell me anything," Rourke replied. "It didn't cost me anything, did it? No, I don't need to go chasing ghosts, Agent Travis. The past is the past. Leave it where it is."

Travis had no further questions for now. He was a little surprised at Rourke's naïveté, but he had neither the time nor the interest to challenge him on it. He went out back to the car. He followed Rourke's directions and wound up outside Jack Farley's house within five minutes. Wolf was on the porch, and raised his head as Travis made his way up the steps.

"Hey, boy," Travis said, and extended a hand toward the dog's muzzle.

The dog seemed insufficiently enthused to respond and laid his head down once more.

Travis knocked on the screen door, and within moments a woman appeared, drying her hands on her apron as she came down the hallway.

"You must be that federal agent feller," she said. "You here to see Jack?"

"Yes, ma'am, I am," Travis replied.

"Well, come on in, then. He's tinkering in back with something or other. I'll fetch him out. Can I get you a drink or something?"

Travis stepped into the cool and shadowed hallway.

"I'm Mrs. Farley, by the way," she said. "Jack's wife."

"A pleasure, Mrs. Farley."

"Some lemonade, I think," the woman said. She nodded toward the doorway on Travis's right. "You go on in there, make yourself at home, and I'll bring you a glass of lemonade."

"I don't want to put you to any trouble," Travis said.

"Lemonade ain't trouble," Mrs. Farley said, smiling. "I've seen plenty of trouble in my time, and it sure as hell ain't a glass of lemonade."

Travis went into the front room and took a seat.

The lemonade came, as did Jack Farley, and Farley seemed surprised to see Travis in his house.

"Do for you?" he asked.

"I came to view the body again, Mr. Farley," Travis explained.

Farley seemed confused. "I don't know what I can do to help you with that, Agent Travis," he said. "Whoever your boy is, he's been gone three days now."

"Three days? The body has gone? Are you sure?"

"Sure I'm sure." Farley settled back in his armchair. "Heard rumor he was a bad 'un. A killer from Europe or someplace. Is that right?"

"I'm sorry, Mr. Farley. Are you saying that the corpse was removed from your morgue?"

"'S what I just said, isn't it? And it was your people that took him. Day after you arrived, Wednesday lunchtime. Couple of suits showed up, all official, said they were from your gang, took him away in an ambulance. Well, I say it was an ambulance, but it was black and it didn't have any official markings on it."

"Do you remember their names, Mr. Farley?"

"Lord, no. Sometimes I struggle to remember my own."

"Try, Mr. Farley. Did they say their names, or did they just show you their identification cards?"

"No, I'm pretty sure the first one said his name. He had another man with him, a younger man, and I don't know if he actually said anything at all. They were only there for a few minutes. They came in, showed their IDs, said they were taking the body, and off they went."

"Did they have a warrant?"

"A warrant?"

"Yes, Mr. Farley. Did they have some sort of official paperwork authorizing them to take the body?"

"Hey, they were federal people, Agent Travis. You showed up on Tuesday, I'm informed by Sheriff Rourke that this is now a federal homicide investigation, that I have to cooperate with the FBI, and then less than a day later, another couple of G-men show up and say they are going to take the body away. I'm not arguing, right? I was getting tired of the stink o' him, and besides, I was told to cooperate in every which way I could."

"But they are supposed to have a warrant, Mr. Farley. In order to take a body out of a jurisdiction, they have to have a warrant."

"Well, how the hell am I supposed to know that? I ain't never been involved in a federal investigation before. Federal means that it crosses all state lines, all county lines, everything. Federal is a little bigger than Seneca Falls, right?"

Travis didn't understand. Why would the body be removed by fellow agents without any preamble, without any attempt to inform him? What the hell was going on here?

"Okay," Travis said. "So you're at your office. You're at the morgue, right? These two men appear. The first one, the older one, he shows you his ID, and he says what?"

"He shows me his ID. He says his name, says he's here from…" Farley frowned. "He said he was from Kansas City. That's right, yes. He said they'd come down from Kansas City and they needed to take the body back for further examination."

"You're sure now, Mr. Farley? He definitely said he was from Kansas City?"

"Yes, I'm sure. *The Wizard of Oz*, right? Dorothy and Toto and whatever."

"Yes, exactly. *The Wizard of Oz*."

"Anyway, they looked the part, they sounded the part, they showed their IDs, and based on what Chas Rourke told me the day before, well, it didn't seem like I had any right to question what they were doing. They were FBI agents, right? They are government people, and you don't argue with the government, not if you have any sense at all."

Travis was not so sure, but he did not voice the thought.

"Okay, so back to their names," Travis said. "Think, Mr. Farley. Just see if you can't cast your mind back to the moment that the older man showed you his ID. Close your eyes; see if you can't picture that moment… see if you can't just get his face in your mind, and he's holding up his card…"

"Car… Carvel…"

"Carvahlo?" Travis ventured.

"Carvahlo!" Farley exclaimed. "That's the one! That's the name right there." He shook his head in disbelief. "That's amazing, Agent Travis. They teach you to do that at the Bureau?"

Travis was shocked by the revelation. He knew Raymond Carvahlo. Carvahlo had been among the very first wave of Unit X draftees into Kansas after he himself had been assigned. He looked at Farley. "Teach me what?"

"Teach you how to get into people's minds and make them remember things that they'd forgotten?"

Travis was still taken aback by the mention of Carvahlo's name, and attendant to that feeling was a sense of being out of the loop. Was there some other agenda being played out here and played out by the very people for whom he worked?

"You okay, Agent Travis?" Farley asked.

"Yes, yes, of course. It's nothing, Mr. Farley. I was just unaware that the body had been requisitioned by the Kansas office; that was all."

"Hey, I wouldn't be too worried about it," Farley said. "If your Bureau is anything like County, then you only find out about new procedures and protocol six months after the fact." Farley laughed. "So, seems if you want to visit with your dead man again, then you're going to have to ask your Kansas buddies what they did with him."

"Yes, it seems so," Travis replied. He set the half-empty glass of lemonade down on the table to his right and rose to his feet.

"Thank you for your time, Mr. Farley," he said.

Farley rose too, walked out to the front with him.

"Just one more thing," Travis said. "Your autopsy report, photographs, fingerprint records—"

"They took the lot, Agent Travis. Said it was federal property, seeing as how it was a federal investigation an' all. Like I said, they looked the part, sounded the part, and I just did what I figured I was supposed to do based on what Chas Rourke had said the day before. They were here and gone within twenty minutes."

"Understood," Travis said. He shook hands with Farley. "Thanks for your help."

"You're welcome, Agent Travis, though I must say you look like you saw a ghost."

"It's fine, Mr. Farley. Perhaps just a little off-color, as they say."

"Well, you take care, son," Farley said.

"Tell your wife thank you for the lemonade."

"Sure will."

Farley closed the door and Travis walked down the path to his car.

35

Travis was back on a side street near the McCaffrey Hotel as three o'clock approached. He sat there oblivious to all around him, his mind turning over the conversation he'd had with Tom Bishop.

So, let me tell you what I want from you. I want you to vigorously investigate this homicide. I want you to vigorously investigate the people that were present when this body was found. I want you to act alone. I want you to use whatever resources you deem fit to employ, but they cannot include this office, nor the office in Wichita.

But Travis was doubtful that Bishop even understood what he was saying. Bishop, just like every rank and file official in the Bureau, merely repeated what he had been told to say. There was the party line, the official response, the expected attitude, and there was nothing beyond that. Hoover had said that Travis lacked imagination, and yet Travis had always felt so very sure that imagination was the last thing required of an agent.

Fekete Kutya. Black Dog. What was this? Who were these people? Why had this body been removed from Seneca Falls? What did the Bureau really want from him? To investigate a murder, or—as Doyle and Valeria Mironescu kept trying to convince him—to investigate the personnel of Carnival Diablo? That's what they believed, and Travis had started to appreciate their seeming paranoia. What could the Bureau possibly want from such people?

We are the outsiders, Agent Doyle. We are the ones nobody wants because we cannot be explained...

But perhaps it had more to do with Doyle's wartime affiliations and loyalties. Was there some connection between this Hungarian killer and the activities Doyle had been involved in after meeting Valeria Mironescu in France in 1943? Did he really become part of this Nazi party Winterhilfswerk organization? Had the Hungarian come to kill Doyle? Was that what had happened? An intended act of vengeance against Doyle for what he had done during the war, and Doyle had killed the man in self-defense? And if so, then what interest did the FBI have in this matter? That would be external intelligence, far beyond the remit of any federal authority.

Travis's mind reeled at the implications. Had he been set up? Had this whole thing been staged? Was this some kind of performance laid on for his entertainment and his alone, or was there a much deeper, far more covert agenda here? Did Bishop even know who had ordered this investigation? Had it come from Section Chief Gale, or even higher? Executive Assistant Director Warren perhaps? How high did this go, and what was the real intention here? More important, if he was unable to speak with Bishop, or if Bishop was actually unaware of the real agenda, then how could he determine the truth? Doyle would have him believe one thing, and yet his affirmed and inherent belief in the integrity of the Bureau denied such a possibility. He did not want to feel as though he was being played with like some sort of marionette, acting out a pre-scripted part while others watched, judging his reactions, his responses, his conclusions.

No, perhaps there was a middle ground, somewhere between the delusions of Edgar Doyle and the official line from Supervisor Bishop. There had to be a reason for the body's removal, the unavailability of those standard resources and personnel as routinely afforded any agent in the field, the fact that no daily situation reports were required, even down to the fact that Travis was here in Seneca Falls at all.

Travis reached into the inner pocket of his jacket. He still possessed the picture of the dead man, a copy of his prints, the outline of his shoes, and the impression of the sole, did the small diagram he'd made of the tattoo behind the man's knee. Beyond these things, and aside from the word of Farley, Rourke, and himself, there was nothing to confirm that the body had ever been here in Seneca Falls. There hadn't even been any operational order issued in writing. How had he been so easily distracted? Simple. His own ego had distracted him, his promotion to senior special agent, the fact that it was his first lead assignment. But it was not only that, for didn't he—always and automatically—trust that he was being told the truth? He had worked with these people for more than five years. He had shared an office with Raymond Carvahlo and Paul Erickson. He had done what was asked of him. He had committed his life to the work that the Bureau was carrying out. Even Unit X itself, a unit ostensibly established by Hoover to work alongside the Bureau laboratory he'd established back in 1932, was there for the very reasons that Hoover had stated. Or was it? What was Behavioral Science? Was this nothing more than a means by which the agents themselves could be viewed and analyzed? Was the clearance he'd been given prior to assignation as he stated, or was there some other ulterior motive?

Travis knew he was making wild guesses. He was now erring toward suspicion of his own people, his own work colleagues, his own friends. But they were not friends, were they? Not really. Special Agent Michael Travis did not have friends. He had acquaintances, associates, contemporaries, peers, and seniors. That was the sum total of his social spectrum. And now he had Doyle and Valeria Mironescu, Gabor Benedek, Chester Greene, and Mr. Slate. He had a collection of the strangest of all strangers, and these people had somehow managed to inveigle their way into his sympathies and sensibilities. Right now, in that moment, who did he want to speak to? He had to be honest. It was Edgar Doyle. He wanted to tell Edgar Doyle that people had come from Kansas, people he knew by name and face, and they had taken away the dead body. If he was completely honest, then he had to confront the fact that they had used their federal authority to remove evidence from the scene of a crime. But for what purpose?

Travis felt claustrophobic. He wound down the window an inch or so and allowed a breeze of fresh air into the car. For a second he wondered whether he wasn't touching the edges of what had befallen his mother. Perhaps it was not some violent impulse that had been passed from father to son, but a strain of insanity from his mother.

And then Travis was struck by the clearest memory of meeting Farley at the mortuary, the viewing of the body, the autopsy report that he'd been given.

Travis got out of the car immediately. He still had that report, right there in his room, and he had a question that needed an answer.

Danny was not at the desk, and Travis went straight on up. The report was still there, precisely where he had left it, and he scanned through Farley's description of the laking and the wound in the back of the man's neck. The laking confirmed that the victim was dead somewhere between twelve and twenty-four hours before the body was hidden beneath the carousel. He wanted something more specific. He hoped that he would be able to determine a closer time frame.

Travis went back downstairs, through to the telephone from which he had called Bishop. He dialed the operator, asked to be connected to Jack Farley, and waited while she put him through to that number.

Mrs. Farley answered the phone, called her husband, and Travis had to raise his voice considerably before Farley really understood what he was asking.

Finally, after the third or fourth time of asking, Farley responded.

"Really, I cannot give you anything beyond what I already have, Agent Travis. You'd have to actually open up his head. From outward appearance, and from what I can recall, the wound in the back of his neck wasn't old. Bruising was still relatively fresh, blood was congealed and hardened, of course, but not so brittle as to be much more than a day old. Like I say, being absolutely exact is not always easy, Agent Travis."

"I understand that, Mr. Farley. So, perhaps you can tell me this much. From what you saw, are we safe to assume that the man was killed no more than twenty-four hours prior to the discovery of his body?"

"Yes, I believe we could safely say that."

"Good. That's much appreciated."

Travis ended the call and went back up to his room.

He sat on the edge of the bed, his gaze directed toward the window but his eyes seeing nothing. If this man was once a member of Fekete Kutya, a known killer, then what possible involvement could he have with the United States Federal Bureau of Investigation?

Considering the little information he had thus far gleaned, it seemed to him that identification of the dead man was still of paramount importance. He *had* to find out. He *had* to know.

His only choice was Kansas City. The Wichita field office was too small, but Unit X in Kansas, the very unit within which he had worked for the last five years, was a strong possibility. If his current assignment was being overseen by Supervisor Bishop and Section Chief Frank Gale, then there was a good chance that records and files existed there. By the time he reached Kansas, it would be close to evening, and the office would be unmanned. He would have to break into Bishop's office, search through his desk, his file cabinets, whatever it took, and there hope to discover something that would confirm or deny what he was now so frightened to believe.

Without proof that there was a conspiracy here, then it was nothing more than supposition.

Travis did not hesitate. Once the decision was made, he went immediately to his car and set out. He drove the fifty miles or so to Emporia, but this time he did not stop for a BLT and a cup of coffee as he had on the way out there. He just kept on going for a further hundred miles or so into Kansas City itself. He played the radio as he drove, catching nothing other than prerecorded programs of music, the odd gospel station, but he needed the noise to stop his thoughts.

Travis arrived in Kansas just after six. He went to his own apartment first, collected his office keys, and then—as he was leaving—he stood for a moment in the doorway. He surveyed the rooms he had inhabited ever since he'd arrived to begin work with Unit X. He remembered how proud he had felt. He remembered how special the assignment had seemed to him. It was a new thing, a brave new thing, and there were only a select few who had been chosen to undertake this project. Now it seemed like something else altogether, and it was not only the possibility of conspiracy that frightened him, but the simple fact that without the Bureau, without this purpose, then who was he, and what would he do?

His apartment seemed like the rooms of a stranger, a hotel room, a room with no personality impressed upon it. Prior to Seneca Falls, he had wanted for nothing. Life had been simple, straightforward, the cases he investigated being all that he'd required to occupy his mind. Now it had all been turned inside out, twisted back upon itself, and he felt as if he was looking at everything from a reversed perspective.

For a moment he again questioned what he was doing, even glanced toward the bookshelf and the letter from Esther that he'd never read, but it did not divert him.

Travis closed the door behind him, went back down to the car, and headed for the office.

36

It was cold, the sky was clear and cloudless, and he sat for a while listening to the cooling tick of the engine. He was a block from the Bureau offices, a couple of minutes' walk, and he did not understand why he was waiting. There was no reason to wait. There was no one there. No one would see him, and—in all likelihood—no one would ever know he had been there. It had to be done.

Travis took a flashlight from the trunk of his car and approached from the rear of the building. He made his way along the alley, left, left again, and down a narrow walkway to the back door. He opened up, stepped inside, closed and then locked the door behind him. His heart raced. There was sweat on the palms of his hands, and he wiped them on his pants.

Bishop's office would be locked, and for this he had no key, but he was not unschooled in accessing locked rooms. He even carried a blank on his own key chain, and employing this along with a straightened paper clip, he managed to open the door without difficulty.

Travis stood for some minutes in Bishop's room. How many times had he been called into this very office? How many times had he sat in this very chair to discuss progress on an ongoing case, to be briefed, debriefed, directed, acknowledged, even commended? More times than he could recall. In fact, the very last conversation he'd had with Bishop, the conversation that resulted in his dispatch to Seneca Falls, had taken place right here less than a week before. It did not seem real that only five days had elapsed since he had listened to Supervisor Bishop's explanation of the situation. He remembered how he'd felt as he left, his intention to set a standard that would presage a stunningly successful and important career. He was SSA Michael Travis, and it was merely a matter of time before he'd be supervisor, special agent in charge, section chief, deputy assistant director, and on it would go, as high as the stratosphere. Those heights now seemed to bear the characteristics of depths, like some strange optical illusion. What was wide was narrow; what was once profound was now a meaningless untruth.

Before he started searching the room, he stood by the door and surveyed the interior. He assumed the viewpoint of someone who had never been there before, taking a mental note of every object within, clarifying in his own mind precisely how it looked. The filing cabinet to the right was imperfectly aligned to its neighbor, the potted plant on the sill was merely an inch from the edge. He took in every detail so as to ensure that he left it just as he'd found it. And then started looking— going through every cabinet in the room, every file, every document. He looked at papers that were stamped three or four levels above his own clearance grade, and yet he did not care. He replaced everything precisely as he had found it and did not consider for a moment that his presence would ever be discovered. And yet he did not find what he was looking for. He found no file with his name, nor that of Seneca Falls, nothing that mentioned Edgar Doyle or the Carnival Diablo. He found no reference to the murder that had taken place, no memorandums addressed to Bishop from anyone in Washington about the "Kansas investigation."

Travis's imagination had been exercised sufficiently for one night, for he felt nothing at all, *wanted* to feel nothing at all. He tried to convince himself that everything had been blown out of proportion, that there was no conspiracy, that he had been blindsided by Edgar Doyle and his people. And then it struck him. What if this was nothing more than a further distraction? What if Doyle was even now disassembling the carnival, taking down the tents, loading everything that he possessed into the convoy of vehicles, and fleeing Seneca Falls as dawn broke?

No. Travis did not believe that was happening. As it stood, Travis considered the likelihood of Doyle's involvement in the murder as real and as possible as that of the Bureau. The old saw applied. He was caught between the devil and the deep blue sea, but which was the devil here?

Travis sat down in Bishop's chair. He could not believe that there was no record of the Seneca Falls assignment in this room. If not here, then there had to be something in Chief Gale's room, unless...

Travis knew then. He knew with certainty. The fire safe. Beneath the floor of the outer office was a metal safe buried in the footings of the building. Impregnable to most everything, it contained material considered to be sensitive or potentially inflammatory until further probative evidence had been obtained. It could be opened by two agents, no less, and one of those had to be Bishop himself. Bishop had a key, and there was a second key provided to each serving agent of the office staff. A further copy of Bishop's key was also held in a strongbox in the outer office, itself securely locked. Travis did not doubt that he could open it, and with both keys he could access the fire safe.

Travis had greater difficulty than he'd predicted with the strongbox. He went through desk drawers in the office until he found some gum.

Chewing it, then kneading it dry between his fingers, he pressed it around the face of the lock to prevent any scratching of the surface. He inserted each key he possessed, testing the levers gently, trying to ascertain where each lever sat. Employing the key that appeared to fit with the greatest ease, ironically the key to his room at the McCaffrey, he applied the finest layer of paper glue. He allowed it to dry, and then he tentatively inserted the key and angled it clockwise until he felt the pressure from the internal levers. Withdrawing the key again with the greatest care, ensuring that he did not make any contact with the outer edge of the lock aperture itself, he scrutinized the teeth. Left in the fine layer of paper adhesive was a clear enough impression of where the levers sat. There were only three, not five, which made the task somewhat easier. The hotel key was not so different from the one required to open the strongbox, and Travis searched the desks until he found a metal comb. Using it as a makeshift file, he started work on modifying the key as best he could. It took a good while. Each time he thought he was close he would try the key, but to no avail. He simply persisted, working at the thing until he felt sure it would turn the levers.

Finally, the strongbox was open. Travis returned the metal comb to the desk from which he'd taken it. He took the copy of Bishop's key, retraced his steps, moved a file cabinet near the door to Bishop's office, and then lifted the boards beneath. He looked down at the fire safe. He held his own key in his right hand, Bishop's key in his left. This was it now. He knelt down, hesitated for one moment more. Now he would find what he was looking for, or he would not. He asked himself whether he wanted to know if he had been played like a pawn in some chess game engineered and created by people he did not know, people he perhaps would never know.

Travis cast aside any final shred of doubt he might have possessed. He turned the key, he heard the levers drop, and then he inserted the second key. He turned it, and the safe was open.

Later he could not have said what he had expected to find. Later he would recognize that the moment he reached into that safe and took out the files within was the moment that everything irrevocably changed. It seemed as if everything he believed in then turned one hundred and eighty degrees and looked back at him with an expression of condescension and superiority.

You are not who you think you are, it said. *What you are doing, and what you think you are doing are not the same thing. And never have been. And you will never really understand how it was that you were so effortlessly fooled and deceived.*

The dead man's face looked back at him. There was no question. It was the same face as that on the picture in his pocket. It was a police precinct mug shot. The man held a board, and upon it was a date, a name, a location. New York City, June 11, 1954. The name given was Andris Varga.

The file itself gave very little further information. It seemed that this Andris Varga had been arrested on suspicion of murder in New York in June of 1954. Whether or not he had been formally charged or arraigned was unclear, but Travis's question as to the man's origin and nationality was confirmed by a handwritten note, author unknown, that stated that Varga was from Kecskemét in Hungary. There was a notation of his height, his weight, notable scars and identifying marks, the latter including details of his tattoos. It was most definitely the same man. And, providing another confirmation of what Doyle had told Travis, Varga was purported to be a member of a Hungarian organized-crime network known as Fekete Kutya.

Michael Travis sat cross-legged on the floor of the Kansas City Field Office with the slim dossier in his lap, and he wondered what the hell he had been thrown into. Who was Andris Varga? What was Fekete Kutya? Why had Varga been arrested in New York on suspicion of murder, and then—more than four years later—wound up dead from a fatal stab wound in the back of his neck, his body summarily deposited beneath the carousel of a traveling carnival organized and run by the strangest collection of misfits that Travis had even encountered?

Travis went through the remainder of the documents and files in the fire safe and found nothing further. This absence, in and of itself, almost directly contradicted the routine and accepted operating basis of the Bureau. Everything was documented; everything was filed; everything was recorded, recoverable, signed, sealed, and accountable to someone. But this was not, it seemed. This was a thing all its own.

And where was Varga's body now? Why had it been taken so swiftly from Seneca Falls, and to whom had it been delivered?

Travis made a note of Varga's name, the New York precinct where he had been photographed, the date of arrest, the case number, and the town of his birth.

He replaced everything as he had found it, locked the safe with Bishop's key and returned it to the strongbox before he used his own key. He cleaned the gum away from the face of the lock, checked to ensure that there were no telltale scratches or finger marks. He replaced the floorboards, moved the file cabinet back to its original position, and surveyed the area to determine if there was any telltale sign of his presence. From what he could see, there was nothing to say that anything out of the ordinary had taken place. He had managed to successfully execute an illegal search of a restricted access safe, read documents that were beyond his clearance grade, and note down details of those documents for his own use. Three charges, any one of which could mean his immediate dismissal from the Bureau.

Travis did not linger. He left the building the way he had come, locked everything securely behind him, and walked the block or so to his car.

By the time he was seated in the Fairlane, he was breathing heavily, not from any degree of physical exertion, but from the sheer mental and emotional burden of what he had discovered.

He had been sent to investigate the murder of a man whose identity was already known to the Bureau, a man who had been arrested on suspicion of murder in New York four years earlier, a man who was a confirmed member of an Eastern European organized-crime syndicate.

This was the truth, and for the first time in his life, the truth seemed a great deal more disturbing than any lie he might have been told.

The truth can hurt. He had heard that before. Michael Travis had never before realized how much.

Despite the hour, Travis knew he could not return to Seneca Falls without addressing one further issue. The badge that Doyle wore, the forget-me-not, the symbol of this Nazi fundraising organization that he had referred to as his shield against all ills.

Travis's first thought was for Sarah Ebner from the Wichita University. She had been aware of Fekete Kutya, and Travis felt certain that she could assist him further. But Wichita was a four-hour drive, and he felt equally certain that she would not appreciate an unannounced visit from the FBI. But what else was there to do? He would not sleep, *could* not sleep, and this matter had to be resolved.

Travis stopped at the bus station and found a bank of phones. He called Information, asked for the residential number of Dr. Sarah Ebner in Wichita, and waited for the connection. Dr. Ebner came on the line almost immediately.

"I need to speak with you, and it is a matter of urgency," Travis said. "I am in Kansas, and I can be there in three or four hours, but I wanted to make sure that you were there, that you would be willing to talk to me so late."

Travis, if he was not mistaken, could hear the wry smile in her voice as she replied.

"Not only are you unschooled in the ways of women, Agent Travis, you are also unfamiliar with idiosyncratic academics, I see," she said. "It is Saturday night, and the only reason I am not on campus is because they tell me I am supposed to stay home weekends. You are more than welcome. Let me give you my address."

Dr. Ebner did so, and Travis wrote it down.

"I shall endeavor to get there as fast as possible," Travis told her.

"And I shall endeavor to have some coffee ready."

Travis stopped at a gas station to fill up. He spoke with the station attendant and determined the fastest route down to Wichita. Though the route he'd taken—I-35 out of Emporia—seemed quicker, the attendant suggested he take 169 southwest to Iola and then head west along 54.

"Might not sound like sense, but you'd be surprised the number of long-distance haulers they run on 35 on a Saturday night. You get a crowd o' those—worse still, you get a bump or a spill—and you're gonna be stuck there till next Tuesday while they sort it out. I figure you should take 169 and hope for the best."

Travis followed the man's advice, and was out on the highway before half past eight. He figured he could make it by eleven if he floored the Fairlane.

Somewhere between Olathe and Paola he knew he was losing all connections to anything certain. He forced himself to think of other things, other memories, other times and places and people.

His attention kept going back to Esther, perhaps occasioned by his return home, her letter now the only thing that seemed of any importance in his apartment.

He remembered the last time he'd seen her, the visit they'd made together to see his mother, the trial, her sentencing, the day he'd sat with her and understood that she didn't even remember who he was.

That was the memory that came, and try as he might, he could not stop it.

37

The events that transpired in the late fall and early winter of 1943 were significant for many reasons. The trial of Janette Travis began on Monday, October twenty-fifth, and concluded on Wednesday, November seventeenth. During those eighteen days, a series of testimonials were presented by both the state prosecutor and the assigned public defender. The public defender, a diligent and spirited man by the name of Nathan Harper, went head-to-head with the much-respected and experienced state prosecutor, Jim Greaves. Whereas Harper possessed a studious bearing and deportment, always on time, always precise in his diction and manner, Greaves possessed a more relaxed and folksy kind of style. He made the jurors smile; he engaged them; he brought himself down to their level and connected with them. Greaves was an academic, possessing more letters after his name than he did within it, but he understood people. He knew something of the life of a Midwest small-town farmer, for such a life was his grandfather's and his grandfather's before that. Greaves was an anomaly in his ancestral line, a man who had struck out of that mold and walked an untrod path to somewhere different. Not necessarily better, but different.

So, in this way, Harper was disadvantaged, not only due to the fact that his client was a self-confessed premeditated murderess, but he was also pitted against someone who had him on the back foot from the get-go.

It was a slow slide into a certain conviction, and those who were present understood that there was no other possible outcome.

Michael Travis did not attend the trial. He knew it was happening, but he did not believe he could face seeing his mother in the witness stand or on the prisoner's bench.

"I can take you," Esther told him. "I'll be there with you."

Michael declined her offer. He felt certain of how it would end, so certain that he did not need to see it played out in painful reality.

Esther, in communication with Howard Redding from State Welfare, learned of the end of the trial and the knowledge that her cousin Janette had been found unanimously guilty, that sentencing would take place at two p.m. on the afternoon of Tuesday, November twenty-third. There was little doubt in anyone's mind that the sentence could or would be anything but death.

Until sentencing, Janette would be held in the Nebraska State Penitentiary in Lincoln. Now the better part of seventy-five years old, NSP had been the only such facility in Nebraska right through to the end of the First World War. Prior to 1903, convict executions had always taken place in the county where the offense had occurred. Subsequently, those executions took place at State, and from 1913, the means of execution was by electric chair instead of hanging. Between 1903 and 1929, there had been seventeen executions, seven of them under the respective jurisdictions of Governors Samuel McKelvie and Adam McMullen. The last execution had been that of one Henry Sherman—a twenty-year-old white farm laborer found guilty of rape and murder—on May 31, 1929, under Governor Arthur J. Weaver. Weaver's term had ended in January of 1931, and during the following decade—the first four years under Charles Bryan, the next six under Robert Leroy Cochran—Old Sparky had not been fired up even once. Cochran's governorship had ended in January of 1941, and though there had yet to be an execution under the new governor, Dwight Griswold, that did not mean that Janette could not be the first. Rumor had it that Griswold was a lenient man, perhaps less the "hanging judge" and more the "strict but compassionate overseer," but—regardless of whatever sense of moral or ethical reservation he might possess about the death penalty—a governor did not possess the power of absolution. A governor governed by the will of the people, and if the people bayed for blood, then blood they would get. Additionally, due to the protracted period of time during which Janette Travis would reside on death row, there was no guarantee that Griswold would even be the governor when her execution date finally arrived.

Esther took it upon herself to convince Michael that he should attend the sentencing hearing.

"I feel it's necessary," she told him. "I know you don't want to go, and believe me, I would not want to go if it were my mother, but I think in years to come, you will regret that you weren't there when your mother needed you most."

"I can go," Michael said, "but what good will it serve?"

Esther took his hand. They were seated across from each other at the kitchen table. It was the afternoon of Sunday the twenty-first.

"Your mother loves you more than life itself," Esther said. "There is no way to avoid that reality. She did what she did to protect herself, of course, but she also did it to protect you." She smiled and shook her head. "I cannot tell you what to think and feel, Michael, and I know it is really difficult for you to speak about these things, but there's no escaping the fact that at some point you're going to have to come out of your shell and face the world."

"Come out of my shell? What do you mean?"

Esther looked at him then, and there was something almost maternal in her expression. It was not something he had seen before, and it unsettled him. She looked at him as an adult to a child, and in that moment—merely a handful of weeks since they had first become intimate—he felt patronized, almost looked down upon.

"Do you not think I know what's going on?" she said. Her voice was calm and measured, strangely sympathetic. "I see you, Michael... I see you every day, and every day my heart breaks for you. You have cried about what happened just once and once only. You never talk about it. Your mother killed your father. She murdered him. He is dead, and she is in prison, and her trial has just ended and they found her guilty—"

"I know—"

"You know in your mind, perhaps," Esther interjected, "but you don't seem to know in your heart."

Michael withdrew his hand from hers.

"Don't," she said.

"Don't what?"

"Don't withdraw even further, sweetheart. You have to have someone love you. Everyone needs someone to love them, and they need to love someone back. That's what makes life worth living. I know you love your mother, and I can't bear to see you hide from what's happening to her."

"I know what's happening, and I am not hiding," Michael said, his tone defensive.

"Michael," she said, and then she smiled in that same manner, and once again she was the adult and he was the child.

"Don't speak to me like that," he said.

Her eyes flashed with hurt. "Like what? What do you mean?" She reached out to take his hand again, but he withdrew it further.

"Like I am a child."

"I am not speaking to you like a child," she said. "I can't believe you think that. I love you, Michael. I really do."

"Then understand that maybe I am different from you, different from anyone else. I don't need to cry and weep and get angry and frightened because of what's happening. I know she's been found guilty, and I know she'll be sentenced to death, and there's nothing I can do about it."

"So, what you're saying is that it will serve no good for you to go and see her?"

"Right."

"And what about her?"

"What *about* her?"

"Well, don't you think she might want to see you? Don't you think it might help her to know that you are there, that you still love her, that she means everything to you?"

"I can't give her something that she didn't give me," Michael said.

"How can you say that? How can you even think that way? She loves you more than you will ever know—"

"Loves me so much she deserted me? Loves me so much that she has taken herself out of my life completely? Loves me so much she is going to die and leave me alone for the rest of my life? Is that how much she loves me?"

Esther looked frightened then, her eyes wide with alarm. "Oh, Michael, I can't believe you think that—"

"Then tell me what I am supposed to think, Esther. Tell me that. Tell me how I am supposed to feel about what is happening. What will happen to me when she is dead? Where will I go? What will I do? If either of them had loved me at all, then maybe he wouldn't have been so bad, so crazy, so violent to her, and she would not have had to kill him. He never laid a hand on me. He never even raised a finger against me. She did not kill him to protect me... She killed him to protect herself."

Esther closed her eyes. She seemed to be gathering herself together at the seams. When she opened her eyes, they were brimming with tears. She finger tipped them away, but they did not stop, and for a moment she sat there and cried in silence.

Eventually, Michael reached out his hand and took hers.

"These past weeks," he said, "I have found out what it means to love someone. I am sixteen years old. I don't know anything about life. I don't understand why this has happened. I don't understand what will happen to me, to us... because I know this will end, Esther. I see that already. Even if we wanted to go on being together, the world wouldn't let us. My mother's gone. That's the truth. If you want to go to this hearing... if you want to go and see her when they tell her that she's going to die, then I'll go with you. I will not be going for myself, but for you. You understand?"

Esther nodded. Her throat was too tight for words.

"Do you want to go?" Michael asked her.

She nodded again. "Ye-es," she stammered. "F-for her, Michael... for he-her sake..."

Michael smiled, but there was little humor or warmth in that smile. "Then we'll go. I'll go with you. We'll tell her that we love her and that we will be thinking of her, and then we'll leave and never see her again."

Esther looked up suddenly, and once again there seemed to be something almost fearful in her expression, as if a facet of Michael's personality had suddenly been revealed to her, a facet that she did not like or understand.

"Is that what you wish?" she asked.

"I have to end it sometime," he said. "What do you want me to do? Go out there every week? Go and see her in prison and remind her of everything she is missing, remind myself of the fact that I have neither a mother nor a father anymore? Is that what you want?"

"I want you to be happy," Esther said.

"I don't think such a thing is possible, is it?"

"Oh, Michael… sweet Michael," she said softly, and couldn't say any more.

And so they went. On a cold Tuesday afternoon in November of 1943, they waited patiently to be admitted to the courtroom.

When at last they took their assigned seats and saw Janette Travis brought up from the cells below, Michael barely recognized his mother. Her expression was so very distant, and she sat gazing into some vague middle ground, perhaps with the vain belief that things were better there.

This was not the mother that Michael remembered, neither in looks nor manner. She had lost an inordinate amount of weight, and her hair—once full and long—was now thin and cut short.

She sat silently at the desk, beside her the public defender, Nathan Harper, and across the small courtroom sat her prosecutor, Jim Greaves.

Janette Travis was greeted by a silence that was more sensed than heard. The room was airless, replete with tension, and that tension was felt in every breath.

Janette looked in Michael's direction, and yet she seemed to be looking right through them. A faint smile crossed her lips, as if noting a pretty child, a cute dog in the street, but nothing more. It really was as if she were elsewhere, her mind still inside a jail cell, endlessly pacing back and forth as if in constant determination of the amount of sadness trapped within the walls.

Michael raised his hand, but Janette's focus had already drifted. He was aware of Esther holding on to the sleeve of his jacket. His chest was like a balloon—as light as air and empty.

Formalities ensued, people entered, a bailiff appeared and shuffled papers ceremoniously.

And then came the judge, and his expression was austere and hard; the shadows cast from the single window to his right made his features as angular and severe as if cut from stone.

Words were spoken—people rose and then were again seated, and finally Janette Travis was asked to stand, and she did so, and her defense attorney stood with her, and she looked at the judge as if she were waiting for him to offer her a cup of coffee, a cigarette perhaps. Nothing more significant than that.

"Janette Alice Travis, having been charged and tried and found guilty of murder in the first degree of James Franklin Travis on May 10, 1927, in the town of Flatwater, against the peace and dignity of the state of Nebraska, it is the judgment of this court that sentence is now heard. It is with a heavy heart that I am obliged to pass down the most severe sentence afforded this crime by the state of Nebraska, that you shall be remanded into the legal custody of the Nebraska State Penitentiary Department at a facility deemed fit for such detention, and there you shall reside until such time as provision can be made for your execution. That is the determination of this court in this case, and I am required by law to inform you of your right to appeal, said appeal to be filed within the due time allocated, the details of which will be afforded to you by your legal counsel."

The judge paused.

Esther's body trembled as she withheld the flood of grief that assaulted her every sense.

Michael sat silent and stoic, his eyes like glass, his heart measuring nothing but the passing of time.

Janette seemed insensate, as if this were nothing of any significance, as if this were no more important than a postponed train or an overdue library book.

"Does the defendant wish to make any further statement at this time?" the judge asked.

Nathan Harper looked at his client. Janette continued staring emotionlessly at the judge. Harper leaned close to her, said something that only she could hear, and then said it again as there seemed to be no recognition of what he was telling her.

And then she smiled. She turned and looked at Michael, at Esther, at the small gathering of onlookers and officials in the courtroom, and said, "Most of the time I had no idea why he was so very angry... but then other times I did know why." She shook her head, and for a moment she seemed again elsewhere, a smile playing across her lips as if recalling some past moment of happiness. Then she turned to the judge and said, "Sometimes I wonder if my punishment for killing him was actually served before he died..."

Janette lowered her head.

"No further statement at this time," Harper told the gathering, and the judge nodded sagely, seemingly unsettled by the few words that the defendant had uttered.

The bailiff stood. "This hearing is hereby adjourned. All rise."

Everyone rose.

The judge got up and left the room.

Those who had business elsewhere departed immediately, and soon there was no one in the room but Michael, Esther, Janette, Nathan Harper, and two officers of the court on each side of the door.

Janette had remained standing, almost trancelike now, looking back and forth from the window to the door as if undecided as to her means of exit.

Harper took her hand and indicated that she should sit. She did so without word or question.

He then crossed the room to speak with Michael and Esther, introduced himself, shook hands, and then lowered his voice.

"She is fragile," he told them. "She is in shock, I believe. Really, for the past three or four weeks, I have not been able to establish with her any understanding of what is going on. She keeps asking me when she will be able to go home." He looked down at the floor, and when he looked back at Michael, there was such a sense of sadness it his eyes, it was almost painful.

"I am sorry to say that she has not asked about you," Harper continued. "I wrestled for a long time with whether or not I should tell you this, but decided that it was best you know. I have met with her three or four times a week, and each time I see her, I have to remind her of my name, my job, what I am meeting her for. Frankly, and it pains me to say this, I am certain she has lost all connection to reality."

Michael held Harper's gaze unerringly. "Perhaps that is best for both myself and her," he said.

Beside them, Esther stifled her sobs with a handkerchief.

"I cannot bear to consider such a thing," Harper said, "but I think you may be right."

"I'll speak to her now," Michael said.

Harper stepped back. Michael walked to the table where his mother sat. He took a chair and sat facing her. He reached out his hand to enclose hers, but she withdrew it. A frown crossed her brow.

Michael said nothing for some seconds, and then he smiled.

"My name is Michael," he said. "Do you remember me?"

Janette smiled back. "Yes, I am sure I remember you," she said. "From church, wasn't it? Didn't I see you in church last week?"

"Yes, ma'am," Michael said. "From church."

"I thought so."

"So, how have you been?"

"Oh, I can't complain," Janette said. "The food is not so good, but it's better than nothing. I keep asking them when I will be finished, but no one seems to know. Sometimes I have a headache thinking about all of it, but it goes away when I sleep."

"Okay," Michael said. "I just wanted to make sure you were okay."

"That's very sweet of you, young man."

Michael smiled, and then he got to his feet.

"Will I see you in church again?" she asked.

"Oh yes," Michael replied. "I would think so."

"Until then."

"Yes, ma'am. Until then."

Janette held out her hand. Michael took it. He felt those slim cool fingers against his palm, and he knew then that she was gone and would never return. Whoever his mother might have been, she had departed long ago. Perhaps she had left immediately after his father, following him even into hell, trying to gain his forgiveness for what she had done.

Michael released her hand, and he turned back to Esther.

"We're going," he said.

They bade their farewells to Nathan Harper, and Harper escorted Janette Travis from the room and into the custody of the court officers.

Michael and Esther left the building immediately, beginning at once their journey home.

Upon arrival, it seemed that Michael had recovered from the ordeal, whereas Esther was traumatized beyond words. She had spoken not a single word on the way back despite Michael's best efforts to encourage her into conversation.

Once inside the house, he poured her a drink, sat while she sipped it, and eventually he held her hand and looked into her eyes as he spoke.

"Esther, listen to me. We knew this was going to happen. We knew this would be the outcome. She knew it too. There is nothing we could have done about it, and there is nothing we can do to change what will happen. I think she wants to die—"

"She... she i-is your mother, Mi-Michael... your mother. Do you not feel anything at all for her?"

Michael frowned. "Of course I feel something for her. Is that what you think? That I feel nothing for her?"

"I don't know what to think," Esther said. "You confuse me. Sometimes I think I understand you, and sometimes you feel like a complete stranger."

"I am as upset as you are, Esther—"

"No, Michael, you aren't. I look in your eyes and I can see that you're not. If it were my mother, I would be tearing myself to pieces right now. I would be inconsolable, and I would be doing everything I could to help her in any possible way. But you?" She paused, looking at Michael, at the way he looked back at her, almost in disbelief at his seeming lack of reaction to what was happening.

Michael knelt before her. He reached up and touched her cheek.

"No, Michael. Don't…"

Michael put his hand around the back of Esther's neck and pulled her close. She resisted at first, as if angry at him for trying to change the direction of things, but she yielded against the warmth of his body and the touch of his fingers on her throat.

"I love you, Esther," he whispered.

"Oh, Michael, don't say that…"

"I love you, Esther, plain and simple. Whether you like it or not, I love you."

She closed her eyes and breathed deeply. She felt guilty then, perhaps for the first time—guilty for loving him in return, guilty for his age, for who he was, for how such a thing would be viewed by others who could never understand what had happened between them.

As if voicing her fears, he said, "And I don't care what people think or what people say. I really don't. You think I feel nothing, well, you're wrong. I feel everything I want to feel, and I make myself invisible for things I don't."

She pulled him tight, tighter, and then she was kissing him.

They made love then, right there on the floor, and it was desperate and hurried, like people possessed, as if each were trying to be inside the other, as if each were trying somehow to get away from who they were and become someone or something else.

And when they were done, they lay beside each other and their breathing slowed, and she turned on her side and watched him, the way his chest rose and fell, the way his hair fell back across his ear.

And it was then—for the last time—that she saw a single tear escape his eye and make its way across his cheek.

38

Away from the confines and formality of the university, Sarah Ebner seemed to be an entirely different woman. Her hair was down, and she was wearing an open-necked blouse and casual slacks instead of the dark suit. Despite the hour, she seemed pleased to see Travis. It was past eleven thirty when he finally reached her door, and she opened it before he'd had a chance to knock.

"You have no idea how much I appreciate this," Travis said.

"Well, strange as though it may sound, Agent Travis, I am intrigued also. I am curious as to what is so important it brings you from Kansas to Wichita on a Saturday night."

"Your expertise," Travis said. "The comment you made regarding your work on national socialism."

"Come in," she said. "I've made coffee."

No more than fifteen minutes later, they sat together in Ebner's study. Again, it was not dissimilar to that of Ralph Saxon, but here the sense of order and organization was far more pronounced. There were distinctly feminine touches between the high-ranged bookshelves and towering columns of texts and dossiers. A manuscript sat on her desk, a good three or four inches thick, and from the scrawls of red ink, the underlinings and margin notes, it appeared to be something she was currently editing.

"Your own work?" Travis asked.

"Yes," she replied. "It's my own crackpot theories on why Communism will ultimately fail, and why the allies should have marched on into Moscow and taken it, just as Churchill advised."

"And you have made studies of national socialism and the Third Reich, yes?"

"Some, yes."

"And you speak German?"

"Yes, I do, as a matter of fact. German, Italian, and French. Not bad for a girl, eh?"

"My misogynistic tendencies have tempered somewhat, Dr. Ebner," Travis said. "After all, who did I call when I needed assistance with this?"

She smiled, and it was such a forgiving smile, Travis couldn't help but see the humor in what he'd said.

"You called me because you had no one else to call, Agent Travis."

"Okay, you got me there," he said. "I wanted to ask you about an organization called Winterhilfswerk."

"Well, all right. A curious question. It means *winter help work*, literally. Winter Relief was the more official name of the program, and it was as it sounds. It was an annual project established by something called the National Socialist People's Welfare Organization. Its motto was 'None Shall Starve Nor Freeze.' It was actually an entirely community-orientated program that went back as far as 1930 or 1931, but Hitler later claimed sole credit for it. It cycled through a six-month period, October to March, and it required donations and contributions of basic necessities like food, clothing, and coal. A lot of the collecting was done by the Hitlerjugend and the Bund Ditcher Mädel, the boys' and girls' organizations. On the face of it, it was a very clever propaganda technique, for it positioned the idea that community was superior to individual, that Hitlerian policy encouraged community responsibility for one another, that children could contribute just as much as adults. It made people think that they were working for the common good of the people as well as the state. In fact, significant donations to the organization made you an ally of the Nazi party without having to formally be a member. Giving to the Winter Relief Program got them off your back."

"And there were badges, medals, awards?"

"Hundreds of them, thousands perhaps. They became collectible items. Badges, pennants, things like this, all known as *abzeichen*, and they were displayed and worn by people to show that they had made contributions. There was even a monthly placard called a *monatstür-plakette*, which you put in your window to show that you'd donated. People who didn't donate were actually reviled, sometimes even the victims of mob violence. Eventually, the Brownshirts were employed to collect money as well, and they collected it with threats and menaces. They would trawl the markets, beer halls, anywhere where people congregated, and oblige people to give as much as they could. What was originally established as a purely philanthropic and community-minded program became something far more sinister and politically motivated."

"In what way?"

"Well, if money was being collected for social welfare from the people themselves, then state and tax monies earmarked for welfare could be diverted to armaments and propaganda. Essentially, if the people themselves paid both taxes and for their own maintenance, then the taxes could be employed for the war effort. The second thing was that those who didn't donate, even those unable to, could be labeled as dissenters, traitors, subversives, anything that seemed to be in vogue, and shipped off to the work camps."

"I wanted to ask you about the badges that were issued. They sometimes used flowers, right?"

"Flowers, yes. Birds too. Insects, nursery rhyme and fairy-tale characters for the children. They had badges depicting German historical personalities and many of Hitler himself."

"And the forget-me-not?"

Sarah Ebner frowned, and a narrow smile played across her lips. "The forget-me-not?" she asked. "You want to know about this badge specifically?"

"Yes, I do."

"Might I ask why?"

"Because I know someone who wears one."

"Presently?"

"Yes, as we speak. Every time I have seen him, he is wearing it."

"And he is American?"

"Irish."

"But he lives here."

"Now he does, yes."

"And he served during the war?"

"According to what information I have, he served in Ireland in collaboration with British military intelligence in routing out and exposing Nazi sympathizers. He then appears to have worked alongside the Resistance in France, but the last two years of the war saw him betray his loyalties and start work for the Nazis."

"And you have concluded this because of the badge he wears?"

"I have, yes."

"Well, I might just have to shatter your preconceptions, Agent Travis."

"Because?"

Ebner leaned back in her chair and sighed. "Well, there is a very strong possibility, Agent Travis, that you are looking at someone who is the diametric opposite of precisely what we've been discussing."

"Meaning?"

"Meaning, very simply, that this man with his forget-me-not badge might have been involved in something that the Nazis would have been very upset about."

"I'm sorry?"

"Have you ever heard of an organization called the Freemasons, Agent Travis?"

Travis's surprise was evident.

"I am sorry," Ebner said. "Of course you have. In fact, you are more than likely already a member of this organization, aren't you?"

"As a matter of fact, no," Travis replied. He couldn't help but think of the conversation he'd had with Doyle, the fact that Doyle himself had spoken of the Freemasons when detailing the history of those who had made studies of the human mind and its capabilities. "I know that Mr. Hoover holds a very significant office in this organization."

Ebner smiled knowingly. "If you know someone is a senior officer in the Freemasons, then they're probably nowhere near as senior as you think, Agent Travis."

"I have to be honest and say that I don't know a great deal about them."

"Well, there's a history all its own, Agent Travis, and I don't need to overwhelm you with that right now. Let's just say that it's a very old organization, and—as with all such fellowships and fraternities—it has two faces, the outward and the inward. Essentially, what it says it does and what it actually does. What you need to know is that the Freemasons were not looked upon as potential allies by the Nazis. In fact, in many countries, anti-Masonry and anti-Semitism are strongly linked, even now, and that harks back to idea that the Freemasons built the Temple of Solomon. As far as the last war is concerned, records were discovered in the Reich Security Main Office that detail the persecution of the Freemasons as enemies of the state. There was a man called Franz Six, and he was responsible not only for creating anti-Semitic propaganda, but also that of anti-Masonry. Masons were considered politically and ideologically subversive, and they were persecuted, as were so many others."

"And the significance of the badge relates to the Masons?"

"It does, yes," Ebner said, "and the fact that you mentioned *that* specific flower intrigues me, because it has two meanings."

"Which are?"

"Well, the forget-me-not emblem was first used in the midtwenties by the Grand Lodge Zur Sonne. It was the symbol for their annual convention in Bremen. Then, just ten or twelve years later, the same badge was selected for the annual Winterhilfswerk drive. In fact, the badge was even made by the same factory. As far as I understand, the forget-me-not badge was worn as a sign of membership by the Freemasons during that period, a badge they could wear without fear of persecution."

"So someone who wears this badge could be a Freemason?"

"Well, the very same badge was chosen as the Masonic emblem for the first Annual Convention of the United Grand Lodges of Germany in 1948. Masons all over the world wear it as a sign of respect and commemoration for those who died during the Holocaust."

Travis leaned back in the chair. "The more I learn, the less I understand," he said.

Ebner smiled. "Sounds like life, Agent Travis."

"No, seriously, I am absolutely baffled by this, Dr. Ebner. I really have no idea what I am dealing with here."

"This relates to the matter we discussed a few days ago? Fekete Kutya and your dead Hungarian?"

"It does, yes."

"Well, the boundaries and borders between most European mainland countries were ever-shifting and disappearing during that period, Agent Travis. Still, there are lands that were one nation before the war and are now considered another. It was a time of unparalleled upheaval, politically, socially, even geographically. People were moved, extradited, expelled, displaced, and even now there are many hundreds of thousands who have yet to be repatriated. It is hard to say who came from where, and when you factor in their religious and political affiliations, you find both pro-Axis and resistance within the same families. There are Nazi war criminals already released from prison, even before Holocaust survivors have managed to establish what actually happened to their own homes and families. I don't believe we've even begun to understand the true horror and tragedy of those years, and I don't imagine we ever will."

Travis was quiet for a time, lost among his own thoughts.

"So what is it that you are trying to establish here, Agent Travis?"

"The true identity of our Hungarian, but more than that, the real reason for his presence in Nebraska. Why he was here, and more important, why he was murdered here and whether the people I suspect of involvement were in fact involved or have been set up."

"And the man with the badge is a primary suspect?"

"Yes, he is."

"And he is Irish, living in America, and worked with British military intelligence exposing Nazi sympathizers in Ireland?"

"So he says."

"And this can't be verified through your own contacts and resources within the Bureau?"

"Uncertain."

"That surprises me greatly, Agent Travis, especially if your man is a Freemason. After all, isn't Mr. Hoover in possession of the greatest intelligence dossier library in the world? If anyone knew whether your Irishman was a white hat or a black hat, it would be the FBI, would it not?"

"One would think so, Dr. Ebner, yes."

"Well, I can see that you are wrestling with something far greater than the history of charitable donations for the Nazi party during the Second World War," she said, again wearing that wry smile. "Is there anything else I can help you with?"

"I don't think so, no," Travis said. "You've been very helpful indeed, and I really appreciate it."

"Well, I don't doubt that you'll get your man, Agent Travis. After all, that's what the movies tell me about you G-men."

"I am beginning to wonder whether the *G* stands for *Gullible*, Dr. Ebner."

"You know where I am," she said. "And I don't keep social hours."

"Appreciated. A voice of sanity in amid all this madness."

Sarah Ebner laughed. "Well, if I am the closest you can get to the voice of sanity, Agent Travis, then you must be dealing with something far darker than I can imagine."

Travis rose and buttoned his jacket. "I think I might be, Dr. Ebner. I really think I might be."

39

The McCaffrey Hotel was silent and cold. Travis let himself into his room. It was a few minutes before two. From his jacket pocket, he took the photo of Andris Varga and put it on the desk beside his typewriter. Beside it he placed the print card and the tattoo diagram. It now seemed so ironic that the tattoo so closely resembled a reversed question mark. The questions he had been asking were now reversing in his own mind. The ones he had asked were not the ones he needed to be asking.

After a while, Travis lay down in his clothes. He did not possess the energy to undress. He held that picture above him, focusing his attention on it, trying to think of nothing but the man's face, the way those dead eyes stared back at him, trying to determine what step he should next take.

If this man was known to the Bureau, if he had in fact been held by the Bureau at any time, then records would exist. But where? Here in Wichita, in Kansas City itself, or perhaps no other place but Washington. Did people like Tom Bishop and Frank Gale know about this? And Clyde Tolson? Did Tolson know? If Tolson knew, then Hoover knew, and if Hoover knew, then it had to be nothing less than a sanctioned operation, and if the execution of a man for a sanctioned operation had taken place, then where did such things end? There are some who can be sacrificed for the greater good. Was that what had happened here? There are some who are worth more to us dead than alive?

And then there was Doyle. Turncoat, or savior for those who would otherwise have been deported to concentration camps across Germany and Poland? And if Doyle was a Freemason, then how did that relate to the Bureau's own support of the Freemason Brotherhood, the fact that Hoover himself was in high office within that organization?

Travis's mind reeled back and forth between what he had believed for so long and the possibilities that were now being presented to him. It seemed ironic that the very thing that was now his greatest source of anxiety was his imagination. That imagination seemed fired up, alive with endless ideas and thoughts, and there was nothing he could do to turn it off. Did he want to turn it off? Did he want to go backward, to undo all of this, to return to his previous certainty, his unalterable perspective on life? He was reminded once more of Wendell Holmes's words: Man's mind, stretched by an idea, never regained its former dimensions. So true, so terribly, painfully true, and yet somehow so real and human and alive. He had been robotic in his attitude, assuming that those above him in the Bureau were to be believed, trusted, relied upon, their integrity and honesty unquestionable. But now—with the removal of the corpse from the Seneca Falls morgue, the disconnection of his communication lines into the Bureau itself, the revelation regarding the Bureau's prior knowledge of Varga—what was the truth? Was he now beyond the bounds of the law himself? Was he now in the firing line if he did not come back with the information they wanted? And what *did* they want?

Travis got up and sat on the edge of the bed once more.

He could not sleep. He could not think. He needed to see Doyle.

Travis left the hotel and drove straight to carnival site, and here he pounded on the door until Valeria Mironescu appeared—sleepy-eyed, still in her robe—and asked him what was going on.

"I need to see Doyle," Travis told her.

"What time is it?"

Travis glanced at his watch. "Nearly three," he said.

"Three? In the morning? For Christ's sake—"

"Valeria, I need to see him. I found out who the dead man was."

"What's happening?" Doyle called out from within the caravan.

"It's Agent Travis. He wants to talk to you," Valeria told him. "He says he's found out who the dead man was."

"What? Seriously? At this time? Tell him to come back later..."

Travis went up the steps and pushed past Valeria Mironescu. "I'm sorry," he said. "I really am, but this can't wait."

"Jesus Christ, Travis, what the hell is going on?" Doyle asked as Travis appeared at the foot of the fold-down bed.

"I went to Kansas City, Mr. Doyle. I went to the Bureau office and I found out who the dead man was."

"Well, that was a bit stupid of them, wasn't it?"

"Stupid? Of whom?"

"Having evidence of the man's identity in the Kansas City FBI office. That, as you Americans say, was really dumb, don't you think?"

"I don't think that's the point, Mr. Doyle. I think the point is that they knew who he was before they even sent me here..."

Doyle leaned up. He was naked, and he pulled the bedclothes up around his chest and put a pillow behind his head. "Now?" he asked. "Do we really have to do this now?"

Travis looked at Doyle in disbelief. He could not fathom Doyle's seeming nonchalance at such a startling revelation.

"Yes, now," Travis said. "This is incredible."

"What is?" Doyle asked.

"That they knew who he was. That they sent me here, all the while knowing precisely who he was."

Doyle shook his head. "Honestly, Michael, I think that's the least of your concerns right now." He reached for a pack of cigarettes and lit one, and then spoke to Valeria. "Looks like we're up, my dear. Would you make some coffee?"

"Of course," she said. "Agent Travis? Coffee for you as well?"

"Coffee?" Travis asked. "You ask me if I want coffee at a time like this?"

Neither Doyle nor Valeria replied. They both looked at him with somewhat bemused expressions.

Travis stood in the middle of the caravan.

"It's a cup of coffee, Agent Travis," Valeria said. "It's not going to make anything better or worse right now. Actually, to be honest, if it's a good cup of coffee, it might make things a little better."

Travis stopped moving for a moment. He didn't speak. He just stood there and looked at Doyle and the woman.

"She's right, Michael," Doyle said. "Just slow down for a minute. I understand—"

"I don't think you do, Mr. Doyle," Travis said. "These are the people I work for. This is like finding out that your parents aren't who you thought. This is like finding out that your wife is actually a Communist—"

Doyle started laughing. "Oh, Christ almighty," he said. "I think it's a great deal more problematic than that, my friend. You have just found out that you are a pawn in a game of chess, Agent Travis. Maybe you're a rook, perhaps a bishop, but certainly you are no king or queen. And the truth, if you really want to know the truth, is that you have always been a pawn, and you will forever be a pawn, because there is a line right there in front of you. You have just seen that line, my friend, and you understand a little of what that line means. I can tell you now that those who cross that line never come back. They can't. They know too much. They threaten the status quo. If you remain behind that line now, then you and I will take a very different path from one another. You will file your report, and I will be in custody, as will Valeria, Gabor, Chester, Mr. Slate, and anyone else who might be considered of use. And then, one day, perhaps soon, perhaps in a year, perhaps in a decade, once our capabilities have been exploited to their maximum effect, we will find ourselves in an untenable position, much the same position as your dead man found himself, and then we will be excused from the game."

"I don't..."

"Understand? Is that what you were going to say, Agent Travis? That you don't understand? Oh, yes, you do, Agent Travis. You understand perfectly well what I am saying, and you have understood it for some considerable time. This is a game—"

"What game? You keep calling it a game—"

"Because that's precisely what it is, my friend. A game of war. A game of politics. A game of human conflict, of money, of power and influence and religious persecution, of the obliteration of civil liberties and basic human rights. This is the game played by dictators and newspapers and drug companies and arms manufacturers and the banks in Switzerland when they agreed to look after all that Nazi gold. This is the game that every government plays when they choose to turn a blind eye to geno-cide and racism and religious persecution. This is the game of who can accumulate the most damning evidence against his opponent and keep it hidden, keep it safe, and then use it to blackmail his way out of criminal prosecution for what he has done. That is the game, Agent Travis, and you have been supporting that game for all your years in the FBI."

Valeria laughed. "The Felonious Bureau of Idiots."

"The Foul Brethren of Injustice—"

"Enough!" Travis said

"You don't have any friends, Agent Travis," Doyle said. "And you actu-ally never have. Not since Esther Faulkner."

Travis looked at Doyle, his eyes even wider. "D-don't you bring Esther into th-this, Doyle."

"She's already here, Michael. Always has been. You carry her around like a mantle over your shoulders."

Travis sat down on the floor with his back against the wall. He pulled his knees up to his chest and linked his hands around his calves.

Valeria poured the coffee. She brought cups to both Doyle and Travis, and then she herself sat on the edge of the bed beside Doyle. She looked down at Travis sympathetically.

"Now you look like the child you once were," Doyle said.

Travis looked at Doyle, at Valeria, and then he shook his head without a word.

"So, tell me," Doyle went on. "Who was our mystery man?"

"I think there is a more pressing and relevant question, Mr. Doyle."

"There is?"

"The question is, who are you?"

"I am many things, Agent Travis. Who would you like for me to be?"

335

"Are you a Freemason?"

Doyle looked surprised, and then he laughed. "My badge?" he asked.

"Your badge."

"You are a hardworking and diligent man, I'll give you that," Doyle said. "Did you wonder for a time whose side I might actually be on?"

"I did, yes."

"Because it would then hold your preconceptions intact. I would remain the bad guy."

"Yes."

"But you didn't really believe it, did you, Agent Travis? Not in your heart?"

"No, I didn't."

"I am glad to hear that. There's hope for you yet."

"You think so? You really think there's hope for me? The whole edifice is coming apart in front of my eyes."

"Perhaps so, but in its place will be something far stronger, I assure you."

"You know that Hoover is a Freemason."

"Of course. He was recently given the grand title of Thirty-Third Degree Inspector General Honorary."

"And you?"

Doyle shook his head. "It is not relevant nor important. Let us just say that everyone has their place, and no matter how high we find ourselves, there is always someone a little higher."

"What are you saying? That—"

"I am saying, Agent Travis, that you have determined the name and nationality of your dead Hungarian, and now it's time to find out who he really was and what he was doing here. I know you know that, and I know that's what you are doing anyway, but sometimes we all need to be reoriented."

"His name was Andris Varga," Travis said. "He was from somewhere called Kecskemét, yes."

"And they knew he was Fekete Kutya?"

"According to the file, yes."

"And was there anything else about him in this file?"

"That he was arrested for murder in June of 1954 in New York."

Doyle was quiet for a little while. He drank his coffee, finished his cigarette, and then he wrapped the uppermost blanket around himself and moved to the end of the bed. He put his feet over the end of the mattress and sat beside Valeria.

"I wonder what he was doing," he said, almost to himself.

"What he was doing?" Travis asked.

"Your Hungarian friend," Doyle said. "I was just wondering what function he performed. They have him in a jail cell in New York. He is a Hungarian immigrant, probably got into the USA illegally, and now he is over a barrel, as they say. I am sure the conversation was very straightforward. It was a choice of doing whatever was asked of him, or he was back on a plane to Hungary that same afternoon. Maybe he had to get out of Hungary for whatever he'd been doing there. If he was Fekete Kutya, then we can be sure he wasn't selling flowers in Batthyány Square, right?"

"I don't know who he was," Travis said. "I don't know what he did in Hungary, and I have no idea why he was here."

"And neither do I," Doyle said, "but we can be sure it wasn't a diplomatic mission to foster better international relationships with the USA."

"So what now?" Travis asked.

"You're asking me? You think I have the answers?"

"Well, I sure as hell don't have any!" Travis said.

"Seems to me you have to just make the decision, Agent Travis," Valeria said.

"The decision? What decision?"

"Whose side you're on," Doyle interjected.

"Like in your Western movies," Valeria said. "It's always so easy to see who are the good guys and who are the bad guys, but it must be very confusing when you start to think that the good guys might—"

"Maybe you're right," Travis interjected. "I don't know. We don't know what happened. We don't know why I was sent here. Not for sure. And if this was nothing more than a test to determine whether I was capable of running an investigation alone, then there will be a very satisfactory explanation as to why Varga was killed, and..." Travis paused, almost as if he was having difficulty believing the words that were coming from his own lips. "For Christ's sake, I still don't know for sure if you people weren't involved in what happened to him."

"Yes, that's true," Doyle said.

"So where does that leave me?" Travis asked.

Doyle raised his cup as if making a toast. "In a caravan in Seneca Falls with a naked Irishman and a beautiful woman, engaged in a conversation that really shouldn't be happening so goddamned early in the morning."

"You think this is funny?" Travis asked.

"Surreal, most definitely."

"My life is upside down, Mr. Doyle. Seriously, completely, and utterly upside down. Left is right; right is left. Gravity doesn't work anymore, you know? You're asking me to throw away my entire life."

"I am not asking you to throw away anything, Agent Travis," Doyle said. "I did not send you to Seneca Falls, and nor did I invite you. We did not do this to you, my friend. The people you work for did this to you—"

"Even though I do not know what has been done to me," Travis said.

"I think you know all too well what has been done to you, and like Valeria says, it is simply a matter of making a decision."

"I have no proof, Mr. Doyle. I have no proof that what I am thinking is even true."

"So go find it, Agent Travis. Go find whatever proof you need, and then we can talk about it once again. That's if you want to keep your eyes open, of course. You can always go for the safe option. That's what most people would do. You may very well be a good person, Michael Travis, and I'm inclined to believe you are. However, the people you work for are not. Ironically, they choose to list their public enemies, even rank them by number, yet they are the worst public enemies of all. They don't rob banks; they rob countries. They don't kill men; they kill nations. There's no way for me to advise you, but I will offer you my help. If you seek further evidence that these people do not have your best interests at heart, then I will do what I can to assist you."

"Why, Mr. Doyle? Why would you want to help me?"

"Why, Agent Travis? I would have thought that was obvious."

"Perhaps not so obvious to me."

"Because you believe that this entire case is about one dead man. I, however, see that as merely a catalyst. I don't know why he's dead. However, someone does know, and I also know that you would not be here without him. I told you this before. You are the reason he died, Michael Travis. Your people needed you inside this carnival. They needed your eyes and ears within this little community. They had questions that they could not answer. They have tried before, and they have failed."

"They have tried before? What do you mean?"

"Beatrice, Nebraska," Doyle said. "Red Oak, Iowa. Bethany, Missouri. Dewey, Oklahoma. I could go on. At first it was simply visits, and though they were supposed to be incognito, it was very obvious. Pairs of men in dark suits driving Ford Fairlanes don't usually attend small-town carnivals. They were just there watching what was happening, taking notes, filing their reports, ticking boxes and coloring inside those very precious lines. And then they became more subtle, or at least believed they were becoming more subtle. They came alone, they returned on alternate days, often dressed differently. Sometimes there was one, other times two. In Dewey, Missouri, there were four of them, and though they arrived in different cars, and though they never actually appeared to speak to one another, it was very obvious who they were and why they were there."

"So how is my being here any different?"

"Because looking from the outside is no good, is it? They wanted someone up close and personal, someone who could ask as many questions as he wished, who could show his ID and walk anywhere he wanted to. Your Mr. Varga was merely a means by which you could have the authority to do these things. You have the law on your side now, and thus you can make us stay, you can make us talk, you can make us do whatever you wish. That is the clever part, you see, and the part that no one would ever think of questioning. The Carnival Diablo is now a crime scene. A murder has been committed. Someone within that carnival must have killed this man, and yet the man has no name, and now I am led to believe that even he has disappeared."

"How do you know that?"

"It is no real secret that the body was removed from the town morgue within twenty-four hours of your arrival, Agent Travis. It was, and that's all that matters. There is very little that goes on in a town such as this that cannot be overheard in any one of the bars or taverns or barbershops. Anything that might engage the attention of Jack Farley will soon be known by Sheriff Rourke and then by Lester McCaffrey. Anything Lester finds out will soon finds its way to his brother, Danny, and anything known by Danny is known by his beautiful sister, Laura. She works in a diner. Need I say more?"

"And if this is true, then why? What do they want of you?"

"Why would they want to determine, once and for all, whether Edgar Doyle could really invade the thoughts of men? If this motley band of freaks and sideshow monstrosities could really read the emotions that people were feeling, could really enable people to remember things they believed they had long ago forgotten?" Doyle shook his head. "I wouldn't even know where to begin with that one, I'm sure. Would you have any idea why the FBI's Unit X would want such people in its employ?"

Travis opened his mouth to speak.

"And yes, before you ask," Doyle interjected, "I know who you work for and which department sent you here. I know a great deal more than you think, my friend."

"It is alarming to consider the implications if what you say is true," Travis said.

"Alarming, or unburdening, depending upon which viewpoint you take. Nothing is better than being free of the lies and untruths that this world seems to trade in so effortlessly and relentlessly. I do not believe what I read in the newspapers. I do not believe the gossip and slander and libel leveled by one man against another. I judge a man from personal experience. In fact, some of the very worst people that the society has

339

pilloried and defamed have proven to be the most worthy, the most courageous and of the highest integrity. My experiences in the war, if nothing else, have taught me that much."

"I don't know what to believe," Travis said.

"The head fights the heart, always," Valeria said. "That seems to be the way of things. Perhaps that is the real lesson of human experience, wouldn't you say?"

"So go," Doyle said. "Go find out who Andris Varga was; see if he didn't do things for your government that no one but a select few were supposed to know. Maybe you will find that there are a great deal more like Andris Varga. Maybe you will discover a perfectly legitimate and rational explanation for everything that has happened here, and you will be able to close your investigation and continue your career. I wish you luck, whatever happens, and I must say that it has been an education to spend time with you, Michael Travis. That much, at least, I know to be true."

Travis could think of nothing further to say. He was exhausted with his own voice, the endless questions, the thoughts that revolved endlessly through his mind, none of them with any kind of satisfactory direction or answer.

He set down the coffee cup beside the small sink, and then he walked to the door of the caravan. He looked back once more at Edgar Doyle and Valeria Mironescu, and though he had known them merely a handful of days, they nevertheless seemed to be the realest and most familiar people in the world.

"Godspeed, Michael Travis," Valeria said.

Travis nodded in acknowledgment, and then he opened the door and went down those narrow steps to the grass.

As he walked to his car, he felt as if he were leaving his entire history behind in his footprints—his father, his mother, the day that he was sent to fetch Sheriff John Baxter and Deputy Harold Fenton; Warden Seymour Cordell, the custodian Max Hibbert, Anthony Scarapetto and all those he had known in juvy; Esther, the little house in Grand Island; those he had known in the army; he saw the face of Don Gerritty as he sat beside him in the diner in Kearney, Nebraska; Bishop and Erickson and Carvahlo, the Bureau psychologist who had tried so hard to take his life to pieces and analyze it. He saw everything as a series of jigsaw pieces laid out, and yet he could not even begin to grasp the image that was before him.

There was one thing he could not yet face, and yet it seemed now to scare him most of all. That he *was* indeed his father's son, that whatever violence had driven his life was there at the edges, ready to overwhelm him at any moment. It was merely a matter of time. He knew that. He was losing his mind by inches, and there was no one there to help him. What if he lost himself altogether and became the man he was always so afraid to become? What if rationality and sanity departed him, just as it had departed his mother, and he fell prey to the raw strain of violence that was even now coursing through his veins? He could feel it multiplying in strength, taking him over, invading every pore of his being and pushing him closer to the dividing line between who he believed he was and who he wished he would never become.

He had never felt so afraid in his life.

He had never felt any emotion with such intensity.

The sound of a crow greeted him as he reached his car.

To his ears, it sounded like bitter and mocking laughter.

40

Travis did not sleep.

Even as dawn broke and the sun crept through the spaces, he knew that what he wanted now was to have failed.

He wanted all of this to have been some kind of test, some kind of complex challenge presented by Bishop and Gale and Tolson and Hoover, some kind of exam to measure his investigatory skills, his nerve, his self-assurance.

That would mean that he had not been wrong, that the Bureau was the Bureau, that the people he worked for were also working for the greater good, the protection of life, liberty, and the pursuit of happiness.

The alternative was the thing he could not face, and yet found himself facing it with greater clarity and certainty as each moment passed. There was now too much for him to explain away. There were too many things that did not make sense. He hated that he could not find the answers. He hated that everything he believed was solid and immovable was now faltering beneath him. There was a line, just as Valeria Mironescu had said. There was a clear and unmistakable line. You stepped over it, or you did not. Step over it, and everything became so simple. You saw what you were expected to see, and you interpreted it the way you were instructed to interpret it. The Bureau would always be right. The Bureau would never be questioned. If you believed something was wrong, it was simply that you had yet to appreciate the bigger picture. There would always be questions without answers, and yet you would learn to live with those questions. You would not question those questions. Your superiors would tell you that a full explanation of the facts was *above your clearance level*, and you would accept such a notion without anything resembling a challenge. You became a company man, a good man, one of the boys. You became just the kind of man to make supervisor, section chief, assistant director.

And if not that, then what?

If Andris Varga had died at the hands of the Bureau, if he had served some purpose and then been *retired from the game*, then what would become of him—Michael Travis—if he chose to no longer play that game?

Did the mind—stretched by such ideas—possess a breaking point? Would he eventually just unravel at the seams? People had mental breakdowns and psychotic episodes. People *lost* their minds, didn't they? Was this why he had been analyzed by the Bureau psychologist before he'd been assigned to Seneca Falls? Not to determine his mental health, not to determine the degree to which he could withstand the rigors of Bureau investigatory work, but simply to determine whether he could actually cope with the truth, if the truth ever came to light?

Travis got out of bed. He went down the hall to the bathroom and took a shower. After he dressed, he stood for a while looking at himself in the mirror beside the door of the room. He did not recognize himself, just as he had not recognized his mother when she walked into the courtroom to hear her sentence.

It was close to eight when he finally went downstairs. The hotel dining room was empty, but he found Laura McCaffrey in the kitchen.

"Well, Agent Travis," she said as he came through the door. "You look like you've had better days."

Travis smiled as best he could. "Late night, early morning, have a long drive ahead of me."

"Where you off to, then?" she asked. "Somewhere exciting?"

"I think I have had enough excitement already, Laura."

"Oh, don't say that. I can imagine you must have one of the most exciting jobs in the world. I've seen that Jimmy Cagney movie, you know?"

"I don't want to disappoint you, Laura, but the reality of what we do and the movies are not that close."

"Oh, you have to allow us our little illusions, Agent Travis. Otherwise, where's the fun?" Laura leaned toward him, and in a mock conspiratorial tone, she whispered, "Makes me feel so much safer knowing you're out there fighting crime and locking up the bad guys."

And then she touched his sleeve, just as she had on the night of the carnival, and the carnival seemed so distant, and what he had seen there seemed so unreal, and there was no doubt in Travis's mind that Laura McCaffrey wanted their relationship to be something significantly more than investigator and potential eyewitness. He had seen it before, but he had not *seen* it.

She winked then, unmistakably, and Travis felt awkward, off guard, then grateful when she punctuated the silence between them with, "So what can I get you? You want some breakfast before you leave?"

"I need to get on the road," Travis said. "I wondered if I could take a sandwich or something."

"A couple of sandwiches, a piece of pie, a flask of coffee, no problem," she said.

"I don't want you to go to any trouble..."

Laura McCaffrey smiled so beautifully and said, "Like I said before, you need to let people do what they do."

"Thank you, Laura."

She hesitated, and then she said, "Were you an orphan by any chance?"

Travis was taken aback. "Why do you ask that, Laura?"

"I don't mean to offend," she said. "Please ignore me. In and out of everyone's affairs, especially when it's none of my business."

"No, really, I'm curious why you asked that question," Travis said.

"Well, there's a way about you, and I've noticed it with people who lost their parents early on. It's nothing too serious. It's just that people like you—" She caught herself then and smiled awkwardly. "I'm sorry. That sounds so rude. I didn't mean that the way it sounded."

"It's okay, Laura... really."

"Well, the thing I've noticed is orphans can't accept help very easily, you know? They have to be in control of everything all the time. They find it really difficult to let people show them how to do things. And they're always so concerned that people shouldn't go to any trouble for them."

"I thought I was just being polite and considerate," Travis said, half joking, knowing in that moment that there was little else he wished to do but stay right there with Laura McCaffrey and forget everything else that was happening. Laura seemed to be the only person in Seneca Falls that made him feel like a real person. To everyone else, he felt like a ghost.

"Well, sure," Laura replied, "but there are certain people who feel that the best thing they can do in life is help others, and if you don't let them do that, then you're responsible for making them unhappy."

"So, what are you saying? That if I don't let you make me some sandwiches, you're going to be unhappy?"

"Right," she said. "Well, maybe I'm saying that if you don't let me make you happy, then I will be..." She blushed. "I'm sorry," she said. "That was ever so forward."

Travis hesitated. Eye contact could not be avoided. He looked at her, she at him, and then he reached out and gently took her hand.

The tiny inhalation she took was audible, as if she was both surprised and relieved.

There should have been words then, but the silence continued for just a few seconds more.

"It's going to be okay," Travis finally said, and his voice cracked.

"It is?" Laura asked.

Travis nodded.

She sighed, and for just a second, she closed her eyes.

Travis released her hand. "So could you make me some sandwiches for the road?" he said. "Please."

"A pleasure," Laura McCaffrey said, seemingly relieved that Travis had so swiftly altered the course of their exchange. She asked him what he liked—ham, cheese, corned beef, and did he want rye or white, and did he like pickles or tomatoes, and did he want his coffee with sugar, with milk, just black?—and Travis told her, and for a moment it seemed that he was in fact a regular person conducting a regular conversation. But he was not, and he knew it, and he knew that Laura McCaffrey would never be able to understand what was happening to him.

When Laura was done, she handed him a sizable paper bag and a flask.

"I want to ask you something," Travis said as he took them from her.

"Shoot," she said.

"It's going to sound odd, but there's a reason for asking."

"Oh, Agent Travis, I work in a small-town diner. You should hear some of the conversations that go on in a place like this."

Travis sat down, indicated she should sit too. "What do you think of the government?"

She laughed. "Okay, well, I sure wasn't expecting that."

"I just want your honest opinion," Travis said.

"Well, here goes. It's something my uncle used to say. It was basically the joke that a democratic election was always the choice between the lesser of two weevils. You get it, right?"

"I get it," Travis said. "Is it a sentiment you agree with?"

"Sure I do," Laura replied. "Doesn't everyone? I mean everyone with even a shred of common sense. I mean, seriously, are we expected to believe that these fellers go into politics because they really care about what happens to the ordinary folks in the street? Surely not. They don't actually think that we believe that, do they?"

"I don't know, Laura."

"Well, I wouldn't want to be saying anything about the government. I wouldn't want to get myself in trouble."

"Really? You think that I'm going to write down what you say and tell someone?"

For just a moment Laura seemed a little distant and serious. "I don't know why you're here," she said. "Not really. I mean, I know why you say you're here. That dead man and everything. But that can't be the real reason, can it? I mean, if it was just about that dead man, then why wouldn't Sheriff Rourke deal with it himself? That's his job, isn't it?"

"Except when it gets a little more complicated than that," Travis

345

replied. "The Bureau deals with crimes that cross state lines, you see, and the carnival—"

"The carnival makes people happy, doesn't it?" Laura said. "I mean, that's the crime they have committed, wouldn't you say? Or have I got this completely wrong?"

Travis frowned. She sounded annoyed, and her tone implied some kind of personal vexation.

"I don't understand," he said. "Have I done something to upset you, Laura?"

She looked shocked then, as if surprised by her own words. "I'm sorry," she said. "Listen to me, talking nonsense again. I'm really very sorry. I didn't mean to speak out of turn."

"It's okay," Travis said. "I'm just a little confused as to why you'd think that I had something to do with what has happened here."

"I know. I didn't mean it to sound that way. It's just that everyone's been talking, obviously. It's a small town, you know? Small towns are like that. Everyone's living out of everyone else's pockets, and if one person has something to say, it isn't an hour before everyone else hears about it."

"And what have people been saying?" Travis asked.

"Well, I don't know that it's any of my business—"

"Really, Laura. It would mean a great deal to me if you'd just tell me what folks are saying."

"People are always going to talk, Michael. You know that. More often than not, it's just a handful of wild rumors all blown up to look like something it's not."

"Tell me the wild rumors. I give you my word they won't go any further."

"Really, you don't want to hear what I've heard."

"I do," Travis said. "I really do."

"Okay, well, here goes. When they arrived—you know, the carnival people—everyone was up in arms. Who are these people and what are they doing here, and what right do they have to come into our town and pitch their tents and whatever? People don't like strangers. Anyway, people started calling up Sheriff Rourke and telling him what he had to do and how he had to do it, but Lester told me the law can't do anything until someone actually breaks the law or whatever, and so Sheriff Rourke just had to let them be. Anyway, the tents went up, and people got excited about the carnival and whatnot. So the carnival opens, and everyone's having a good time and word gets out. Saturday night comes and there's ten times the number of people there. And people see they're just circus folk, that they're not crazy or dangerous or anything, and they're trying to make a living just like everyone else. The fact that they're a bit wild and different doesn't make them bad, does it?"

Travis didn't speak. He didn't want to interrupt her.

"And then there was a dead man there, and everyone was wondering who the hell he was and what had happened. Then word got out that he was a gangster or something. I mean, if he wasn't a gangster, then why would the FBI be involved? Maybe he'd come to kill someone, you know? But who would he want to kill in Seneca Falls? Perhaps it was someone in the carnival that he was supposed to kill. Like that Mr. Doyle, or maybe the big guy, the giant, you know? And if that was the case, then who were these people? I mean, who were they really? Was this some kind of cover operation for crooks on the run from the authorities and other gangsters? Everyone was trying to find out more from Jack Farley and Chas Rourke. Jack's wife said the dead guy had already killed a bunch of people. Said he was from somewhere in Eastern Europe. That's all that she'd managed to get out of her husband."

Laura paused for a moment, and then she sighed.

"It all changed after that," she went on. "When you let them open the carnival again, you see? After that, folks figured it couldn't be anything to do with the carnival itself. I mean, how could it? If they had really done something bad, the FBI would never have let them open again. And so everyone started wondering whether it was all a setup, you know?"

"A setup?" Travis asked, amazed at how out of control and random the rumors had been about the death of Andris Varga.

"Yes, a setup," Laura said. "I mean, he was a killer after all, wasn't he? And if he hadn't been murdered by anyone at the carnival, then maybe he had been murdered by the authorities, and they needed to clean things up and make sure there were no loose ends. That's why you were here. You had some kind of special instruction to make sure there were no witnesses and informants. People even got scared, you know? We started to wonder whether or not someone would suddenly have a heart attack, or maybe there would be another unexplained murder."

Travis had never heard such a thing in all his life. He was stunned by the revelation. He could not believe that this was the townsfolk's explanation for his presence in Seneca Falls. He started to smile, to laugh even.

He soon stopped laughing when he realized that Laura wasn't sharing the joke.

"And you believe this?" he asked her. "You think that the dead man was killed by the authorities, and that they sent me here to clean it all up and make it disappear?"

"Wouldn't be the first time, would it?" Laura asked. "It's true, isn't it? I mean, the whole thing with the authorities. I mean, they can do whatever they like with anyone, can't they? My sister's neighbor said that the government can just make someone vanish, and not only do they vanish, but every record of them just disappears as well. It's like they never even existed."

"That's just crazy talk, Laura," Travis said, at once amazed that a woman such as this would possess such notions, but even as he heard his own response, he felt that his words possessed an element of hollowness and self-doubt. "I'm sorry to disappoint you, but I am not in Seneca Falls to cover up a government murder."

"Well, I just hope that's the truth, because now I've put myself right in the firing line."

"You honestly believe that I'm the kind of person who would be capable of that?"

"Well, to be truthful, I don't really know who you are, 'cept that you grew up with no parents and you don't much care for people helping you. You could be anyone, couldn't you? Your name might not even be what you say it is. We don't know a thing about you, and yet you can come in here and ask all the questions you like and we're obliged to answer them. If you want to hear something uncomfortable, then you'd do worse than to listen to my uncle. He says the only difference between a Communist dictatorship and the United States is the longitude and latitude. Now, I don't happen to agree with him, and I know his views can be a little forceful and intolerant, but I read some of the stuff in the papers about Senator McCarthy and all those people in Hollywood that he terrorized, and I start to wonder about whether what my uncle says is true. I mean, really, that's not so different, is it? Putting people in prison for their political beliefs and goodness knows what else. Telling them that they have to give up the names of their friends and whoever else, otherwise they'll lock them up and throw away the key. Seems to me that Senator Joe McCarthy and your Mr. Hoover might be two eggs out of the same box, though I know it's really dreadful to say something like that, seeing as how you're a federal agent and everything."

Laura looked down at her hands. She had been twisting a cloth between her fingers the whole time. "And now I've run my mouth off and said a great deal more than I intended to say, but you asked me, and if you've got to arrest me, then so be it. Danny always said I was never afraid to share my opinion, even when it was clear that no one else wanted to hear it."

"Arrest you?" Travis asked. "And what would I arrest you for?"

"Oh, I don't know," she said. "Some of those un-American activities, probably."

Travis didn't know what to think. Laura McCaffrey certainly had a viewpoint, and yes, she had shared it with him, but had he been asked to predict what she would say, it would have been very far from what he'd just heard. For one so young, she seemed to carry a great weight of cynicism.

Her manner changed then; she softened noticeably and said, "You seem like a good man, Michael Travis. I felt that from the first time I met you. Intense, serious, very dedicated to what you were doing, but a good man. Danny says I can see things in people that other folks don't see. That's part of the reason I was so interested in what was happening at the carnival. All that stuff, reading people's minds, telling the future, all the gypsy things you hear about. That kind of thing fascinates me. Always has, probably always will. Anyway, I met you and you seemed too focused and committed, but there was something so lost about you, and I just felt..."

Laura looked up at Travis. Were there tears in her eyes?

"What, Laura? You felt what?"

"I don't know, Michael. You just seemed like the loneliest person in the whole world."

Travis reached out and touched her hand. "Well, if I wasn't then, I think I probably am now," he said.

"Well, whatever they say about you, I still think you're a decent man," Laura said. "Maybe Danny is wrong. Maybe I can no more read people than I can read Japanese, but there's something good about you. I feel that. I also think that you're going to do the right thing."

"And you wouldn't happen to know what that was, would you?" Travis asked.

"Oh, I think we always know what the right thing is, wouldn't you say? I think we're just wired that way. I think being a decent person comes naturally to most of us. The bad guys are the ones who have it rough. I think they have to work extra hard to overcome basic human nature, you know?"

"I appreciate your optimism, though my experience tells me that it might be unfounded."

"Hey, maybe you've just been spending too much time around the wrong kind of people," she replied. "And I hope you're not mad at me. Maybe I said some things I shouldn't have said."

"Maybe you did," Travis replied, "but that doesn't mean I didn't need to hear them." He reached out his hand then, closed it over hers, and she looked at him with an expression he had never seen before. As if she had been waiting for him to reach out to her forever. "And no, I am not mad at you," he added. "Could never be mad at you, Laura."

She closed her eyes for a second and breathed deeply. "And you're not going to arrest me or my uncle for being Communists?"

"Oh, sure I am," Travis said. "Didn't I mention that? Both of you, probably your brothers as well, because I'm sure we can nail them for something, even if we have to fabricate some evidence."

"We'll have to go on the run, then," Laura said.

"Hey, you could run away with Doyle and the others."

"Great idea. Run away with the circus. Always wanted to do that."

Travis reached for the bag and the flask.

"Thanks for the sandwiches," he said.

"You're very welcome, Michael Travis," she replied, and then walked with him to the foyer of the hotel.

"Take care," she said.

"I'll do my best."

Travis crossed the street to his car. Before he got in, he glanced back. She was still there, watching him from the window, and when she caught his eye, she raised her hand as if to wave farewell.

He smiled. He did not know whether or not she would see that smile, but he believed she would know it was there.

There was something about the woman that broke his heart. That was the truth. It was perhaps not her, but all she represented. The things he did not have and perhaps would never have.

For the first time, he believed he had made a mistake. Not just an error, not just a wrong step, but a real honest-to-God mistake.

He had trusted everyone above himself. He had believed what he'd been told, and now he was starting to see it for what it was. The curtain had been drawn, and behind the scenes there was something disturbing and malignant. The world as he saw it was not the world as it was. He had been fooled. He knew that now. He had failed to confront that fact for as long as he could manage.

Andris Varga had not been killed by anyone but his own people. Either that, or they were intimately complicit.

Of this he now felt sure.

Michael Travis started the car, and pulled away from the curb. He felt an indescribable weight on his shoulders, and yet for the first time realized he had been carrying that weight for as long as he could recall. It was everything his father had tried to frighten out of him, everything from which his mother had tried to free him.

There was the line. Right before him. Right there in his line of sight. He would step over it, or he would not.

The decision had been made.

Travis glanced in the rearview mirror as Seneca Falls receded into the distance. A small town in the middle of Kansas. Nothing more than that. Probably of insufficient size to even figure on anything beyond a county map. Nevertheless, everything had happened here, and it was here that everything would end.

Travis looked back at the endless road before him, running away toward the horizon like a dark ribbon.

If he knew one thing and one thing only, it was that the life he'd known was now over.

When he reached the highway, he pulled over. He got out of the car and paced up and down. He breathed deeply—in, out, in, out—until he started to feel dizzy. He had to learn the truth about Andris Varga. What had happened between his arrest in June of 1954 and his death in August of 1958? Discover that, and such information would go a long way toward assisting him in making the decision he had to make.

The road that stretched to Travis's left and right was symbolic. It was one way or the other. He could not rest where he was. He could not just let it all slide, forget about it, give up this case and head back to Kansas. Maybe there were people who could do such a thing. Maybe that was the kind of person that the Bureau wanted—the unthinking, unquestioning, the trusting and doubtless—but Travis could not be that person.

And if Andris Varga had been murdered by the FBI and placed here as a means by which Travis could infiltrate this group of people, then what else did that mean? It meant that everything else that Doyle had said could be true. The newspapers, the government, the drug companies, the arms manufacturers, the banks, the police, the entirety of the legal and judicial machine was riddled with corruption and lies, professing to defend the rights and civil liberties of the common man and yet serving only itself. Keep people afraid, you keep them in check. Foster suspicion, distrust, paranoia, and you controlled them. It was that simple.

Travis walked back to the car. He got in and started the engine. If he could not go to Wichita or Kansas, then he would drive south to Oklahoma City. He knew no one there, and—notwithstanding the possibility that every Bureau field office in the country had been alerted to his identity and the fact that he was to be afforded no assistance—there was no reason he could not access information from there and make some progress on learning what he could of Andris Varga.

It would be another three-hour drive, a straight run down 35 through Wichita and across the state line. Whether the office would be open, he did not know. It was Sunday, granted, but the federal government ran its own calendar. The Oklahoma office would be manned if there was some reason for it to be manned.

Regardless, he had already broken into one office, and he could do it again.

It was now no longer an investigation concerning an unknown Hungarian and a carnival of oddities; it was an investigation into the very organization for whom he worked.

The line was there, and he was going to cross it.

41

The fact that neither of the agents in the Oklahoma City office had heard of Travis raised doubts in his mind. Had they heard of him, it would have confirmed two things: that the Kansas City office had forewarned them that Travis might appear and that Travis was onto something that the Bureau wished to keep under wraps. But then again, even as he was introducing himself to the Oklahoma agents, Travis saw the flaw in his own thinking. Their ignorance could simply mean that maximum care was being taken to preserve the confidentiality of the Seneca Falls investigation. Surely only those who were directly involved in such a cover-up would be apprised of all the facts? Regardless, Travis knew that nothing would move forward until he established the precise whereabouts and movements of Andris Varga prior to his death, and the only way that such a thing seemed feasible was with Bureau resources.

The agents seemed eager to assist Travis in whichever way they could. Ostensibly, he was just another agent in the field; it would have been strange for them to do anything other than offer their unconditional assistance. The junior man, half a dozen years younger than Travis, was called Alan Lacey. The senior agent, of the same rank as Travis but three or four years older, was called Donald Kline. Kline took the lead, asked questions, ventured suggestions. He looked closely at the picture that Travis showed him, the print card, the small diagram of the tattoo.

"You say he is Hungarian?" Kline asked.

"Yes, name of Andris Varga."

"I worked in New York before I was posted here," Kline said. "Had a partner who dealt directly with those coming in from Hungary, among other places. This was a couple of years ago, primarily political asylum applications. I am sure there were Hungarians. Or maybe Czechoslovakians..." Kline paused in thought. "No, I'm sure it was Hungary. It was at the time of the civil unrest in '56."

"Do you remember any details?"

"No specifics," Kline said. "The Bureau was interested in the potential espionage aspect, most of Eastern Europe being Communist, but it ran far above my partner's clearance level and he didn't move on it. That kind of thing goes out of federal jurisdiction into national security, and then the CIA pick it up."

"You ever hear of people with tattoos like this?" Travis asked.

"No, never heard of that before."

"Do you remember any names?"

"I don't think he ever mentioned names. And even if he had, it would have been nothing more than an offhand comment, you know? And more than two years ago."

"Do you remember the name of the operation?"

"Yes, that I do remember. It was called Chrysanthemum."

"Operation Chrysanthemum. And it was a political asylum operation?"

"I really don't know any specifics, Agent Travis. I'm sorry."

"Do you know if the case was directed from the New York office?"

"Yes, I'm sure it was. That's where I was posted at the time. I've only been down here six months. I was four years in D.C., six years in New York, and now I'm here for as long as needed."

"Do you still know anyone in the New York office?"

"Sure, I know all of them... all of them who are still there, for sure."

Travis looked at Kline, then at Lacey, and then back at Kline.

"I'm sorry, Agent Lacey..."

Lacey smiled and shrugged. "I'm heading out to lunch anyway. You want I should bring you something back?"

Travis declined, but Kline asked for a sandwich, ham on rye, and a bottle of root beer.

Once Lacey had gone, Travis asked Kline to sit with him in Kline's office. He closed the door behind him, and when he sat down, Kline already had an anxious expression on his face.

"What's the deal here, Travis?"

"I don't know that I can actually give you a clear answer on that, Kline, but I am going to ask for your help anyway."

"Is there something going on here that I should be worried about?"

"Probably, yes," Travis replied, "but, again, I don't know that I can be specific about why you should be worried."

"Are you doing something under the radar?"

"No, not at all. This is a legitimate and authorized investigation, but there's an aspect of it that concerns me, and that degree of concern has encouraged me to seek assistance outside the state of Kansas. Let's just leave it at that for now."

Kline squinted suspiciously. "That doesn't sound so good to me, Travis. Something isn't right here. Not right at all."

"Well, do you want to know enough so that you become implicated, or do you want to help a fellow agent just out of the goodness of your heart?"

"Implicated in what?"

"A potential internal situation that could prove difficult to explain away."

"Inside the Bureau?"

"Inside, perhaps outside as well. I am not sure."

"I shouldn't have said anything," Kline said.

"About what?"

"About those cases back in '56, the Hungarians and whatever." He smiled sardonically. "Of all the field offices in all the world, you had to walk into mine."

"New York would have been the first office I would have contacted anyway," Travis said, thinking of the arrest sheet he had found in the Kansas City office fire safe. "I already have information that leads me in that direction. You haven't told me anything that I wouldn't have discovered with one phone call."

"So, if you're willing to call New York and ask them questions, why do you need me?"

"Because I want to avoid having my name come up, if at all possible."

"Okay," Kline said, the hesitation evident in his voice. "Now I'm really not liking the sound of this. This is a transparent network, my friend. The Bureau is the Bureau. Just because I'm out in Oklahoma doesn't give me any greater distance from this. If I'm going to be putting my hand in a hornet's nest, I want to know why, and I want to know what the implications are."

Travis leaned back and took a moment to breathe. He could not, and he did not wish to tell Kline anything, not only for the sake of self-preservation, but also because Kline hadn't done anything to warrant the backlash he might experience if this went the wrong way.

"Sometimes you do something on trust," Travis said. "It is a small thing, a seemingly inconsequential thing to you, but for someone else it's of great significance."

"I can do without this, Travis," Kline interjected. "You want my help, then tell me the truth. If you are not prepared to trust me with the truth, then how can you expect me to assist you in any capacity? I am not naive, Agent Travis. I am not some greenhorn, three weeks out of Quantico looking to impress someone. You either come clean on this, or you go ask someone else to help you out."

Travis weighed up the options that faced him. If he requested the information he wanted from New York, they would be onto him immediately, especially if the information he requested was linked to Varga. If he had Kline do it, then the alert would take a little longer, but it would still happen. Of that he was sure. If the information he requested was not connected to Varga, or—more to the point—if this was not in fact the conspiracy that Edgar Doyle had led him to believe it was, then he would still be left with a dead body, a name he was not supposed to know, and an unresolved homicide investigation.

"Okay," Travis said. "I will tell you as much as I can."

"And you will answer my questions when you are done, if I have any," Kline said.

"If I can answer them, I will," Travis replied.

"Understood. So what the hell is going on here?"

Travis briefed him as succinctly as he could, leaving out as much as he could without making it obvious.

"So this dead guy, this Andris Varga... you are telling me that he was killed by one of our people?"

"There is that possibility, yes. One of our people, or someone within the intelligence community."

"No evidence to suggest that's what happened?"

"No, no evidence."

"Just a suspicion that there's more going on here than you're being told?"

"Exactly."

Kline smiled ruefully. "Well, that wouldn't be a first, now, would it?"

Travis didn't respond. He had displayed as much of his hand as he was prepared to at this stage, and he did not know how Kline would respond. His mouth was dry, his hands moist with sweat, and he could feel his heartbeat in his temples.

"So, if I call New York, what do you want?" Kline asked.

"I want you to call someone you know, someone who might be prepared to send us some information and delay filing the data request for a little while. I just need a head start, Agent Kline, if only for a few hours."

"Okay, like I asked, what do you want?"

"I want you to give them the dead man's name and get any information that is flagged as related, whether that is other names, ongoing investigations or inquiries, even closed cases... anything that can be found."

Kline sat for a while in silence.

"And what will happen then?"

"I don't know, Agent Kline. I won't actually know until I get some information back. Right now I have a handful of suppositions and nothing even remotely reliable."

"And if this is something that I hope it's not?"

"Then you can make a decision as to whether you want to know or not. Perhaps it would be better if you didn't know."

"I don't believe there is ever a situation where it is better not to know, Agent Travis."

"Then you and I are of the same mind," Travis replied.

Kline shifted his chair closer to the desk and reached for the telephone. "It is Sunday," he said. "There'll be somebody there, but there's no way to guarantee they will help us. We may just get a brush-off until tomorrow."

"Try," Travis said. "That's all I can ask of you."

Kline dialed the number.

Travis rose from his chair and walked to the window of Kline's office. He was caught between the need to know and the hope that he was wrong, beneath even that the knowledge that here was the pattern of his life. He had made every choice—leaving Esther, joining the army, the Bureau, never committing to anything that required an individual determination—simply because he was afraid of making a mistake. And had that not been the greatest mistake of all?

Travis turned back as Kline started talking to someone.

"Yes, Hungarian, far as I know. Hang on a moment..." Kline covered the mouthpiece. "V-A-R-G-A, right?" he asked Travis.

"Yes, that's correct."

Kline went back to the call. He spelled the name, said that he needed anything they had, anything that was flagged as related. He then asked if there was a supervisor or a section chief in the office.

"Okay," Kline said. "If you could get onto that right away, and just teletype everything you've got as soon as you find it, that would be really appreciated."

The call ended. Kline set down the receiver.

"The angels are on your side," he told Travis. "No supervisor, no section chief. Don't know who that was, but he was a new kid, sounded about fifteen. Seemed happy to have something to do. If he even remembers to file a data request, no one is going to see it until tomorrow."

"Unless there's an alert on the file itself, and then it will just be automatically flagged," Travis said. Such a thing was not uncommon. Back when he'd been chasing Tony Scarapetto, every single file relating to Scarapetto, William Murchison, Luke Barrett, Madeline Jarvis, and any other known associates had carried such a flag. If you filed or requested data on any one of them, there was a call within half an hour. Was there new information? Who was chasing what? Had there been a fresh sighting of Scarapetto or Barrett? Perhaps this would be the same. Maybe as soon as New York started transmitting information regarding Varga, there would be a call from Washington.

"You need to settle down," Kline said. "I don't know what the hell is going on in your head, Travis, but you are wound like a clock spring, my friend, and something is going to snap. Seems to me you are imagining the worst without any evidence to suggest that the worst is what you're going to get."

"You're right," Travis said. "I am going around in circles on this thing."

"Well, I don't much care to know what it is you're thinking until we have something substantial to back it up. Assumption, as they say, is the mother of all fuckups."

Travis laughed suddenly, surprising even himself. He had not heard the expression for as long as he could recall, perhaps as far back as the army. Agents did not use such expressions. It was not Bureau policy. You were polite, professional, mannered, conservative, always distant, unattached, objective. The Bureau was not a job; it was a way of life. It was not a career, it was a vocation. And it required everything of you, everything you had and everything you could give.

"Stop it," Kline said, snapping Travis out of his reverie. "Enough, okay? Think about something else for a minute, would you? You're gonna drive yourself crazy."

"How old are you?" Travis asked.

"Thirty-six, thirty-seven in a couple of months. Why d'you ask?"

"You married? Got kids?"

Kline smiled, frowned a little. "No, and no."

"You dating someone?"

"What's with the third degree?"

"Isn't this what people talk about, Kline, or have you forgotten as well?"

"Oh, Lord, are we having a crisis of faith, Travis?" Kline said, and there was a tone of mock concern in his voice.

"A crisis of faith? Maybe," Travis replied.

"Been there, done that, as they say."

"You doubt the Bureau?"

"You really want to have this conversation, Travis? Is that what you want?"

"I think we're already having it," Travis replied.

"You don't think most everyone goes through this at some point? You're not that unique, my friend."

Kline reached for a cigarette and lit it. "You know what I think we do sometimes, Agent Travis?"

"What do you think we do, Agent Kline?"

"I think we are there to make sure that the decent, hardworking citizens of this country never see behind the curtain."

"The curtain?"

"You've seen *The Wizard of Oz*, right?"

"No, I can't say that I have. Heard of it, sure."

"Oh hell, Travis, where have you been?"

"I don't know," Travis said. "I honestly don't know where I've been. That's the question I've been asking myself for the last few days. What have I been doing? Where have I been? Who am I?"

"Oh, Christ almighty, you really have got it bad, haven't you?"

Travis waved the comment aside. "You know, these past few days I have seen things, heard things, experienced things that I didn't even believe were possible."

"Sounds to me like you're having a little more than a crisis of faith, my friend," Kline said.

The teleprinter in the back office started to chug, but Travis didn't even seem to hear it.

"Maybe it is a crisis of faith," Travis went on. "Maybe it's something else entirely." He sighed deeply. "You ever get to the point where you feel it would be best to try not thinking at all?"

"A good few times," Kline replied. "Look, this doesn't have to be as big a deal as you're making it. There are always going to be boundaries and limits to what we can and cannot know. That's the way it works. That's the way any organization works. Sometimes something happens, and you look at it out of context and it seems like the worst thing in the world, and then you get the context and it makes perfect sense. Like a disease, for example. You got a disease, and there's a bunch of guys in white coats trying to figure out a cure for this disease, and they come up with this, that, and the other, and they try it out and it makes some people sicker. They go back to the drawing board, and they figure it out again. They get a bunch of volunteers to test this thing on, and half of them up and die. They do more tests, they try another formula, and finally they get it right. Now they have a real honest-to-God life-saving cure, and it works for everyone. Okay, so they killed ten or fifteen people on the way, but now they have something that saves hundreds, maybe thousands of lives. So are they heroes, or are they murderers? Depends on the context, see?"

"I don't know the context of why Andris Varga was killed," Travis said. "I don't know why his body was put where it was, and I don't know why I was sent down there to find out."

"So, you're trying to make a jigsaw piece fit, and you don't even have a box with the picture on right now. You don't even know what you're looking at, my friend, and that's the worst kind of perspective from which to form a viewpoint."

"You're right," Travis said. "You're absolutely right."

"Of course I'm right," Kline said, smiling. "I'm from New York."

The pair of them got up and headed back to check on the teleprinter.

"Here we are," Kline said, indicating merely one line on the first page. "Chrysanthemum, the name of that operation that was running out of New York."

There was a sequence of operational code names, all of them meaningless—Sahara, Navajo, Hannibal, Paperclip, Chatter, Bluebird, and Artichoke. Beside each name was a confidentiality classification, each of them of a level prohibiting access to anyone beneath the rank of associate deputy director, just two steps beneath Director Hoover himself. There was reference to something called Venona and the Communist Party of the United States of America.

"I don't understand this at all," Kline said. "This is all kind of meaning—"

The phone rang, interrupting his comment. He was gone for no more than a minute, and when he returned, the teleprinter had stopped.

"That was New York," he said. "I don't know if you're going to like this or not. The agent I spoke to, Hendry, says that the first page is simply a list of all the file headings where the name Varga is referenced. There's no guarantee that it's the same Varga as your dead guy, but that's what he's got. The second and third pages are simply a list of all the cases that fall under those headings. That is a lot of files, hundreds he says, and they are all classified at the uppermost level. He can't give us any more than what you have in your hand right now."

"Which is nothing more than a shopping list of things we can't buy, right?"

"Right."

Travis looked over the second and third pages. There were streams of names—Rudolf Abel, Sidney Gottlieb, Donald Ewen Cameron, and then an entire paragraph devoted to Operation Pastorius. Travis knew of Pastorius, and the US Supreme Court *Ex parte Quirin* case that upheld the verdict of a military tribunal from the early 1940s. Pastorius had been a German plan for internal sabotage of strategic US economic targets such as hydroelectric plants, railroad repair shops, Hell Gate Bridge in New York and Penn Station, New Jersey. Eight Germans had been involved, two of them US citizens, all of them having previously lived on the US mainland. The eight had been rapidly trained, were given close to two hundred thousand dollars, and then sent from France to the East Coast of the United States in two U-boats. The anticipated two-year campaign of sabotage didn't even begin, and the case itself was almost legendary in Bureau history, not only for its bizarre nature, but also because of the way in which the leader of the sabotage team, George John Dasch, had volunteered his own surrender to US authorities. After landing at Amagansett, New York, Dasch and three other members of the team—Ernst Burger, Richard Quirin, and Heinrich Heinck—took a train into New York City. Dasch lost his nerve immediately and traveled on to Washington, where he turned himself in to the FBI office. He was believed to be crazy until he put eighty-four thousand dollars on an assistant director's desk. He was then interrogated for several hours, and over the subsequent two weeks, Burger and the other six Germans were picked up. Roosevelt ordered a military trial. All eight were found guilty and sentenced to death, but that sentence was commuted in the case of Dasch and Burger due to the fact that they had cooperated with the tribunal. The other six confederates had been executed in August of 1942.

Beneath this, almost as an aside, was a small reference to both Frank Olson and Harold Blauer. It was that line that prompted a noticeable physical reaction in Travis. He shuddered and looked up from the pages he was studying.

"So?" Kline asked.

Disguising his reaction as best he could, Travis said, "So, as you say, not a great deal to go on. Names of operations that I am not familiar with and lists of files that we can't access."

"Matters of national security, right?"

"Seems that way."

"Some things are not for the common man, my friend. Our minds are weak, and if we knew what was really going on, then our brains would burst with the pressure."

"You think it's funny?" Travis asked.

"I think that sometimes things get so serious that you have to force yourself to laugh about them. Otherwise you lose your sanity."

"I can't laugh about it," Travis said. "I can't even try to laugh about it. The more I see, the more I realize that I see nothing at all. It almost seems calculated, the degree to which I am unable to follow any line of investigation."

"And there is the seed of paranoia," Kline said. "Keep on thinking that, and they'll have you in Bellevue before you know it."

Travis thought of Blauer, the injections he'd been given, the threat of committal to that very same hospital hanging over his head.

"Maybe that'd be the best place for me, the way I feel right now," he said sardonically.

"And there's your sense of humor, Agent Travis. A little dark, very cynical, but still alive. However, that isn't even funny. Don't even joke about winding up in Bellevue."

"You ever hear of Frank Olson or Harold Blauer?" Travis asked.

Kline thought for a moment, then shook his head. "Can't say I have. Why?"

"Just another couple of names I've come across among all of this."

"Our people?"

"No, not ours. It doesn't matter. Unrelated."

Kline got up from the desk. "So where to now?" he asked. "Where do you go from here?"

"I have more questions now than when I arrived," Travis said. "I need to know what these projects are." He indicated the cover sheet on the desk. "I mean, what the hell are Bluebird, Mongoose, and MK Ultra?"

"Ours is not to question why, right?"

"That may be the viewpoint at the top, but I can't just walk away now. I have come too far to just let it go."

"Well," Kline said matter-of-factly, "that's where you and I differ, my friend, because I can let it go, and I am going to do just that."

"Even if there is something going on here that actually contradicts the reason for being in the Bureau in the first place?"

Kline laughed, but the sound was forced and shallow. "*Especially* if there is something going on that contradicts my reason for being in the Bureau."

"I don't understand that, Kline. I really don't understand that at all."

"It's the greater good, Travis. You understand the principle of the greater good. That's precisely and exactly what we are doing. Because you'd go crazy trying to figure out the possible ramifications of what was really behind everything. There are some things that we will never understand. Of that I am sure. There are some things that we are not even capable of comprehending. There are better men than us, Travis. Smarter, more effective, more competent, and they have shouldered a responsibility that would crush us in an instant. You want to make decisions for a city, a nation, the entire population as a whole? Well, you go right ahead. That is not the game I am playing, and that is not a game I believe I ever want to play."

"You're going to turn a blind eye to this? Really?"

"Really."

"And if they come down here asking after me, what then?"

"They won't, I'm sure. If they do, what can I say? You were here. You asked for some help. I made a call to New York, I printed out a couple of pages for you, and off you went."

Travis picked up the sheets of paper, folded them in half, in half again, and tucked them into his jacket pocket. He got up and walked to the door. "All I can ask of you is that you say nothing until you are asked. Can you do that much for me?"

"Sure I can. I don't even know why you wanted that information, and I didn't look at it. You are a senior special agent in the field, working on an authorized and legitimate homicide investigation. For some reason, you wound up here, needed some help. It is within my official remit to extend interoffice courtesies. After all, we are a *federal* network, are we not?"

Travis looked at Kline for a moment. The man's expression said everything that needed to be said. He saw the line, and he chose to step back from it. It was more comfortable that way. It short-circuited the anxiety before it started eating you up from inside.

"When did you stop asking the important questions?" Travis asked.

"And what would they be, Agent Travis?"

"Who am I? What am I doing here? Where am I going? What is my reason for being?"

"How do you know that I ever asked myself those questions? Seems to me that if you know that there'll never be a satisfactory answer, then why bother yourself with the question?"

"Because... because..."

"Because what, Agent Travis?"

Travis knew there was no point. Kline was not going to be an ally. "It doesn't matter," Travis said. "Just forget it."

Kline smiled. "I already have, my friend. I already have."

Travis thanked Kline. He did not shake the man's hand. He left the Oklahoma City office and he walked down the street to his car.

42

By the time Travis arrived back in Seneca Falls, it was close to six. The run back had been slower. He had stopped twice, once at a roadside diner to get coffee, the second time for gas. He was tired, no question, but it was not merely a deep-seated physical fatigue that he was experiencing, but something far beyond that. It was psychological, emotional perhaps. It was as if he had been excommunicated from his body, had the hell beaten out of him, and then he'd just been put back in his body and left at the side of the road. There were no bruises, no broken bones, nothing visible, but he felt as if he had been though a hurricane and somehow survived.

He returned to the McCaffrey Hotel and found Laura there in the foyer. Just seeing her, Travis experienced a collision of seemingly contrary emotions.

"Agent Travis," she said warmly. "I wondered whether you would be back today."

"No Danny?" Travis asked.

"Oh, Danny has a hot date. One of those rare occasions when he actually makes it out of here. There's a girl in El Dorado, and she just might be the one."

Travis smiled, started laughing.

"What's so funny?"

"Sorry, it's just that it sounded like a line from a song. There's a girl in El Dorado and she just might be the one."

"You've had a long day," she said.

"Yes. I'm beat."

"You want some dinner?"

"I don't know that I have the energy to eat dinner."

"I have some steaks in back. I could fry you a steak."

"No, please don't go to any trouble for me," Travis said.

She smiled that endearing smile. "You just don't learn, do you?"

Travis didn't know what to say.

"You're not often lost for words, are you, Agent Travis?"

"Not often, no."

"I don't mean to make you feel awkward, but you are a guest in our hotel, and meals are part of the service, and if the cook were here, or even Danny, then I am sure that neither of them would have a problem with making you some dinner. As far as I can tell, you've existed on little but sandwiches since you arrived. A man has to eat, doesn't he?"

"Did you have dinner, Laura?"

"As a matter of fact, I didn't. I tend to skip dinner a couple of times a week. I am trying to stay slim."

"Well, I don't think you need to worry about staying slim, Laura"

Laura looked at him askance. "Are you flirting with me, Agent Travis?"

Travis said nothing. He was feeling something different from abject dismay and confusion and was savoring it.

"Well?" Laura prompted.

"I find myself a little unsteady on my feet in such a situation, if you know what I mean."

Laura leaned forward against the desk. "And what kind of situation might that be, Secret Agent Travis?"

He laughed, shook his head. "I don't know, Laura... just dealing with people on an informal basis, just as acquaintances, friends perhaps."

"Are we acquaintances, Agent Travis?"

"I would say we were."

"And could we even be friends?"

Travis looked at her. There was no doubt in his mind now. She was trying to coax him out of himself. She was trying to wrong-step him enough so his defenses would crack. Was he that obvious? Was he just wearing a facade that everyone could see through like glass? And didn't he now want those defenses to crack? Didn't he want to just unwind and unravel? Wouldn't he give anything just to be himself for the first time since... since Esther?

He felt something rising in his chest, like a plume of slow-motion water, just filling him up from inside, flooding through him, and there was a sense of electricity through his veins, his nerves, through every muscle, through every inch of his physical being.

He felt his cheeks color, and he glanced down at the floor.

"Have I upset you?" Laura asked.

"N-no, Laura, not at all. I'm sorry. It has been a very long day and I am tired, and I really don't think I have the energy to even eat dinner, though I really do appreciate your offer."

"Maybe a cup of hot tea, then?" she asked.

"Y-yes, of course. That would be good," Travis said, unable to refuse her. He wanted to be there. He wanted to be near her. As he watched her step from behind the desk, he felt a compelling urge to put his hand on her shoulder, to tell her...

She glanced back. "Come on, then. I'll make tea, but I'll not wait on you."

Travis followed her out back to the kitchen. He took a seat at the small table near the sink.

"So, the hotel," he said eventually. "What's the deal with the hotel? You and your brother seem very young to own and run a hotel."

"Well," she said, "it belongs to all three of us—myself, Danny, and Lester. Our parents bought it back in the thirties, made a real success of it, and then my father went to war and didn't come back."

"I'm sorry to hear that."

"My ma... well, it just broke her heart, you know? Understandably, of course. They'd been childhood sweethearts, married in their teens, and then he's just gone. In 1947 she went out to stay with her sister in Fort Scott, and she wasn't there a month before we heard she'd passed. We had absolutely no warning at all. She just went to sleep one night and didn't wake up."

"Died of a broken heart," Travis said.

"That's the only explanation I have," Laura said. "Like what Chester Greene said about those Native Americans Indians, you know? They can just decide to die, and then they're dead."

The water had boiled, and Laura busied herself with making tea. She brought cups and milk to the table and then sat facing Travis.

"Why aren't you married, Laura?" Travis asked.

She smiled wistfully. "Because I am a firm believer in one marriage for life, Michael, and I have yet to meet a man with whom I would be prepared to spend the rest of my life." She poured the tea. "And now I am asking the same question of you."

"The job," Travis said. "It takes over everything, really. I don't think I really grasped the extent to which I *was* the job until I came here."

"I must say that it does seem very strict, very formal, you know? I can't imagine you going to the drive-in or to a dance or something. I think it must take a very particular kind of person to do that, to give up all the usual things, to make that degree of sacrifice. I find it very noble."

"Really?"

"Yes, of course. I mean, my brother is a cop, and he has a wife and kids and he does barbecues and he drinks a beer every once in a while. I love him dearly, but he's still my brother and that gives me the right to make fun of him. When he's a cop he's a cop, but at the end of his shift, when he goes home and takes his uniform off, well, he's just my brother again, you know? He's someone's husband, someone's dad, and my brother. But with you…" She looked up at Travis, almost as if she was now concerned that she would say something improper.

Travis smiled, put her at ease. "Go on," he said. "I am armed, but I am unlikely to shoot you."

She laughed. "Well, you seem so serious. And I mean pretty much *always*. It must be an awful strain to be that serious and intense every hour of every day. Have you always been like that, or is that what's expected of you?" She blushed then, looked away.

"What?" Travis asked. "What is it?"

"No," she said. "I can't possibly tell you."

"It's okay. Really, I won't be upset. I promise."

She laughed again, looked too embarrassed for words. "It's terrible," she said. "It's just the most awful thing, really."

Now Travis had to know. "Laura, please. Tell me what it is."

"It's just something someone said. Jack Farley, you know? He said something and it was very funny, but it was also kind of awful."

"Tell me what Jack Farley said."

"I can't," Laura replied. "Really, I can't."

"Well, that's that then," Travis said. "I'm going to have to arrest you for withholding evidence, obstruction of justice, probably a few other things. I might have to handcuff you."

"You promise you won't tell him that I told you?"

Travis merely raised his eyebrows.

"Oh, Lord, this is too bad. He said… well, he said that you were so stiff you probably put your shirt on before you ironed it. He said that anytime the Feds needed to bash a door down, all they had to do was pick you and bash your head against it."

"He said that, did he?"

"He did, and I feel just awful now, Michael. I really shouldn't have said that, but I just thought of it and I couldn't help laughing."

"Well, that I understand, because I keep thinking about what Danny told me about you, and it was just too funny for words, but I could never bring myself to repeat it."

Laura stopped laughing. "What? What did he say? Oh man, I'm gonna knock him black-and-blue if he said something bad about me."

"I can't say a word. I promised. I made an oath."

"Hey, that's not fair. I told you what Jack Farley said."

"Sure you did, but did you make an oath not to repeat it? I don't think you did. Anyway, I work for the federal government, and we have to sign stuff that says if we make an oath we keep it until death."

Laura didn't speak.

"See, I thought so. I knew it. No such oath was made. Well, I gave my word as a gentleman and as a federal agent not to repeat what your brother told me about you."

"Oh God, it was awful, wasn't it? Was it about when I got sick in church?"

Travis shook his head.

"Oh no, I know what he told you," she exclaimed. "I don't believe it. I just don't believe he would have told you that. It was when we went skinny-dipping and they hid my clothes, didn't he? He did, right? Oh my, that's just the worst thing ever. How could he do that? I am so mad at him. I am really, really mad at him!"

Travis could keep a straight face no longer. He started laughing, and once he started, he could not stop.

Finally she understood.

"That is so mean, Michael Travis! I cannot believe you tricked me like that! Oh, that is just an awful thing to do to someone."

"I'm sorry," he said. "I couldn't help myself."

"But you were laughing," she said. "It was worth it to see you laugh."

Travis was aware then that he did laugh, *really* laugh, if only for a moment.

"I think maybe you forgot somewhere along the line, huh?" Laura said. "The kind of work you do... I bet it's really hard to let go of that stuff at the end of the day."

"Sometimes, sure, but then that's the choice you make."

"Like I said before, I think it's very noble."

"Now I'm not so sure," Travis replied.

"You don't think it's noble, to sacrifice that much of yourself for your work?"

"I thought so. Now I'm starting to see something else." He waved it aside. "I don't want to talk about it, Laura. I can't talk about it. Let's change the subject, okay?"

"Sure, if you want. So, what's happening with the carnival now? Are you all done investigating them?"

"I can't tell you that either."

"Okay, well... well, is it likely that the carnival will be able to move on soon?"

Travis smiled weakly. "Sorry."

Laura laughed. "Right, so how do you think the weather's going to be?"

Travis smiled. He reached out and took her hand. It was an impulsive action, something he didn't even think about, even as he was doing it, and when he felt her hand within his, it created a sensation deep within him that he hadn't experienced for as long as he could recall.

Travis withdrew.

"What are you afraid of, Michael?" Laura asked, her expression something close to serious.

"Afraid of?" he echoed. "I'm not afraid of anything. I chase bad guys, remember?"

"Not out there," she said. "In here." She paused, and then she reached up and placed her hand to her chest. "Is it so very wrong for two people to like each other, to spend some time together, to talk to each other?"

Travis couldn't speak.

"Maybe I am way off here," Laura went on, "but it seems to me that you and I... well, we kind of hit it off, if you know what I mean." She looked up at him, and though she had not voiced the question, the question was all too evident in her eyes.

Travis did not contradict her. He did not refute what she was implying.

"So, if two people meet, and there's a possibility they could be friends, perhaps even more than friends, then why shouldn't they talk to each other, Michael? Because they're afraid it might not work out? Because they're concerned about what other people might think? Seems to me that most of the epitaphs on folks' gravestones should say something about not doing things for fear that they won't work. That's why people give up, as far as I can see. That's why people don't even start things, because they're worried that it might not work, that people might think they're dumb or whatever. But who cares?"

"I care," Travis said. "I actually really care, Laura. I have watched you since the first time I saw you, and yes, I felt something, and yes, I hoped somewhere in amongst everything that's happening here that there might be some way to become friends with you. To be honest, I have wanted to think about you, but I have forced myself not to."

"I want you to think about me, Michael Travis," Laura said. "Does that make things clear enough for you?" She reached out her hand, and just as Travis had impulsively reached for her, he now withdrew.

"You don't understand," he said.

"Then explain it to me. I am not stupid."

"I know you're not stupid, Laura. I wasn't suggesting that you were."

"You're closing down again, Michael. I can see it. I told you before, what Danny said about how I could see through people. Well, I'm not saying that I know a great deal about you at all, save the fact that there are two of you living inside the same body, and one of them keeps squashing the other one down, and you're not the only person who does that. In fact, most everybody does that, and some of them don't even realize it. All I know is one thing, and I know this for sure. You go on living like that, and you'll never find out what it is to be happy."

"Maybe some of us are not destined to be happy."

"Maybe you're right."

"Maybe you think you see me for who I am, and maybe you're wrong."

"Maybe I am," Laura said.

"Maybe—"

"Maybe you should shut up for once."

Travis smiled. "I guess I should."

"So, Secret Agent Travis, are we doing this or not?"

Travis hesitated.

"That's my answer," Laura said, and she got up from the kitchen table.

Travis watched her as she rose, and he said nothing.

"Arc you not exhausted with pretending, Michael?" she asked.

"I guess I am," he replied. "In more ways than one."

She smiled, and it was a sincere and genuine smile. "It's a shame," she said. "More sad than just a shame. You seem like a good man to me. There are less of those than you think. I figured that maybe..." She looked away—toward the sink, down at the floor—then back to Travis. "Never mind," she said, her tone one of disappointment.

Travis wanted to say something, anything, to bring her back, but he knew she was going, and there was little he could do now to stop her.

"Sleep well, Michael," she said, and she left him there alone in the kitchen.

43

Travis fell asleep with thoughts of Laura McCaffrey, and he awoke to find the same thoughts present. What had he expected? That sleep would somehow miraculously wash away his emotions? He knew he could not afford himself the luxury of analyzing what had happened the previous night, and yet he so wanted to.

Downstairs, he was both relieved and disappointed to find Laura absent.

Danny was there, offered Travis breakfast, but Travis declined.

"You were off somewhere yesterday, Laura tells me," Danny said, seemingly for no other reason than to prompt a conversation.

Travis was aware that it was close to ten, that he had slept far longer than usual, and yet that deep sense of internal fatigue was still very much present.

"Just had some matters to attend to out of town," Travis replied.

"I understand that you and she had some words last night," Danny went on, the tone in his voice one of caution.

"What makes you think that?" Travis asked.

"She was not so happy when she got home. I asked what was wrong. She said that you and she had a disagreement about something."

"Is that what she called it?"

"That was the word she used, yes."

"I think it might have been a difference of opinion, but I don't believe it was a disagreement."

"None of my business really, is it?" Danny said.

"She's your sister. You're going to be concerned for her welfare, naturally."

"You know she..." Danny McCaffrey looked awkward.

"Danny, seriously, I am here to do a job. This is not a good time to be getting—"

Danny raised his hand. "Enough said," he replied. "I am sorry. It *isn't* any of my business, and I am simply concerned for her welfare. How she might or might not feel is not your fault. Not directly, at least. It's not as though you've done something to encourage the way she feels."

"I have to go now," Travis said. "I am sorry that there is some problem here, but I cannot deal with it right now, you understand?"

"I understand, Agent Travis."

"If you see your sister, please pass on my best wishes to her."

"I'll do that."

"Thank you."

"And are you going to be back for dinner this evening?"

"I don't know," Travis said. "Best not to expect me. I am not sure what will happen today."

Danny said nothing further, just stood and watched as Travis headed out to his car.

Travis didn't look back. It had been another awkward moment, another conversation that he really couldn't afford the time to undertake, but life seemed to just go on happening irrespective of whether or not he did anything to ignore it or change its direction. He could not deflect and avoid forever, but at least he could postpone.

Travis drove out to see Doyle, the sheets of paper still in his pocket from Oklahoma City. Doyle was seated outside the caravan, an empty chair beside him, a small folding table before him, upon which sat a pot of coffee, two cups, an ashtray, and a packet of cigarettes.

"I hope you appreciate the effort I have made for you, Agent Travis," he said. "Please take a seat. Have some coffee, and let's hear the latest news in this ever-changing saga of bullshit and lies."

Travis didn't challenge Doyle. He merely sat down, took the printout from his pocket and handed it over.

Doyle read through it, and then he placed it before him on the table and folded his hands together in his lap. He didn't look at Travis as he spoke, but toward Seneca Falls and the line of trees near the highway, beyond that to the horizon.

"I suppose the thing that surprises me most," Doyle said, "is that you are surprised by any of this." He reached out and tapped the papers on the table. "You know what Paperclip was... what it *is*?"

"No, I don't," Travis replied.

"Well, it was a little project that the Office of Strategic Services undertook at the end of the war. Berlin had fallen, Hitler was dead, and someone started to wonder about Wernher von Braun and Arthur Rudolph and Hubertus Strughold, all those brilliant minds that had empowered Hitler's visions of world domination with aircraft and bombs and whatever else they could dream up. Those minds were still there, still working, and the worst thing that could happen is that those minds would be found in the employ of the Russians or the British. The Allied agreement counted for nothing in the face of that possibility. So they took all those

372

brilliant minds out of Germany in an operation masterminded by the Joint Intelligence Objectives Agency. They created false employment histories, false biographies, and wiped out any record that these people had ever been active members of the National Socialist Party or the Nazi regime. More than a hundred of them came to the United States, including Wagner, Neubert, Poppel, dozens more. The cream of the crop, so to speak. And that little performance was nothing in comparison to some of the other projects that you have here. The other stuff is altogether more sinister and horrifying, believe me."

"More than those responsible for the worst war in human history evading justice?"

"Oh, they didn't just evade justice, my naive and trusting friend, they are even now living the high life in the United States. These people figured on something called the Osenberg List, named after the head of the German Military Research Association."

Doyle lit a cigarette and leaned forward, his elbows on his knees, his expression intense, focused.

"You see, after Stalingrad, the Germans needed all the physicists and mathematicians and engineers they could muster to work on new rocket technology. They recalled more than four thousand rocketeers from frontline duty and sent them back to the northeast of Germany. Germany fell regardless, and that Osenberg List wound up in the hands of British military intelligence. They gave it to US intelligence and then to a certain Major Staver in US Army Ordnance. He understood what those names represented, and he selected those he wanted in the United States."

"And they are here, right here in the United States, and they have never been called to account for what they did?"

"Yes, they are here, and no, they will never be called to account."

"How do you know this?" Travis asked.

Doyle smiled. "The same way you know how to secure evidence, take fingerprints, manage an investigation. The same way you know the ranking system of the FBI and how to ascend it. The same way anyone knows what they know... experience, familiarity, personal involvement, connections." Doyle paused, as if he planned to say something further and had then changed his mind. "Because I am who I am, Agent Travis. Because I was there from the start... but we will talk of that later."

"And you said that this Paperclip operation was nothing compared to some of the other operations?"

"That's right."

"Meaning?"

"The names you have ... MK Ultra, Chatter, Artichoke ... those are the very programs for which they want people like me, Agent Travis."

"And they deal with what?"

"Well, let's take a regular guy on the street, a guy who has his worries and troubles like everyone else, and maybe he figures he needs some help, you know? He goes to see his doctor, and the doctor refers him to a psychiatrist. He tells the psychiatrist that he's been feeling depressed, that he isn't so good these days. The psychiatrist listens, he makes some notes. He learns that the man has no wife, no kids, that his parents are dead, that he is, in essence, a loner. And so our depressed and unfortunate man becomes a candidate for a special type of research that is being done. The psychiatrist picks up the telephone and makes a call. Within two hours, there is someone there to collect the man, to take him to a special clinic, to cure him of his depression with a new experimental treatment. This is what he's told, and he believes it. In fact, he is quite happy to believe anything as long as it will cure him of his problems. So the man goes to the special clinic. He trusts these professionals. He knows that he doesn't understand his own mind, but these people, with all these letters after their names, with their white coats and their special language, well, they must know what's going on. That's what they do. Just as a man knows how to build a wall or fix a car, there are people who know how to fix a human being, right?"

"Right," Travis said. "Of course."

"Wrong. No. Of course not."

"This is a real scenario you're describing here?"

"One of hundreds, if not thousands," Doyle replied.

"So what happened to the man?"

"Let's call him John, okay? John goes with the men to the clinic. As soon as he arrives, he's given a shot of sodium pentothal. He's locked in a room for three days without food. He's given water, but nothing to eat. Every time he falls asleep, someone wakes him up. There's no windows, he's naked, and he doesn't know where he is, whether it's day or night, what time it is, nothing. He's completely disorientated. He starts to imagine things; he starts to hallucinate. He will say or do anything that he's instructed to. This goes on for a week. Then he is given food. He's allowed to sleep. He's permitted to go outside, to walk around, to look at the trees. He starts to feel better, he becomes a little more himself, and then suddenly everything changes. He is given an injection of LSD. You know what LSD is, Agent Travis?"

"I do, yes."

"You know where it came from, why it was developed?"

"I don't."

374

"Albert Hofmann, a Swiss scientist first synthesized it in 1938. The Germans were very interested in its potential to incapacitate a nation in preparation for an invasion. A few years ago, the CIA got wind of what it could do, and they started using it with far greater regularity. They gave it to teenagers, students, teachers, academics, even their own operatives, and they made extensive studies to see if it could serve any purpose in mind control and chemical warfare. The fact that it produced paranoia, schizophrenia, delusions, even permanent brain damage was all just collateral damage. This was vital research; this was for the sake of national security and the fight against Communism. They had to be in control, they had to know what a man could be made to do, with or without his agreement." Doyle leaned forward and extinguished his cigarette in the ashtray. "And that, my friend, is just a tiny, tiny glimpse of what you have on that sheet of paper."

"And the connection between this and the other operations?"

"Well, let's take Paperclip, for example. Paperclip not only gave us the rocket men and physicists, it also brought the doctors, surgeons, neurologists, and psychiatrists too. It brought out the very people who'd gotten their hands dirty in the concentration camps under the auspices of people like Josef Mengele. Those people are now the backbone of American Military Intelligence mind and behavior modification and control practices. The CIA and the Federal Bureau of Investigation are taking care of America's national and international security issues with knowledge about the human mind that came out of Auschwitz. Sterilization, electric shock treatments, operations without anesthesia, to what degree could a human being be subjected to mental and physical torture before death—all these things were tried and tested there in Germany and Poland, and these were the very people who did these things. Operation Paperclip gave birth to Artichoke, nothing more than an investigation into interrogation techniques overseen by the CIA's Office of Scientific Intelligence."

"This is just too incredible—"

"It is not difficult to comprehend, Agent Travis. It has been said that politics will never learn from history, but I beg to differ. The current US administration is well versed in the language of Machiavelli and the Borgias, believe me."

"So now? What we have here? A dead Hungarian, a name I am not supposed to know, a body that has just vanished into nowhere. What does that have to do with the CIA and Nazi rocket scientists?"

"It is one and the same thing, I am afraid, Agent Travis."

"How? How can that be?"

"MK Ultra. Your Hungarian, why he was in New York, why he was

375

arrested, how he ended up here in Seneca Falls four years later with a hole in the back of his head. I could be wrong, of course, but everything that has happened here is directing me toward MK Ultra."

"And that is what, exactly?"

"Human behavioral engineering. Sanctioned at the highest level, running at more levels through this society than I can even count and utterly terrifying in its ramifications and implications. They employ LSD, sensory deprivation techniques, isolation, physical torture, mental and emotional abuse at a level that you cannot even begin to appreciate, even so far as trying to create sexual fixations and obsessions through the use of hypnotic repetition of images and words. They hope to determine the very limits of human endurance—physical, mental and emotional—to see whether they can change a subject's loyalties, discover things about a subject that even the subject themselves has forgotten. It is headed by someone who is right there on your piece of paper. Sidney Gottlieb, real name Joseph Scheider, a club-footed stutterer from the Bronx who became a chemist, specialized in poisons, wound up heading the chemical division of the CIA's Technical Services Staff. His assignment was authorized by Dulles himself, his instruction being to discover if there wasn't some drug or technique that could be used to control a man's mind, all of this in the supposed direction of fighting the Cold War. Gottlieb actually said that he hoped to find a technique that would crush the human psyche to the point that it would admit to anything."

"Honestly, if this is true, the consequences—"

"Oh, it is true, my friend. As true as daylight and darkness. You know, the funding for this came from a certain long-established and well-respected foundation whose stated purpose is to promote the well-being of mankind throughout the world." Doyle laughed sarcastically. "This very American foundation was so generous as to support Josef Mengele in those vital eugenics programs he was working on before he was assigned to Auschwitz. Oh, of course they do a huge amount of beneficial things, I am sure, but the connection to Mengele and Gottlieb alone means they're off my Christmas card list."

"But this is all CIA, Mr. Doyle. I am not CIA. I have never had anything to do with the CIA. I am an agent of the Federal Bureau of Investigation."

"You think they're different? Of course, in name they're different, in stated purposes they're different, but it's all the same playground, my friend. You don't think that Dulles and Hoover talk to each other. You don't think there are phone calls and lunch meetings and favors granted and concessions made. You do this for me, I'll do this for you. It's all the same bullshit. And one and all, right the way to the highest echelons, we are overseen and dictated to by the Freemason hierarchy, a hierarchy that cannot be sidestepped, bypassed, avoided, or negated. Loyalty to that Brotherhood is paramount, and the oaths that are taken can never be violated for fear of excommunication and disavowal."

"So I am working for an organization that is involved in secret mind control experiments, all of it sanctioned by the CIA, funded by some well-respected foundation, and overseen by the Freemasons?"

Doyle laughed again, this time quite heartedly. "Well, I have to say that putting it like that makes you sound like a mad conspiracy theorist, but in a nutshell, yes."

"You sound like the crazy conspiracy theorist, Mr. Doyle, if you don't mind me saying."

Doyle smiled ruefully. "Oh, I don't mind at all, Agent Travis. I have been called a great deal worse than that."

"And now?"

Doyle reached out and closed his hand over Travis's. "You have to make a decision about what to do, Agent Travis," he said. "And when I say make a decision about what to do, I am not talking about whether or not you should ask Laura McCaffrey out on a date."

Travis's reaction was sudden. He looked shocked, and then he started laughing, and before he knew it, his eyes were filled with tears and he was having difficulty breathing.

"St-stop do-doing that," he gasped. "Stop fu-fucking doing th-that, for Christ's sake!"

Doyle leaned forward and held Travis's shoulders as Travis gathered himself together.

"I am sorry," Doyle said, "but every once in a while I feel I have to do something to shake you out of your comfort zone."

"I think you have accomplished that," Travis said.

"Well, now I have seen you laugh, I have seen you shocked, offended, upset, angry. We're doing pretty good, wouldn't you say, Agent Travis?"

Travis knew there was no going back. What Doyle had told him made sense, but for all the wrong reasons. He did not know what to do or think, least of all how to extricate himself from this nightmare with anything remaining of his former life.

"Tough, huh?" Doyle said.

Travis nodded.

"You want to know what they have in store for me, for Valeria, for Chester Greene? You want to know why they've made so many attempts to infiltrate our little family?"

"Yes," Travis said. "I want to know everything. Absolutely everything."

44

Before Doyle could say another word, the door of the caravan opened and Valeria appeared. She was dressed in her robe, her hair tousled, her expression that of someone just awoken.

For some reason, Travis was reminded of those mornings he'd awoken beside Esther, and on the heels of that thought came a thought of Laura McCaffrey, and he felt himself slip away from familiar moorings even further. His mind resisted what his heart wanted. He hated how he felt, but he did not see any way to change it.

"Breakfast," Valeria said matter-of-factly. "I know it's officially closer to lunchtime, but nevertheless..."

"Breakfast would be good," Doyle said.

"I'm all right, thank you," Travis said as she started to close the door.

"Hey, you'll eat what's put in front of you and be grateful for it," Valeria replied. "You don't eat anywhere near enough as it is. Don't smoke, don't drink, don't dance for sure. Lord knows who raised you."

Valeria closed the door behind herself before he could respond.

"Don't make her mad," Doyle said. "I have learned this at my peril."

"Enough said," Travis replied.

Doyle lit a cigarette and stretched his legs out in front of him. "This has been a long time coming, in all honesty. I knew this kind of thing would happen. There were moments when I thought I'd slipped out of the net, but I realize now that they will never really let me go."

"What net? What do you mean?"

"Let me give you a little education," Doyle said. "Let's talk about the American intelligence community, though that term sometimes seems like the greatest oxymoron of all time. They're nowhere near as intelligent as they like to believe they are, and despite the fact that they're all supposed to work together, hence *community*, they actually lie to one another just as much as any prison population you could mention. Let's take the director of the CIA, for example. Let's start at the top, shall we? Right now, the director of the Central Intelligence Agency is a man called Allen Welsh Dulles. He was Office of Strategic Services, and then, when the OSS was dissolved in the latter part of 1945, all of its functions were transferred to different state departments. Then came the National Security Act of 1947. That was the beginning of the CIA, ostensibly a civilian-staffed intelligence-gathering organization, and yet Truman's first CIA director was a US Navy admiral." Doyle smiled thoughtfully. "You know what their motto is?"

"Not a clue."

"John, Chapter eight, verse thirty-two. And you shall know the truth, and the truth shall make you free. Can you imagine anything more ironic and contradictory than that? And such arrogance. Such immeasurable and unbelievable arrogance." Doyle shook his head. "It completely beggars belief, to be honest. Anyway, that was the start of it. In June of the following year, there was something called a National Security Council Directive. This gave the CIA authority to carry out covert operations against anyone who was considered a hostile foreign group. There was a clever little rider in the wording of that directive, you see, for it not only gave authority to attack perceived enemies, but it also gave the CIA permission to withhold information regarding their own activities from anyone that they considered unauthorized. And if you're wondering who falls into the category of unauthorized, then it's everyone but themselves. Free rein didn't stop there, however. In 1949 they passed the CIA Act, and that gave them clearance to withhold their own financial and administrative procedures, exempted them from having to disclose the number of employees, their titles, salaries, and additionally gave them the authority to create what was known as 'essential aliens'—"

"And what the hell is an essential alien?" Travis asked.

"Well, it is a foreign national who isn't really a foreign national. It's a false identity, a cover story, a fabricated identity that has all the paperwork necessary to prove that they are indeed someone that they are not, every little facet of it created, sanctioned, and funded by the agency."

"Seriously?"

"Seriously, but this is just the tip of the iceberg. That was all within the first two years of the agency's existence. When Eisenhower became president, he wanted an agency that would back him in the Cold War. Eisenhower was Supreme Commander of the Allied Forces, remember. I don't think he could get through a day without knowing that he was at war with something. So Communism it was, and everything was perceived as some kind of potential red infiltration. That NSC Directive of 1947 gave him all the legal and political leverage he needed. He just had to say something was a threat to US national security, and bang, they were on the hit list. As far as Ike was concerned, Dulles was the golden boy. Ike was in the Oval Office in January of '53. Dulles was appointed

379

as director of the CIA just seven weeks later. It was a match made in heaven." Doyle paused. "More accurately, a match made in hell."

Doyle leaned forward, elbows on his knees, his hands together. He looked at Travis, and there was a sadness in the man's eyes.

"Anyway, the director is required to report on all activities in a timely and punctual manner to the Congress intelligence communities. That's how they word it. Timely and punctual. What is timely? What is punctual? Who the hell knows, eh? This requirement is given a good degree of . . . shall we say, flexibility? The president can advise the director as to his interests, the director can carry out covert operations to support those interests, but never has to actually report that it was done. That way the president's hands stay clean." Doyle smiled sardonically. "If the shit hits the fan, then the chain of command ends with the director, though in truth it never actually gets that high. Someone way down the totem pole always takes the head shot, but even then it's only nominal blame. They are quietly pensioned off, given a nice property in Martha's Vineyard, and that's the end of that. It's a perfectly designed self-protecting mechanism, answerable to no one, no oversight committee, no internal investigations worth a hill of beans, a free license and unlimited funding."

Doyle leaned back and reached for his cigarettes.

"It has been said that the collective body of Congress intelligence agencies—the NSA, the Department of Justice, the Attorney General's Office, the Department of the Interior and so many others—know some parts of the truth. No one knows all of it, not even the president or the director of the CIA. Information combined, the president and director understand significantly more than seventy or eighty percent of what there is to know about America's involvement in world affairs. The rest is known by the deputy director and the attendant legion of cohorts, contacts, agents, double agents, sleepers, moles, plants, scalp hunters, authenticated sources, floaters, friends, handlers, gamekeepers, and controllers. Worlds within worlds. Universes within universes."

Doyle lit his cigarette. "And then we come to your gang, my friend. Hoover's little band of merry men. I have to say that as far as the intelligence community is concerned, the FBI is something of a wild card. The FBI is Hoover's creation, and he is a very smart man indeed. Crazy as a shithouse rat, but very smart. The FBI is national, internal, supposedly uninterested in externally sourced threats to life, liberty, and the pursuit of happiness. But when Hoover gets involved in anti-Communist activities, when he takes his marching orders from the Oval Office and those orders come via the director of the CIA, then we have a situation where someone is not playing ball, as they say."

"And is that what has been happening?" Travis asked. "The president has been directing the FBI through the CIA?"

"Not exactly. Hoover would never stand for such a thing. They all walk on eggshells around Hoover. Hoover has his files, and they all know that if they ruffle his feathers, then their files will find their way to his desk, and phone calls will be made. They all have their dirty little secrets, you see? And even if Hoover doesn't know every one of their secrets, it doesn't stop them believing that he might know. The paranoid always manage to create that sense of paranoia around them. Hoover doesn't like agents who are too short, too tall, who have sweaty hands, who can't maintain steady eye contact, except when it doesn't suit him, of course. He is a fickle man, Agent Travis. A fickle man with a great deal of power, and thus he is the most dangerous kind of all." Doyle shrugged. "And yet who knows what really goes on, my friend? Perhaps everything that goes on in the Oval Office is taped, but I can't imagine those tapes will ever see the light of day."

"So, where do you come into all of this?" Travis asked. "I am still not seeing the picture here. Why on earth would someone like Dulles, or even Hoover, for that matter, be interested in a man like you? You own and run a traveling carnival. You are not exactly a threat to national security, surely?"

"Or so one would believe," Doyle replied. "I am trying to paint a picture here, perhaps to build a jigsaw puzzle, you know? I am one part of it, as is Valeria, as is Chester Greene and Gabor Benedek, but on our own we mean nothing. However, you put all those pieces together, and you have something that means an entirely different thing. The whole is always greater than the sum of its parts."

"So there's more?"

Doyle laughed. "I have described some small part of a snowflake, Agent Travis. Beneath the snowflake is an iceberg, and this iceberg is far bigger than the one that sank the Titanic. We need to be specific here, though. I understand that this is a great deal of information to take in, and some of it sounds just too fantastic for words, but when you start to break it down and analyze it, then you begin to see where this thing is headed."

"Mind control," Travis said. "Behavior modification, making people do things that they have no control over, creating double agents and sleepers and whatever else they believe they need in order to fight the Cold War. That's what you're telling me, isn't it? That we are just part of some grand and master plan to eradicate the threat of Communism?"

"Yes, to a degree, but that is the socially acceptable face of it," Doyle said. "These people want a certain thing, and they enforce those wants on everyone else. They see it as some kind of divine ordination. They are laboring beneath the most fantastic self-created delusions and paranoias imaginable. They are part of the Freemason Brotherhood, and they feel that their calling comes from God. They believe that they are responsible for the world complete. They believe that psychiatric mind control techniques can be employed to effect political ends. These men fall well within the boundaries of their own classification for numerous mental disorders and yet would never subject themselves to the treatment they order for others. They are not crazy, you see? Everyone else is. You know Dulles, such a model of integrity and decency, is believed to have had more than a hundred extramarital affairs. That information from his own sister. These people shake one another's hands, they pat one another's backs, they safeguard their own positions, and they protect their vested interests. Behind the scenes, these are the very people who possess major financial shareholdings in the newspaper industry, the media channels, the medical and psychiatric drug companies, the arms manufacturers. They say they want peace, but they want war. They say they want well people and good mental health, but in reality they push ever harder to classify even the simplest difficulties as mental diseases, and thus they rake in millions in government appropriations for the research and development of so-called cures for the these imaginary diseases. It is a spider's web of internal corruption, ulterior motives, and hidden agendas. These people make the Borgias look like children squabbling at a church picnic."

"And they want you?"

"Yes, they want me."

"And Valeria and Chester and everyone else."

"Not everyone. Perhaps not Gabor or the Bellancas or Akiko. Those are our friends. Those are the outcasts and unwanteds that we have collected along the way. They are good people, and they have thrown their lot in with us out of support and camaraderie. They are gypsies, and they wish to remain gypsies, and for no other reason than a real sense of exhaustion with the world as it is. They have reached the point now where they simply want nothing further to do with it."

"But they do want you... for what you can do, right?"

"For what they believe I can do, Agent Travis."

"Reading minds."

"Not minds, perhaps, but people. You can tell a great deal about someone just by looking at them without preconceptions and fixed ideas. You can see who they are from how they talk, how they listen, whether they look at you, don't look at you. You can see if someone is telling the truth, lying, whatever else might be going on. But the simple art of seeing what is there in front of you, of asking questions, of interviewing someone to learn what they know, has become a dark art. It has been corrupted, twisted, a perverse compulsion to know everything, and it all went to hell."

"So why do they *really* want you, Mr. Doyle? Who are you? How do you know all these things? What do they hope to gain by creating a situation like this, killing a man and putting his body here? Why try to create something for which you could be blackmailed?"

"If I told you that, then *I* would have to kill *you*, Agent Travis."

"So tell me," Travis said, "and then kill me, because if even a fragment of this is true then I cannot go on working for the FBI. And if it is true, and they are so afraid of what you might say or do, then why not just kill you and everyone else here? That would seem to be the swiftest and simplest solution. If they have all this power and influence that you speak of, how are you even still alive?"

"For three reasons," Doyle replied. "First, because these people still have to be seen to be lawful. That's a trap they have effectively created for themselves. That is why I was so surprised that you found documentation in one of the FBI offices regarding the dead man. That was just asking for trouble. These people write the law, and then they have to be careful to be seen as paragons of virtue when it comes to the application of the very laws they themselves have authored. One can do what one wishes, Agent Travis, as long as one is not caught red-handed doing what one wishes."

"And the second reason?" Travis asked.

"The second reason is that they cannot kill me, Agent Travis. Even if Hoover was given *carte blanche* to make me disappear by those to whom he defers, he still would not do it. He would not issue that order."

"Why not?"

Doyle smiled sardonically. It was obvious he was not going to answer the question.

Travis held Doyle's gaze, but Doyle was implacable.

"And the third?"

"That reason I cannot give you, Agent Travis. If you knew that, then yes, I *really* would have to kill you."

"You know, this is the organization to which I have devoted my life for the better part of a decade," Travis said, "and before that I was in the army—not for long, granted, but still I was there. I believed I was doing the right thing, and I am fighting with this like you wouldn't believe."

"I know you are, Agent Travis."

"Do you? Do you really know what I am going through, Mr. Doyle?"

"Yes, I do."

"I don't believe you do, but I am not going to argue with you," Travis said.

"I know everything, Agent Travis. I know everything there is to know about how this all started, about who is behind it, about why they are really doing it, and what their intentions are."

"You have yet to explain *how* you know all of this, Mr. Doyle. You have yet to give me any real evidence that what you are saying is actually true. How do I know that you are not as corrupt and deceitful as those that you are accusing?"

"You don't know, Agent Travis. The only thing I am trying to do is appeal to your fundamental awareness of truth. As for how I know these things, well, I saw it for what it was, I saw where it was going, and I chose to leave it behind."

Travis frowned.

"It's not hard to understand," Doyle said. "You know a little of my history, a little of my background. I came here to America for a very simple reason. It was an escape route, my way out of everything that had happened during the war. But the US authorities knew who I was, and they knew of my reputation, and thus began a lengthy courtship to which I finally succumbed. Let us say that the carnival continued for a number of years without me, the years between early 1950 and the latter months of 1953, and during those three years, my beautiful Valeria saw very little of me."

"Where were you? What were you doing?"

"He was causing untold amounts of trouble," Valeria said as she came down the steps from the caravan. "And now, just to change the mood, we are going to eat."

Travis sat forward. "Seriously," he said, "what were you doing?"

"Later," Doyle replied. He reached out and grabbed the edge of Valeria's skirt. He pulled her close, and without rising from his chair, he put his hand around her waist. "Valeria has made breakfast. We eat, we have some more coffee, and then we talk again."

"Are you not already bored with war stories, Agent Travis?" Valeria asked.

"God, no! This is unbelievable. I want to know everything."

"Everything?" she asked. "Maybe when you know everything, you will wish that you had never asked."

"How could you say that? You have to know everything. You can't just ignore the truth."

"I would agree, but there is always a penalty for knowing the truth."

"A penalty?"

"A sacrifice to be made, let us say. There is always a sacrifice that has to be made."

"What kind of sacrifice?" Travis asked.

"Look at us," Valeria said. "We live in caravans; we are on the run; we never settle down; we cannot raise a child."

"But you are free," Travis said. "That much at least."

"Free?" she asked. "To be free one has to be free *from* something, Agent Travis. Are we free to do what we wish? Are we free to speak our minds, express our opinions, follow our own political and religious ideals? No, I don't believe we are. But, regardless, we are free to eat breakfast, no?"

Doyle laughed and got up. "Come on, Travis," he said. "Even the freedom fighters of the world have to stop for bacon and pancakes."

45

"They appealed to the better angels of my nature," Doyle said. "They got to me by talking about ideals that I really believed in. I was not young and naive. I was not the hot-headed firebrand I had been at thirty. I wasn't even the committed reactionary and resistance fighter I had been in my thirties and forties. The war was over. I was out of Europe. I had made it back into America, and I was with Valeria."

Doyle reached out and took her hand. He squeezed it affectionately, and she smiled. The three of them were seated around the small table in the caravan, and the meal Valeria had prepared was laid out before them. It was only as he took a seat that Travis realized how hungry he actually was.

"I was fifty-something," Doyle went on. "I was emotionally stable, of sound mind and body, and they came to me and they told me their story. They seduced me. They knew how to get me. They treated me as more than equal, as someone important. Maybe they appealed to my ego..." Doyle seemed thoughtful for a moment, and then he shook his head. "No, it can't have been that, as I don't believe I have an ego."

There was silence for a moment, and then Valeria started laughing.

Doyle laughed too.

"The first man without an ego," Valeria said. "Of course, yes. Edgar Doyle has no ego at all."

"So that's what they did," Doyle went on. "They spoke to me about the need to understand what people were really capable of, about the power of the mind, about human endurance and tolerance. They said they were organizing studies to learn as much as they could and that the motive behind it was purely defensive."

"And the enemy was?"

"The Russians, of course. The Communists. Hell, even Churchill said that the allies should've just kept on going right into Moscow. He was the one who coined the term 'iron curtain.' He saw the division of East and West Berlin, and he realized that this would become the frontline in an entirely different kind of war. The American intelligence community told me that they needed as many people like me as they could find, not only for my wartime experience, but for what I could do…" Doyle paused, and then he added, "For what they believed I could do, you see? They imagined me to be something I was not. They imagined that I had stepped through some sort of looking glass, and I could see right into the hearts and minds of men. They wanted to know if such a faculty was innate, if it was inherent in all people and if there was something that could be done to rehabilitate such a faculty. They had teams of doctors, neurologists, psychiatrists, psychologists, specialists in Freudian psychoanalytic techniques, everything from hypnotists to brain surgeons, and between us we were charged with the task of not only understanding the real parameters of the brain and mind, but also ways and means by which such parameters could be exaggerated, extended, increased."

"All of this under the auspices of the CIA?" Travis asked.

Doyle shrugged. "The CIA, the FBI, the ABC, or the XYZ, it didn't matter who was behind it. It was just a US intelligence-managed, government-funded operation." Doyle looked at Travis unerringly, and once again there was the sly and knowing smile on his lips. "Now any offshoot or exploratory division or department that ventures into territory such as this falls under the bureaucratic umbrella of Unit X."

"Unit X," Travis said, "is the name of the department I work for in Kansas City."

"I know, Agent Travis. I told you already that I know exactly and precisely who you work for. I am not unfamiliar with some of the other cast members in this particular performance. Unit X is a generic term. It covers everything they don't want people asking questions about."

"I've been in Kansas for five years," Travis explained. "I was told that it was a new thing, an experimental division, and we've been involved in interviewing convicted killers, sociopaths, terrorists, whoever else we're directed to interview, all with a view to better understanding the rationale and motivations of such people."

"Hell of a shame you haven't been able to interview Hoover and Dulles, eh?" Valeria said.

"Well, Unit X is a great deal older than just five years, my friend," Doyle said. "Even the things I was involved in were part of Unit X, and that was in 1950."

"And it was never a defensive program?" Travis asked.

"Oh, very far from it," Doyle replied. "It was very much an offensive action. They were on the attack. They wanted to develop interrogative techniques, techniques with which a man's loyalty and political adherence could be manipulated and altered. They wanted mind control, the ability to send people crazy. They wanted to build the perfect assassin. Literally, they wanted to be able to take a Russian agent, turn him, send him back in, have him kill a political figure, and then put the gun in his own mouth and pull the trigger. That's what they wanted, and everything we were doing, every project and experiment and trial we undertook, was designed to achieve that end. They even began work on what they called remote viewing, the ability to divorce the spiritual awareness of an individual from the body and then have that spiritual awareness be somewhere else, not only aware of that other location, but able to report back what was seen and heard. In essence, the perfect eavesdropping system."

Doyle paused to refill his coffee cup.

"And so it continues. Even as we speak, a program has been established in Canada under the control of a Scottish psychiatrist called Donald Cameron. He is working on something called 'psychic driving,' designed to wipe out memory and reprogram the way in which a human being thinks and feels. Cameron, ironically, was a member of the Nuremberg Medical Tribunal, publicly condemning the techniques that had been employed by individuals such as Mengele in Auschwitz."

Travis sat in silence. He was now no longer shocked, and that seemed to be the worst consequence of this seemingly endless litany of damning revelations. He was being given a view of the world from the side of the stage, and from this vantage point he could see behind the scenes, behind the curtain, and the reality of what he was seeing repulsed and horrified him.

"And you were right there at the start of this," Travis said.

"I was."

"And you got out."

"I got out."

"And they want you back?"

"Whether they want me back or not is beside the point, Agent Travis. Your Mr. Hoover feels that he owns me. Once you are involved in any aspect of such operations, he believes that your life is his for the taking. The federal authorities can always call on you, can always make demands of you, however unreasonable, and only by stepping out of that loop completely can you preserve some sense of identity." Doyle waved his hand out toward the collection of caravans and tents. "Hence, I live like a gypsy under an assumed name, and I keep moving, I keep running, and even then there is no guarantee that they won't finally get me."

"And my presence here—"

"Is just another step toward better understanding my intentions, perhaps securing a murder charge against me, even accomplice to murder along with everyone else here, and then they have us over a barrel. It becomes a choice of fulfilling their wishes or seeing Valeria, Gabor,

Akiko, even the Bellancas extradited. That is what they have planned, I am sure."

"And Edgar Doyle isn't even your real name."

"No, it's not."

"What is your name?"

Doyle smiled and wagged his finger at Travis. "If I told you that—"

"You'd have to kill me, right?"

"Right."

"And Chester Greene was in this program?"

"He was."

"And Oscar Haynes?"

Doyle nodded just once.

"But not Gabor?"

"I don't want to talk about specific people," Doyle said. "There is no real reason for you to know, and the less that you know, the less you can be asked to compromise."

"I hate myself for being so ignorant, so naive, so trusting."

"It's not necessary to feel that way, and it won't serve any purpose. You can't go back and undo the events themselves, only the effect they've had on you. The past is gone; the present's here; the future's unknown. Some people will never see. Simply put, they're afraid to look. Some people look, yet when they find something that threatens the status quo, they run away and pretend that they saw nothing. Others—like you, like me perhaps—didn't know they were looking, but when they see the truth, they recognize it for what it is. It's never comfortable, in all honesty, but I believe that ignorance is worse."

"Yes," Travis said. "I think ignorance is worse."

"It has been a tough journey for you," Doyle said. "And in such a short time."

"But I am still alive," Travis said. "Unlike Varga, eh?"

"He must have become a liability," Doyle ventured. "Maybe he could serve no further purpose. Maybe he found out something he shouldn't have. I don't know. And so his body became a useful prop for infiltrating this little community once again. Even in death, he could be employed for something covert. And then, if some evidence could be manufactured to make me responsible for his death, then maybe I could be blackmailed into silence, into cooperation, into... well, whatever they have in mind."

"And that's what they want of me," Travis said. "To drive back to Kansas with a report that confirms that not only is this a federal case, and thus deserving of the Bureau's attentions, but also that you can be charged with homicide."

"And Valeria, Oscar, Chester, Gabor, any one of them could be labeled as accomplices. The Carnival Diablo is done and over with, I am in custody, and then those that they wish to exploit will be given the choice… cooperation, or stay in prison for the rest of our lives. The only thing I know for sure is that their intentions are not good."

"I see that now," Travis said. "It still makes no sense why they don't just kill you. They could kill all of you. They could cover it up without any difficulty at all. It seems they have done worse, and they've done it many times."

"I have my shield," Doyle said, and touched the small blue forget-me-not on his lapel.

"So what does that—" Travis started

Doyle raised his hand. "You have to make a choice, Agent Travis."

Travis smiled wearily, and yet there was an element of defiance in his tone. "My name is Michael," he said, "and the choice has already been made. I have spent my life afraid. Afraid to upset people, afraid to disagree, afraid even to have a relationship. I was even terrified at the prospect of having children in case I carried some strain of psychopathic intent from my father. I don't see that I can go on doing this, not now that I understand what has been happening, and yet my immediate concerns are not for my own self-preservation, but yours."

"We are survivors," Doyle said. "I figured you would've guessed that by now. I think you should consider your own welfare the priority now."

"But, as you said, surviving is not freedom, and in order to be free, you have to be free from something. I cannot even comprehend how it would be to live under such a shadow of threat and oppression."

"Well, all of us live under the same shadow, Michael. The only difference between myself and Sheriff Rourke, for example, is that I know it and he doesn't. People are not really afraid until they see the monster, and often having seen the monster they convince themselves it was nothing more than imagination."

"I think I have to stop waiting for the monster to find me."

"Whatever you choose, Michael, whatever you choose."

"I need time to think," Travis said. "I am going back to the hotel. I just need a little time to think."

Travis got up from the table. He walked to the door, and as he opened it, he looked back at Edgar Doyle and Valeria Mironescu.

No one spoke. For once, it seemed that all that needed saying had already been said.

46

It was past one by the time Travis arrived at the McCaffrey, and the message that awaited him did not come as a surprise.

"Someone called Bishop has been after you," Danny told Travis. "He called Sheriff Rourke, and Rourke came down here looking for you. Anyway, the message was simply that you were to call him as soon as possible. He said it was important."

Travis did not doubt that Bishop now knew of his visit to Oklahoma City, his data request, the material that had been forwarded via Donald Kline. And if Bishop knew what he was looking into, then alarm bells would be ringing. And yet there was always another possibility, that Bishop was just as much in the dark about the true nature of what was happening here as Travis had been. Six days had passed. Travis had not filed any reports—at Bishop's request, of course—but how long would Bishop be permitted to let Travis work alone without Bishop having to answer up to his own superiors, especially if the real target of this investigation was Edgar Doyle?

To be safe, Travis would have to assume that Bishop knew at least some part of this, at least a greater part than Travis, and that everyone above Travis—Section Chief Frank Gale, Executive Assistant Director Bradley Warren, Tolson and Hoover themselves—were knowing and willing co-conspirators in this charade. And for what purpose, and where would it end?

Travis knew he'd have to call Bishop. If he didn't, Bishop would send someone to find out what was going on. Perhaps Bishop would come in person. Kansas City was little more than an hour away.

No, he could not delay. He would call Bishop immediately, and thus he asked once again if he could use the private line in the kitchen.

"Sure thing," Danny told him. "You know where it is."

Travis went on back and was surprised to find Laura there. He felt momentarily awkward, and then told her he needed to make a private call.

"Of course," she said, evidently uncertain as to how she should now be around him. She had presented him with an invitation to be himself, to share a little of that self with her, and he had—in essence—refused her. It had not been a direct rejection, and even as he stood there by the table, waiting for just a moment as she made her way to the door, he felt the compelling need to stop her, to try to explain what was really going on. Once again, as with all matters beyond the scope of regulation and protocol, she beat him to the punch.

"Michael," she said.

"Laura."

"Last night, when we spoke..." She looked at him, and there was sadness in her eyes. "I did not mean to presume anything, and I am sorry if I—"

"You have nothing to be sorry for," Travis said. "Really, honestly, seriously, you have nothing at all to be sorry for."

"I thought that perhaps I had... well, you know, assumed something." She smiled hesitantly. "And you know what they say about assumption, right?"

Travis felt his heart in his temples. He needed to tell her what he was thinking, what he was feeling, but he could not. Not yet. Not until he knew his own mind.

"Something is happening here," he said, knowing how little he could say and yet desperately wanting her to understand that he just needed some time to deal with his own world as it fell apart. For that's how it felt—as if the world within which he had lived for as long as he could remember was nothing more than a house of cards.

Laura looked expectantly at Travis. "What is happening here?"

"This case," he said.

"What about it? Is it over? Are you leaving?"

"I wish I were," Travis replied. "Not to be away from here. Not that. But to be somewhere else, not having to deal with what I'm facing right now."

He thought back to the moment he had discovered Andris Varga's police record in the floor safe, the simple and inescapable truth that the Bureau—whoever or whatever that was—had known who Varga was before they'd even given Travis his assignment briefing. That—in hindsight—had really been the turning point in his own understanding of what he was doing.

"Sit down for a moment, Laura," he said.

She shook her head. "I don't want to sit down, Michael. I have to go. I have to be at the diner."

"You can't understand what is happening," he said. "Not that you *can't*, but there's just too many things that I cannot tell you. That's what I mean. I want to tell you, but it's just that—"

"I don't want to know why, Michael," Laura said. "I don't need to know why you can't do something. You have a job to do. I understand that. I also appreciate that whatever you are doing is confidential, and to be honest, I don't think I want to know all the details of some murder investigation."

"It has gone so far beyond a simple murder investigation," Travis said.

"Is there such a thing as a *simple* murder investigation?" she said, almost smiling.

"What I'm trying to say, Laura, is that there are some decisions I have to make. They relate to what I am doing here. Not the case, not the dead man. I'm talking about my life. The whole of my life. Who I am, why I am doing this job at all."

"Are you serious?"

"I've never been more serious, Laura."

"What's happened? Did something happen here?"

"Everything happened here," Travis said. "At first I thought it was everything that I didn't want, and now I think it might be the opposite."

"And did I even appear among all these happenings, or was I just a distraction on the sidelines?"

Travis laughed suddenly, a reaction to her question, but also a reaction to so many other things.

"Laura... you were anything *but* a distraction on the sidelines. In fact, I would go so far as to say that you were the catalyst for a great deal of what I am trying to deal with right now."

Laura blushed visibly.

"I am sorry," Travis said. "I didn't mean to embarrass you."

"And I didn't mean to say what I said last night."

"About what?"

"About you pretending."

"But it was true."

"It might have been true, but sometimes it doesn't need to be said. It was hurtful."

Travis smiled. He reached out his hand toward her. She hesitated for a moment, and then she reached back.

"I want to tell you a great deal," he said, "but I can't. I have things to do, and I don't know what will happen as a result. I am in a very uncertain position, and it may go very wrong indeed. If it does go wrong, I don't want you to get caught in the crossfire. It doesn't concern you, and it doesn't need to concern you, and even though that might sound like an attempt to avoid what is happening here, it isn't."

Travis squeezed her hand reassuringly, and then he let go.

"I am going to wait for you to do whatever you have to do, Michael

Travis, and when it is done, you can explain these things to me. However, I am not as quiet and well mannered a young lady as you might believe. I am a troublemaker, and I say what I think. If you upset me, I will..." She paused for a moment and then added, "Well, just don't upset me, okay?"

"I won't."

"I'll take that as a promise, and I believe you might just be a man of your word."

"I am... I try to be."

"I am trusting you, but only for so long. I have wasted too much time expecting people to be something they're not."

"I believe I have done the same," Travis replied.

"So now I am going to work," Laura said, "and maybe I'll see you later, okay?"

"Yes," Travis said, and just reached out toward her once more as she left the kitchen.

Travis paused for a moment. He tried to focus himself on the matter at hand. He did not know what to expect from Bishop, but there was only one way to find out.

Travis dialed out. The phone rang barely twice before it was lifted at the other end. Travis asked for Bishop, and Bishop was there immediately.

"Special Agent Travis," Bishop said.

"You called, sir?"

"I did. I wanted an update on your progress. It's almost a week since you arrived. I expect you are coming to some sort of conclusion in your findings."

"I am, sir, yes."

"And so?" Bishop asked.

"I understood that you required a full and final report, not an ongoing commentary of events."

"That is correct, Travis, but I am being asked questions, and I need answers for those questions."

"I have a couple of questions first, if that is okay with you."

"You have questions?"

"Yes, I do."

"Okay, fire away."

"I was curious as to why a daily report was not required in this case," Travis said. "A daily report is the administrative backbone of any investigation. It is something we are required to provide in all instances, and there have never been any exceptions. I was wondering why this case was different."

"Because this case *is* different, Agent Travis," Bishop said.

"Can you explain that, sir?"

"I don't know that I can enlighten you a great deal more than I have already. Just like you, I receive orders. They are not to be contradicted, of course, and sometimes they are not to be questioned. That is the essence of duty, Agent Travis."

"So you don't know?"

"No, I don't know."

"Very well."

"So, your conclusions, Agent Travis?"

"I have some other questions," Travis said.

Bishop was silent for a moment, and then he said, "Okay," but his tone was measured and patient, as if Travis was now testing his patience.

"I have learned the identity of the dead man."

"You have?" Bishop said, and it was most definitely a question. There was no doubt in Travis's mind that Bishop was surprised.

"You seem surprised, sir," Travis said.

"Not at all, Travis. You have had a week. I would have expected this much at the very least."

"I have learned some other things about his identity, also his past, and they are of significant concern to me."

"Concern?"

"Yes, concern."

"And what is it that concerns you, Travis?"

"Where he came from."

"Before Seneca Falls?"

"No, sir. Before he arrived in the United States."

Again there was a moment's silence, almost as if Bishop was taking a moment to absorb, to process, to ascertain what he could or could not say in response. Either that, or Travis was feeding his own suspicion and paranoia.

"You don't want to know where he was from?" Travis asked.

"I want to read it in your final report, Travis," Bishop said.

"Did you already know where he was from, sir?"

The silence this time was longer, noticeably so.

"What are you asking me, Travis?" Bishop said.

"I am asking for a clearer explanation of the nature of this case, sir. I am asking for a better understanding of the actual purpose of this investigation. I am asking you to tell me the truth about why I was sent here to Seneca Falls."

"I think it's time you returned to Kansas City," Bishop said. "Perhaps it was a mistake to assign you to this case alone. Possibly you were not ready to manage such an investigation single-handedly."

"I have more questions, sir," Travis said.

"Enough with the questions," Bishop replied, his voice now edged with irritation. "As I said, it is time to come back to Kansas. You can make a full report of what you have learned thus far, and we can make a determination of the best—"

"Where is the body, sir?" Travis interjected.

"I am sorry?"

"Where is the body? The dead body, sir, remember?"

"I do not appreciate the tone, Travis—"

"And I do not appreciate being misled or lied to or being—"

"Okay, I have had about as much of this as I am prepared to take, Agent Travis. I expect you back here within two hours. That's no later than four thirty, you understand? And that is a direct order."

Travis did not respond.

"Agent Travis, I have just issued an order. I expect that order to be complied with on an immediate basis."

"Tell me why the body was taken away, sir," Travis said. "Tell me where they took the body of Andris Varga, the assassin, the Hungarian hired killer who belonged to Black Dog? Tell me why the body was removed from Seneca Falls without informing me. After all, am I not heading up this investigation?"

"Travis, seriously—"

"Seriously what, sir? Seriously *what*?"

"I don't think you have the slightest comprehension of what is actually happening here—"

"Oh, I think I'm starting to get a pretty good grasp of it."

"I am filing a report about this conversation right now."

"Excellent. I am pleased to hear that. And where will that report be going? To Section Chief Gale, Executive Assistant Director Warren, to Mr. Tolson, perhaps even to the director himself? Or will it be going to Sidney Gottlieb and Allen Dulles?"

"Travis, you have no idea what you are saying. You cannot even begin to appreciate the amount of trouble—"

"Oh, I think I can, sir. That's the problem. I *can* appreciate the amount of trouble, and—"

"And nothing, Agent Travis. As I said, I expect you back here within two hours. By the end of the day I will need a full and detailed report of everything that has happened in Seneca Falls, and I am sure that others besides myself will be very interested to hear what you have to say about these allegations."

"Allegations? I haven't made any allegations."

"Accusations, inferences, whatever you want to call them. You know precisely what I am referring to. Suggesting that there was some other agenda in sending you to oversee this investigation, implying that something untoward occurred regarding the removal of the body. I think you understand well enough that the Bureau has a very firm and intractable policy regarding being wholly responsible for the things we say, both verbally and in writing. That is not something I should have to remind you of, Agent Travis."

"Perhaps it is something that Mr. Hoover needs to be reminded of," Travis replied.

"How dare you—"

"How dare *you*, sir. You sent me here. You knew who Andris Varga was before I even arrived, didn't you? I think you have made it very clear by your complete inability to even answer a straight question that there is a hidden agenda here, that I have been misled, that I have been lied to—"

"Misled? Lied to? These are matters of the gravest national security, Agent Travis, and I don't think you are—"

"Are what, sir?"

Bishop fell silent.

Travis's heart was racing, his hands sweating. For a moment he felt he might lose his balance.

"I am advising you to come to Kansas immediately," Bishop said, his voice now calm and quietly insistent.

"If you want to see me in person, then you come here," Travis replied, and then he hung up.

Travis stood there in the kitchen of the McCaffrey Hotel, and though he did not fully understand the implications of what he had done, he also knew that there was nothing else he *could* have done.

He imagined that his heart would have been beating out of his chest, that he would have felt some deep and profound sense of terror, but he did not. It was not that he felt nothing, because he did, but what he felt was not what he had expected.

There was a measured calmness in his thoughts, and though he believed that the conversation he had just conducted with Tom Bishop would mark the end of his career in the Bureau, this did not trouble him.

The thing that troubled him more than anything else was that he might never learn the truth.

Simply stated, it had to end. One way or another, it had to end.

47

Travis drove back to see Doyle. He was alone in the caravan.

"They're recalling me," Travis said. "I was ordered back to Kansas. My supervisor called. I asked him some questions that he didn't actually answer. I told him I wasn't going back."

"You have thrown your toys out of the pram," Doyle replied. He looked at Travis with a crooked smile, as if the news that Travis had brought was no news at all. "So much for having a little time to think about what you're going to do, eh?"

"Where is Valeria?" Travis asked.

"I told her to take all of those who are not directly involved in this away."

"Involved in *this*. What is *this*, as you understand it?"

"Whatever it is that you think is going to happen now, the reality will be a lot worse," Doyle said. "I have to say that this was inevitable. This... this fiasco has been waiting in the wings for me for a long time."

"But not for me," Travis said. "I feel like I have just been manipulated into a situation that was not of my creating—"

"Ah, well, that's where we shall differ again, my friend."

"How so?"

"We create our own lives, Agent Travis. We are responsible for everything that happens to us, even those things that we believe are externally motivated. Thought and decision are superior to everything. The power of thought is the power of the mind, and the mind dictates the body, and the body does just as it's told. If you're in a hole, then you dug it. That's just the nature of things, like it or not."

Travis shook his head dismissively. "That makes no sense. That can't be. You're telling me that I am responsible for what's happening here?"

"Of course you are. Who else is responsible?"

"Well, the people who sent me. My supervisor, my section chief, all the people you spoke of—"

"That very well may be the case, Michael, but they chose *you* to come down here, and they chose *you* because of who you are and what they

398

believed *you* might do. So why you? That's another question yet to be answered, is it not?"

Travis was silent. He was afraid now, and there was a claustrophobic tension in his chest, his throat, even his head. The impulse was to run, but where to?

"There's nowhere to go," Doyle said. "Whatever you feel, it's right there inside you. You run away, you just take it with you."

"So what's going to happen now?" Travis asked.

"The gang of thugs that organized this crapshoot are on their way here. If they ordered you back to Kansas and you said no, then they're on their way here, no doubt about it."

"And what do we do?"

"Who is your senior?"

"The man who sent me here is my supervisor, Tom Bishop, but the section chief is a man called Frank Gale."

"Seriously? Frank is the section chief over this?" Doyle laughed dryly. "Oh, this will be fun. When we last crossed swords, he wasn't a section chief, but I am sure that the added seniority and authority have done nothing but exaggerate the sheer stupidity and arrogance of the man."

"He was the one who established the unit I work for in Kansas. The direction for the unit came directly from Executive Assistant Director Bradley—"

"Warren," Doyle interjected.

Travis should have been surprised, but he was not. He had passed the point of being surprised by anything Doyle said. "You know him as well, right?"

"Bradley Warren? Oh yes, indeed. Bradley Warren and I go back a long, long way. Warren was there right at the start, early 1950 when I came in. He and I shared many a conversation. Seems like we have a crew of old familiars on the way, eh? And when you have a moment, you should ask Oscar Haynes about what a warm, generous, and wonderful man Bradley Warren truly is."

"Well, Warren is above Gale, and he directs the unit on a day-to-day basis. Whether or not he reports directly to Hoover, I don't know."

"Oh, I am sure he does. Nothing happens in your Bureau without Mr. Hoover being fully aware of every detail."

"I know," Travis said. "I am well aware of that. That is why I am trapped. There is no one I can go to."

"And there is also another possibility you have to consider."

"Which is?"

"That the director himself might make a visit."

Now Travis was surprised, and he shook his head in disbelief.

"Don't look so shocked, Michael. If you think that such a thing is impossible, then you have underestimated the degree to which I am a threat to the man."

"But Hoover? Hoover will come here?"

"Not only that, but he might very well have already organized your unexplained disappearance."

"What?" Travis said. "What on earth are you talking about? Of course they're not coming to kill me."

"Maybe," Doyle said. "What they may very well do is give you a choice, and if you don't choose right, then they are definitely going to kill you. They might kill you right away, or they might ship you off to some psychiatric institute, and there you will become a guinea pig for more barbaric drug trials under the supervision of some outright horror of a human being like Donald Cameron or Sidney Gottlieb."

"They cannot do that!" Travis said, visibly stunned by Doyle's words. "How can they do that? What—"

"They did it to Harold Blauer, Frank Olson, our friend Andris Varga," Doyle said. "They were not the first, and they sure as hell won't be the last. I don't know who Varga really was, but I don't doubt for a second that he was in the employ of the FBI or the CIA, perhaps even both, and that was the way he paid for his American liberty. The price of freedom, eh? Nevertheless, once he'd exhausted his usefulness, they killed him and used him to get you close to us. Anyway, details are pointless now. The simple truth is that you are no longer playing by the rules. You are no longer being a good company man. I can imagine they are very interested in seeing that you don't speak to anyone about this odd murder that took place in a small town called Seneca Falls."

Doyle sat down.

Travis continued pacing. He was too agitated and disturbed to keep still.

"So this is it?" Travis said. "I am just supposed to wait here for them to come down and do whatever the hell they want to me?"

"Yes, that is what you're supposed to do," Doyle said. "Whether or not that is actually what you do is your decision."

"Well, of course I am not going to do nothing!" Travis said. "But what do I do? I can't very well just shoot whoever shows up and hope for the best."

"You could do worse than that," Doyle said.

The door opened behind Travis and he stepped back.

Valeria stood there for a moment, and then she said, "They won't go."

Doyle frowned. "Sorry?"

"I told them that people were on the way. I told the Bellancas and

Akiko and Gabor, and they said they were not going. They said that if you were in trouble, then they were in trouble too. Even John Ryan said that if there was going to be any fighting, then he was in. He said you would understand that, Irishman to Irishman."

Doyle turned to Travis. "See? Real friends? What do they say—a friend helps you move, a real friend helps you move a body?"

"So what's happening here? We're going to have a running gun battle with the FBI?"

"You have a gun, maybe. I don't have one. Don't believe in them." He turned to Valeria. "We don't have any guns, do we, sweetheart?"

"Not that I'm aware of, no."

"Sorry to disappoint you, Michael. Seems that a running gun battle with the FBI isn't in the cards today."

"Jesus Christ, I can't believe you're being so damned nonchalant about this! The FBI is on its way, Doyle. The FBI will send people here, they *will* be armed, and if what you say is true, if they really are here to take me in and do whatever they're going to do with you, then we need to do something."

"And what would you suggest, Michael? They are federal, after all. They can cross state jurisdictions with impunity. They are accountable to no one but Hoover and the president himself. What would you have us do? Run for our lives? We have been running for long enough now. And, frankly, I think it has gone beyond that, dear friend. If they have finally resorted to murder, then we have gone as far as we can go. They're not coming to negotiate, Michael. They're coming to get their own way once and for all."

"So, what are you going to do? Just quit? Just let them come? Just hold up your hands and be defeated? How can you do that? How can you even consider such a thing?"

"We're not going to hold up our hands, Michael," Doyle said. "Be defeated? I would never even consider such a thing. We're going to let them come; we're even going to make them welcome, and we will listen to what they have to say. That's the plan."

"The plan? That's not a plan!"

Valeria crossed the caravan and sat beside Doyle. She reached out and took his hand.

"Are you willing to die, Michael?" Doyle asked.

"To die? No, of course not. Of course I am not willing to die."

"Then today you will probably die," Doyle said matter-of-factly.

"Edgar, seriously, stop teasing him," Valeria said.

"He needs to face the reality of what is happening, my sweet," Doyle said. "He needs to understand and appreciate that his life is over."

"What? What the hell are you saying?" Travis exclaimed.

"I am saying that this is the end of the line for you, dear Michael Travis. How old are you?"

"How old am I? What the hell does that have to do with anything?"

"It's just a question. How old are you?"

"I am thirty-one," Travis said.

"Well, that was your hand this time around. That was your deal. What you've done is what you've done, and what you've seen is what you've seen, and here is where it all comes to a conclusion. If I were you, just to make a point, I would go out in blaze of glory. A real Western-style shoot-out between you and a few of your colleagues, if you can manage that. Better still, if you can kill Gale and Warren, then the world will owe you a tremendous debt."

"I am not going to kill Frank Gale and Bradley Warren—"

"Why the hell not, eh? They wouldn't even think twice about killing you. In fact, even if they aren't on their way right now to make sure the job is done properly, they will have assigned it to someone who won't think twice either. That I can guarantee, no question about it. Hence my question, are you willing to die?"

"I don't want to die—"

"That's not the question, Michael," Doyle interjected. "I didn't ask if you *wanted* to die. I asked if you were *willing* to die."

"No, I am not willing to die," Travis said.

"Then you need to change your mind, my friend."

"What? What the hell—"

"You have to decide that today is a perfectly acceptable day to die. That is all I am suggesting."

"I don't even understand you anymore," Travis said. "All I know for sure is that is that in about forty minutes or so, Tom Bishop and Frank Gale and whoever the hell else decides to come along for the ride, will be here with a host of agents and an arsenal of weapons. I have a Bureau-issue .38 revolver, and you have nothing."

"Oh, believe me, Agent Travis, we have something a great deal more powerful than the Bureau's arsenal of weapons," Doyle said, smiling.

"More powerful than guns?" Travis said. "What have you got? A tank?"

"Not at all," Doyle said. "What we have, my poor, dear, unfortunate, anxious, doubting Thomas, is a shadow play... a shadow play of smoke and mirrors to rival their own, I believe."

48

They had gathered in the central marquee. Akiko Mimasuya was there, as were the Bellanca brothers, Gabor Benedek, Chester Greene, Mr. Slate, Oscar Haynes, even John Ryan. Strangely enough, it was seeing that mute old man that put everything in perspective. The previous Tuesday, the fifth, and Travis had sat listening to Supervisor Bishop as he outlined the situation in Seneca Falls. Ryan had been the one to show him where the body of Andris Varga had been found. Between that moment and now, Travis's entire life had been turned back to front and upside down.

The assembly was waiting for Doyle, and Doyle came in after Travis, Valeria Mironescu beside him.

"People are coming," Doyle said. "Government people." He looked at Slate, Haynes, and Greene. "Among them will be people you know, of course, and we are going to have to deal with this."

"Finally," Haynes said. "This has been a long time coming, Edgar."

"Not long enough," Greene added. "They're never going to let it lie, are they?"

"You knew they never would, Chester. This is what they do."

"And you others... really, you don't need to be here. This doesn't concern you."

"If it concerns you, then it concerns us," Benedek said. "We already discussed it. We already told Valeria."

"And if I ask you to leave?" Doyle said.

"Ask," Benedek said. "See what good it does."

"I don't have a plan," Doyle said. "I don't know what they will do if they don't get their own way."

"They'll do what they always do," Haynes said. "They'll behave like spoiled children."

"It might get noisy."

"So let it get noisy," Slate said. "To hell with them, Edgar. We've run away for long enough. We knew they'd find us, we knew it would eventually come to this, and we either face them down or..." He shook his head resignedly. "Hell, we don't have a choice, right?"

"And what about him?" Greene asked, nodding toward Travis.

"Special Agent Michael Travis," Doyle said, taking a step to his right and putting his hand on Travis's shoulder, "has a Bureau-issued .38 revolver about his person, and I, for one, am hoping that he shoots both Frank Gale and Bradley Warren."

"Gale and Warren are coming?" Slate asked.

"Edgar told me that some of you knew them," Travis said.

"We know them very well," Haynes replied. "Too well, you could say."

"If I am not misjudging the situation, I believe that Mr. Hoover may be gracing us with a visit as well."

Haynes smiled. There was something altogether mischievous in his expression.

"And we use what we know to our advantage," Doyle said. "What we know is the only weapon we have. And everyone else... really, I do appreciate your support and loyalty, but for this I need you to make yourselves invisible, at least for a while. Stay here, of course, but out of sight. If it gets noisy, then come running, but I don't believe it will."

"Stay with me," Valeria said to the assembly. "Let's go to the caravans, and we'll wait there."

"That's what I want," Doyle said. "Really."

Benedek was the first to move, and then Akiko, the Bellancas and Ryan followed him without protest.

Valeria took Doyle's hands, kissed him, then put her arms around him. She whispered something that only he could hear, and he said, "I promise. Absolutely, I promise."

She didn't say anything else. She did not look at Travis, nor back at Doyle as she escorted Benedek and the others away from the marquee.

Travis looked at the men in front of him, just four of them, and he wondered how the hell they were going to face down the might of the Federal Bureau of Investigation.

"Do not worry about what you don't yet know," Greene said.

"I am terrified," Travis said.

"Of what they will do to you?" Slate asked.

"Yes, of course."

Slate smiled. "Hell, man, the worst they can do is kill you, and that isn't so bad. You get a chance to start all over, or so I've heard."

"I don't want to die," Travis said.

"He's in love," Doyle explained.

"I am not in love," Travis countered.

"Of course you're not, my friend," Doyle replied, laughing. "And I'm not a crazy old Irishman."

"With the McCaffrey girl, right?" Haynes asked, his question rhetorical. "The cop's sister."

"I know the one," Slate added. "Good choice, Agent Travis."

"You people—" Travis started.

"We're teasing you," Doyle said. "You show them how scared you are, they'll know. They'll take advantage of that. That's what I've been trying to tell you. You think you're so implacable, so impregnable, but you walk around with whatever emotion you're trying to hide painted all over your face. If you're not careful, that'll be your undoing, Michael Travis. Don't ever take up poker. I mean that."

"So what do we do?" Travis asked. "That's a real question now, okay? That's not just me passing the time of day. I want to know what we're actually going to do when a fleet of sedans turns up here and a host of suits get out of them."

"We're going to meet them right here," Doyle said. "We're going to listen to what they have to say, and then we're going to make a judgment call."

"I think we know what they're going to say," Greene said.

"People can change, Chester," Doyle replied, the sarcasm obvious in his tone.

"You know as well as I that these people don't change, Edgar."

"Michael did," Slate said.

"But he was here," Haynes interjected.

"Granted," Doyle replied. "Okay, so maybe they won't have changed. Hell, I'm just stalling. You keep asking me what to do, and to be honest, I don't know. I don't have all the answers all the time."

"Really?" Slate asked. "Hell, Doyle, you should have told me that right from the get-go. I'd have run away with Barnum and Bailey."

"They wouldn't have had you, you crazy son of a bitch."

"Okay, enough!" Travis said. "That's it. This is utter madness. I give up. Just let them come and do whatever the hell they like. Trying to get anything sensible out of you people is... well, it's just impossible."

"You give up?" Doyle asked.

"They can bring whatever the hell they like. They can do whatever the hell they like. I don't care anymore."

"Well, that's more like it," Doyle said. "That kind of attitude is a lot better than whatever you had going on before."

"You are unbelievable," Travis said. He moved left and sat down at one of the tables where they had previously eaten.

"Oscar... why don't you go get a bottle of wine, eh?" Doyle asked. "Let's have a glass of wine before the shit hits the fan."

"Good plan," Haynes said, and headed out of the tent.

"You'll join us, of course, Michael," Doyle said, taking a seat beside Travis.

"Sure. What the hell. Let's get drunk. How about that for a plan? Seems like the best idea I've heard so far."

"Don't be facetious, Agent Travis," Slate said. "It doesn't suit you."

Travis looked at Slate. Slate smiled. Then Travis started laughing, and he couldn't stop himself. He laughed until Doyle had to slap him on the back to help him catch his breath.

"Jesus, what was the joke?" Haynes asked as he approached the table bearing wine and glasses.

"You had to be there," Doyle explained.

"They are just goading me further," Travis said.

"Well, someone has to," Haynes replied. "You stay that serious for too long you... well, you'd just die of loneliness, right?"

"So I am starting to believe," Travis said.

Haynes opened the wine, poured some for each of them.

"To what shall we drink?" Slate asked Doyle.

Doyle was quiet for a moment, and then he raised his glass.

"To J. Edgar, to Mr. Dulles, to Gottlieb and Cameron and the whole stinking crew of them. May they burn in hell forever."

Slate raised his glass, Greene, Haynes, then Travis, and in unison they echoed, "May they burn in hell forever."

49

It was Larry Youngman who first saw the convoy of cars making their way along the farm road to the west of the Seneca Falls town limits. There were at least three or four dark sedans and a black Lincoln Continental.

Larry had been out to see a friend in Marion, up near the edge of the lake, and he returned southward along 7 and then cut back northeast on I-35. The cars he saw must have come in from Kansas, for that's the only other way that 35 went. He was almost home when he saw them, and they sped by as if on some urgent mission. They were gone by the time he reached the slip road that would take him down to his own place.

It was midafternoon, and yet the sky already held the promise of evening. It was cooler than the previous day, and Larry stood on the porch and looked back toward the highway. There was a sense of foreboding in his thoughts, though he could not have explained why. It was just a feeling, that was all, and he did not like it.

As he turned back toward the front door, he heard someone calling his name. He glanced in the direction from which the sound had come, but he knew before he looked that it had been nothing more than his imagination. And as he entered the dark hallway, he thought of what had happened at the carnival, what he'd learned of his son, the fate of the man who'd killed him. He *knew* that the little guy had been bang on the money. There was no doubt in his mind. It had given him a sense of peace, no question there, but at the same time it had scared him a little. It had opened a door, and through that door he had seen something that made him aware of all he had missed. How he could have done with such information twenty years ago, even fifteen, ten. He had carried that weight for two decades, that mystery like a second shadow, and now it was over.

The thing that had struck him after his conversation in the Tavern was that his own boy, eleven years old when he died, would now have been pretty much the same age as the man asking the questions. Special Agent Michael Travis, Federal Bureau of Investigation. Hell of an intense young man, Larry reckoned, and had there been a couple of men like that on the case way back when, then maybe the truth of what had happened to

David would have been discovered so much earlier. The guy who did it killed himself. He had been haunted by guilt, and he had done himself in. Was that any real form of justice? Larry Youngman didn't believe so. He would have wanted to look that man in the eye and tell him what he thought of him. Accidents happen, sure. People make mistakes. But there is a hell of a difference between recognizing it and taking responsibility for it, as opposed to running like a frightened rabbit and never telling a living soul. *You killed my boy.* That's what he would have said. *You killed my boy, mister, and I want you to know that when you did that, you killed a little piece of me as well. Hell, you killed a big piece. You tore out my heart and threw it on the ground, you dumb son of a bitch. Then you done stomped on it with the biggest boots you could find. That's what you done.*

But Larry Youngman never did see the man who had left his child for dead. No, that man had found himself some special hot place in hell before Larry even knew that he'd put a gun in his mouth and pulled the trigger.

Larry paused. He was troubled. He shook his head as if trying to ease an insistent ringing in his ears, and then he took a deep breath.

Something had happened here, and now something else was happening, and though he didn't have the faintest clue what it might be, he still knew that it didn't sit well with him.

All he knew in that moment is that he felt impelled to go down there. That's the only way he could describe how he felt. He needed to go down there—not to ask questions of Chester Greene, not to try to find out anything further regarding the man who had killed David. It was nothing like that. He just needed to go, and that was that.

Larry Youngman hadn't even taken his coat off. He simply turned and walked back out of the house, pausing momentarily to lift his rifle down from the gun rack in the hallway. Why he took it, again he did not know, but he felt he might need it. He also felt that he would take his time to get there, make a deal of it, use the scenic route, and thus when he eased up the hand brake and pulled away up the drive, he figured on getting out to the carnival after a good while. He believed he would know when to show up, and had you asked him why he believed this, he would have looked at you with an expression so vacant he might not have been there at all.

The second person to see that line of sedans and Lincolns was Danny McCaffrey. He was up on the second floor of the hotel, and for some reason had suddenly felt the need to look out of the window at the far end of the hallway. He caught sight of the third and fourth cars as they turned at the end of the road and headed out toward the fields. He knew where they were going, but he—just like Larry Youngman—did not know why. For some reason, he thought of Laura and the few awkward words he had shared with Michael Travis. He liked Travis, but he did not like what he represented. More accurately, he knew that Laura liked Michael Travis, and though he would never have attempted to dissuade her from pursuing what she believed was right for herself, he did not care much for the future she would find with such a man. From his own limited understanding, he appreciated that the lifestyle of a federal agent was in no way comparable to the lifestyle of a Sheriff's Department deputy like his brother, Lester. From what he had seen in Travis, the man had been subsumed by the job. Such a thing was not in fact a job, but a vocation, akin perhaps to joining some strict religious order or taking a vow of silence. Danny did not believe that Laura—free-spirited as she was—would find much happiness there. But what could he say? What could he do? There was no governing the heart, and there certainly was no governing the heart of a woman. Knowing Laura, how impulsive she could sometimes be, Danny reckoned that if Travis showed up on her doorstep and told her to run away with him, she probably would. She'd certainly got it into her mind that there was something there. The man was under her skin, and Danny McCaffrey didn't care much for the potential trouble of such an infatuation.

Danny turned away from the window and went back to the business of preparing vacated rooms for new guests. For some strange reason he believed that something was about to happen that would take any such decisions and considerations out of Laura's control, perhaps even out of Michael Travis's. He believed this without any reason to believe it, and it unsettled him. He tried to push it out of his mind, but it would not go. It nagged at him, and he walked back to the window and looked down into the street. He did not see Travis's car, but that was no surprise. As the days had elapsed, he had seen less and less of Travis. He did see Larry Youngman drive past, however, and he instinctively raised his hand, even though he knew that Larry could never have seen him there at the window.

Larry's car passed silently, and then the street was empty once more.

For some reason Danny thought of old Monty Finch, how he'd died after he was robbed by someone with a pillowcase over their head. Laura had said it was someone that Monty knew, even someone related. And it had been. The darnedest thing. Creepy, to be honest. That kind of thing had never sat well with Danny, though Laura seemed ever more fascinated, especially now that these carnival people had rocked up in Seneca Falls. A good deal of things had been stirred up, and folks couldn't stop talking about them.

Danny hesitated at the top of the stairwell. He looked back toward the window, thought once more of Larry's pickup passing in the street below, and he recalled what had happened that first night of the carnival, how that dwarf guy had told Larry about his kid. He remembered that Thin Man as well, Oscar something-or-other, and how he'd seen him twice now, and there was something about that man that made Danny feel like he was just as transparent as glass. In fact, all of them made him feel that way, as if they could see right through him. It was a scary feeling, but also strangely liberating, as if to have no secrets at all would give you some kind of freedom. People spent so much time worrying about what other people thought of them, even people they didn't know, and if everyone knew everything, then there'd be nothing left to hide.

Danny shook his head. He was thinking foolish things. Why was he thinking like this? These were the kind of thoughts he'd expect from Laura.

Danny figured it was time to talk to Michael Travis, but this time a real conversation, a real man-to-man discussion about what was going on, what was likely to go on, and bring it to a head, one way or the other.

That's what Danny McCaffrey told himself as he searched for his car keys and found his jacket.

In truth, he just felt compelled to go down there—not even to see Travis, not even to see the dwarf who had so fascinated Laura. Not even to see that human skeleton, Oscar whatever-his-name-was, and remind himself of how transparent the man made him feel. It was not one specific thing, but simply a sense of urgency that overtook his thoughts. Danny just felt that he *had* to go. And so he went, but he drove around the back way, the long route, and he took his time. For some reason he didn't want to arrive too soon.

Too soon for what?

Danny shook his head, as if to flick his bangs out of his eyes, and he caught sight of his own reflection in the rearview. He looked anxious. That's the only way he could describe what he saw. Anxious, even a little afraid, and for this he had no explanation at all.

The last person to see that line of cars as they finally crossed the far side of town and made their way down toward the tree line that defined Seneca's limits was Chas Rourke.

Rourke had been sheriff of Seneca Falls for four years, and never during those past four years had he felt less like the sheriff than he had during the previous week. Ever since the arrival of the federal agent, he'd felt his position as the local law enforcement representative had not only been compromised, but overtaken. He had cooperated as requested, but had found that cooperation did not mean *cooperation* in the usual sense. It had been more like *Stay out of it* or *Don't get in the way*. Since he'd first taken Travis down to see the body, Travis had barely shared a word with him. Save for that conversation about what had happened at the carnival. The thing about Bobby Alberstein. It had been obvious that Travis hadn't believed a word of what he'd said, but that didn't concern Rourke. What others thought was what others thought, and more often than not, anything you said merely confirmed what they had already decided.

So, whether or not Special Agent Michael Travis of the Kansas City branch of the Federal Bureau of Investigation considered Chas Rourke a nut or not was of no great concern to Rourke. He had carried the ghost of what he had done to Bobby Alberstein for a good many years, and it had been like a drag anchor on his heart. Kids could be vicious, downright evil in some instances, and that was not him. He was not a bad person, had never been a *bad* person, but that didn't mean he hadn't done a few bad things. Like that time with Mary-Ellen Faber at the drive-in outside of Eureka and how what he thought she was interested in and what she was *actually* interested in were two very different things altogether. Even now, the better part of twenty-five years on, he still felt the color rise in his cheeks when he considered that night. No, there were bad people, and there were good people who sometimes did bad things. Between the two there was a whole world of difference.

Like the guy who ran down Larry Youngman's kid. Okay, he did a bad thing, a seriously bad thing, but the mere fact that his own guilt had driven him to suicide said a great deal about his inherent nature. Truly evil people, irrespective of whether or not Chas Rourke had ever met one in person or not, wouldn't have thought twice about killing someone. He'd seen things on the TV, read stuff in magazines. There were folks who didn't seem to possess an atom of goodness in them, and for a man to feel sufficient a burden of guilt to take his own life told Rourke that there must have been some good in him despite what he did.

Like these carnival folks. Okay, so there'd been a good helping of noise and fuss when they turned up, but in reality they'd been no trouble at all. Okay, so someone had died, but something told him that those folks didn't have anything to do with it. Hell, if they had been real suspects in a homicide, Mr. Six Foot of Starch Travis would never have permitted them to open up the carnival again. And Jack Farley had told him that the corpse had been taken away by federal people the very day after Travis's arrival. No, the carnival people—freak show though they might be—did not seem to him to be bad people at all. He had made no effort to really try to understand what they'd done or how they'd done it, but they'd managed to not only make people feel good about them, but about themselves as well. Larry Youngman, laconic though he was, was visibly happier. He really did look like a man who'd gotten a load off. And himself? Knowing what he now knew about Bobby Alberstein (and yes, he had been tempted to make a call, to even drive out there and see the man and shake his hand and offer to buy him a drink, but in the long run of things had decided that it would be better to just let it be), even he had felt lighter. Like he'd been carrying around a suitcase full of bricks and someone had told him it was okay to leave it behind.

Something important had happened here, and it seemed that something was still happening. The convoy of dark sedans he'd seen was about as out of place driving through Seneca Falls as the Carnival Diablo had been when it first rocked up.

This was his town. He was the sheriff, after all. If something was awry, if some kind of law enforcement business required attention, then it would be him doing the attending. Federal these people may be, but that did not give them license to depose him and negate his authority. This was the United States of America. There was a Constitution, there was a Bill of Rights, and no one had the authority to overturn such things. Not even the FBI.

And so Sheriff Chas Rourke, determined to know what was going on in his town, put on his hat and went to find Lester McCaffrey. It would be a little while before he located him, out there in the diner where his sister worked, taking some kind of unauthorized break, it seemed.

" 'S up, Sheriff?" Lester asked him, wiping mayonnaise from his chin with a napkin.

"Off down to see the carnival folks. Want you to come with me."

"Some trouble down there?" Laura asked.

"Laura... I need you to stay here. I'm taking your brother 'cause he's my deputy, but there ain't no such thing as deputy's sister now, is there? Not officially speaking."

"I'm just interested, Sheriff, that's all," Laura said.

"Well, I have no doubt that Lester will give you the full lowdown as and when there is any lowdown to give, right, Lester?"

Lester seemed offended. "What d'you mean, Sheriff? I don't go discussing police business with my sister."

"And you're here just interrogating that chicken salad sandwich about a bank robbery and that there glass of root beer as an accomplice. Get your hat, Lester. We're taking a drive."

Lester looked at his sister. Laura shook her head and just took the plate and the glass from the table and disappeared in back.

"What's going on?" Lester asked as he slid out from the booth seat and set his gun belt right.

"Could be something, could be nothing," Rourke said. "Just seen a convoy of cars head down toward the carnival fields, and we're going to go look see what they're up to."

"Good enough," Lester said, and followed Sheriff Rourke out of the diner and across the street.

Laura came from the kitchen and stood watching as both the sheriff's car and that of her brother pulled away from the opposite curb and headed for the highway.

She knew that Michael Travis was not at the hotel. She had been over there a little while earlier helping Danny clean up, and Travis's car had not been evident in its absence.

Laura did not herself drive, and so she called Danny. There was no answer on the private apartment phone, nor the phone in the kitchen. Even the desk phone in reception rang out before being answered.

So she called Jack Farley at the morgue, told him that something was happening and that she wanted to go down to where the carnival was pitched. It took a while for him to understand what she was saying, but he got it, said he was more than happy to help, would pick her up from the diner in fifteen minutes. He did as he had promised, and Laura McCaffrey was outside the diner with her overcoat and her purse as he pulled up.

Farley shoved Wolf back into the rear seat, and Laura got in.

"What's going on, then?" Farley asked her.

"I have no idea, Jack," she told him, "but I can't help feeling the way I did when old Monty Finch got robbed."

Jack didn't say another word. He tugged the car into gear, turned back the way he'd come, and headed out the same way as Rourke and Laura's brother had done just a little while before.

50

I t was immediately evident that neither Tom Bishop nor Frank Gale were strangers to those gathered in the tent.

Behind them came Executive Assistant Director Bradley Warren, a man Travis had met on no more than three or four occasions, and as soon as he stepped from the rear of one of the sedans on the road beside the field, Travis heard Doyle say, "Oh, they have indeed sent the big guns."

Behind Bishop, Gale, and Warren were Raymond Carvahlo, Paul Erickson, and two or three others whom Travis did not recognize. Travis could only assume that they were Warren's escort unit. To be here so quickly, Warren must already have been in Kansas.

Gale approached Doyle, and on his face was an expression of condescension.

"So, what are you calling yourself now, you spineless son of a bitch?"

Doyle laughed softly. "You know very well, Frank."

"Ironic choice of name, don't you think? Edgar?"

"I thought it was fitting."

Gale paused for a moment, looking Doyle up and down. "You're looking well, I must say."

"Sad to say I cannot return the compliment, Frank. You don't look too good at all. You've put on a good few years and more than a good few pounds. Perhaps the constant diet of lies and bullshit is finally catching up with you."

Gale smiled sarcastically and then turned to the assembled gathering. He scanned the faces before him, and then he went back to Doyle.

"Time for you to take responsibility for your past," Gale said. He glanced back at Warren, and Warren nodded.

"He came," Doyle said matter-of-factly. "I am impressed. What did he do? Fly from D.C.?"

"Neither here nor there, Doyle," Gale said. "You go on back and deal with him. Personally, I am hoping that I never have to see your face again."

"Reciprocated," Doyle said, and started toward the Lincoln.

Travis stood there watching, and though Doyle had intimated that Hoover himself might come, he found it almost impossible to believe.

"Special Agent Travis," Gale said. "I hear word you've been causing a little flurry of excitement down here."

Travis continued to watch Doyle until Doyle had climbed into the rear of the car. The door slammed with authority, and he looked back at Gale.

"I have questions, sir, and I have not been able to obtain any satisfactory answers," Travis said. He felt uneasy. Now he felt the sense of urgency and fear that he'd anticipated when speaking to Bishop on the phone. A delayed reaction, perhaps.

Warren and Bishop stood back a little way behind Gale, their expressions somewhere between dismay and superiority.

"Is that what you believe you're here for, son?" Gale said. "To obtain satisfactory answers?"

"I believe I am here for the reason I was assigned to this case," Travis said.

"Which was?"

"To determine who was responsible for the death of Andris Varga."

Gale smiled, glanced back at Warren.

"You are not denying that the dead man was Andris Varga?" Travis asked.

Gale frowned. "Deny? What do you mean, deny? You are interrogating *me* now, Agent Travis?"

"I am asking a question, sir, that is all. As a result of my investigation, I learned the identity of the dead man. I am asking whether or not his identity was known to the Bureau before I was even sent here."

"Bishop told me about this allegation . . . this thing you had somehow managed to convince yourself of."

"So you're telling me that you did not know that this man's name was Andris Varga, that you were unaware of the fact that he belonged to this Fekete Kutya organization?"

"This what organization? Fek-what?" Gale asked.

"He is lying," Chester Greene said. He stepped forward and stood to Travis's right.

"Chester Greene," Gale said. "The one and only."

"You are lying, Gale," Oscar Haynes added. "It is obvious you are lying."

"Haynes," Gale said. "How are you, Oscar? Still telling bullshit stories about John Dillinger?" Gale turned to look at Mr. Slate. "And you," he added. "The one and only Harold Lamb, the whore's son."

"You know them all," Travis said, and in that moment he realized that

415

what he had most feared, and yet what he had known for so long, was true.

Warren stepped forward. "I am Executive Assistant Director Bradley Warren."

"I know who you are, sir."

"I am issuing you a direct order now, Special Agent Travis. I am ordering you to step away from these people, to walk to the car over there, to sit in the back and wait for me."

"I cannot do that, sir."

"And why can't you do that, Agent Travis?"

"Because I believe that there is going to be a further attempt to fabricate evidence, to perpetrate a miscarriage of justice—"

Warren looked back at Gale, and for a moment it seemed as though they were sharing some private joke at everyone else's expense.

"Listen to yourself," Warren said. "Do you know how ridiculous you sound? I am the executive assistant director, you are a special agent—"

"Senior special agent," Travis interjected.

There was a flash of irritation in Warren's expression.

"Do as you're ordered, Travis," Gale said, stepping forward to stand beside Warren.

"Stay right where you are," Slate said, taking a step forward to stand beside Travis.

Haynes and Greene moved forward also, the two of them behind Slate and Travis.

In echo, Carvahlo, Erickson, and Bishop came up behind Warren and Gale.

Travis indicated Carvahlo with a nod of his head. "You took the body out of here on Wednesday, you and someone else. Were you with him, Erickson?"

Neither Carvahlo nor Erickson responded.

"Some people know when to keep their mouths shut," Bishop said.

Gale glanced back at Bishop. "Enough from you," he said. "Had you run this as closely as you were instructed, we would not be in this farcical situation right now. I have a great deal more important things to be doing than—"

"Than housework?" Travis asked. "Isn't that what this is? A little extracurricular housework?"

"You have no idea—" Gale started.

"Andris Varga," Travis replied. "Fekete Kutya, arrested in New York City in June of 1954. What he's been doing since then is anybody's guess. Maybe just taking care of those odd bits of housework that you are too superior to dirty your hands with, eh?"

Gale glared at Travis.

Travis felt a sense of vindicated indignation rising in his chest. He was waiting for a denial, and that was all. A clear, uncomplicated, unequivocal statement of denial regarding any aspect of this, and—as of that moment—no such denial had been forthcoming.

"And what about Frank Olson?" Travis asked. "And Harold Blauer—"

"Enough!" Warren said. "You say one more word and I will—"

"What, sir? What will you do?"

"You, my poor, misguided, deluded friend," Gale said, "have ended what could have been a very illustrious and rewarding career. You listened to what Doyle told you? You *believed* what he told you? The bullshit, the conspiracy, the lunatic ravings of a paranoid madman? Oh come on. Seriously, I cannot believe that you have been taken in by these sideshow freaks."

"What about Joseph Pruitt?" Slate interjected. "He was another sideshow freak, wasn't he? Or was he different? What about Kathleen Caldwell, Timothy Reynolds, Otto—"

"I said that's enough!" Warren barked. His face had reddened considerably, and he stared at Slate with an expression of such intense hatred that Travis believed he might actually have backed him off.

But Slate merely smiled knowingly and said, "The roll call goes on, my friend, and you know it does."

"Whatever names you mentioned are nothing to do with me," Warren said.

"Still lying," Chester Greene said. "And not too good at it, either."

Warren turned on Greene. "You shut your fucking mouth, you fucking abomination!"

Slate raised his right hand, and he started to count off the names on his seven fingers. "Joseph Pruitt, Kathleen Caldwell, Timothy Reynolds, Otto den Braber, Lawrence Carson, Linda Glatt—"

Gale stepped past Warren, and before Warren could even say a word, there was a gun pointed directly at Slate's head. The muzzle was mere inches from his eyes.

"What the hell are you doing?" Warren shouted. "Jesus Christ, Frank. Put the fucking gun away!"

"Just give me the word, sir," Gale said. "Just give me the word and I'll kill the son of a bitch."

"Gale! Put the gun away!" Warren commanded. "Put the goddamned gun away right fucking now!"

"He can't," Slate said. "He is demonstrating his authority, just exactly as he does with ... what's his name now, Frank? That young and handsome

417

university lecturer you are sleeping with? The secret little life that you so desperately hide from your wife, your children, your fellow agents—"

"You... you..." Gale started, his eyes wide, his face a seething mask of absolute disgust. He raised his hand and brought the gun down across Slate's nose. There was an audible crack as the bone gave, and Slate dropped to his knees, his hands clutching his face, blood pouring from between his fingers.

Warren grabbed Gale's arm and twisted it hard behind Gale's back. Gale dropped the gun and Warren kicked it to Bishop. Bishop picked up the gun and put it in the pocket of his overcoat.

"Carvahlo, Erickson, take Gale to the car. Lock him in. Get an agent to stay with him and come directly back."

Carvahlo and Erickson did as they were ordered, and Gale was hurried away to one of the sedans.

Travis helped Slate to his feet, and then Haynes and Greene walked him to a bench where they sat him down.

"Fetch Valeria and Akiko," Travis said. "Have them come and take care of Mr. Slate."

"Oh, Valeria is still here, is she?" Warren asked. "I always wondered what it was she saw in Doyle. But then, perhaps gypsy whores are not renowned for their taste in men."

"If you are looking to provoke me into some sort of violence, Mr. Warren, then think again. I am not going to give you the slightest justification for shooting me."

"Oh, I don't need to shoot you, Agent Travis. I have every single one of you sewn up in a neat conspiracy to pervert the course of justice, withholding evidence, accomplice to murder, and I am sure we can throw in a couple of extradition warrants for that Romanian bitch and that Japanese—"

Warren stopped talking as Valeria and Akiko appeared through the doorway of the marquee. They hurried to where Mr. Slate sat nursing his shattered nose, and without a word they escorted him out of the marquee and away toward the caravans.

Carvahlo and Erickson returned, and they stood with Warren and Bishop.

Travis took a step forward, Greene and Haynes to his left. Travis's hand was in his jacket pocket, his fingers around the grip of his .38. He felt things he had never felt before, so far beyond even the mental and emotional disorientation that had assaulted his senses during the previous days. He was certain now. Neither Gale nor Warren had denied a thing. The people surrounding him were known to the Bureau—by name, by immediate history—and the tone and attitude with which Warren and

Gale had confronted Travis said all that needed to be said. They wanted him to step down, to color inside the lines, to be a good company man and help them make this disappear. But this was not why he was here, not now, and he was more than willing to do whatever was required to ensure the safety and survival of Doyle and the others. His loyalties lay with Doyle and Greene, with Haynes and Valeria, and somehow, some way, these loyalties seemed now constant with his own. What had been discovered in Seneca Falls was not what he had expected.

"You are finished, Agent Travis," Warren said. "You do understand that, don't you?"

Travis looked back at the man, the arrogant expression, the self-satisfied smugness of everything he believed he was, and he shook his head. "I understand that I have been deceived, Mr. Warren."

"What do you want me to say, Travis? You want me to tell you the truth, the real truth? You want me to explain every decision, every action, every considered consequence and implication of all that we do? We are responsible for the safety of a nation. We are responsible for the well-being and security of every man, woman and child in the United States of America. That is our charge, Agent Travis. That is the burden we carry, and there are very few people whose shoulders are broad enough and strong enough to bear such a burden."

"You believe your own propaganda, don't you?" Haynes said.

"You can shut your fucking mouth, Haynes," Warren said. "This is between me and Agent Travis. This has nothing to do with you. You are nothing but a distraction."

"This has everything to do with these people," Travis said. "You wanted them charged and convicted of crimes that not only did they know nothing about, but crimes that you sanctioned—"

"You think you can stop us, Travis? You honestly believe that you can stop us? One man?"

"I am not one man," Travis said.

"Oh, you think these lunatics will stand by you when we put them in jail, when we send that Romanian bitch back where she came from, when we put Benedek on a boat and send him home to Budapest?"

"You know them all, don't you?" Travis said. "You know more about these people than I do. This is all some kind of bullshit game to you, isn't it? These aren't real people, and these aren't real lives, are they?"

"They are not *American* lives, Travis! You made an oath, remember? I do solemnly swear that I will support and defend the Constitution of the United States against all enemies, foreign and domestic, that I will bear true faith and allegiance to the same, that I take this obligation freely, without any mental reservation or purpose of evasion, and that I will well

419

and faithfully discharge the duties of the office on which I am about to enter. So help me God. You remember that, Travis, or is your memory as compromised as your loyalties?"

"There is nothing wrong with my memory, Mr. Warren, nor my loyalties. There is a great deal wrong with your loyalties, however—"

"I am fulfilling my duty, Agent Travis—"

"By killing people, by planting evidence to incriminate others, by perverting every single basic—"

"I am doing what I have been ordered to do! I am following orders, and those orders have been issued from the highest offices and for the greatest good. This is not a personal issue, Travis. This is an issue for all of us, for the nation, for the American people!"

"It was personal for Andris Varga," Travis said.

"Enough about Varga!" Warren said. "You think anyone really gives a single solitary damn about Varga? He was nothing. He was nobody. He did what he was asked to do, and that was that."

"Did he kill for you, Mr. Warren?" Travis asked. "Is that what you had him do? Did he murder people for you, people who got in the way of the greater good?"

Warren turned suddenly to Bishop and Erickson. "Take him. Arrest him. Do it now!"

Bishop stepped forward.

Travis withdrew his hand from his pocket and pointed his .38 directly at Warren. He expected then to feel the spirit of his father within him, as he intended to unleash violence, as he intended to shoot Bradley Warren right where he stood.

Travis waited for the rush of blood, the way it would fill his mind with fears of what he could be capable of... but there was nothing. He felt merely distant and calculating, unafraid of what would now happen.

Warren's expression relaxed, as if he now had Travis precisely where he wanted.

"He is threatening me with a firearm," Warren said. "I will count to three, and if he has not lowered his gun, then you shoot him dead right where he stands."

"I don't reckon anyone's gonna be shootin' anyone."

Travis turned at the sound of a familiar voice. It was Sheriff Rourke, in his hands a rifle, beside him Lester McCaffrey, also armed, and behind them came Larry Youngman, Jack Farley, Laura McCaffrey, and her brother Danny.

"Sheriff, stand down," Warren said. "This is federal business. This is no longer your jurisdiction."

"Oh, I think it is my jurisdiction, especially when it comes to the law,

Mr. Warren. I heard pretty much everything you've said, and I have to say that I am on Mr. Travis's side of the fight, and that side suits me just fine." Rourke raised his rifle at waist height and aimed it toward Bishop and Erickson. "If you fine gentlemen would just back away a step or two, that would be very much appreciated."

"You will do no such thing!" Warren said to Bishop and Erickson.

The agents near the cars started forward, now uncertain as to what was expected of them.

"Oh, we can have ourselves a Mexican standoff right here and now," Rourke said, "but I got a rifle here, and my deputy is a damned fine shot with his sidearm, and then we got Larry with a thirty-ought and he can take the wing off of a bird at three hundred feet. Jack Farley's got himself a pump action, and though I am sure he doesn't even have a license for it, that won't stop him using it. You wanna dance, then we'll dance with you, sir, but I reckon you've got about zero chance of getting out of here without some holes in you."

"You are dealing with the Federal Bureau of Investigation—"

"Sounds to me like I'm dealing with a handful of crooks and liars, whether they be federal or otherwise. All I know is that there was a dead body here, and then all of a sudden there was no dead body anymore. Maybe you had every right to take it away. I'm not questioning those rights, but I sure as hell know that there was no warrant, there was no court order, and unless you are prepared to give us our dead body back, then it seems to me you got yourselves quite a problem."

"Federal authority supersedes any authority you might have, Sheriff Rourke."

Rourke smiled. "Oh, I am flattered that you bothered to find out my name before you got here, sir. That's much appreciated. Wouldn't like to think I was just a nobody in the grand scheme of things you got all worked out here." Rourke tightened his grip on the gun. He moved forward and nodded in acknowledgment as he passed Travis. "And as far as federal superseding local, I have no argument with that, sir, but I am sure that nowhere in your federal books does it say that your authority supersedes the law itself."

"You know nothing—"

"I reckon I know enough, sir."

"And what are you going to do, eh Sheriff? Arrest us?"

"I may just do that, sir."

"And for what?"

"Some of those things that Mr. Travis here has been talking about. That would be a good start. Murder more than likely. If not directly, then at least accomplice. Conspiracy to obstruct justice, withholding evidence, illegal and unauthorized removal of evidence, grievous assault against Mr. Slate, and then we'll add a few charges of disturbing the peace for good measure, just so you understand that your coming down here and upsetting my town is not appreciated."

"You are an idiot, Sheriff."

"I may be an idiot, sir, but I am still sheriff and I still have a gun, and unless you back off right now, I will put a hole through your chest, so help me God."

Warren looked at Greene, at Haynes, then at Travis.

"Time to leave us be," Travis said. "Walk away, take Gale and Bishop and all the rest of them with you. File whatever report you want to file, but leave us be. This is over, Mr. Warren, and if you ever consider pursuing this, the entire town of Seneca Falls will stand and give evidence against you. You know what you did; we know it too, and there are just too many people now, too many voices, and we are not going to be silent."

"This does not end here, Travis. You are no longer a federal agent. I have the authority to strip you of your rank, your position, your job. It's all finished for you, you understand?"

"We will have to agree to differ, Mr. Warren. As far as I am concerned, it has only just begun. And I am sure that Mr. Hoover and Mr. Doyle are—"

As if cued, the rear door of the Continental opened and Warren turned to see Doyle step out. His expression was implacable. He merely nodded at Warren.

Warren hesitated for a second, no more, and then he hurried back to the car.

Doyle joined Travis and the others. He acknowledged Rourke and Lester McCaffrey, Larry Youngman and Jack Farley.

"What's happening?" Travis asked.

Doyle smiled and shook his head.

Warren leaned in through the rear door of the vehicle. He was there no more than a minute, and then he returned to where Doyle and Travis stood with the others.

Warren glared at Doyle, at Travis, and then he held out his hand.

"Your ID, Mr. Travis," he said calmly. "And your sidearm."

Travis hesitated.

"Give them to him," Doyle said.

Travis withdrew his wallet and handed it over. He also gave Warren his gun.

Warren paused for just a second, and then he told Bishop, Carvahlo, and Erickson that they were leaving.

Bishop looked as if there was something he wished to say, but Warren raised his hand to silence him.

"Now, Agent Bishop," he said matter-of-factly.

Warren looked at Doyle once more, and there was such resentment and hostility in that expression it was almost tangible.

"Always a pleasure, Bradley," Doyle said. "Safe journey, eh?"

Warren sneered and then headed to the car.

The assembled crowd in the marquee—Travis, Doyle, Oscar Haynes and Chester Greene, Sheriff Rourke, both Laura and Lester McCaffrey, Larry Youngman and Jack Farley—stood there in silence until the convoy of vehicles had disappeared along the highway.

Shortly thereafter, the sound of engines faded into silence, and still no one said a word.

51

Valeria appeared, in her hands a blood-soaked cloth.

"How is Slate?" Doyle asked.

"He'll live."

"Good," he said.

"And they have gone?"

"Yes, they've gone," Doyle replied, a sardonic smile on his face.

"Are we good?"

"We're good."

She leaned up and kissed him, and then she turned to the assembled crowd and told them that they were all leaving, that Doyle needed to speak to Travis alone.

No one said a word to Travis. Some did not even look at him, save Laura, who approached him, touched his hand, and then left quickly with her brother.

In less than a minute, the marquee was empty but for Travis and Doyle. Doyle crossed to one of the tables and sat down.

Travis took a seat facing him. "That was Hoover," he said.

Doyle smiled. "My old friend, John Edgar. Indeed it was."

"And you spoke with him and he went away."

"He did, and he took his own little carnival with him."

"What did you say to him? What do you have on him?"

"Me? What do I have on him?" Doyle shook his head. "I have nothing on him, Michael. Nothing I could prove, nothing that isn't already suspected, nothing that hasn't been talked about many times before."

"I don't understand... Then how did you make him go away?"

"Sometimes things happen simply because you believe they will."

"You *wished* him away?"

Doyle laughed. "Oh, I'm not talking about what I believe, Michael. I'm talking about what our friend Mr. Hoover believes."

"But you must have done something. You must have said something. If he is so afraid of what you can expose about him, then why didn't he kill you a long time ago?"

"Because I am protected, just as I told you before," Doyle said, and touched—once again—the small badge on his lapel.

"Do you know how many Freemasons were murdered during the Holocaust, Michael?"

"I didn't," Travis said. "I spoke to someone about your badge. Someone who told me that the Freemasons had been persecuted, but she didn't tell me about their being murdered."

"Well, they were. They say that as many as a quarter of a million were killed in the concentration camps. Think about it . . . the Freemasons, the Masons of the Temple of Solomon. They were a Jewish organization in the beginning. And good people, so many of them, and yet—as with all organizations—there are those who seek to use that authority for their own ends, and not all of them good. My friend John Edgar—let's say my once-friend John Edgar—was a man who took a different route."

"The last years of the war," Travis said.

"The last years of the war, absolutely," Doyle said. "Larouche, Lepage, the French-Canadian Resistance network. The German anti-Nazi movement. British military intelligence, the OSS under Bill Sullivan . . . what were we doing out there? We were bringing the engineers and doctors, the scientists, the bureaucrats and ambassadors, the teachers and judges and anyone else who might have a place in rebuilding the new Germany out of there before the Nazis rounded them up and killed them. And they were Freemasons, so many of them, and we saved thousands of lives, and for that, among other things, I earned a place of favor with those who our Man of the Year, Mr. Hoover, wants so much to impress and please. Like I told you before, even men like Hoover and Dulles have those before whom they kneel. J. Edgar Hoover cannot kill me, Michael. He would not dare."

"And Varga?"

"Varga was a ploy. Somewhere in amidst all of Hoover's paranoid delusions and imaginings he thought he could perhaps sully my reputation, and thus be forgiven if he dealt with me the way he wanted to. If he could prove I was a murderer, then perhaps he would be granted a pardon for making me disappear. He wanted me gone, Michael, has wanted me gone ever since I walked away from Unit X and everything they were doing. I am you so many years ago. That's all there is to it."

"And Varga was Hungarian? He was Fekete Kutya?"

"Andris Varga was a hired gun, a paid killer, and he upset enough influential people in Hungary to make his position there untenable. He got out of Hungary, arrived in New York, was arrested in '54, and then he went back to Budapest in '56 to take care of some things that would serve US interests."

Doyle leaned forward. "I'll tell you something curious about Hungary. Up until August of 1956, the US ambassador was a man called Christian Ravndal. He knew that Hungary needed help. He knew they wanted US credit and imports. They needed American wheat and cotton. Ravndal appealed to Eisenhower. Hungary was willing to lift travel restrictions, to make concessions, to be more accommodating to the United States. The Hungarian Ministry of Internal Affairs got wind of this and slowed everything down to appease the Soviets. Eisenhower took complete advantage of it by doing nothing at all. Eisenhower recalled Ravndal and sent in his place a man by the name of Edward Tailes. Tailes arrived in Budapest on November the second, just forty-eight hours before Soviet tanks rolled into the city to crush the revolution. Tailes was there to make sure that Hungary failed in its attempt to overturn Soviet rule. Why? Because it would bolster the growing sense of paranoia about Communism, the international condemnation of Soviet political occupation of Eastern European countries. And Tailes? He was gone just three months later, in February of 1957."

"And Varga was there with Tailes?"

"Yes, I'm sure he was, though I doubt there's any record of it. Tailes needed someone, maybe even more than one, and they would have gone as native Hungarians, able to take care of cleanup operations, able to infiltrate anti-Soviet resistance units in Budapest, whatever was needed to undermine that revolution. The Americans wanted the world to hate the Communists, to fear the possibility of Communist invasion in South America, Southeast Asia, Europe, even Britain. In that way, America could continue to do whatever it wished in the name of fighting Communism. Even Joe McCarthy has ingratiated himself into the favors of the Kennedy family and the Catholic majority, and the witch hunt goes on through every strata and level of society. They have everyone looking under their beds for Commies."

"And when Varga came back, they needed to make sure he never spoke of it."

"Of course, just as they need to make sure that a thousand other people never speak of a thousand other things."

"But what about Hoover himself? You know something about him, don't you? Something important—"

"No more than many other people, Michael, but I was part of Unit X because of what I could read and understand about men, you see? What Hoover thinks we know and what we actually know don't even have to be the same thing for Hoover's paranoia to be fed. Like why was a birth certificate not filed until after the death of both his mother and his father? You know, Hoover was forty-three years of age before he was even registered as having been born. And why did that birth certificate say he was born in January of 1895 in Washington D.C. when his baptismal record states he was born in June? And who were J. Edgar's parents? I mean, who were they really? His mother, Anna Marie Scheitlin, the niece of the US Swiss Honorary Consul, his father one Dickerson Hoover of Washington D.C., or was he *really* the son of Ivery Hoover, descendant of the Pike County, Mississippi, Hoovers, themselves no more than plantation slaves? There are many who say that Hoover was actually born in New Orleans, and then he was taken to D.C. to be raised by Dickerson Hoover and his wife, that he even had a stepbrother. And if that's the case, and he *was* the son of Ivery Hoover, then his paternal grandmother was instrumental in establishing an Underground Railroad movement that integrated light-skinned blacks into white society after the Civil War. And there we have J. Edgar, part of the Kappa Alpha Order at George Washington University. And his mother, if this Anna Marie Scheitlin was in fact his mother, was an honorary guardian of that fraternity, well known as a college auxiliary of the Ku Klux Klan. And how did Hoover avoid conscription in the First War? He was made a clerk at the Justice Department under John Lord O'Brian, special assistant to the attorney general for war work. And who was O'Brian? Mentor and law partner to Bill Donovan, head of the OSS. It becomes even more complex the deeper you go, but the simple fact is that Woodrow Wilson reinstituted segregation throughout the entirety of the federal service network, and had anyone taken the time to dig a little into John Edgar's past, well, there would have been no place for him in the Justice Department, and he would never have been appointed to the Bureau of Investigation, and he would never have been permitted entry to the Freemasons, for one condition of membership is that you are freeborn, neither a slave nor a descendant of slaves."

Doyle looked away for a moment, and then he smiled sardonically. "The truth of who you are is in your blood, right? You can never escape your history, and your past will always find you."

"He has given you power that you don't have," Travis said.

"He has given a great many people power they do not have, and never will," Doyle replied. "Your own fears are the only thing that ever give people power over you, and Hoover has more than all of us combined."

"And what you are saying is true, about Hoover's ancestors? He wasn't the son of Dickerson Hoover and this Scheitlin woman?"

"Hoover knows the truth, Tolson too, I'm sure. It is Hoover's fear that we know more than we do that builds a cage of shadows around him."

"And he cannot risk harming you because of what you did in the war, the fact that there are those above him who won't sanction it?"

Doyle did not reply. He merely looked at Travis, a half smile on his lips.

"Something else," Travis said. "There is some other reason, isn't there?"

"A man such as this sees danger when there is none. He sees rumors and hearsay as the worst kind of threat, Michael. Fear is strong and pervasive. It possesses the power to override anything so simple as the truth. Why do you think he has spent all these years amassing so much evidence of others' wrongdoing? Offense is the best form of defense. He was a lawyer, first and foremost, and that is one of the oldest adages in the book. And a man like that does all he can to surround himself with men of like minds, and if he cannot find them, then he tries to make them."

Doyle sighed and shook his head. "No, our friend Mr. Hoover has nothing to worry about but his own shadow. As is the case with most men."

"And that includes me," Travis said. "As you said, a man cannot escape his own past."

"And sometimes a man can find out that his past was not what he believed it to be."

Doyle took a cigarette from his pocket and lit it.

Travis smiled ruefully. "Hell of a thing, Rourke and the others showing up when they did. Might not be so lucky next time."

"You still believe in luck, Michael?"

Travis didn't answer the question, but said, "So, what do you think made them do that? Why did they rally together like that? They didn't owe you that, did they?"

"They didn't, no."

There was silence for a moment, and then Travis said, "Did you make them come and help us?"

Doyle didn't reply.

"Did you do that, Edgar?"

"Sometimes people do things that you can't so easily explain," Doyle said. "Like getting up in the middle of the night and typing words that they don't even remember they knew."

Travis's eyes widened.

"And before you ask, I had nothing to do with that one."

"Really?"

"Really. The subconscious can be a very powerful thing, Michael. All of this, everything we experience." Doyle smiled ruefully. "I went to the woods because I wished to live deliberately, to front only the essential facts of life, and see if I could not learn what it had to teach, and not, when I came to die, discover that I had not lived."

"Thoreau," Michael said.

"You know Thoreau?" Doyle asked.

"Not personally, no."

"I am suitably impressed."

"That I can read?"

Doyle laughed. "That you read something so subversive and anti-establishment."

"I read everything I could get my hands on at one time, and then time seemed to run away with itself."

"Then we shall chase it down and capture it once more."

"And now?" Travis asked.

"I will do what I always do," Doyle said. "I will keep on moving. More important, I feel sure that you will not be welcome in Kansas. I think you might just be a little unemployed, eh?"

"Yes," Travis said. "Unemployed and probably unemployable."

"So what will you do? I would ask you to come with us, but there's nothing you can do, and I don't have the time to teach you card tricks and fire-breathing. Besides, I don't think the life of a gypsy is one that would suit you."

Travis laughed, just briefly, and then the expression on his face was strangely nostalgic.

"There's somewhere I need to go," he said, "and I need to get back to Olathe as well. I cannot stay in the apartment now, and there's something I have to collect from there."

"And what would that be, Michael?"

"A letter."

"Just a letter?"

"I don't think it's *just* a letter, no. It's something that I have not faced, something I have not dealt with for many years, and if I am starting my life again, then I need to face it."

"And who is this letter from?"

Travis smiled wryly. "Oh, Mr. Doyle, don't disappoint me. If you are as good as Mr. Hoover thinks you are, then you know very well who that letter is from."

Doyle nodded, but said nothing. He rose from the bench and stood for a moment.

"You are leaving now?" Travis asked.

"There is no reason for me to stay," Doyle said. "There is no murder investigation, there is no Andris Varga, and Valeria tells me that Bolivar, Missouri, seems ready for some magic and wonder."

"And they are not interested in me?" Travis asked.

"Hell, Hoover even said you could keep the Fairlane."

"So there it is," Travis said.

"There it is, my friend."

Travis extended his hand. Doyle took it. They maintained that grip, each looking back at the other for a good half minute, and then Doyle said, "I am not Irish, Michael. And my name is not Edgar Doyle."

"I have thought as much for a good while."

"My name will change, and you won't find me."

"I don't plan to look for you."

"Everything else I have told you is the truth, however, though there are some things that I have not said. Not because I didn't trust you, but because there was no need for you to know."

"Such as the real nature of your relationship to Mr. Hoover."

Doyle looked back at Travis, and—but for an almost imperceptible flicker in his eyes—Doyle's expression did not change at all.

And then Doyle smiled and gripped Travis's shoulder firmly. "Live a good life, eh?"

"I will do my best, Edgar."

"I know you will, Michael ... I know you will."

52

Clyde Tolson, assistant director of the Federal Bureau of Investigation, was a precise man, not only in his dress, but also in his manner, his speech, his actions. A Missourian by birth, a lawyer by study, an FBI man by default, Tolson had formerly worked for three different secretaries of war—Baker, Weeks, and Davis. Upon first application to join the Bureau, believing that such experience would advance his law career, Tolson was rejected. However, he reapplied and was accepted in 1927, achieving successive promotions to the rank of assistant director within three years. Hoover called Tolson his alter ego. Other people had a different term for him. Despite being present when Alvin Karpis was arrested, having engaged in gunplay with the New York gangster Harry Brunette, even fulfilling an operational role in the capture of Nazi saboteurs, Dasch and Burger, Tolson was more an administrator, a policy maker, a desk man.

And so, on the afternoon of Tuesday, August 19, 1958, Clyde Tolson was the man who met with Executive Assistant Director Bradley Warren in Tolson's D.C. office. Warren knew Tolson well enough, respected him more for his judicious and measured attitude than anything else, and though Warren himself was among those who had—on more than one occasion—questioned the nature of Director Hoover's relationship with Assistant Director Tolson, Warren was also sufficiently careful never to allow such thoughts to become words. Hoover's sudden and fickle mood changes were legendary, and the merest hint that some impropriety had taken place between the two men would have seen Warren dismissed just as easily as he himself had dismissed Michael Travis.

The meeting took place at three in the afternoon, and present was a stenographer, seated quietly in the corner of the room, her machine audible only in the conversational pauses. However, the word *conversation* did not perhaps apply. More accurately, it was a debrief, an admission of assignment failure, and a stern reprimand.

"The director is not pleased, and that is perhaps an understatement," Tolson began.

"I understand his response completely," Warren said. "However—"

"There is no *however*, Mr. Warren. This has been, to put it mildly, a

431

monumental disaster. You realize that your section chief, Frank Gale, was in fact maintaining a homosexual relationship with a university lecturer by the name of Stephen Longmuir?"

"Yes, sir, I realize that now."

"You also realize that the suicide of a Bureau section chief is not well received by the director?"

"Yes, sir."

"And do you have even the slightest appreciation of the amount of time and money and effort and energy it takes to keep something like this out of the newspapers?"

"No, sir. I do not."

"Well, I do, Mr. Warren, and it is not insignificant, let me assure you."

"I have no doubt, sir."

"So, not only do we have a failed assignment, and to be honest, that in itself is hard enough to fathom, considering how little was actually required of this Michael Travis, but we have a compromised department, a dead section chief, and the objective of this assignment now seems even further away than it was before we started."

Tolson paused. The stenographer became audible.

"So, what do you have to tell me, Mr. Warren?"

"We got it wrong, sir."

"You did, indeed. I would have expected a little more of an explana-tion, however."

"The agent we assigned failed to carry out his orders in every regard."

"So it seems. And he is where now?"

"We don't know, sir."

"He has been dismissed?"

"Yes, he has. I dismissed him personally."

"And what do we have on him?"

"Sir?"

"Material, information... This Agent Travis, what do we have on him?"

"Very little, sir, as far as I can tell. He was somewhat of a loner. Lived alone, no relationship, didn't seem to make friends, no real social life."

"A blank page, then?"

"You could say that, yes sir."

"Good, so write a biography for him. Give him some background that can be exposed if he ever decides to resurface and cause trouble. We have had enough to deal with already without further embarrassments and unpleasantness."

"Yes, sir."

"And these people we were supposed to bring home?"

"They won't be coming home, sir."

"Well, I can imagine that Dulles and his crowd of thugs will be far more disappointed in that than either myself or the director. I never did much care for that sort of thing, personally. You start in that direction and it can't lead to anything but trouble, wouldn't you say, Mr. Warren?"

"Yes, sir, I would."

"Well, okay. Is there anything else?"

"No, sir. I don't think so."

"Very well."

"Just one question, sir."

"Yes, Mr. Warren?"

"Are we going to just let Travis disappear, Doyle and the others too?"

"I cannot answer that question directly. I am not at liberty to divulge the director's longer-term intentions. However, I will say this much. The work that has been undertaken in this field by Gottlieb and Cameron, among others, has proven to be unreliable, certainly as far as immediate and applicable results are concerned. It has been a considerable financial burden as well, and even with the seemingly endless Communist challenges to contend with, the director feels that we should be returning to good, solid, proven investigative techniques. He feels that our association with the CIA has not been productive for the Bureau. It is his Bureau, and he wishes to direct its energies and resources toward more relevant and immediate concerns."

Tolson paused, and then he smiled sardonically. He glanced over at the stenographer, and she nodded in acknowledgment.

"There are those who believe that one of Joe Kennedy's boys might actually make it to the White House, God forbid."

The stenographer did not transcribe Tolson's comment.

"So we leave Doyle and the others be? We let Travis go as well?"

"What can I say, Mr. Warren? They are all small fish, are they not? Most of them swim in seas populated with far bigger fish. There is a natural order in such things, and sometimes it is better to let nature take its course than to fight it."

"You do not believe they will be the cause of further trouble?"

"You are being too imaginative. If Doyle and Travis and the others surface, then we will deal with it. Contingency plans are in place for all such eventualities. You should know that by now."

"Yes, sir."

"Good. Well, your timely and succinct report was appreciated, despite the ultimate outcome of the operation. Though, having said that, the damage control we undertook has kept all reference to what happened off the radar, as they say."

"It could have been worse."

"Not for Frank Gale, I wouldn't have thought," Tolson said, and there was a slightly mocking tone in his voice that Warren didn't like at all.

"One's improprieties and proclivities, if and where they exist, should never be a matter for discussion or revelation, save with those who are directly engaged in such things, wouldn't you say?"

"Yes, sir, of course."

"Excellent. You are a good man, Warren. I have always liked you. You know where your loyalties lie, and that is acknowledged. I have discussed this most recent case with the director, and he feels that you are not to be held directly accountable for what happened. Bishop will survive too. He shows promise, as do Carvahlo and Erickson. The failing was with this Michael Travis, and with Frank Gale, of course, but that unpleasantness is now well and truly behind us."

Tolson rose from his desk.

Warren rose too, and together they walked to the door of the office.

Tolson extended his hand, and he and Warren shook.

"And Mr. Gale's name shall not be uttered again. Are we clear on that point?"

"Absolutely, sir."

"The Bureau does not forget, Mr. Warren, but I am sure that you are already fully aware of this."

"Yes, sir."

Warren headed out of the office and down the corridor. Present in his mind was one overriding and inescapable certainty: He understood that Frank Gale would have undoubtedly resigned, acceded to a divorce, have suffered the most extreme public and private humiliation, but the Frank Gale that Warren knew would never have committed suicide.

There were other Andris Vargas, and they were always available when a little housework was required.

This was the way of things. It was all for the greater good. Such knowledge carried a burden of responsibility, but those who were insufficiently strong to bear such a burden were also unsuited for public office.

It took a certain kind of man, and those such as Frank Gale and Michael Travis were evidently not of the required caliber.

By the time Tolson's door was closed and Bradley Warren had made it to the top of the stairs, Tolson had already dismissed the stenographer and placed a call through to another department.

"Yes," he said, "I wanted to let you know that Mr. Warren is to be admitted for treatment as soon as possible."

A moment's pause.

"Yes, of course," he went on. "And I think perhaps that Dr. Cameron might wish to supervise this case personally."

Tolson replaced the receiver and leaned back in his chair.

He closed his eyes for a moment, and then he rose and walked to a small safe in the corner of the room. He opened it, withdrew a file, and returned to his desk. He leafed through pages, through photographs, all faces that he knew, faces that were so familiar, until he came to one in particular. The gunmetal gray hair, now close to white at the temples, aged the man so, but the expression was unmistakable. So many times Mr. Hoover had taken this file from the very same safe and looked at this image, as if believing that to look at it enough would somehow change the past. But the past had not changed and never would.

Attached to the photograph was a certificate of birth, now yellowed, ragged at the edges, more than sixty years old. Tolson scanned the parents' names printed thereon—Dickerson Hoover and Anna Marie Scheitlin, and the name of the child registered on Tuesday, July 6, 1897, just four days after its birth.

From his desk drawer Tolson took a lighter and held it beneath the corner of the certificate. He watched as it started to smolder and catch. There was little smoke, and Tolson dropped it into the trash basket and stood over it until it was finally consumed.

Returning to the file, he once again looked at the photograph that had accompanied the certificate. He slid it back among its neighbors, suspecting that despite everything that had happened between them, the director might wish to keep at least one photograph of his stepbrother.

The file back in the safe, Tolson looked at his desk calendar.

He smiled. So unlike him to forget such a thing, but he and the director were leaving for a weekend in Martha's Vineyard the following evening.

That would be good. A welcome respite, and too long overdue.

STATUS REPORT
Reference: AV-067980-011E
Originator: SSA Raymond Carvahlo
Recipient: Section Chief Tom Bishop
*Please confirm that Operation Black Dog has now been retired. I
need to submit completion documentation on behalf of Unit X.*

STATUS REPORT
Reference: AV-067980-011E
Originator: Section Chief Tom Bishop
Recipient: SSA Raymond Carvahlo
*Black Dog is retired. Unit X has been reassigned to Operations
Oswald, Camelot, and Bloody Elm. All three operations are class 7
security clearance and above only. As covered in the most recent
briefing, I am transferring to Dallas, TX, for the foreseeable future,
and will be supervising one of the aforementioned operations. Your
promotion to section chief has been approved by the assistant
director, and we are awaiting confirmation from the director. On
a more personal note, your continued diligence is acknowledged
and appreciated. No doubt we shall work together again at some
point in the future, and until then I wish you success in your new
posting.*

COMM EXCHANGE TERMINATED AT 11:22 a.m. BY SSA TOM
BISHOP

54

The nineteenth of August, 1958.

Sixteen years.

Sixteen years to the day since his mother had murdered his father.

Michael Travis could not believe that the house had stood empty for sixteen years.

Successive winters had begun a slow and irrevocable decay, the steps up to the porch now gone, the outer door a bare and rotted frame, the screen itself long since vanished. Rust had taken the locks, the latches, the striker plates, and even the floor beneath his feet felt insubstantial as he made his way through the ground floor, pausing for a moment at the top of the basement stairwell, peering into the darkness, unable to face the prospect of going down there.

And so he did not.

He walked back to the hallway near the front door and looked toward the kitchen.

Even as he stood there, he could hear her voice, those small fragments of songs she used to sing—"Over the Rainbow" and "A Nightingale Sang in Berkeley Square."

Perhaps he should have been afraid, but he was not.

Perhaps he should have been concerned that the Bureau would now never let him be, that he had broken the faith, crossed the lines, committed the ultimate betrayal.

He did not know what he felt, not really, but it certainly wasn't fear or trepidation or anxiety.

He felt free of something, as if he'd been released from some unknown jail.

He had tried to explain it to Laura, but she had said—as she had said so many times—that he did not need to put everything into words. Not everything needed a label. Not everything needed a box. *Some things*, she said, *just are.*

Travis did not risk an ascent to the second floor of the house. The banister had sagged and now leaned outward like some crazy optical illusion. What was meant to be straight was twisted, and what was meant to be twisted was straight. Like his thoughts, perhaps.

There were many things with which he would wrestle. He knew that. He was prepared for that.

A stone recovered from the sea will always carry salt.

There are some things that would always be part of identity, personality, *self*, and to consider anything other than acceptance would be to attempt erasure of something that could not be erased.

Take any number of layers away, and fingerprints always return. Innate, inherent, whatever word might be used, there are some aspects of a person that would always be that person.

Perhaps that was the soul; perhaps it was something else.

Michael Travis did not know, but he knew that in time he would stop fighting himself and the rest of the world. Perhaps there were some questions that could never be answered in this life, because the answers could only be found after this life was done.

And so, finally, he came to the room where it had all happened.

He approached it tentatively, as if on eggshells, and he heard nothing, not even his own breathing, not even his own heart, and he waited for that voice to start in his head.

You think your mother would be proud of you? Jesus, you are a sick kid; you know that?

And he felt his pulse then, that quickening sensation, that awareness on his skin, *under* his skin.

You think you have the right to judge me? You don't have the right to even speak to me, let alone judge me, you self-righteous hypocritical son of a bitch!

And he placed his hand against the wall as if to steady himself, even though he knew he was not going to lose his balance. Not now. Not again. Not ever.

And I'll tell you now, that ain't never had more meaning than it does right now. Son of a bitch. You are a son of a bitch. Because she was a bitch, kiddo. She was a fucking nasty fucking bitch, and I hope she burns in hell forever...

And the table came into view, the chair also, the chair where he had sat in life, in death also; the chair from where Jimmy had risen and walked forward, the sound of cockroaches scuttling across the plates, the smell of rotted food, the *drip-drip-drip* of blood as it spooled out between items of crockery and cutlery to find the edge of that table.

And there was nothing.

Not a sound. Not a word. Nothing for him to see and nothing in his mind. The table was still standing, the chair also, but the seat had gone, the back also, and whatever color the fabric might have been had long since disappeared, bleached out by daylight, by damp, by time.

In that moment, Michael Travis believed that he was in front of himself, as if he could turn around right there and then and see his own face looking back.

He shuddered. It was a strange and disorientating sensation, and then it passed, almost as quickly as it had come.

He stood for a moment longer, trying to feel anything at all, but the house was empty, as were his feelings for it, the only extant memory that of his mother in the kitchen, her voice gentle and melodic.

If happy little bluebirds fly... beyond the rainbow... why, oh why can't I?

And then the memory was gone.

Michael retraced his steps and left the house. He paused for a moment on the veranda, and then he walked to the edge and stepped down.

From his jacket pocket, he withdrew the letter that he had recovered from his apartment in Olathe. He had left everything behind but for a few articles of clothing. Even the book he had given Esther so many years before had stayed there on the bookshelf.

Michael

Just one word on the front.

He turned it over and opened it.

There were two sheets of paper. The first was from Esther, and even as he read her words, he felt a wave of emotions deep enough to drown him forever.

January 28, 1950

Dear Michael,

The truth can both hurt and heal. I trust that what I am telling you now will bring you more of the latter and none of the former.

Your mother, dead now more than two years, never lost her mind. She was never crazy. She knew who you were, and she always knew who you were. She made two decisions in her life, both of them harder than any decision I have ever had to make, harder than any decision I will now ever have to make. The first was to end the suffering she endured from Jimmy and also any possibility that Jimmy might hurt you. The second was to leave you long before her death. She knew that you would only suffer more if she did not disconnect. And so she feigned her madness, and she pretended to you and the rest of the world that she no longer recognized you. It broke her heart, but she did not believe she had a choice. Once she had decided, there was no going back.

I was there with her in the very last moments of her life, and she wanted me to tell you how much she loved you, how much she had always loved you, and that she wished you all the happiness in the world.

And she gave me something for you, and this I have enclosed.

She said that she never told you for fear that you might—perhaps in anger—say something to Jimmy, and if he knew of this, then he would have reason to really hurt both you and her. And even after his death, she could not bring herself to tell you, for fear that you might think her a liar, that if she had withheld this from you, then what else had she not communicated?

There was nothing else she did not tell you. She wanted you to know that.

And so, facing my own death as I do, I want to send my blessings as well, Michael.

I loved you with all my heart, just as your mother did, and I trust that you will find happiness in whatever you decide to do with your life.

Take care, my sweet.

Esther.

Tears were on the page before Michael had finished reading. The ink bloomed and spread, and words merged together here and there. He folded the page, and before he tucked it back in the envelope, he withdrew the second page.

It was a birth certificate, and it was a moment before he appreciated that it was his own.

Michael Travis
Birth registered in Howard County, Nebraska, this day 12 May 1927
Name of mother: Janette Alice Travis
Name of father: unknown

Travis looked at the word again. *Unknown.*

There was something written on the other side of the certificate, and when he turned it, he saw his mother's unmistakable hand.

I am sorry, my darling. You lived with a lie. Jimmy was not your father. You father's name was Jack Fredericksen, and no, he does not know and never will. He died in the fall of 1931. He was a good man, and though I should have married him, it seemed that Fate had a different path mapped out. Whatever happened, I always did what I thought was best. I hope you will forgive me. x

Michael held the paper in his hand.

Doyle's words came back to him.

And sometimes a man can find out that his past was not what he believed it to be.

He did not know what to feel. He was unsure that he would ever know what to feel.

He was not his father's son.

Michael stood slowly. He took four, five, six steps away from the veranda. He paused for a moment and then glanced back over his shoulder at the house of his childhood. There was nothing there. He believed that whatever ghosts might have followed him had finally been laid to rest.

Reaching the Fairlane, he looked once more at his mother's words. He folded that page, tucked it into the envelope, put the envelope in his pocket.

It was no more than four or five hours back to Seneca Falls, and there was a girl he needed to see.

He caught sight of his own shadow then, stretching out before him across the cracked and arid earth.

Somewhere a crow laughed.

The setting sun had reached the tops of those too-familiar trees, and Michael Travis felt that final ghost of warmth upon his face.

He started the engine and drove south.

There was silence all around him and silence within.